Regarding Anna

Florence Osmund

DISCLAIMER

This is a work of fiction. Names, characters, places, and incidents are either the product of the author's imagination or are used fictitiously. Any resemblance to actual persons, living or dead, business establishments, events, or locales is entirely coincidental.

ACKNOWLEDGEMENTS

I wish to thank the following people for their assistance in creating this book.

To my editor, Carrie Cantor, thank you for your insightful feedback, being patient with me as I struggled with the right POV and narrative tense for this story, challenging me when I needed it, and making the story better.

I wish to acknowledge graphic designer, Deborah Bradseth of Tugboat Design, for an intriguing cover design and meticulous print and e-book formatting.

And a special thanks to Marge Bousson, for catching things no one else did—like you have to let a cake right out of the oven cool first before you can frost it—and other things.

∽ TABLE OF CONTENTS ∾

CHAPTER ONE	The Kindness of Strangers	1
CHAPTER TWO	The Back Room	5
CHAPTER THREE	Saved By the Bush	11
CHAPTER FOUR	Rumors	17
CHAPTER FIVE	That Was No Poker Game	23
CHAPTER SIX	Indigent, Unclaimed, and Unknown	30
CHAPTER SEVEN	"Arrest That Woman!"	36
CHAPTER EIGHT	"I Hate Coffee"	41
CHAPTER NINE	Ties to Mexico	50
CHAPTER TEN	The Real Bird-Dogger	54
CHAPTER ELEVEN	She's No Misstep	59
CHAPTER TWELVE	"She Called Him Al"	68
CHAPTER THIRTEEN	He Pulled Into Where?	77
CHAPTER FOURTEEN	The Ninety-Pound Wuss	80
CHAPTER FIFTEEN	An Ethical Dilemma	88
CHAPTER SIXTEEN	Doing the Right Thing	93
CHAPTER SEVENTEEN	One of Us Is Wrong	96
CHAPTER EIGHTEEN	The Cavalry	101
CHAPTER NINETEEN	Treasures or Trash?	107
CHAPTER TWENTY	The Key	113
CHAPTER TWENTY-ONE	She Wants to Talk	118

CHAPTER TWENTY-TWO	Minnie	130
CHAPTER TWENTY-THREE	Emotional Overload	135
CHAPTER TWENTY-FOUR	The Will	144
CHAPTER TWENTY-FIVE	"You're Not Alone"	149
CHAPTER TWENTY-SIX	A Loud Knock	152
CHAPTER TWENTY-SEVEN	Desperation	159
CHAPTER TWENTY-EIGHT	Roommates	165
CHAPTER TWENTY-NINE	The Connecting Puzzle Pieces	168
CHAPTER THIRTY	It Was Elmer	175
CHAPTER THIRTY-ONE	Revoked	181
CHAPTER THIRTY-TWO	Happy Birthday to Me	191
CHAPTER THIRTY-THREE	The No. 54 Bus	196
CHAPTER THIRTY-FOUR	The Floor Safe	203
CHAPTER THIRTY-FIVE	Open Floodgates!	207
CHAPTER THIRTY-SIX	The Trunk	210
CHAPTER THIRTY-SEVEN	Anna's Letters	214
CHAPTER THIRTY-EIGHT	Bad Timing	224
CHAPTER THIRTY-NINE	The Photo	230
CHAPTER FORTY	A Rhetorical Question	238
CHAPTER FORTY-ONE	Regarding Anna	243
EPILOGUE		254

Regarding Anna

ONE

The Kindness of Strangers

Under different circumstances I could have been a carefree twenty-two-year-old driving to Oak Street Beach for a much-needed reprieve from the sweltering heat instead of sitting on the No. 54 bus headed for a shady neighborhood on Chicago's South Side in search of Erma Fincutter. I had no one but myself to blame for my discontent—I could have simply accepted my uncertain parentage four years ago and moved on with my life in a more conventional way. But if I was right about things, all the aggravation I would endure in search of the truth would pay off in the end. If I was right about things.

Erma Fincutter was a missing teenager whose mother had hired me to find her. I'd named it the Green Teen case—Erma had been wearing a green coat the day she ran away. Naming cases helped me distance myself from the people whose reason for contacting me was almost always something unfortunate. Being a private investigator was not a particularly heartening profession.

If I had a car it would have taken me all of twenty minutes to reach my destination, and I wouldn't have been stuck sitting so close to Mr. Body Odor and listening to the two crabby old hens behind me complain about everything. The bus was full. Summer sweat dripped off the brows of most of the passengers, and the thick air that held us captive in tight quarters wasn't moving.

Louise Fincutter, the child's mother, suspected her daughter had fled to a side of her family about which Louise knew very little—she had divorced Erma's mixed-race father just a few months after their wedding, calling the marriage the biggest mistake of her life. After locating Erma's two half-brothers and having reason to believe she was with them, I was obligated to pay them a visit regardless of the neighborhood. It was broad daylight, so I figured I'd be safe.

The second I stepped off the bus, I realized I was out of my element. Cheerless houses with boarded-up windows lined a potholed street cluttered with beat-up cars and a variety of trash. An unidentifiable smell permeated the air. I was tempted to turn around, hop on a bus headed in the opposite direction, and go home. But I had a job to do.

I walked a block. My stomach churned, telling me to reconsider. But if I turned back, it would have meant I was incapable of doing the job, and I wasn't about to make that admission. I had too much at stake personally.

Stares from the pedestrians and people hanging out of car windows driving down Twenty-fourth Street seemed more sinister the farther I went, and the address I was looking for was another three blocks away. My brain knew I shouldn't continue, but the message hadn't gotten to my legs yet.

As my uneasiness heightened, I tried to imagine who lived here, what their days were like, how they ended up here. I thought about children growing up in this kind of environment, the opportunities they probably didn't even know they were missing. I thought about my own situation, and all of a sudden my troubles didn't seem so bad.

"Yo, gorgeous. You loss er somepin'?"

I nearly jumped out of my shoes at the sound of the male voice. Still walking, I turned my head and saw a dark-skinned man with a huge scar running down the side of his face approaching me. The bile reached my throat so fast I didn't know if I could get the words out.

"I know where I'm going," I managed to say. I pumped my legs faster, even though it felt as though my knees could have buckled under me at any second.

He grabbed my arm and forced me to look at him. The scar appeared too aged for such a young face.

"Look, sweetheart, you be in the wrong 'hood. You keep goin' in *that* direction, I promise you, you'll find trouble."

I sensed he was right.

"Howdya git here?"

"The bus."

"Which one?"

I didn't know if he was trying to help me or had some other motive.

"The fifty-four."

"C'mon, I'll walk ya back there."

"Can you let go of my arm…please?"

He dropped my arm with a thrust.

"I appreciate your kindness, but really…" I knew that sounded lame, but it was all I had.

"Uh-huh. Best know I got betta things to do with my time."

He turned around and headed toward the bus stop. I wasn't sure what to do. I wasn't sure what he *expected* me to do, but it didn't matter much because my legs felt frozen.

He turned around.

"I'm tellin' you, don't you bein' around here if you don't want to get hurt." He gestured for me to follow him.

His walk was fast and full of attitude, and I couldn't keep up without running.

"What in the hell are you doin' here anyway?" he asked without turning around.

"I'm looking for someone. Erma Fincutter." Right after I said it, I realized I shouldn't have given out her name.

"Breed bitch?"

"Excuse me?"

He turned around to face me. "She mixed? Looks white. 'Bout sixteen, seventeen?"

"Yes."

The man shook his head. "Stupid private dick. You'll back outta this one if you know what's good for ya." He glanced down the street. "Here's your bus. I'd get on it if I was you." He disappeared behind a parked van.

I was embarrassed and offended by his remarks, but that didn't keep me from getting on the bus. I had gone on this mission totally unprepared and forgetful of just about everything I had been taught—like the importance of traveling with a partner and dressing appropriately for the mission. Criminals can spot parole officers, process servers, undercover cops, and PIs a mile away.

Being a PI isn't what most people think it is. Forget about images of Sherlock Holmes and Philip Marlowe sitting back in their brown-leather high-back chairs in dimly lit offices talking to a steady stream of clients with intriguing cases who waltz through their doors. That rarely happens in real life—even to seasoned PIs. Your average PI collects information much like a garbage man collects trash but without the perks. When garbage men find treasures among the trash, it's finders keepers. But when PIs find treasures, they belong to someone else.

I so wanted to help Mrs. Fincutter find her daughter—she was relying on me. After she had reported Erma missing to the police, they had called the hospitals, checked with her friends, gone to places where runaways tend to congregate, and called a few other precincts to see if anything had turned up, but that had been about it. Unfortunately, when no crime has been committed, the police tend to treat these types of cases as low priority.

I never wanted to be a private investigator. After high school, I'd had aspirations of becoming an interior decorator and had even enrolled in classes at Morton Community College. But when my parents died from carbon monoxide poisoning in their home three months before my eighteenth birthday, with no relatives to take me in, I was left to fend for myself. And that was when everything changed.

As soon as I got off the bus, I walked home and dragged out the ironing board. Ironing relieved stress for me. If I didn't have any clothes or bed sheets that needed it, I'd iron anything—underwear, towels, the bedspread. I even ironed a package of cheesecloth once—the kind you use to cook a turkey.

If I'd had a car to take to that South Side neighborhood, I wouldn't have run into Mr. Scarface nor would I have felt the need to iron a pair of sweatpants, three pairs of socks, two dishrags, a ski hat that I hadn't worn in years, and the white apron from the Raggedy Ann doll I'd cherished since I was three.

And if my parents hadn't died in March of 1960, I wouldn't have found what I did in their attic leading me to believe a woman named Anna Thalia Vargas was my real mother—and that she was murdered, and I was kidnapped, when I was seven months old.

TWO

The Back Room

In the office the next day, I got a call from the circuit court asking me to serve a subpoena to someone in Englewood. Fortunately, I had managed to get appointed by Cook County to be a licensed process-server, and the measly ten-dollar fee I got for each person I served was, in fact, making a difference. Unfortunately, the witnesses being served often resided in the worst neighborhoods, and no matter where they lived, they typically didn't want to be served, making this the least favorite part of my job.

"Do you know anyone large and intimidating who can go with me to serve subpoenas?" I asked Elmer after I finished the call. "Someone cheap."

Elmer was the attorney from whom I was renting office space. I had met him when I'd answered the ad he posted for someone to share eight hundred square feet of leased office space on West Irving Park Road. The building was located near Six Corners, the largest shopping district in Chicago outside of downtown. More important to me was the fact that it was less than a mile from the apartment on Belle Plaine Avenue where Anna Vargas died, making it convenient for me to work on my own case, the one I called Attic Finds.

"Sure, I know some people," he said as he put out his cigarette.

Elmer reminded me a little of Gregory Peck, but not as handsome. He was middle-aged, tall, thin-faced, with a full head of dark hair. I was surprised on my first day at the office to catch him checking me out when he thought I wasn't paying attention. I'd never exactly dazzled anyone with my looks—I'm twenty-two years old, five-foot-six, weigh 125 pounds, and have plain-Jane brown hair and eyes—so I don't know why he was eying me that way.

"Would you be interested in subleasing the apartment upstairs?" he asked in his usual monotone. "I could give it to you pretty cheap. My last tenant just moved out...without notice and without paying me this month's rent."

I hadn't realized there *was* an apartment above our office, which was a tiny brick storefront building in a row of buildings all so uniform that I always had to check the street number over the door to make sure I was entering the right one. Closer to Six Corners the buildings had matching awnings with the names of the businesses on them. Here there were no awnings and every third storefront was vacant.

To say I could have afforded an apartment would have been a lie—I couldn't even afford my basic living expenses. I had duct tape on the sole of one of my shoes, cut my own hair, and still wore clothes from high school.

"Maybe. What's it like?" I asked him.

"Want to see it?"

Elmer led me outside to a door not more than fifteen feet from our office that I had never noticed before—some PI I was. He led the way up a dingy, narrow staircase that smelled like dirty socks. When we reached the top of the stairs, I followed him into the apartment.

While I didn't see any actual rotting garbage, inside it smelled like maybe there had been some there recently. I tried not to breathe in too deeply.

"He didn't keep it very clean," he said.

No kidding.

The entire apartment was visible from where I was standing. The furniture—which appeared to have come from a thrift store, garage sale, or someone's curb—included a flowered sofa that had three bricks serving as one of its legs and two shapeless cushions, one of which had a nice, neat cigarette burn right in its center. Two mismatched armless side chairs complemented the sofa along with a coffee table that I wouldn't have trusted to hold anything weighing over a pound. A TV stand and a three-fixture pole lamp that was missing one of its cone-shaped plastic shades completed the décor. All the comforts of home.

I walked over to the only window in the room and gave the yellowed paper shade a gentle tug. When it came crashing to the floor, I looked at Elmer.

"It comes 'as is.'"

The view out the window left a lot to be desired: a rusted streetlight in the foreground, and in the background an even row of unsightly rooftops belonging to the time-worn brick buildings across the street, one of which had been completely boarded up.

"Where's the bed?"

He pointed to the sofa. "It converts."

I peeked into the filthy bathroom to confirm the existence of a toilet, sink, and bathtub.

"You'd have it cleaned before I moved in, right?"

"I'll split the cost with you."

"Elmer..."

"I'll have it cleaned."

"How much?"

"It comes furnished."

Like that made a difference.

"I'll give it to you for sixty-five a month. Plus another sixty-five security deposit."

"Sixty-five! I'll give you fifty, and that shade has to be fixed. I'll throw in a free skip search to find your last tenant." My father had taught me the fine art of negotiating when we went to the Maxwell Street flea markets.

"Fifty-five, and you've got yourself a deal."

"First month's rent not due for thirty days, and you've got *yourself* a deal."

We shook on it and retreated to our respective offices. Despite the deplorable condition of the place, I was grateful to have it. It was time to leave the Millers' house, even if it meant a steady diet of ramen noodles for dinner for a while. I'd been living with the family of my best friend, Beth Miller, ever since my parents had died.

The Millers had allowed me to stay with them even though early on I'd made some bad choices by dropping out of community college and taking a waitress job at a crummy diner outside of town. There I met some older kids and got into my share of trouble. I tried cigarettes in order to fit in with them and had my first taste of alcohol followed by my first hangover—the kind where you wake up the next morning fearing you're going to throw up and then a while later fearing you won't. Then they introduced me to marijuana, and one late night after getting high we all got a terrible case of the munchies and went to a nearby pizza parlor. After we devoured three large pizzas and a couple of pitchers of beer, one of them started talking about "dine and dash," a term unfamiliar to me. Before I knew it, they were gone, and I was left sitting there like an idiot. The restaurant manager said he would call the police if I didn't pay the bill. Mr. Miller came to my rescue. It took three paychecks to pay him back.

With some unsolicited but much-needed guidance from the Millers, I came to my senses, quit that waitress job for one in a more respectable restaurant and part of town, and re-enrolled in college.

I was feeling down from the previous day's failed attempt at finding the missing teen, nervous about the deal I had just struck with Elmer, and hungry. I pulled out a box of Cheez-Its from my desk drawer and popped a few in my mouth—not as satisfying as one of those thick ham-and-cheese sandwiches on soft rye bread from the deli down the street but better than nothing.

A small stack of bills beckoned me from atop the secondhand filing cabinet I had purchased at a garage sale, but instead my eyes rested above them on a cheap print of Navy Pier that had been my father's. That and my private investigator license were the only things hanging on my office walls. A Parker mother-of-pearl pen-and-pencil set I had picked up at a pawn shop for almost nothing and a brass nameplate GRACE THALIA LINDROTH that the Millers had given me were the only things on my desk.

I had been in business for three months and had just one client, Louise Fincutter, the mother of the missing teen, and I wasn't even sure if she could pay me. I hadn't had the heart to ask her for a retainer, which went against my common sense and everything I had learned in school, but I felt sorry for her. I needed to stop doing that—I had logged nearly twenty hours trying to find her daughter and had no income to show for it.

Elmer didn't appear to be doing much better. He had hardly any clients, at least not ones who came to his office. He didn't leave the office much, which made me think he didn't spend much time in court. He spent a lot of time on the phone, usually with the door closed as he chain-smoked, leaving me to keep an eye out for walk-ins. He groused about how much things cost all the time and how he was going to have to cut back on this or that. He never cracked a smile, and he never mentioned having any family.

Still, I couldn't be too critical of Elmer. He'd been nice to me and had said he'd throw me work when he had it—finding people, gathering evidence—stuff like that. And he didn't charge me much for rent.

The layout of the office worked pretty well. Inside the front door, there was a reception desk with a free-standing wall behind it. Berghorn & Associates had been the only signage on the wall until my name was put under it—smaller than his. If someone had actually sat at the reception desk, people walking in the door wouldn't have been able to see much of my sign at all, but what could I expect for only seventy-five dollars a month in rent?

After much thought, I had decided to name my agency NSU Investigative Services—professional sounding, short and sweet. NSU stood for No Stone Unturned. Maybe a little corny, but I thought it worked.

We each had two rooms—a front office on either side of the reception desk that faced the street and a small room in the back. Behind the reception desk was a bathroom with two doors—one on my side and one on his.

I used the back room strictly for my Attic Finds case. Spread out on a large table was everything I had collected from my parents' home that I believed could possibly provide clues to Anna Vargas's life and death. The most promising pieces of evidence had come from my parents' attic—a place in our home that had been off limits for me my entire life, a place I had trepidatiously explored after they were gone.

Two newspaper articles had immediately caught my attention. The earlier one stated a woman named Anna Thalia Vargas had been found dead in her Chicago apartment on January 23, 1943. One dated a week later referred to her death as a homicide.

There I had also found several pieces of jewelry, a dozen or so photos, a Bible with Anna's name in it, some clothing, and lots of miscellaneous paperwork—116 pieces total, all packed into one box and hidden behind several plastic crates of clothes and toys I had outgrown.

A baby girl named Celina appeared in many of the photos—at least that was the name that had been written on the backs of them—and I believed that baby to be me. One I found particularly interesting was of a young dark-haired woman holding baby Celina while seated in a rocking chair. Another was of the same woman standing, holding a baby. CELINA THALIA VARGAS—JUST HOME FROM THE HOSPITAL had been written on the back of that one. Thalia was my middle name too.

But the photo I was the most curious about was one of a man holding what appeared to be the same baby. He was turned sideways and looking down, so you couldn't see much of his face. I was dying to know who that man was.

A photo I had found tucked inside the Bible was the clue that had convinced me I was the baby. On the back of it had been written SHE HAS MY EYES. It was a photo of the same young dark-haired woman holding a baby wearing a red polka-dot dress. As soon as I saw it, I ran to my dresser drawer where I kept my own family photographs and found one of me wearing the same little dress. On the back, my mother had written 4 MOS—SHE'S SITTING UP NOW.

All this evidence had led me to believe that Anna Vargas was my real mother, but what had me even more troubled was that in order for my parents to have had this evidence hidden in their attic meant they could have had something to do with her death.

The essence of my life was in this back room. There were truths that needed to be uncovered, and I felt that my whole future depended on it. It was all up to me—no one had been interested in helping me solve a twenty-year-old murder case—not the police, not even a private investigator I had contacted. That's why I had changed my studies to law enforcement, served a two-year apprenticeship, and gotten my PI license. How I wished I could scoop up all the tiny bits and pieces of the Attic Finds evidence, toss them in the air, and watch them land in such a way that everything made complete sense. I supposed that was the dreamer in me.

My life was, well, pretty pathetic. I'd never wanted to be a private investigator. The only reason I'd gone down that road was to get answers so as to be able to go on to do something else. I had no friends to speak of, no hobbies, no social life. I didn't care too much what I wore or how I looked, never pampered myself. If a guy had asked me out on a date, I wouldn't have known how to act.

I wasn't happy, but I fully intended to be one day. I was reminded of a list I had found in my mother's dresser drawer titled "The Seven Keys to Happiness." It appeared to have been torn out of a magazine article. I still remember them.

1. Safety and security
2. Relationships with family and friends
3. Being comfortable with one's self
4. Having achievable goals
5. Good health
6. Maintaining a positive attitude
7. Helping others

With the exception of number six, sort of, and a hint of number seven, I didn't have any of these, and sadder yet was that the only one I was doing anything about was number three. I wished she had torn out the whole article. No, come to think of it, that might have depressed me even more.

My thoughts were interrupted by the sound of Elmer slapping that day's *Tribune* down on the reception desk, letting me know he was finished with it. I was checking the Used Cars section every day, hoping that at some point I would be able to afford one of my own. I went out to the reception desk and opened the paper to Used Cars, ready to torture myself again looking at what I knew I couldn't have, especially now with the added expense of an apartment.

The ads were the same as always: used cars ranged from $50 to $550. I couldn't imagine that a car costing $50 would be much good, and there was no way I could afford $550 without dipping into my meager savings, which I wanted to preserve for a real emergency.

Elmer walked out of his office and peered at the open paper.

"Looking for a car?"

Conversations with him were always short and to the point. Never any small talk.

"Yes."

"Don't look in there—too many people trying to pawn off their problems on you. If you want, I can put you in touch with someone who'll sell you a decent car for a reasonable price...and will even service it for you when you need it."

Of course, I would have to figure out a way to pay for a car in addition to several other essential items...like a new pair of shoes. I was getting low on duct tape.

THREE

Saved By the Bush

"**G**race, since Beth is a no-show, would you like one of us to help you get settled in?" Mrs. Miller asked.

Beth had promised to help me move but then had called at the last minute to say she wasn't feeling well. She had just recently eloped with her boyfriend and was living in Brookfield. I could see the sadness in Mrs. Miller's face—now she was losing my presence in the house as well.

All my worldly possessions were in the back seat and trunk of my new car—a 1952 Chevy Bel Air I had bought from Bob Conway of Big Bob's Used Autos. It wasn't bad for a twelve-year-old car. Tan with a maroon top—a car that would blend in well no matter where my job took me. And he was letting me pay it off on time.

"I'll be fine," I told her. "There's not that much to settle." I was smiling but privately bummed out that Beth wasn't there for this turning point in my life.

"Do keep in touch, dear, and if it doesn't work out for you, you know you're always welcome here."

Mrs. Miller was cool.

On the drive to my new place, I thought about what a milestone it was—my being completely on my own—and wondered if other people my age experienced the same sick feeling in their stomach contemplating whether they were going to make it or fall flat on their face. I had to make it. I pulled into one of the parking spaces behind my apartment and carried as much as I could up the narrow staircase.

I opened the door and was greeted by the overwhelming presence of Pine-Sol—a scent I never did like very much, but I supposed it beat the stench of garbage that had been left behind by the previous tenant. After putting away my belongings in their new places, I jumped back in the car and drove to the address on Belle Plaine Avenue where Anna Vargas had once lived...and where she had also died. Armed with the camera I used for work, I headed for the Portage Park neighborhood where I believed I was born and where it had all begun. I had been by the house several times before—the No. 80 bus stopped within just a few blocks of it—but visiting it in my own car as a licensed PI was different.

It was a cool day, unusually cool for September. I searched for the lever that controlled the heater in an attempt to take the chill out of the car, but it appeared to be non-working. I would have to get Bob to look at that for me. I hoped that was the worst thing I found wrong with it.

I first drove by my old house, which was out of my way, but I hadn't been by it since I'd lived there four years earlier and was curious to see if anything had changed. The memory of the day I had discovered the lifeless bodies of my parents there still haunted me and probably always will. I had just come home after attending my final interior design class before spring break. I had grabbed a hamburger with Beth, who'd dropped me off in front of my house.

As soon as I opened the back door, I sensed something was wrong. I called out for my mom, who was always there, to let her know I was home. When she didn't answer, I went looking for her.

Within minutes, I became a little lightheaded. Thinking it was just my body reacting to not seeing my mother in her usual places in the house, I continued searching for her. Finally, I looked in the basement, and that's where I found both of them—stretched out on the floor, face-down. I called to them, and when they didn't move, I went to my mother, who was closest to the stairs, and shook her shoulder. By that time, I was experiencing a heaviness in my chest and felt like I was going to be sick, so I ran upstairs and called for an ambulance. Then I went to the back door and stuck my head out for a breath of fresh air.

When the ambulance attendants arrived, they ordered me out of the house. I went next door to use the neighbor's phone to summon Beth who arrived just as they were transporting my parents' bodies out of the house on stretchers. She brought me to her home where I was comforted by her and her parents.

I was later told my parents died from carbon monoxide poisoning caused by a faulty furnace. They'd left no will, and I was underage with few rights. Unfortunately, I was also just a naive kid who didn't know enough to ask the right questions.

Shortly after they died, North Community Bank sent me a letter saying I would have to move out of my home in thirty days. How the bank got away with that, I don't know. I know now they had no business sending a minor that kind of notice. Furthermore, the law was that you had to give someone ninety days to move.

Lucky for me, the Millers took me in and treated me like a second daughter. Beth and I shared a bedroom, but with each of us working different shifts and going to school part-time and Beth's succession of boyfriends, we didn't see too much of each other.

The only things I inherited from my parents were the items I managed to remove from our home that held the most meaning for me, including the box full of things that I assumed belonged to Anna Vargas that now lay strewn on my back room evidence tables and a $1,000 death-benefit check from the Soo Line Railroad where my father had worked as a general laborer for many years. I used part of that money to pay for school tuition and books, my business license, insurance, and basic equipment.

I turned onto Ferdinand Street and parked the car where I had a clear view of my old house. It didn't look the same as it did when I lived there. It was the same color, had the same tall evergreens framing the side and back yards, even had the same black mailbox with the heart-shaped red sticker I had put on it when I was little. Yet it didn't look the same. Smaller I thought. It looked a lot smaller.

It was a nice neighborhood for families, especially with the park right across the street. We'd been less than five miles from Lake Michigan but had never once gone there. I wasn't sure why. I had taken swimming lessons when I was ten.

Thinking back, I realized we hadn't done much of anything as a family. My father worked long hours, and my mother rarely left the house. We never really went anywhere.

My mother had been overprotective of me. I'd had to come home right after school, even in high school. I assumed she expected me to be like her and stay home all the time. She did allow Beth to come over, but it was only on rare occasions that she allowed me go to Beth's house. That was probably why I'd earned such good grades—I had nothing else to do but study. When I wasn't studying, I learned to entertain myself by making up outrageous stories in my head about what my life would have been like if this happened or that happened. Stupid stories. Nothing better to do.

My mother was always somewhere in the background—doing whatever was required of her to be a mother to me and a wife to my father. She didn't seem to have a life of her own. My father was controlling. I remember times when he told her things that even I knew weren't true, but she believed him. Like, one time she said she wanted to plant a vegetable garden in the backyard, and he convinced her that the dirt had to be sent to a laboratory for analysis first to make sure it was safe. She never planted the garden.

My father ruled the house—there was no mistake about that—and he knew how to make my mother feel grateful for it. But he had his good side too. He would compliment her cooking or what she was wearing or how she had rearranged the furniture. And he supported her in whatever it was she wanted to do—as long as it didn't require her to leave the house. I learned to stay out of the middle of their relationship, even if it did make me feel isolated and alone much of the time.

I think my parents loved me—each in their own way—even if they weren't my real parents.

I studied my old house for several minutes until the recurring image of their bodies lying on the basement floor compelled me to turn on the car engine and start driving away. Fifteen minutes later, I was on Belle Plaine Avenue, a tree-lined street with well-maintained older homes on decent-sized lots. The newspaper articles had referred to Anna's residence as an apartment, which I never did understand—this was a neighborhood of single-family homes.

Arriving at the address, I pulled over and parked across the street in a spot where I had a good view. Anna's home, the place where she died, looked like every other house on the street. It was an old white clapboard house with green shutters, two-stories, almost a perfect cube in shape. A variety of bushes, evergreens, and small ornamental trees landscaped the yard.

When I eased my car past the house and driveway, I was surprised to catch a glimpse of an outside stairway in the back leading up to the second story, something I had never noticed before. A ride around the block and into the alley allowed full view of the back of the house. The stairs were situated ten or so feet away from the house and led up to a deck that provided a partial cover for the ground-level patio. It was only then I understood the references to Anna's apartment—the house was a two-flat.

I rolled down my window, took a few pictures, and drove back to the front of the house where I took a few more. I couldn't wait to get them developed—it was helpful to have visuals when trying to solve a case.

A sharp rap on my passenger-side window startled me. The older woman I saw through the glass couldn't have been more than five feet tall. The shawl she wore carelessly wrapped around her chubby little body looked like something she'd grabbed before rushing out the door.

I reached over and rolled down the window nearest to her. She bent forward a bit to get a better look at me, her facial expression hostile.

"What are you doing here?" Her clenched fists rested on her hips, or maybe that was her waist. It was hard to tell.

"Um, nothing really, I was just admiring these homes."

"And taking pictures. Who are you?"

Something pinched inside my stomach. She was small but looked like she could throw a good punch if she had to.

"I'm Ginger Godfrey." I'd been taught in one of my college classes to use a fake name in some circumstances. I figured this was one of them. "I love this house," I told her. "I was just driving down the street and said to myself, 'If I ever get married and have a family, which I'm not sure I'll ever get to do given the string of loser boyfriends I've had lately. Anyway, if I do, this is the type of house I want to have. You know what I mean?"

One interrogation technique I had learned was that if you sensed someone was going to give you a hard time, you should try to distract them with personal information about yourself. I hoped it was okay just to make stuff up. I didn't remember if we had covered that.

Her face contorted into a sneer, and for a moment I thought she was going to blow a gasket or something. She swiped a wisp of her mousy brown hair off her forehead and took a step closer to my car.

"You don't own that house, do you? I must say you have a real gem there if you do. Yep. I'll bet it's gorgeous on the inside too. But I'm sorry. You must be getting cold. It's even cold in here, so you must be freezing."

"Get off my block. And stop taking pictures, or I'll call the police."

"May I ask you just one question?"

Her glare didn't waver.

"That beautiful bush in your front yard...is that a winterberry bush?"

I wasn't sure how long I should wait for her to say something.

"The only reason I ask is because my parents—they're deceased now—my mother tried many times to grow one in our backyard. She would try everything to keep them alive, but they never did survive, and when each one died, well, she was heartbroken. That's the only reason I asked. You must have given yours some pretty special attention." I didn't have to make up that story about my mother. It was true.

She took another step closer and poked her head in. Her face softened.

"The trick is in the watering," she said in a completely different tone. "They don't like to go to bed with wet feet."

"Go to bed?"

"At night. They don't like to be watered at night."

"Really? My mother used to water them every evening."

The woman gasped.

"Worst thing she could have done?"

"Oh, my...yes."

"It's cold. I better let you go."

She gave me a sympathetic look. "Would you like to see it up close?"

Bingo!

"Yes. That would be lovely."

I got out of the car and triumphantly followed her across the street.

"They do better a little farther south, but if you know what you're doing, they can thrive up here too. They like full sun, you know." She glanced over at me. "But not midday. That's when I pull down the canopy, so it's in the shade. And then when the sun reaches about two o'clock, I pull it back up."

Up close, the bush *was* beautiful, nothing like the ones I'd seen my mother struggling with.

"They can get twelve feet high and just as wide if you don't trim them."

"No kidding."

She caressed one of the branches. "They're like my children."

"Well, it shows. Your landscaping is beautiful. You do all this yourself?"

She nodded.

"Someday, when I have a house of my own, can I come to you for advice?"

Her expression melted into a soft smile. "Would you like to come in for a cup of coffee, Miss Godfrey?"

I had a feeling someone who cared so well for a winterberry bush couldn't be all bad.

FOUR

Rumors

"**A** cup of coffee would hit the spot, Mrs..."

"Lawless. But please call me Minnie. And may I call you Ginger?"

"Yes, of course."

I followed her up the front steps and into the foyer. It wasn't often that a real-life situation in investigative work turned into a textbook example of how to do it right. I was proud of myself—this stranger had just invited me into her home. But then it occurred to me that all I'd offered her were lies, and that didn't seem right. They hadn't covered *that* in class.

Minnie pointed to the living room. "Please make yourself comfortable. I'll put a pot of coffee on for us."

While she was in the kitchen, I took in as much as I could—even things that didn't seem important right then could have meaning later on. I made notes on a small pad of paper I kept in my purse.

It was eerily quiet in the living room—the faint sounds of Minnie fussing around the kitchen were all I heard. I couldn't even hear a car go by, and the street couldn't have been more than thirty feet from the house. With the windows closed, it was possible no one would have heard a commotion going on in there, like the day Anna had been murdered.

A fireplace flanked by built-in bookcases that held more knickknacks, photographs, and houseplants than books took up most of one wall. Leaded-glass doors beneath the shelves revealed cabinets filled with cardboard boxes.

I took a seat at one end of the long upholstered sofa in front of the three windows facing the street. On the other side of the room were two cushioned side chairs separated by a large round two-tiered end table. The soft blue and brown tones in the furniture's fabric made the room warm and inviting.

The throw rug in the middle of the room looked familiar to me, but the pattern was common—blue borders, maroon and blue flowers, beige background—so I figured I had probably seen similar ones before. I must have stared at it too long—it made me a little uneasy.

My eyes were drawn to the far wall where there hung a handmade tapestry depicting a long, narrow cobblestone walk meandering through a lush summer garden. A black cat sat on the walk three quarters of the way into the garden, seemingly taking pleasure in the essence of the flowers. There was a feeling about the room that reminded me of our old living room.

"You have a lovely home, Minnie," I practically shouted so she could hear me in the kitchen.

A minute later, she reentered the living room, and as she neared me the unmistakable scent of Cashmere Bouquet talcum powder tugged me back to my childhood when my mother used to hug me close to her chest and say, "I'm so glad you're mine." I never thought anything about it then, but now I wondered what she had meant by that.

"This is just how I pictured this house inside...warm and cozy. Did you raise a family here?"

She gave me a blank stare.

"I'm sorry. I didn't mean to pry."

"So, Ginger, are you from around here?"

"I live near Six Corners, not too far from here."

"And what brings you to this neighborhood?"

I was prepared for that question but didn't feel good about telling yet another lie.

"I went to school with a girl who now lives in Minneapolis but was in town visiting her cousin who lives just a few blocks from here. We had a nice visit."

"Oh, really? What's her name?"

"My friend? Susan Grady."

"No, I meant her cousin."

"Well, her first name is Charlotte, but I don't think I ever heard her last name. Nice girl." I took a sip of coffee, which I never did like. I didn't much like myself just then either.

"Don't know anyone named Charlotte in this neighborhood."

"Well, maybe she hasn't lived here that long. I didn't ask."

"A few blocks in which direction?"

"Um, let's see." I twisted the upper half of my body around to glance out the window and buy some time. "I seem to be a little turned around. I think it's that direction," I told her, pointing across the street. "But I'm not sure now." With my luck, she knew who lived in every house within a two-mile radius.

"No, it can't be there, unless of course, they just moved in, and then it could be the old Jefferson house. I heard there are new owners, but they're older, maybe in their seventies."

"I didn't see anyone else in the house, but maybe they were out. In fact, I'm sure of it. Charlotte was pretty young to own that house all by herself."

"Hmmm."

Minnie's facial expression told me she may have been thinking about how she could find out more about who bought the Jefferson house. All I could think of right then was a line from some poem I had to read in school: "Oh, what a tangled web we weave..."

"Have you lived here long, Minnie?"

"I bought this house in 1943. May 29. The day Rosie the Riveter was on the cover of the *Saturday Evening Post*." She beamed. "I know what events happened on important days of my life. Like on the day I was born, right at the beginning of World War I, Germany declared war on France that day."

She was quite a character.

"That winterberry bush," she said. "It looked like it was about to take its last breath when I bought this place. If I hadn't come along, it would have died for sure."

"You must have a way with plants."

She appeared to be silently reminiscing, so I gave her several seconds to come back to the conversation.

"I bought this house after I lost my daughter and husband."

"I'm sorry."

"I couldn't bear to keep living in the house we had when we got married, so I sold it and bought this one. I was so lonely, and that's what attracted me to this place. I thought maybe the boarders would be company for me."

"Boarders?"

"When I bought it, there were three boarders upstairs. Four rooms, three boarders. But not for long. One by one, they left, and I didn't bother replacing them. Turns out they weren't company at all—just a bunch of weirdoes. One of them even died up there."

It was hard to think with my heart racing so fast. "I just assumed this was a single-family home. It looks like—"

"This house was originally built as a single-family home, but someone who lived here before me must have turned the upstairs into a boardinghouse. That's why there are outside stairs in the back. They were added so the boarders would have a separate entrance."

The story was getting more interesting by the minute.

"If it was during the war, maybe the owner needed the money," I added.

"I suppose. I never met her, the owner that is. I didn't find out until after I was settled in here that she was actually murdered in this house—right here in this room."

So Anna actually owned this house. I hadn't considered that.

"No kidding. What happened?"

"I don't know for sure." She lowered her voice to a whisper. "But I *do* know there was some hanky-panky going on between her and one of the boarders."

"Really? What kind?"

"Well...there were rumors."

It was all I could do to contain the excitement mounting in my chest.

"Rumors?"

"They were having an affair," she whispered.

"How scandalous. It would make for a good book though. I'll have to keep that in mind."

"Are you a writer then?"

"Yes. Well, I would like to be one. So far, all I've done is collect ideas. So do tell, what were the rumors?"

"I shouldn't say. They were just rumors, and—"

A ringing phone interrupted her. Minnie walked across the room to answer it. The conversation was brief.

"Ginger, dear, I completely forgot about my hair appointment. They're going to hold it for me, so I have to run."

"Can I give you a lift somewhere?"

"I was going to call a taxi."

"Oh, don't do that. I'll give you a ride."

"Well, okay. It *would* be faster that way."

Minnie threw on a coat, and we walked to my car.

"Where are we going?" I asked her.

"Near your house—Six Corners."

Realizing there was now not much more time to get information from her, I got right to it. "So, Minnie, tell me more about the juicy rumors you heard about the people who used to live in your house. I love gossip."

"Well, I don't really know exactly what went on there before I moved in, but don't you think it strange that— Oh, look, there's Mrs. Jedlecker! That old battle-ax. She stole my Sunday paper from me once, right off my sidewalk! I like her granddaughter though. Reminds me of..." Her voice trailed off.

"Of who, Minnie?"

"Muriel."

"Muriel?"

"My little girl."

No matter how important it was to maintain my investigator role, I just couldn't. The sadness in her voice was heartbreaking. "How old was she?"

"Six." She paused. "Just six years old. Her first day of school. September 9, 1942. The war was in full swing by then. Everyone was in it—it may have been easier to list the countries that *weren't* in it. September 9..." The sound of her voice appeared to be coming from a different place. "Clarence drove her to school that day. He had the radio on, and when the newscaster said Japan had just dropped a bomb on us—not in Hawaii like Pearl Harbor, but in Oregon—he lost control of the car and ran into a tree."

"How awful."

"By the time I got to the hospital, Muriel was gone, and Clarence was hanging on by a thread. He told me what happened. I didn't tell him about Muriel, but I'm sure he found out soon enough...when he passed over to the other side."

I was trying not to tear up, but it was hard not to. I didn't know what to say, so I kept silent for the next couple of blocks. The rumors didn't seem all that important then.

Minnie broke the silence. "Don't you think it strange that the woman didn't close off the inside stairway to the second floor when she took in boarders? After all, those stairs were in her bedroom. There it is, dear. On the right. See the awning?"

We're there already?

I pulled over, and before I'd come to a complete stop, Minnie had the door open. "Thank you for the lift, Ginger! Do keep in touch, dear!"

It was all I could do to collect myself and drive away—first, the unexpected news about the house having had boarders; then, Minnie on the verge of telling me something provocative about Anna, followed by the tragic story of how she'd lost her husband and daughter. I wasn't sure which of these bombshells was causing my stomach to swirl like it was.

It was four o'clock, and I was just minutes from home. I decided to forego stopping in at the office before climbing up to my apartment. I needed to sort things out without distractions.

I parked the car behind my building and walked through the alley to the front. I was almost past our office windows when I heard a rap on the glass and saw Elmer waving me in. He met me at the door.

"You have a visitor."

Louise Fincutter, the mother of the missing teen, started talking before I'd even sat down. "I got a call from one of Erma's friends who said she'd heard from her. Apparently, she left the house on the South Side where her two half-brothers live and hopped on a bus to Detroit looking for her father."

"How long ago was this?"

"The call? This morning."

"Do you know how long ago she got on the bus?"

"I asked that question too, but her friend didn't think to ask her that."

"What else did Erma tell her?"

"Just that one of her half-brothers gave her some money to look for their father and told her if she found him to let them know."

"Do you know where he is?"

"The last I heard he was in jail, but that was some years ago. I'm sure he's out by now."

"Well, I can check that out. In jail in Detroit?"

"I can only assume that because that's where he's from and where he went after we parted ways. I know it's not here in Chicago, because I have a sister who works at the County Clerk's Office, and she checked that out for me. Flora. You interviewed her when you first took my case."

"Yes, I remember her. The County Clerk's Office, you say?"

"Yes. She's been there for years."

"It would be nice to have an inside contact there. Sometimes—"

"Say no more. I'll talk to her."

Louise gave me more information about her ex-husband before leaving.

I went upstairs with visions of a long bath and a glass or two of Mad Dog, the only wine I could afford. Weighing heavily on my mind was how I was going to manage to continue the search for Erma Fincutter if she was in Detroit looking for her ex-con father.

⊙ FIVE ⊙

That Was No Poker Game

I wasn't in my office five minutes, hadn't even gotten my coat off, when the phone rang. I couldn't imagine who would be calling before eight o'clock. The sun was barely up.

The man introduced himself as Jeff Porter. He suspected his daughter's husband was "shady" and wanted a background check on him. He said he'd bring the retainer check over shortly. He sounded anxious. I named this case Shady Lane.

Since I'd started the business four months earlier, my workload had consisted of mostly skip traces, public record searches, and process serving. A background check would be a nice change of pace, and it paid more.

The tinkling bell told me someone had just walked in the front door. Too early for Elmer. I should have locked the door until we officially opened at nine.

"May I help you?"

A middle-aged woman dressed to the nines and a foot taller than me held out her gloved hand. "Lucie Barnett." She glanced at the NSU sign behind the reception desk. "Are you with NSU?" she asked.

Her handshake was so soft, it was barely noticeable. I introduced myself and led the way into my office. She closed the door behind us.

"I need your services."

"Okay. What is it you need?"

"I want to know where my husband Nathan goes on Thursday nights."

I explained my retainer fee, and before I could finish she had her wallet open.

I spent the next twenty minutes asking Mrs. Barnett questions about her husband and his suspicious behavior: Had he suddenly started taking better care of himself? Was he using different cologne? Was she getting hang-up calls at the house? Had he been working late? Had he been less interested in…"intimacy"?

She answered no to all of them.

She told me she wanted answers immediately and was willing to pay extra for it. Christmas was a month away, and she wanted to have just the right gift for him—new golf clubs if he'd been a good boy and divorce papers if he hadn't.

I named this one Thursdays Out.

Between Shady Lane, Thursdays Out, process-serving, and skip traces, I had a full caseload. My next visit to Minnie would have to wait until after the New Year. In the meantime, I thought I'd send her a little thank-you note and tell her I looked forward to chatting with her again...soon.

When Elmer came in, he brought with him Danny Davis, someone for me to consider taking along on jobs when I didn't feel comfortable going it alone. From a purely physical standpoint, he was perfect—over six feet tall, built like a sumo wrestler, with a face only a mother could love.

I spent an hour with Danny discussing my business and his background, all the while trying to determine whether we were compatible. In the end, I liked the guy. The only thing tough about him was his appearance—his personality and demeanor appeared to be just the opposite. I told him what I was prepared to pay, and he accepted my offer, which was conditional upon a favorable background check.

I didn't need Danny for my Thursdays Out case, which I delved into, doing as much preliminary investigating as I could before Thursday when I could actually surveil Nathan Barnett. I didn't find anything incriminating or even the least bit suspicious in the man's background. He had been a lieutenant in the Army during World War II and had worked for Morton Salt in their engineering department for the past eight years.

While working on Thursdays Out, I'd made calls to the Detroit police, hospitals, and homeless shelters looking for Erma Fincutter and wove in aspects of the Shady Lane case, one of which was to clarify Jeff Porter's son-in-law's age. I questioned it because I'd read in the military record I pulled that he'd been a Navy SEAL during the Korean War, but based on the photograph Jeff had given me, the man looked way too young to have served in the military during that time period. I looked into the SEAL age requirements and did the math—one could have been as young as twenty-eight or as old as fifty-two to have been a SEAL between 1950 and 1953 during the Korean War. In the photo, he looked to be in his early twenties, at the most. A call to Jeff confirmed my suspicion—his son-in-law claimed to be twenty-five and had never mentioned serving in the armed forces. Something didn't add up.

The days flew by as I continued with my cases and a growing number of skip traces. I tried, on several different occasions, to make plans with Beth, whom I missed terribly, but between my unpredictable hours and her busy life with hubby, we never seemed to make a connection.

Lucie called me on Wednesday to tell me that the excuse her husband was using for this particular Thursday was a poker game with his golf buddies. The Barnetts lived in the Conrad Hilton Hotel—I couldn't even begin to imagine what that would be like—so it wasn't going to be easy catching him leave. The hotel was on South Michigan Avenue overlooking Grant Park, and there was no place to park where I could observe him leaving the building.

At six-thirty the following evening, I drove into the Conrad Hilton parking garage, pulled a ticket, and rode around the multi-floor structure until a spot opened up near enough to the exit where I could observe who was leaving. Lucie had told me they were having room service for dinner at six o'clock. My task was to sit in the car and wait for a dark blue Mercedes with license plate number FT1033 to exit the garage.

I didn't mind the waiting time—it gave me an opportunity to reflect on my own case, which had been neglected lately. Minnie was the key to my learning more about what had gone on in the boardinghouse. Sure, I had gotten her to invite me in, but as I had witnessed first-hand, she could be a tough cookie. How much she revealed would depend on me. If I could glean more information about the boarders, especially the one involved in the "hanky-panky," I was sure I'd be closer to knowing who Anna was and how she had died.

At exactly seven-forty, I saw the blue Mercedes exit, so I turned on the ignition, paid the attendant sixty-five cents, and away I went. He turned right out of the garage, toward the park. Then he turned right on Michigan Avenue, and before I knew it, we were on Lake Shore Drive, headed south.

Even though the sun had set an hour earlier, I could still see hear the waves of Lake Michigan rise and fall along the shoreline, creating a virtual playground for the noisy seagulls fluttering above them. I passed the Field Museum and Shedd Aquarium, then Soldier Field, Burnham Harbor, and McCormick Place while keeping an eye on Barnett two cars ahead of me.

Right before the Forty-seventh Street exit ramp, I took my eyes off of his car for just an instant and lost sight of it. I figured he must have taken that exit, but I couldn't get off the Drive until Fifty-first Street. At that point, I felt there was no use continuing. If he had gotten off at the last exit, he'd be long gone by now.

Tailing someone was not an easy thing to do, especially on the crowded streets of a major city.

I exited at Fifty-first Street and drove until I came to Drexel Boulevard, the first major road. In an attempt to circle back to the Drive, I turned right and then right again. I had no sense of direction, and it was poorly lit in that area. I hoped I was going the right way.

I was at the corner of Ellis and Fiftieth when I spotted a car just like Barnett's parked in someone's driveway. I drove past it and affirmed by the license plate that it was his car. What luck! I turned around at the end of the block and parked across the street several houses away.

The neighborhood was a mixture of unremarkable two-story single family homes, a small playground, and what may have been a church at the end of the block. I took out my notepad and jotted some things down and then pulled up closer to the house and snapped several pictures showing the address above the door, the draperied front windows, and Barnett's lone car in the driveway. I observed no other cars parked on the street, so I snapped a few photos of the empty roadway to provide evidence as to the unlikelihood of a poker game going on where Barnett was spending his evening.

I proceeded to drive around the block, hoping there was an alley behind the house. There was none, so I returned to my original vantage point and waited. My mind drifted to Minnie. How would I get a chance to talk with her again? She wasn't listed in the phone book. Then I remembered I had a connection to someone at Illinois Bell who could get unlisted numbers for me—in exchange for a few bucks. But after thinking on that a little more, I nixed the idea. Minnie would be suspicious as to how I knew her number. My best play would be to drop by her house again, this time with a better reason for being in the neighborhood.

After an hour, Barnett's car remained the only one in the driveway. No one had even driven down the street since I'd arrived. I pictured him in the house with some woman, romancing her, telling her whatever he thought she wanted to hear, lying about having a wife, lying about—

In the midst of my rambling thoughts, the front door opened and Mr. Barnett walked out followed by another man whose face I couldn't see very well. I picked up my camera and start snapping pictures. It was dark—a full moon would have helped.

Even under the best of conditions, taking surveillance photos was tricky. You had to position yourself so as not to be seen. You didn't know what the suspect's next move would be. You had no control over the field conditions. You had to take the photos at a distance. And you had to be prepared to back off if necessary.

The darkness helped me stay hidden but worked against my getting good photos. I took multiple snapshots with varying aperture and shutter speeds and hoped at least one of them turned out. I didn't have very sophisticated equipment— just a secondhand 35 mm camera I had picked up at a pawn shop. I didn't have a telephoto lens or anything like that. At least I was able to snap a few photos of the two men as they moved down the walkway away from the house.

When they reached the sidewalk, they turned left and headed away from me. I started my car and drove past them so I could get a better look at the other man, but Barnett was blocking my view of him. I raced to the corner, made a right, and turned around in the first driveway I could. I parked on the street where I could watch them approach the corner. Then I snapped several photos of them walking toward the church, up the steps, and into the building.

I couldn't make out the words on the sign in front of the church from my position, so I drove closer to it. KAM ISAIAH ISRAEL. It was a synagogue. I snapped a quick photo and kept on driving down the block to park in my original spot where I would be able to see them exit.

Lucie had mentioned Christmas during our discussion, not Hanukkah, so I wondered about the Jewish connection.

I didn't know what was going on, but it was a far cry from a poker party.

I waited and watched for thirty minutes, wishing my heater worked, as the temperature outside had dropped significantly since I'd left home on this adventure. Another thing I couldn't afford to get fixed.

When they emerged from the synagogue, I turned on both my engine and headlights in order to get a better look at the other guy. He was wearing one of those Jewish caps, but I didn't know enough about the religion to know whether that meant he was a rabbi or just Jewish.

The two men shook hands as I drove by. I went around the block headed toward home when I met up with Barnett in his car at the corner of Fiftieth and Woodlawn. He waved me through the intersection. I wanted him to go first, but he waited for me to go. *For Pete's sake, just go.* I looked the other way, pretending not to see him, until he finally drove through.

Light from a streetlamp was shining into my car, and I tried to hold my head down as much as possible, but even so I was pretty sure he had seen my face. Time for a change in my appearance. After he turned onto Lake Shore Drive, I followed him, wearing the big floppy hat I kept in the car for such occasions.

I followed him to the garage of the Conrad Hilton, where he parked in a reserved space. My only option was to drive past him. I parked in the first vacant spot and headed toward the elevator.

Once in the hotel's expansive lobby, I found a pay phone from which I called Lucie to tell her where I was and what I had seen. She said she knew of no one at that address and had no idea what her husband might have been doing there. The part about the synagogue really threw her. I had no theories to offer. After ten minutes on the phone, he still hadn't returned to their apartment. We talked for another few minutes, and when he still hadn't returned, I told her I'd look around the hotel and call her back.

I walked through the lobby until I reached the lounge. At the far end of the bar sat Lucie's husband sipping a drink. I sat directly behind him at a small cocktail table for two and ordered a soda. It was a nice bar—not too dark, sleek furniture, just a few patrons, and not very much cigarette smoke. The pianist was playing a Johnny Mathis song I liked.

It was obvious that the bartender knew Barnett. They chatted while he dried the glassware. When Barnett finished his drink, he said, "Put it on my tab," and left. I followed him out at a safe distance until he disappeared behind an elevator door, and I took a final photo.

I gave him a few minutes and then called Lucie to ask if he had returned. When she told me she could hear him coming in, I told her I would write up my surveillance report and call her in the morning.

Heading home, I swung through the Portage Park neighborhood, scouting for an excuse to give Minnie on my next visit as to why I was in that area again, but I didn't see anything, except maybe Portage Park itself, so I pulled into it. It was a sizeable park with a baseball field, swimming pool, tennis courts, and nice landscaping. I drove up to the Cultural Arts building and took a brochure from the display case in the outside vestibule.

When I got home, I turned on my twelve-inch black-and-white TV to see Granny Clampett trying to get Mr. Drysdale to eat possum stew on *The Beverly Hillbillies*. It was kind of a silly show, but it didn't matter because my mind was on the mysterious Mr. Barnett.

I wondered what I would do if I knew my husband was cheating on me. Would I give him a second chance or leave him? It seemed a little unfair not to give someone a second chance, but how could you ever trust him again? And if you didn't have trust, what did you have? Mrs. Barnett was set to leave her husband if he was being unfaithful. I wondered what their marriage was like.

I tried to fall asleep, but my mind drifted to the boarders who used to live in Anna's house. Some of them could still be around and able to shed light on her—how she lived, who her friends were, what kind of landlady she was. I made a mental note to track down Flora Walsh the next time I was at City Hall and ask her if she could find Anna's death certificate, something I had no luck in finding without an inside connection in that department. I made another mental note to thank Louise for putting me in touch with Flora.

* * *

The next day, when I arrived at my office, Elmer greeted me at the door.

"You have a visitor." He gave me a look that said he was annoyed. It was one minute after nine. If he was going to freak out because I was late by one minute, it was too bad. Who did he think he was—my boss?

Seated in my office was Mrs. Barnett. "It's nice to see you again," I said as I sat down in my desk chair and scrambled for the Thursdays Out file. "I'm afraid I haven't had the chance to prepare a report for you quite yet." What did she think... that I worked through the night?

"That's okay. You can put it in the mail to me. I'm always the one who gets the mail." She gave me a quick smile. "I wanted to tell you in person what is going on with my husband." She paused while she brushed an imaginary piece of lint or something off her lap. "My husband lost his mother when he was very young, and unbeknownst to me until now, she was Jewish. His father was a Lutheran, so Judaism was never part of his life. For the past six months, my husband has been studying Jewish history, its culture, and its religious practices under the guidance of Rabbi Ascherman, all in order to have a bar mitzvah."

She closed her eyes for a brief moment, and when she opened them, they were teary. "It had always bothered him, but he had never said a word about it to me."

"Was he eventually going to tell you?"

"He said he wanted to complete the process first before he said anything. Just his way, I guess."

"Did you confront him when he got home? Is that how you found out about this?"

"I did. And he told me he wasn't surprised I knew where he was because after he left the rabbi's home last night, some crazy woman in a ridiculous-looking hat had followed him all the way to our apartment."

"Oops."

"Don't worry. Everything turned out fine."

"I'm glad it did." It was clear I needed to work on my undercover disguises.

"What is the balance of my bill? I would like to pay that now."

Lucie settled her account with me, and after she left I glanced at the check she had written—it was fifty dollars more than what she owed. She probably felt sorry for me, but I didn't care. I was too busy thinking about the skirt steak I was going to attempt to cook on my beat-up hotplate that night.

◆ SIX ◆

Indigent, Unclaimed, and Unknown

The Millers, bless their hearts, had invited me to spend Thanksgiving Day with them. Otherwise I would have been stuck in the six hundred square feet of pathetic space I called home heating up a frozen turkey TV dinner in the toaster oven and then eating it from a tray on my lap. I had often missed the Millers during those first months on my own. Mostly I missed sitting around a table at mealtime, talking with other people. Or maybe it was just the table itself.

"Mom, Dad, there's something we want to tell you," Beth said.

Beth, her husband, her parents, and I had just finished a fabulous turkey dinner and had congregated in the living room. Beth was sitting in her mother's rocking chair smiling from ear to ear. Her husband stood behind her. The Millers and I stopped our conversation and focused on the two of them.

"We're going to have a baby."

Mrs. Miller began to wail—whether in delight or horror, I didn't know. Mr. Miller tried to calm her down. Then Beth began to cry, and her husband appeared like he was about to faint. The dog went crazy—apparently, he didn't like to hear people crying. Beth's father yelled at the dog. The dog got scared and bolted out of the room, almost taking a potted dieffenbachia with him. I wasn't sure what I was supposed to do, so I just sat there...like the fifth wheel that I was.

It took a while for everyone to calm down. By the end of the day, it still wasn't clear to me how Beth's parents truly felt about the baby—I knew they weren't crazy about Beth's husband. But I was happy for her, even if it did feel like it diminished our "best friends" status a little more. After all, it was natural for people to go on with their lives I kept telling myself.

* * *

Thanksgiving Day came and went, and I was left having to face the rest of the holiday weekend alone. I would have jumped in my car and gone somewhere, done something, but money was too tight. I would have visited a relative if I'd had one. Would have reorganized my only closet, but then what would I do seven minutes later when that was done?

On Saturday, I took the "L" downtown to watch the Christmas parade, something I'd never done as a child, even though Christmas had been my mother's favorite holiday. We would start decorating the house weeks in advance. She'd always insisted on having a live Christmas tree, which my father grudgingly brought home at the last minute when they were cheaper. I hated when the Christmas season was over—that was when Mom always seemed the saddest.

The train was crowded, and I had to stand the whole way to Jackson Street. I went with the crowd—I had no other choice—toward State Street. I had heard on the radio that they expected more than 500,000 people downtown watching the parade. I believed it because at least half that many had stepped on my toes trying to get a good viewing spot.

The parade lasted two hours, about an hour longer than the younger children's attention spans. I recognized a few people—Mayor Daley of course, Ray Rayner and Bob Bell from Bozo's Circus, radio DJ Jerry G. Bishop, and Hugh Hefner. I wasn't sure why Hugh Hefner would be in a Christmas parade, but there he was. I rode home on another crammed "L" car and somehow made it through the rest of the weekend.

I spent the following week working on my cases. I was unexpectedly busy: besides the Green Teen and Shady Lane cases and several skip traces, I was hired to conduct an asset check for someone who thought he might be the beneficiary of a large inheritance, and I had to pick up three subpoenas at the courthouse for process serving. Though I'd resolved to put my own case on hold until after the first of the year, I at least had Flora hot on the trail of Anna's death certificate.

Flora called me the week before Christmas but not to talk about Anna.

"Erma called me," she said.

"From Detroit?"

"Yes. She said she needed money to come home."

"She called you and not her mom?"

"She sounded scared. Maybe she was afraid to face Louise."

"So what did you do?"

"Nothing. She hung up before I could do anything."

"Do you know why she hung up?"

"All she said was, 'Forget it. I have to go.' Louise and I are thinking about going there."

"Well, I'm having no luck trying to find her with phone calls. Do be careful if you go."

It occurred to me that maybe it should have my place to go to Detroit as soon as I had heard Erma had gone there. The more I thought about it, the more I knew that was what I should have done, and now I felt bad about it.

* * *

I was in the back room of my office in search of another box of file folders when something on the evidence table caught my eye. I was very organized and had all the documents for my case separated into nice neat piles. But one of the photographs—the one of the woman sitting in a rocking chair holding a baby—was out of place. And it wasn't as though I might have brushed up against the table or something and it had moved a few inches. Someone had tampered with it.

I examined all the other evidence, and nothing else seemed out of place.

On the way back to my office, I heard the door tinkle and found a young boy, maybe twelve or thirteen, standing in front of the reception desk.

"May I help you?"

"I'm here to see Mr. Berghorn."

"Here's not here at the moment. Was he expecting you?"

"No. We just took a chance he'd be here."

"May I take a message for him?"

"No. Well, yes. We live next door to him, and my parents sent me in here to tell him there was a...a thing that happened in his backyard today."

"What sort of thing?"

"Uh, this mean old dog was loose, and he bit three kids, and Animal Control came out and shot it. In Mr. Berghorn's backyard. Close to his back porch. And my parents didn't want him to go ape or anything when he came home and saw a mess of blood."

"How awful." I had been curious about where Elmer lived but had never had an opportunity to ask him. "Where do you live?"

"In the Austin neighborhood. Across from Levin Park."

That's where I grew up. "Really? What street are you on?"

"Ferdinand. On the corner. I gotta go. My parents are waitin' in the car. Thanks, lady."

I pictured my old house, the second one from the corner of Ferdinand and Long Avenue, directly across the street from Levin Park. I wished I could have talked to that boy longer.

I went back to working on Shady Lane. An hour later, Elmer returned and poked his head in my office. I told him about the conversation I'd had with his neighbor. Then I mentioned that I used to live in his neighborhood. His demeanor puzzled me—the longer I talked, the paler he got.

"Are you all right?" I asked him. "That wasn't your dog, was it?"

"No," he said. He turned and headed for his office. I got up and followed him.

"The boy said you live across from Levin Park."

"It's not really across from the park. It's down a ways."

"Really? What's your address? I grew up on that street."

He was sitting in his chair now, reaching for the pack of Marlboros on his desk. "I'm in the...5600 block."

"No kidding. I lived at 5405."

"Small world. Anything else?" he asked.

"No, that was—"

"Good. Could you close my door on your way out?"

"Elmer?"

"What is it?" The edge to his tone rubbed me the wrong way. Don't take it out on me, fella. I'm not the one who got blood on your house.

"May I ask you a question?"

"Later."

I closed his door, maybe a little too hard, and went back to my desk.

When Elmer came out two hours later, he stopped by my office.

"Sorry about before. I have a lot on my mind." His apology sounded indifferent. "What did you want to ask me?"

"I keep the door to my back room locked. Do the cleaning people have keys to it?"

"Uh...I'm not sure. No one has ever locked it before. Why do you ask?"

"Nothing much. I just found something out of place this morning, and—"

"I'll talk to them. You don't want them to clean in there or anything?"

"No. I'll do it myself."

"I'll take care of it."

A few minutes after Elmer left, Flora called to tell me she had looked everywhere there was to look and couldn't find a death certificate for Anna Vargas. We agreed that was odd, because I knew she was dead—it had been in the paper—and she had died in Cook County. Why wouldn't there have been a death certificate?

I spent the next couple of hours tagging the evidence in my back room like I should have done from the beginning.

* * *

With nothing better to do, I worked on Christmas Eve, but even so my spirits were high. The previous day, I had received a check for the Shady Lane case, one that would keep my head above water for the next month. Turned out Jeff Porter's son-in-law wasn't who he said he was. The name and Social Security number Jeff had given to me for him had belonged to a man who was killed in an automobile accident two days before his thirty-second birthday. His son-in-law was really a jobless drug addict with a criminal record that included three counts of wire fraud, burglary, and drug possession. Nice guy. Jeff had been able to help his daughter out of a situation that could have destroyed her life.

I had learned something from the Shady Lane case—you can charge more for cases that have the outcome your client desires. Not that I would ever have padded a bill, but you can bet I didn't cheat myself out of anything on that case like I sometimes did.

Flora Walsh turned out to be a wonderful contact in the Cook County Clerk's Office. While she hadn't managed to locate Anna's death certificate, she had been able to tell me where Anna was buried. I had decided Christmas Eve would be a good day to visit her grave.

It was a twenty-five-mile drive down Cicero Avenue to the cemetery in Oak Forest, a small city southwest of downtown Chicago. Flora had told me to look for Oak Forest Hospital, as Cook County Cemetery was adjacent to it.

The more I thought about Anna on the drive to her gravesite, the more connected I felt with her. Or maybe it was that deep down I wanted someone to feel connected with her, and I was all she had. Or maybe it was the other way around.

I found the cemetery and paused a moment at the small sign by the side of the gravel road leading to the public graves.

COOK COUNTY CEMETERY

FINAL RESTING PLACE

FOR THE

INDIGENT, UNCLAIMED, AND UNKNOWN

The harsh reality of that place was heartbreaking. Couldn't they have come up with a more sympathetic sign?

The grounds were expansive and modestly landscaped. The light freezing drizzle caused my windshield to ice up, making it difficult to read the signs. My budget constraints had forced me to choose between repairing the heater and repairing the windshield defroster. I had opted for the heater.

I found Section K and parked the car. Lot number 131 was right in the middle of the section. I walked through rows of graves until I found Anna's. The twelve-by-four-inch flat stone marking her grave was no different from the thousands of others surrounding it. With the side of my foot, I pushed back the sod that had crept onto the marker.

ANNA T. VARGAS
AUG. 1, 1904 – JAN. 23, 1943

"I wish I knew who you were, Anna," I whispered. "What you were all about and how I fit in." I let the tears run down my cheeks until the weight in my chest subsided. I took a photograph of the marker and quietly left.

I sat in my car for I didn't know how long, and it was only when the depthless sorrow I felt over seeing her grave left my body that I felt the numbness of familial disconnect. Like I had been robbed of one of the most fundamental privileges in life—being raised by a loving mother. I told myself I shouldn't feel that way—I had in fact been raised by a woman who loved me. But I felt deprived nonetheless.

Guilt overcame me on the drive home. My mother deserved better.

I had planned to go out that evening and eat in a decent restaurant—something I hadn't done in ages—but after the visit to Anna's grave, I didn't feel much like it.

* * *

The holidays were behind me, and I had to admit I felt pretty good about my first year—well, partial year—in business. In addition to handling numerous subpoenas and background checks, I had managed thirty-one cases—six significant enough to be assigned a pet name—in addition to my own.

Lying in bed on New Year's Eve thinking about everything that had happened during the past year and what was yet to come, I thought about making a new year's resolution, but then decided against it when I realized the only promise I was going to make to myself in 1965 was to get a life.

⌒ SEVEN ⌒

"Arrest That Woman!"

On my way to visit Minnie, I drove to my old neighborhood because now I was really curious as to where Elmer lived. Once I was on Ferdinand Street and approaching my old address, I pulled over to the curb. To the right of my old house, on the corner, was another small bungalow that could have been the house where the young boy lived. But according to Elmer, he and the boy's family lived two blocks down.

I drove to where Elmer said he lived. The boy had said they were on the corner and Elmer lived next door. One corner had a gas station on it. Another one was an empty lot. Either house on the remaining two corners could have been the boy's house, but neither was across from Levin Park, unless in the boy's mind a block and a half away qualified as "across from."

I drove to Minnie's, thinking something wasn't jiving with what the boy had told me and what Elmer had said, but then I had to take into account that the boy was only a child and it probably wasn't a good idea to take what he'd said so literally.

I arrived at Minnie's a little nervous about knocking on her door and wondering if it was too soon since our first visit. The last thing I wanted to do was come across as nosy or pushy—that could scare her away. But I was so excited to talk with her again, I couldn't bear to wait any longer. And given the way we had left it the last time, I was sure she'd be fine with my stopping by.

On the way to her front door, I rehearsed the story of why I was in the neighborhood. I took in a deep breath and rang the doorbell.

A couple minutes later, Minnie opened the door. Her sour face left no room for doubt that she was not happy to see me.

"How dare you show your face here!"

"What, why? What's the matter, Minnie?"

She shook a finger at me. "Don't you 'Minnie' me, Miss Lindroth. I know who you are!"

It took me a few seconds to gather my thoughts. "Minnie, I can explain."

She closed the door, but not before I could get my foot halfway inside.

"Please let me explain," I told her through the gap. "I'll tell you everything."

"Get your foot out of the door, or I'll call the police."

"Minnie, please. I'm sorry I lied to you, but when I tell you why, I think you'll understand."

"You have no idea what I will or won't understand, so don't even go there. Now get out!"

She tightened the pressure on my foot until I had no choice but to pull it out. When I did, the door closed with a loud thud, followed by the sound of a lock engaging.

I looked down at my foot and the remnant of crumpled duct tape that was caught between the door and the jamb.

I had lost her—my only lifeline—and I had no one to blame but myself. I walked toward my car with the feeling of defeat pushing down on me so firmly it was hard to breathe. If only I hadn't pretended to be someone else, right now I would be sitting in her living room learning more about the woman I thought was my mother. I wondered how many lies I had told her when we first met. Stupid PI work.

I drove home feeling like such a failure...in everything.

I appealed to the gods for dry weather for a while—that had been my last piece of duct tape.

* * *

One good thing came from all the sporadic thoughts I had throughout the next several nights—I figured out a possible way to get back into Minnie's good graces. I knew it was a long shot but figured I had nothing to lose. Correction. I had $11.75 to lose if it didn't work, money I had to withdraw from my meager savings account.

It took me a while, but I finally found a garden center in Wilmette willing to order a winterberry bush for me. A week later, they called to tell me it was in.

I drove to Chalet Garden Center where a friendly face greeted me inside, and when I told her my reason for coming, she chuckled.

"I have your special bush in the back, Miss Lindroth."

I guess I might have gone on a bit on the phone with them about how important getting this particular bush had been to me, even after they'd explained that January in Illinois wasn't the time to plant anything, let alone something as finicky as a winterberry bush. On top of that, I had told them it had to be a mature bush—not some puny little seedling. I didn't care what they thought. I was determined. And desperate.

She came out with a cart that held a parcel wrapped in burlap about the size of a fifty-five-gallon drum. Apparently, they had listened.

I asked her if it could withstand being outdoors overnight if I left it wrapped like it was. She said it should be okay. It was too heavy and bulky for me to carry to my car, so she called for someone to help me.

I was excited and nervous at the same time about what I was about to do, and it took me until I was almost halfway home to ask myself how in the hell was I going to lift that thing out of the trunk and maneuver it down Minnie's front walk and up the front steps to her porch. I laughed out loud. What else could I have done? Cry, I supposed. But then what good would that have done?

It was close to five o'clock when I arrived home, the last sign of the sun barely visible above the low neighborhood buildings. I parked the car and went up to my apartment, still chuckling as I imagined myself dragging this massive bush up to Minnie's porch in the dead of night.

All I had in the apartment for dinner was a can of chili, which I heated up on the hotplate. I poured myself a glass of Mad Dog, and while the chili was heating sat down with a pad and paper and began writing. The words I chose had to be just the right ones. A rough draft was done by the time dinner was ready.

If I made the delivery too early or too late in the evening, I risked getting caught. Someone might even call the police. So I decided to do it early in the morning, before the sun came up.

By the time I'd finished eating, I had the final draft of what I wanted to say to Minnie. I read it for the umpteenth time and then sealed it in an envelope.

* * *

The alarm jolted me out of bed at four-thirty A.M., and I quickly put on some old clothes and headed out. Fortunately, the mild weather meant I didn't need to wear a winter coat and risk getting it dirty—I couldn't afford an expensive dry-cleaning bill.

At that hour of the morning, there was no traffic, so it took me little time to get to Minnie's. When I pulled up in front of her house, there was no one in sight and the neighboring homes were dark.

I opened the trunk. The bush had conveniently rolled to the back, and I couldn't reach it without bending over the edge of the trunk on my stomach and extending my arms as far as they could go. My feet were off the ground as I pulled on the beastly shrub with all my strength. It moved a few inches.

I let go and stood upright to catch my breath before I dove in for another try. That time I managed to pull the bush close to the edge of the trunk. Now to get it out.

I figured I could probably lift twenty-five pounds. This bush was a lot heavier than that, and it was an awkward shape. I grasped it at its trunk and pulled up. It moved, but not much. I tried again, and it moved a little more. I took in a deep breath, gave it all I had, and managed to raise the bush up onto the edge of the trunk.

I was now holding on to the damn thing for dear life so it didn't either fall back into the trunk or onto the street, but I didn't know if I had the strength to lower it to the ground without dropping it.

"What are you doing?" The raspy baritone voice startled me so that I lost the little control I had over the bush. Then I lost my balance and fell down onto the asphalt squarely on my butt with the bush in my lap and the burlap-wrapped upper half of it tight up against my face. I tilted my head back and looked up to meet the policeman's gaze.

I expected him to say something else, but he didn't, so I said the only thing that came to mind.

"Hi."

"What are you doing?" he repeated.

Now, I could have responded to that question in a couple of different ways, and the first answer that came to me was pretty sarcastic, so I chose another one.

"I'm trying to deliver a bush. I don't suppose you could help me get this thing off of me."

He walked around me at a slow gait, shined a blinding light in my face, and said, "I'd hate to get my uniform dirty. It just came back from the laundry."

I counted to five. It was a good thing I did because what I almost blurted out would have definitely gotten me into more trouble than I was already in. I looked down at what little I could see of my lap and realized the burlap wrapping around the roots had broken, and there was dirt everywhere. I managed to push the bush off my lap just as a second police car arrived on the scene. This one had his red lights blaring.

"What seems to be the trouble?" he asked the first cop.

I pulled myself up off the pavement and brushed myself off the best I could.

"Her story is she's delivering a bush."

"A bush."

"A winterberry bush," I explained for no useful reason.

One by one, lights came on in the surrounding homes, and people were peeking out their windows and doors to see what the commotion was all about. A man wearing nothing but boxer shorts came out of the house I was parked in front of and stood on his porch staring at us. Only in his underwear and it was forty-something degrees out there.

Then my worst fear became reality. Minnie, wearing a plaid nightgown, fuzzy slippers, and a shawl around her shoulders, marched toward us like Sergeant Carter out to get Gomer Pyle after he'd done something incredibly stupid.

"Arrest that woman!" she shouted.

"Calm down, lady. She hasn't done anything illegal...that we know of."

"I know her! She's an imposter!"

"What do you mean she's an imposter?"

It was getting more absurd by the minute. Now all the neighbors were out on their porches watching us.

"Officer, I can ex—"

"I'll get to you," he said before I could finish my sentence.

He turned to Minnie. "Now what were you saying?"

"She lied to me...about who she was. Gave me a phony name and other lies too."

The policeman turned toward me. "Is that true?"

"I was desperate to get to know her, and I shouldn't have lied. That's why I'm here with this winterberry bush. I wanted to make amends. Apologize to her. It's a peace offering." The longer I spoke, the more pathetic I sounded...even to me.

Minnie grunted something inaudible, turned back toward her house, and walked away.

"Take her away," she shouted.

"What do we do with the bush?" the second cop asked the first one.

"Throw it away. Find a dumpster in an alley somewhere," he said.

Minnie stopped walking and turned around. She looked directly at me. "It's a winterberry bush?" she asked.

I nodded. "With a note to you inside."

She walked back to us and glared at cop number one.

"You can't mistreat a precious bush like that by throwing it in a dumpster." She gestured toward me. "Now, her...well, *she's* a different story."

"Ma'am, what do you suggest we do with the bush? We can't exactly plant it anywhere," the cop said sarcastically.

"Can you put it in my garage? Someone has to rescue the poor thing."

"Yes, ma'am. We can do that." The cop turned toward me. "I suggest you leave this neighborhood and don't come back."

"Yes, sir."

Completely disheartened, I drove home and went back to bed.

∽ EIGHT ✍

"I Hate Coffee"

A week after the ill-fated winterberry bush incident, I was still feeling embarrassed and totally stupid. Though Minnie now had my phone number and address, I was not optimistic she'd ever contact me. I doubted she'd even read the letter I had tucked inside the burlap wrapping. She probably burned it.

I tried to move forward on my case by following up on the scant information I had gleaned from Minnie during our first meeting, but after several false starts, I was no further along.

It could be that Minnie had told me everything she knew about the boarders and the "hanky-panky" that went on in the house before she'd bought it. If that was the case, I wouldn't have felt so bummed out about having ruined my relationship with her. If that was the case.

* * *

I woke up at two-thirty in the morning, shivering. Damn heat had gone out again. Past experience told me it was no use calling Elmer—it wouldn't be fixed until Monday morning anyway. I donned two sweaters, put the only other blanket I owned on top of the one already on the bed, and then draped the bedspread over that.

After thirty minutes, I decided that wasn't working, so I got up and put a kettle on the hotplate for a cup of tea and then left the rest of the water boiling, hoping the steam would provide a little heat for the room.

It was Sunday. I wasn't sure what to do with myself at such an early hour—I had ironed everything in sight. No use turning on the television—all that was on were test patterns this time of day. Why were they on anyway? What did they test?

No use going down to my office—the heating systems were connected.

December had been a good month, and I had a little extra cash, so I decided to drive over to Lou Mitchell's and have myself one of their big breakfast skillets, something I hadn't had in years. I knew they opened early.

I got dressed and jumped in my car, the comforting taste of eggs, bacon, and hash browns the only thing on my mind. The car's heater was still out, so it was a chilly ride to Lou's. I arrived at five-fifteen and had to wait for a table—the restaurant was packed.

After eating the best breakfast I'd had in a very long time as slowly as I could, I paid the bill and headed home, wishing there was somewhere else I could go that was warm and didn't cost anything. No place came to mind.

I was at the bottom of the long staircase leading to my apartment when I heard my phone ringing. I couldn't imagine who would be calling at that hour.

I raced up the stairs.

"Hello."

"Miss Lindroth?" It was Minnie.

"Yes."

"Where have you been?"

Quickly reminding myself it would serve no purpose to be sarcastic, I put on my diplomacy hat and answered her.

"I just walked in the door after having breakfast at Lou Mitchell's. Is this Minnie?"

"Pretty extravagant for someone who lives in a one-room apartment over a two-bit lawyer's office."

I took in a deep breath and reminded myself of what she meant to me.

"Actually, that's my office too. And thank you for contacting me."

"Well, I wasn't going to, but then I thought to myself, you owe me one big apology, young lady."

"I know I do. Would you like it over the phone or may I come over?" I silently begged her not to hang up.

"I suppose."

You suppose what? "When would be a good time?"

"Would I be calling now if it wasn't a good time?"

I took a chance she meant an in-person visit. "I'll be there in a few minutes then. Can I bring anything?"

"How about the truth?"

She was a tough old bird, but I deserved that retort.

"I promise you that."

As I drove, I started to rehearse what I was going to say, but then put the kibosh on that thought—better not to come in with a prepared speech. I decided to wing it and just tell the truth—like I should have done before. I would leave my PI hat in the car.

I was at the stop sign at Belle Plaine and Lawter when my car conked out. Talk about bad timing! I was less than five blocks from her house. I pumped the gas a few times and tried to start it. Nothing. I repeated the process until I became sickened by the smell of gas.

I felt the blood rise up in my neck. I threw the car into neutral, turned the steering wheel toward the curb, jumped out, and pushed it out of the lane of traffic. Then I locked the car and hoofed it to Minnie's.

She was standing in the doorway waiting for me—a scowl on her face, clenched fists resting on her hips.

"Took you long enough. Where's your car?"

"It died a ways down the street."

"Where?"

I told her which corner.

"You're just going to leave it there?"

I wondered if she was going to invite me in or if we were going to have this conversation outside until one of us froze to death.

"I can call my mechanic if I may use your phone."

"How soon can he get here?"

What difference does it make? "I don't know. It's pretty early to call and—"

"C'mon in. What do you want to do—freeze out here?"

I wondered what her husband was like.

Minnie left me standing in the foyer. I didn't know if I should stay there, saunter in and sit down in the living room, or follow her into the kitchen. I could hear her talking on the phone.

"Pat? Yeah, this is Minnie. There's a tan and maroon Chevy broken down at Belle Plaine and Lawter. Might be a while before the mechanic can get here. Can you make sure it's not towed?" She paused to listen to the response. "Okay, thanks. And Patty, if old lady Shuffleherbottom complains, tell her to stick it in her ear." She paused again. "Whatever. Bye."

She approached me with an emotionless expression on her face.

"Sit down, for Pete's sake, and I'll put a pot of coffee on."

"Minnie."

"Yes."

"I hate coffee."

Her glare was penetrating.

"I'm just being really honest here."

"How about Scotch then?"

"It's a little early for that, don't you think?" I knew as soon as the words left my lips that it was the wrong thing to say. "But then I've never tried it, so what the heck."

"Good, because I never drink alone." She paused. "Who am I kidding? I always drink alone. I'll pour you a small one. Maybe you'll like it. Maybe you won't. But you'll never know until you've tried."

After she poured the drinks and handed me one, she sat down on the opposite end of the sofa and held up her glass. "To the truth then?"

I held up my glass as well. "To the truth."

I took a sip and tried not to wince as it took a burning glide down my throat. How could anyone drink this stuff? But then it was barely seven A.M. Surely, that made a difference. Or maybe it was an acquired taste.

"Talk," she said.

I wasn't sure if I could. "Okay," I stammered. "Here's the short version. I have reason to believe my real mother was Anna Vargas, the woman who was killed in this house right before you bought it. I'm looking for answers, and you have some knowledge of what went on here. That's all I ever wanted from you. I promise."

"Then why didn't you just tell me that in the first place?"

"I have a private investigator's license, and I think I got carried away with assuming that role instead of being me—just a lonely girl searching for the truth."

"You don't look so lonely to me."

"Minnie, my parents, the two people who raised me, died in our home from carbon monoxide poisoning when I was seventeen. I just spent Christmas and New Year's by myself in an apartment not much bigger than your living room, and I'm living on a shoestring budget not knowing if I can make the next month's rent."

She didn't say anything for several seconds.

"I'm not at all happy with the way you've conducted yourself. You ought to be ashamed."

"I *am* ashamed of the way I handled myself, and I apologize to you for that."

"Look, Gracie. I may not have gone to some fancy school like you, but that doesn't mean I don't know how to get to the bottom of things. So if you're done feeling sorry for yourself, let's get down to business. What makes you think Anna Vargas was your mother?"

The only person who had ever called me Gracie was my mother. I pleaded with my emotions to remain under control.

I told her about the box of mementoes and other things I'd found in the attic, including the photo of the woman I was convinced was Anna holding a baby I was convinced was me. Then I told her about the second photo of the woman in the rocking chair and the inscription on the back, CELINA THALIA VARGAS—JUST HOME FROM THE HOSPITAL, and my own photo of me as a baby wearing the same dress as the baby in the first photograph.

"What does that prove? Maybe your mother and Anna knew each other."

"But the inscription on the back of the one in the rocking chair wasn't one a friend would write—it's something a mother would write."

"All babies look alike. Maybe that wasn't you."

"But the dress—"

"Walk into any Monkey Wards. They have more than one copy of the same dress."

"And here's the other thing, Minnie. My middle name is Thalia. And the baby she's holding has the same middle name. And guess what Anna's middle name was. Thalia. That's a pretty uncommon name, don't you think?"

"Well, I'll give you that."

"So you'll help me?"

She shrugged. "I'll tell you everything I know, but I'm not sure how much that will help you."

"Thank you."

"God only knows why, but I like you."

"I like you too."

"Of course you do—you want something from me."

"No, it's—"

"How's the Scotch?"

"It's beginning to grow on me."

"Another?"

"Maybe just half, and while you're pouring, may I ask you something?"

"Do you see anything stopping you?"

"What made you change your mind on talking to me?"

She turned to face me and heaved an audible sigh. "You put a lot of thought into that winterberry bush, and a lot of effort getting it here, even if it was utterly stupid to think it would survive a winter planting. But stupidity aside, I was touched by what you did—says something about your character."

She handed me my glass and sat back down.

"So do you want to know what I know, or do you want to spend the next hour getting all sappy over each other?"

"I like a little sap now and again."

"Well, I don't, so here's what I know." She looked down at her lap and played with one of the buttons on her dress. For a brief moment, I thought she was going to say something else that would fit into the category of "sappy," but then she didn't.

"I think I told you after I lost my Clarence and little Muriel, I couldn't live in that house any longer, so I sold it and bought this place. It was the summer of

'43. Apparently, Anna didn't have a will or any family because I bought it from the state. And the funny thing is that less than a week after I bought it, someone offered to buy it from me for a thousand dollars more than what I paid for it. Can you imagine that?"

"Do you remember the name of the person who wanted to buy it?"

"No. But I never throw anything away. If I wrote it down, I probably still have it somewhere. I'll hunt for it if you like, even though I don't know how it will help you."

"I'd appreciate that. And if you don't mind me seeing all the closing documents, they may reveal something as well."

"Okay. Like I said, I don't throw anything out."

"I'm sorry. Go on."

"I didn't know what had happened to Anna before I bought the house, and when I found out, I was horrified."

"You had started to tell me last time about some rumors going around about Anna."

"Let me tell you about the boarders first. Then I think the rumors will make more sense."

I was feeling a little buzz from the alcohol and was afraid I'd forget some of what she had told me by the time I got home. "Do you mind if I take notes?"

"Be my guest. The boarders. They were something else. Let me tell you about the dead one first—Mark Smith. I bought the house in late May, moved in all my things within a week. Met all but Mr. Smith that same week. Didn't meet him until a month later when the rent was due. Before that, I had knocked on his door to introduce myself a few times, and even though I knew he was in there, he didn't answer. Then, late one evening, I couldn't sleep and went to the kitchen to warm up a glass of milk. As I was drinking it, I saw a dark figure pass by the window. Well, I grabbed a baseball bat I keep for just such occasions and stood by the back door ready to clobber the person in case they tried to break in."

"You must have been scared to death."

"Nothing much scares me, sweetie, but I suppose my heart was pounding a little fast. Anyway, he didn't try to break in. Instead he slipped an envelope under the door. I opened it, and inside was seven dollars and fifty cents and a note that read 'July rent from Mark Smith.' So I dashed outside—I'm in my nightgown, mind you—and I reach the bottom of the outside staircase just as he reaches the top, and I yell up at him, 'Hey you. I'm Minnie Lawless. Nice to meet you.'

"He looks at me—I can barely see his face. He gives me a little wave, and disappears inside. And that's pretty much how it was until he died."

"How did he die?"

"As far as I know, he had a heart attack. At least that's what the paper said. All I know is one morning I went to the A&P to buy groceries, and when I got home, there was an ambulance out front. The police came, and I asked them what I was supposed to do with the little stuff he had. And after they looked around, they said throw it out unless I wanted anything. There wasn't anything to speak of—worn-out clothes, some books, an old Philco radio, and a pile of newspapers."

"How old was he?"

"He was an older man, maybe in his seventies. Then there was Henry Sikes. Pale-faced little busybody. Mousy-looking, that's what he was, afraid of his own shadow, but into everybody's business. And he wasn't even a decent busybody... you know, one who shares what he knows. No, he stuck his nose in where it didn't belong and then kept it all to himself. Except about Anna, but I'll get to that.

"The last character was... Give me a minute to think of his name. And I use the term 'his' loosely. Ah, yes, Dorian Ross. I know he was a man—no woman I know has an Adam's apple—but he dressed like a woman. The whole nine yards. Full makeup, blond wig, dresses, and high heels. Hell, he had prettier clothes than I did. Can you imagine that? A real weirdo."

"Any idea where he is now?"

"No, and I don't want to know."

"You said before there were four rooms upstairs."

"Two large ones—I charged seven-fifty for those. And two smaller ones for five bucks. One bathroom. Would you like to see them?"

"Yes, of course."

"C'mon. I'll take you up the inside staircase, and you'll see how the rumor story fits in."

We walked through the foyer and down a hallway to the back of the house.

"This is my bedroom," she said as we entered a good-sized room. It was sparsely decorated with a double bed and matching dresser; two nightstands; a well-worn overstuffed armchair; the winterberry bush I had given her, now planted in a large terra-cotta pot; and a rocking chair.

I couldn't take my eyes off the rocking chair.

"What's the matter, Gracie?"

"That's the chair!"

"What chair, dear?"

"The same rocking chair Anna was sitting in as she held me. It's in the photo!"

"It can't be. I..." Her voice trailed off.

"You what? Where did you get it?"

"I don't remember. This is a very common chair. You could buy one like it anywhere back then." She paused a moment. "Come to think of it, it *was* left here.

I found it in the basement and thought it was a shame to leave it down there. It was in such good shape and all. So I brought it up here."

Minnie led me to the far corner of the room toward a five-foot artificial tree, which she dragged out of the way to reveal an enclosed staircase. I followed her up the stairs.

"My guess is that my bedroom was originally the dining room when this house was first built, and they walled off the stairs when it was converted to a boardinghouse. That's the only way this staircase makes any sense."

I followed her to the top of the stairs where it was so dark I could hardly see her. When she opened the door, light came through along with a good whiff of cold stale air.

We entered a bedroom. She twirled around to face me. "So do you get the rumor now?"

"I see two bedrooms connected by a staircase. Are you saying Anna and whoever was in this bedroom were having an affair?"

"According to Mouse-face, they were."

"So who lived in this room?"

"Don't know. This room was empty when I bought it."

"Mouse-face, I mean Henry, didn't divulge who he was?" I asked.

"No. C'mon, I'll show you the rest."

We walked across the hallway to a smaller room.

"Henry lived in this one."

"Do you know anything about him? Where he went after he left here?"

"No. He left right after Smith died, the same day, in fact. No goodbye. No forwarding address. Didn't even ask for a refund on the unused rent money."

We went back into the hallway and into another small room.

"Cross-dresser's," she said.

The last room had belonged to Mark Smith, the elderly man who had died there.

"That's it. Have you seen enough?"

"I guess so."

"I'll show you the rest of the downstairs," she said as we descended the staircase. "It's not much, but it suits me well enough. After all, I've been here almost twenty-two years."

We entered the kitchen where I used her phone to call my mechanic, who said he'd drive to the car and try to get it started. He said he'd call me to let me know if he succeeded.

"I haven't done anything in here. It's all original," she told me.

The kitchen was good-sized, but with the large counter-height island in the middle, we had to walk single file around it. It was an interesting piece of furniture with drawers and cupboard space underneath and a swing-out seat where one could sit and peel potatoes, shuck corn...or something. I had never seen anything like it.

Minnie led me to a small room next to the kitchen where there were baskets of yarn, fabric, and ribbon everywhere. A treadle sewing machine was in the corner.

"I use this as a sewing room, but I have a feeling it may have been a nursery at one time."

"What makes you think that?"

"Because there was pink-and-white-flowered wallpaper in here when I bought it. Looked to me like a baby's room. Took me weeks to peel the damn stuff off."

I was sure she didn't realize how that sounded to me—that "damn stuff" might have been what I had viewed as my world back then.

The closet door was ajar, and I peeked in. My heart raced.

"You mean this wallpaper?"

"Mm-hm. I forgot I didn't take it down in the closet. Too damn hard to get off."

After my parents died, I went through all their things and took with me anything I thought was important or of any value. One of the things I threw away was a partial roll of pink-and-white-flowered wallpaper—just like in the closet. At least, I was pretty sure it was the same. I remember wondering why the heck it had been stuffed in the back of the closet my father used for his clothes. I wished I had been able to save everything from that house.

"Are you all right, Gracie?"

"I think I need to sit down."

We went back to the living room.

"And it wasn't wallpaper that was hung in any of the rooms in your house?"

"No. I'm thinking it's connected to the wallpaper here."

"That doesn't make any sense. Why would your parents have some of the wallpaper Anna had in the nursery here?"

"I don't know. It's one more puzzle piece."

"Has this been helpful, dear?"

"You have no idea."

Minnie got up to answer a ringing phone.

"Bob says your car should be fine now. Something about your idle. If you still can't start it, he said to call him back."

"Minnie, can we keep in touch?"

"You think I'd spend this much time with you if—"

"Do you think the winterberry bush will make it?"

"I doubt it, but it won't be because I didn't try everything to save it."

Probably best that I didn't further that thread of conversation—too much opportunity for it going downhill.

NINE

Ties to Mexico

"This is stupid," he said. "I didn't see anything."

The man was not happy to see us at his door on an early Monday morning, especially after I told him he was being called as a witness in a mugging case. I had brought Danny with me to serve him the subpoena, since the address was in a sketchy neighborhood on the West Side.

"Then your testimony won't take very long," I explained.

He raised his voice. "You're taking me from my work, lady. I have a family to feed."

The reason for being subpoenaed usually didn't matter—most people were not happy to be served, so I was always ready for a bad reaction.

Danny took a step closer to him. "Just who do you think you're talking to...sir?"

"Give me the damn paper," the man said. He signed it and thrust it back to me.

Had Danny not been there, I would have had to have put up with that man's rant for a lot longer, and then he still might not have signed.

After dropping Danny off at a bus stop, I returned to my office to prepare a list of things to check out at City Hall where I planned to go a little later in the day. But before I knew it, it was noon, and I had six new subpoenas, three skip traces, and another runaway teen. I decided to defer my trip to City Hall.

At six o'clock, I called it a day. Before I went upstairs to my apartment, I grabbed several items from the Attic Finds evidence table thinking maybe something would strike me as important in light of what Minnie had recently told me.

Once upstairs, I ate an overdone Swanson TV dinner, tuned in the radio to a jazz station, and sorted the documents I had found in my parents' attic into three piles: receipts, bank statements, and contacts.

There were roughly fifty receipts bundled together with a thick rubber band— all related to the house on Belle Plaine Avenue, now Minnie's house. I sorted them by type and date and ended up with three piles—home improvements, rent, and purchases. The home-improvement receipts went all the way back to 1939, and some of them were so vague it was hard to tell what they were for. Like the one that said "basement build-out" under Description of Work. What did that mean? How did one build out a basement? Weren't basements built when the house was built? You either had one or you didn't.

I was even more confused upon noticing that the basement build-out receipt had my parents' Ferdinand Street address on it and not Anna's. I fanned through all the receipts—only that one had the Ferdinand address. It was dated July 14, 1943. I had just seen my first birthday.

I moved on to the rent receipts, which were just scraps of paper, but they included dates—for every month in 1942 and January of 1943. Anna died on January 23, 1943. There were no names on the receipts, just initials.

MS   I assumed this was Mark Smith. Thirteen receipts, one for each month, each one dated the first day of the month.

HS   Henry Sikes, aka Mouse-face. Ten receipts between March 1942 and January 1943, each one dated between the first of the month and the tenth. On one was written late again.

DR   Dorian Ross, the cross-dresser. Six receipts between July and December 1942, each one dated toward the end of the month.

The initials matched the names of the boarders Minnie had given me and supported her statement that they all lived there when she bought the house. This was important—I could trust Minnie's memory.

The rent receipt dates told me a little something about the boarders. Mark Smith had been punctual and consistent with his payments. Henry Sikes had often been late and inconsistent with his, and Dorian Ross had always been early. I wasn't sure if that information would ever be useful, but it was interesting.

No receipts for the fourth boarder. Perhaps the boarder with whom Anna was having an affair hadn't paid any rent? If so, what did that say about Anna?

There were five receipts for purchases over $50, all of which had purchase dates in 1939.

1. $59.95 – RCA floor-model radio-phonograph, model 39-19F
2. $79.50 – Maytag electric washer, model 108, porcelain tub
3. $1,758.76 – 939 Buick Roadmaster, black with red interior

4. $129.35 – 12-piece mahogany bedroom set
5.   Torn receipt for a combination floor safe – no price information

I didn't think the average middle-class person could have purchased most of these items—whoever had purchased them had money. Two things stood out: the "floor safe" and the washing machine. For some odd reason I remembered one day when I was nine or ten years old, our neighbor Mrs. Hindslip had knocked on our back door presumably to borrow a cup of sugar, but at the time I thought she was just being nosy and wanted to make chitchat with my mother. Mom never talked with any of our neighbors. I told her Mom was in the basement doing laundry. She edged her way closer to the basement door and asked me if the sound that was coming from down there was an automatic washer. I didn't know, so I told her I'd go down and ask her. When I asked my mother about the washer, she told me to tell Mrs. Hindslip she was busy and I was not to let anyone inside our house again, neighbors included. When I went back upstairs, Mrs. Hindslip was gone.

I never did understand what that was all about. When I asked my mother about it later, she didn't want to talk about it. That washer broke when I was in high school, and my parents bought another one. I wished I knew if that first one had been a Maytag model 108.

It occurred to me that I might have been going about this all wrong. Maybe I should have been examining things I'd salvaged from my parents' home for possible ties to Anna Vargas instead of the other way around. I wished I had more of their things. God only knows what happened to them.

I picked up the stack of bank statements, each of which was for the year ending December 1942.

>   North Community Bank, balance of $7,801.11
>   San Diego Bank, balance of $1.00
>   Banco Nacional de Mexico, balance of 39,219 pesos

There was no indication of the account numbers or the owner of the accounts, since the tops of the statements had been torn off. I had no idea what that meant, but it made me even more curious about the whole situation.

I spread out the three business cards.

>   IGNACIO RAMIREZ, ASESOR
>   PETRÓLEOS MEXICANOS
>   VERACRUZ, MEXICO

MARTIN TORRES, ATTORNEY
HIGGINS, FLETCHER & McKENZIE
SAN DIEGO, CALIFORNIA

KENNETH ANDERSON, FINANCIAL ADVISOR
AMERIPRISE FINANCIAL
CHICAGO, ILLINOIS

Two names—Tymon Kossak and Essie—with phone numbers had been written on two separate scraps of paper.

If these records had belonged to Anna Vargas—and I was sure they had—then it appeared she had ties to Mexico. Her last name, Vargas, sounded like it could be Mexican. If she was my mother, I might be Mexican, or part Mexican. But then again, Vargas could have been her married name.

I fetched my phone directory and found a Tymon Kossak with an address on the Northwest Side. I was familiar with that part of town, as I had served a couple of subpoenas there. Polish neighborhood. Nice people. The phone number was different from the one written on the scrap of paper, so I wasn't sure if the address was meaningful.

I didn't think I had what it took to peruse the phone book for anyone having a first name of Essie, especially considering the likelihood that the name was short for something else. But it occurred to me that the phone books in the late thirties were likely a lot smaller, and the main branch of the Chicago Public Library had old phone books for all the major cities.

It was past ten, and I was spent. I put everything back in the box, did my paltry beauty routine, and crawled under the covers.

Just as my brain began making its moony journey into that relaxed state I so enjoyed, I remembered a letter among the attic finds written by someone named Nacho. Had he—I assumed Nacho was a male—mentioned Veracruz in it? The answer to that question would have to wait.

∞ TEN ∞

The Real Bird-Dogger

The next day, I spent the afternoon at City Hall going through boxes of Cook County voter registration records, finding nothing even close to the 1943-and-earlier records I was seeking. This work was pure drudgery—the boxes were unorganized, unlabeled, and uninteresting. The room itself was horrible—dim lighting, dust on everything, and no air movement.

The fact that World War II had been raging throughout the early 1940s didn't help matters—fewer people had registered to vote. And I imagined boardinghouse residents would have been even less likely to register than other people, wartime or not.

Finally, the forty-eighth box brought me some hope. I found a voter registration form from September 1945, right after the war ended. The next three boxes were full of wartime voter forms.

At 4:15, after spending most of the day there, I was asked to leave so that the staff could begin closing up. I had gone through only about one third of the boxes. My lungs felt as though they had been coated with dust; I had managed to get two paper cuts; and I was hungry. Tomorrow would be another day.

On my way out, I stopped by Property Taxes and learned that Anna had bought the house on November 10, 1939. Oddly, there was no record of Minnie having bought it in 1943. I also learned my family's old house on Ferdinand Street had sold on July 29, 1960, to a Canadian entity named Waddershins Trust. Trusts were a pain to trace, and the fact that this one was Canadian made it that much more difficult.

I walked the four blocks to the library from City Hall, even though it was below freezing. The fresh air on my face and in my lungs was invigorating.

I loved Chicago's main library with its domed Tiffany glass ceiling in the center, the grand staircase leading to the second floor, and all the wonderful quotes from historical authors high up on the walls, each one crafted from a different material—colored stones, stained glass, and mother of pearl.

For copies of old phonebooks, I was directed to the microfilm room. Anna had owned the boardinghouse from the end of 1939 to the beginning of 1943, so I planned to concentrate on phone books from 1940 through 1942.

I knew finding Essie wouldn't be easy. I got as comfortable as I could in the stiff wooden chair provided to me and began the arduous task of searching for her name—page by page, column by column, line by line. After two hours, I found a listing for Esmeralda Noe with an address on Warner Avenue, which I knew to be the street just north of Anna's house. The phone number didn't match the handwritten one I'd found, but it was promising none the same.

I asked the reference librarian where I could find a Spanish-to-English dictionary and if there were any reference materials that would help me locate someone in Mexico. She directed me to the dictionary and suggested the Consulate General of Mexico. I asked her if she had any reference materials on Mexican companies, and she again directed me to the consulate's office.

The Spanish dictionary told me asesor meant advisor, so it appeared that Mr. Ramirez had been an advisor to Petróleos Mexicanos. I found *petróleo* in the dictionary and confirmed that it meant petroleum, as I had expected.

While driving home, I mentally prioritized what to do next—finding out more about Tymon Kossak and Esmeralda Noe was high on the list. My next visits would be to the Department of Motor Vehicles, the Social Security Administration, the County Assessor's Office, the Recorder of Deeds, and the Clerk of the Circuit Court.

* * *

I decided to combine my visit to Esmeralda's neighborhood with another visit to Minnie. I called Minnie first, and she said my timing was perfect as she had some information for me.

Minnie was smiling as she opened her front door. "Come in! Come in! I have something for you."

It was hard to believe this was the same woman who less than a month earlier had told police to preserve the winterberry bush but didn't care what happened to me.

We sat in the front room where she handed me several documents. The first one was a letter giving a senior vice president with the First National Bank of Chicago power of attorney over Anna's estate. Next was a copy of a cashier's check for $500 from Minnie made out to the same bank, followed by a copy of the deed and the Seller's Certification.

I looked up at Minnie's wide grin.

"So I did good, huh?"

"You did excellent."

"You can keep everything. I had copies made for you."

"Thank you. What do I owe you?"

"Are you kidding? People do things for..."

She didn't have to finish in order for me to get the message.

"On another subject, do you remember anything besides that rocking chair that was left behind in the basement...or anywhere else in the house for that matter?"

Minnie gave that some thought. "There probably was, but I don't remember anymore. You can look in the basement if you like. I don't use it for anything but the washer and dryer."

"Let's go."

We made our way down the steep concrete stairs to a dark, dank basement. Minnie turned on the only light—a bare bulb hanging from the ceiling near the middle of the basement's only room.

"How do you even see to do laundry down here?"

"It's not easy."

She pulled out a lantern from a large metal cabinet located near the steps and turned it on. "Here, use this."

The lantern helped as we walked around the perimeter of the basement—past Minnie's laundry area, the furnace, the water heater, a pile of old gardening tools, and a corner shelving unit that held paint cans, small pieces of lumber, and some other tools. I observed a fern stand next to the shelving and shone the light on it.

"This is nice. Is it yours?" I asked her.

"No. That must have been left behind. You can have it, if you like."

"I can?"

"Sure. Take it."

It was heavy—too heavy for me to wrangle up the stairs.

"Do you mind if I come back for it with a helper?"

"Sure. Come whenever you like."

"Minnie, what's in here?" I asked, pointing to a walled-off section in the corner near the stairs.

"Nothing. It's not a room or anything."

"Something has to be back there. There's no door?"

"Not that I know of."

I shined the lantern on every inch of the two cement walls and found no door. The space was square-shaped, roughly ten feet on each side.

"Do you have access to the basement from outside?"

"No. Just the stairs we came down."

"Well, that's pretty odd then."

"Maybe it was an old cistern that someone closed off when it was no longer needed."

"What's a cistern?"

"Houses used to have them to catch rainwater, before indoor plumbing."

"Can we look outside at this corner of the house?"

"Seen enough down here then?"

"Yep."

I followed Minnie up the stairs. We grabbed our coats and headed for the northwest corner of the house.

We saw no evidence of anything on the outside of the house that remotely resembled something that would have caught rainwater.

"Is this your bedroom?" I asked her, pointing to the corner of the house above the walled-off room.

"Yes."

I was baffled.

When we went back inside, Minnie put on a pot of tea. Five minutes later, she joined me in the living room with the tea and a plate of chocolate chip cookies.

I took a bite of cookie. "Homemade?"

"You can't tell?"

"Of course, I can." What was I thinking? "Minnie, do you know any more about Anna's death than what you've already told me? Even if it's something small, it could help."

"What I told you I heard from Henry. He had his nose in everybody's business, so I figured he knew things."

"Nothing more about the man who lived in the room above your bedroom, the one he seemed to think Anna was having an affair with?"

"Now that you mention it, I do remember one thing. He said something about the man's wife...but I don't remember what."

"So this guy was married?"

"I think he gave me that impression, but it's been so long..."

"I know. If you do remember, will you let me know right away?"

"Yes, of course."

"One more thing, Minnie. Do you know anyone by the name of Esmeralda Noe on Warner Avenue?"

"No, I can't say that I do. What block?"

"Same block as this."

"You know which house?"

I gave her the address.

Minnie thought for several seconds. "That's either Vineta Stone's house or the Rigby place. No one by that name in either of those families. But let me give that some thought. I may be able to come up with something."

We ended our visit with some idle chitchat, and as I was getting ready to leave, Minnie handed me a brown bag.

"Some cookies for the road."

It took me two minutes to drive to the address on Warner where Esmeralda had once lived. I parked down the street a little and munched on a cookie while I observed the house. Five minutes into my quasi surveillance, there was a loud rap on my window. It was Minnie motioning me to let her in.

"Is something wrong?" I asked her as she seated herself next to me.

"You bet there's something wrong. How dare you work behind my back to find out about this Esmeralda person?"

I just stared at her.

"I told you I'd handle this."

"You did?"

"Don't you listen when I talk? Am I just whistling in the wind when I talk to you?"

"I..."

"What do you want to know about her?"

"Who?"

"Esmeralda Noe. Who else would I be talking about?"

After I explained the possible connection with Anna, she opened the car door and proceeded to get out. Before closing the door, she grabbed the bag of cookies and waved me on.

"Go on home now. You leave this to me."

And with that, she walked off...with the rest of the cookies.

She's No Misstep

I had just returned to the office from City Hall, having spent the entire day chasing down erroneous leads, and was tired—physically and emotionally.

"I'm thinking of hiring a Girl Friday," Elmer said. I hadn't heard that term in a long while. "She can answer your phone as well, but I'll have to up your rent to cover the expense."

Here it comes. "How much?"

"I think fifteen dollars would be fair."

With minimum wage at $1.25 an hour, I quickly figured that would be worth ten or twelve hours a month, so maybe a half-hour of her time a day. If she was any good, maybe I could delegate some of my grunt work which often piled up.

"I'm good with that."

And so now I was able to say I had an assistant. Well, sort of. A receptionist anyway and someone to answer the phone. I hoped she wasn't too tall or too wide—my company name on the wall behind where she would sit was obscure enough as it was.

Business was good, and I should have been delighted with my ample workload and that I was able to support myself, but it took me away from my own case, and that was the reason I had gotten into this business in the first place. There was a term for that—some kind of irony—but I was too tired to think about it.

I spent an hour wrapping things up and headed for home.

I could hear my phone ringing from the bottom of the stairwell, so I pounded up the steps in an attempt to get to it before it stopped.

"Where have you been? I've been trying to reach you for a half hour."

There was no mistaking Minnie's voice.

"I was in my office. Why?"

"Why are you working so late?"

"Is anything wrong?"

"Nothing's wrong. I just have that information for you."

"What information?"

"What information? About Essie, of course."

"Already?"

"Yes, already. What do you think, I'm some kind of deadbeat that I don't come through with my promises?"

"No, not at all. I'm just—"

"Here's what I have. Esmeralda Noe—or Essie, as she was called—and Anna were friends. Essie moved to Cicero soon after Anna died. Do you have a pencil?"

I scrambled for a pencil and a piece of paper. "Shoot."

"1407 South Fiftieth Court. Her phone number is 555-4543, and she works for Baird & Warner."

I was speechless.

"Don't you have anything to say?"

"I love you?"

"Don't get smart with me."

"I wasn't, Minnie. I meant it. You're incredible."

"Got any more?"

"Any more—"

"People you want to locate."

"Only if I can pay you what a skip tracer would get."

"I don't know what the hell a skip tracer is or what one is worth, but I do like my Scotch."

"Got a pencil?"

"Shoot."

"Tymon Kossak." I gave her his address. "Now that's all the way on the Northwest Side, so—"

She cut me off. "Don't worry about me."

She hung up before I had a chance to tell her what I wanted to find out about him.

* * *

The next day, I was in the back room scrutinizing documents when Elmer walked in with a pretty young blonde by his side.

"Miss Lindroth, this is Naomi Step. She's accepted the Girl Friday position."

She would have been tall even without the three-inch heels she was wearing—so much for my sign. Tall and slim with a big chest that she showcased in a tight red sweater.

We talked for a couple of minutes. Her silvery soft-spoken voice reminded me of Marilyn Monroe singing "Happy Birthday" to the late John F. Kennedy. I watched them leave and wondered if the smooth sashay of her hips from side to side in that snug skirt was any indication of her personality. I hoped she could at least take a phone message without messing it up. Nice choice, Elmer.

I retrieved the letter to Anna from Nacho. My memory had been right—there was mention of Veracruz, so I figured there may have been some tie-in of the letter to the business card for Ignacio Ramirez. I went back to my office and called the library to see if they had anything on Mexican genealogy, surnames, nicknames, and the like. The reference librarian told me they did not.

Two minutes later, in walked—I mean, in *wiggled*—Naomi.

"Yes, Miss Step." Oh, dear. I couldn't call her that.

"Please call me Naomi."

Gladly.

"I couldn't help but overhear your phone conversation. I think I can help you."

"Really?" This ought to be good.

"I speak fluent Spanish."

"Really?" I have to stop saying that.

"What nickname are you interested in?"

"Nacho."

"It's short for Ignacio."

"You're sure?"

"Positive. I lived in Boca del Rio for six years."

I pointed to the last line of the letter. "Can you tell me what this means?"

She bent over my desk, providing me with an eyeful of cleavage. "I love you and miss you."

It was a good thing nobody walked in at that precise moment.

"Well, I don't know what to say...except thank you."

"You're welcome," she said and strutted out of my office. She picked up her purse and headed toward the front door. "See you two tomorrow."

A minute later, Elmer poked his head in. "Never judge a book by its cover." Then he left too.

Lesson learned.

I reread the letter.

April 18, 1939

My Dear Anna,

I hope this letter finds you safe and well. Do write me soon to
the PO Box in Veracruz.

You left just in time. I relocated your aunt the following week.
It was too dangerous for her to stay here. When things calm
down, I will let you know our whereabouts. At least for now
she is safe and away from this madness. I will leave too after
I fulfill my commitment to Pemex. The good times have come
to an end, but I am not sad about this, as we have sufficient
resources to last us the rest of our lives.

I know you have made a connection with MT and are working
on a plan of your own. You are in good hands.

Te amo y te extraño.
Nacho

The letter was dated seven months before Anna had bought the boardinghouse.
The reference to Anna's aunt made me think Nacho may have been Anna's uncle.
Nacho was likely Ignacio Ramirez, an advisor to the Mexican national oil company
in Veracruz. I assumed the reference to MT was to Martin Torres, the San Diego
attorney. Maybe I was filling in too many blanks, but everything did seem to fit.

* * *

The next day I was in my office, busy with piles of paperwork, silently grousing
over the amount of work I had to do ahead of my own case, when Naomi came into
my office. She sat down in one of the guest chairs.

"You're very busy."

I nodded.

"Could I help you with anything?"

"Maybe."

"I'm a pretty quick learner. You'll only have to tell me something once, and I
don't mind figuring things out for myself."

"If you don't mind phone work, you could help me out a lot with the bird-dogging that's required for most of my cases. Have you talked to Elmer about this? Is he okay with you helping me more?"

She lowered her voice. "I did, and he's okay with it as long as it doesn't distract me from his work, but he did say you may have to pick up more of my salary."

That was Elmer—always concerned about money.

"That would be okay with me, but don't tell him that."

"May I make a suggestion?"

"Sure."

"If I'm going to do more phone work, can we get a regular office phone?"

"I'm not sure what you mean."

"I have two extension phones on my desk, one for your line and one for Mr. Berghorn's. And I have no line for myself. It would be much more efficient if I had one phone with both your lines, a third and fourth line for me, and a hold button. That way I can see when you're on the phone without getting up from my desk, and I can put people on hold instead of having to place the phone down on the desk until you pick up. And the newer models have a built-in intercom so I could talk to you without coming into your office. It'll save time."

I was impressed. "I like the idea. Want to pitch it to Elmer?"

She winked at me. "Consider it bought."

I liked her.

Danny would be there any minute to assist with serving two subpoenas in a couple of rough neighborhoods, one of which was home to several Chicago Outfit hangouts. Those thugs wouldn't have much interest in me, but I didn't want to take any chances. I had read a few years earlier about this one man who had been hanged on a meat hook by his fellow Outfit mobsters and tortured for days until he finally died of shock. Apparently, they believed he had become an FBI informant. You didn't want to mess with these guys.

I glanced out my window and saw Danny approaching. He hadn't been to our office since Naomi had started. I got up from my desk pretending to be busy putting on my coat so I could catch his reaction.

"May I help you?" Naomi asked him. She was wearing a tight low-cut pink sweater that revealed the exact shape of her ample breasts. Unfortunately, what Danny wasn't able to see was the short pencil skirt she was wearing with a slit more than halfway up the back.

He stood in front of her with a gapped-mouth stare. His lips were moving but no words came out. It was all I could do to keep from laughing out loud.

"Sir, may I help you?" she asked a second time.

It would have been cruel of me not to rescue him.

"Danny, this is Naomi Step. Naomi, this is Danny Davis." I turned to Danny.

"Naomi is our new office staff member." To Naomi I said, "And Danny is my number-one field technician."

Danny was silent on the walk to my car. After we had driven a few minutes, I said, "So what do you think of Naomi?"

He didn't respond immediately. "I refuse to answer that question on the grounds that it may incriminate me."

We served the first subpoena without incident, a court appearance for a parole violation. The second subpoena, the one in Chicago Outfit territory, didn't go as smoothly. A woman answered the door, and before I had even finished explaining my business, Danny nudged me with his elbow and mumbled, "Let's go."

I gave him a puzzled look.

Danny apologized to the woman for the bother and led me away from the house. When we were out of earshot, I asked him just what he was doing.

"I'll tell you in the car."

I don't get paid the whole fee if I don't deliver the documents, so I was expecting a very good explanation.

When we were a block away, Danny said, "You couldn't see from your vantage point, but I could see a man inside holding a gun."

"Oh, dear! No, I didn't see that."

"So what do you do now?"

"I return the subpoena, tell them what happened, and they will probably get a sheriff or someone to serve it."

What if Danny hadn't been with me? I contemplated the incident on the drive back to my office. Even though I needed the money, I decided I didn't want to be a process server any longer.

When I parked the car behind my office, Danny said goodbye and headed toward the bus stop.

"Wait, Danny. I want to pay you for today."

"But you didn't even get to deliver one of them."

"I still get paid something. Just not as much."

He waved and said, "Naomi was enough payment for me for today."

I liked that boy.

Naomi handed me a message from Minnie. I was a little surprised as it had been just two days since she had taken on the task of finding Tymon Kossak. I called her back right away.

"Tymon was Anna's handyman," Minnie explained. "And he still lives on North Cleaver Street."

"Minnie, you're amazing."

"Don't you want to know what I found out from him?"

"You talked with him?"

"You think I went to all that trouble to find him and then not talk to him?"

I had never asked her to talk to him. She didn't know what questions to ask, or how to ask them, or anything else about this business.

"Well—"

"We chatted. I asked a lot of questions, and he answered."

"Who did you tell him you were? And how did you explain all the questions?"

"Do you want a lesson in the art of talking to someone without raising suspicion, or do you want to know what I found?"

"Sorry, please continue."

"You know that walled-in room in my basement? Well, I found out from him you can access it from my bedroom."

"Your bedroom? Where in your bedroom?"

"There's a trapdoor in the floor, under the rug."

"And you didn't know it was there?"

"You'll see when you come over—it's barely noticeable, plus the rug's been over it all these years."

"When can I come over so we can go down there?"

"Are you telling me you think I uncovered a secret door under the rug in my bedroom and didn't look down there?"

"No, ma'am. Go on."

"There's no ladder or anything. Just an opening like the one to the attic."

There's an attic?

"And?"

"The room was empty."

All that buildup for...nothing.

"But I did find one thing—a torn receipt from Victor Lock & Safe Company. It was snagged on the rough edges of the opening under the trapdoor. Does that mean anything to you?"

"It sure does. I think I may have the other half!"

"Well, then you're going to love this part because someone wrote what looks to me like numbers to a combination lock."

"What are they?"

"L4, R29, L60."

"Is there a date on that half?"

"January 8, 1940."

I was so excited I couldn't stand it but calmed down in a matter of seconds when I realized I didn't actually have much of anything.

"Well, if I ever find the safe, I'm all set. You're sure there was nothing else down there."

"Not now, but according to Tymon, the one time he went down there for her, he saw boxes and artwork stacked against the wall."

"No safe?"

"He said there was something in the corner that was covered with a tarp or something. I asked him how big, and he said it was maybe three feet high and a foot and a half wide, so it could have been a safe."

"Anything else?"

"That's not enough?"

"Well, yes. I just... You did great. How did you leave it with him?"

"The old coot asked me for my phone number."

"You didn't give it to him."

"I sure did. He was her handyman, for Crissake. He knows more!"

* * *

"My family moved to Mexico when I was ten," Naomi said. "My father had some kind of business there—we were never sure what exactly it was that he did. I left when I was eighteen right after my mother died." Naomi and I were seated at Gene & Georgetti's, one of my favorite Italian restaurants. Buying her dinner was a small price to pay for the tremendous help she had been all week.

"Is he still there?"

"I don't know, and I don't care. He's a mean person."

I asked her how hard it would be to locate someone in Mexico.

"Not hard if you know the right people."

I told her about Ignacio Ramirez and Petróleos Mexicanos.

"Pemex. That's what it's called in Mexico."

"You're familiar with the company then?"

"Anyone who has ever lived in Mexico is familiar with Pemex. They have a monopoly on oil. It's huge. The Mexican government owns it, and..."

"And there's a lot of corruption?"

"Sí. Mucha corrupción."

"Do you think you could help me locate someone who worked for Pemex in the thirties?"

"I could try. It may cost a little in phone calls. I don't think Elmer will go for that."

"He gives me an itemized phone bill each month with my calls underlined in red and I reimburse him, so it'll be okay."

"Do you want me to arrange for two separate bills with the phone company?"

"You can do that?"

"Of course."

"Naomi?"

"Yes."

"I'm so glad you're here."

TWELVE

"She Called Him Al"

"Oh, look who's here! It's my neighbor, Grace." Minnie winked at me as she greeted me at the door and mouthed she had a surprise for me.

"C'mon in, dear. I have company, but that doesn't matter. We can all visit."

I gave her a quizzical look. "Here's a little something I picked up for you, Minnie," I said as I handed her a bottle of Scotch that luckily was still in the brown paper bag from the liquor store.

She peeked in the bag. "Oh, goodie. That bath powder I like so much." She leaned in and gave me a peck on the cheek. "You're so thoughtful!"

I didn't know what was going on, but Minnie could have given the lead actress in *The Three Faces of Eve* a run for her money with that performance.

When she introduced me to the man in her living room, Tymon Kossak, goose bumps rose on my skin. He was older than I had pictured, with a thin layer of graying hair on his head that had been plastered down with something that looked a little gooey. Judging from his appearance, he appeared to be somewhere in his sixties, which meant he must have been in his late thirties or early forties when he was Anna's handyman.

We introduced ourselves and shook hands. Tymon and I sat on opposite ends of the sofa. Minnie headed for the kitchen.

We made small talk until Minnie returned—I couldn't do much more than that, not knowing what she had already told him. I didn't want to blow it.

Minnie returned with a tray of glasses.

"I hope you drink Scotch, Tymon."

"I've been known to take a nip now and then," he said.

"It's funny that you dropped over, Grace, because I was just telling Tymon how you two have something in common."

"Oh? What would that be?"

Minnie shot me a playful look.

"Tymon here used to work for your Aunt Anna."

Aunt Anna?

"No kidding. What did you do for her?"

"Handyman work. Little of this, little of that."

"Here? In this house?"

"Yes."

"I've not met very many people who knew her, so this is pretty special. Did you know her well?"

His stare made me uncomfortable.

"I said, did you know her well?"

"I'm sorry. Yes, pretty well."

"Were you working for her up until she died?"

"Yes."

I could tell he was uncomfortable too.

"You know, they never did solve that case," I told him.

"I know, but they didn't try very hard either."

I could hardly believe I was having this discussion and prayed my thumping heart wouldn't leap out of my chest.

"What do you mean?"

"For starters, they never interviewed me, and I was in and out of this house all the time."

"So you never talked to the police?"

"I went to the police station that same day, told them who I was, thinking maybe I could shed some light on what happened to her, but they had no one there to talk to me at the time and said someone would be touch."

"And they didn't get back to you?"

"I left my name and number, but they never called."

"So do you know what happened?"

"No."

The day was overcast and it was dark in Minnie's house, so I could have been wrong about seeing tears building up in his eyes.

"And what about the baby? What do you think happened to...was it a boy or a girl?"

He didn't say anything right away—he just stared at me and shook his head. Finally, he said, "What baby?"

"Anna had a daughter...right?"

Tymon shook his head no, but the look in his eyes revealed there was something more he was thinking that he wasn't saying.

"You never saw a baby?"

He looked away from me.

"You said you were in and out of here all the time."

He looked back at me with a blank stare and nodded.

I decided to drop the subject...for the time being.

"Tymon, what would you have told the police if they *had* questioned you?"

"For starters, I would have told them this place was picked clean before they got there."

"Picked clean?"

"Almost everything was gone—most of her furniture, what was stored in the basement, even most of her clothes. Just enough left to show someone lived there."

"No kidding. Now, I would think that would have been important for the police to know."

"I thought so too. And when I finally found someone at the precinct who would talk to me, I told him that."

"What did he say?"

"He listened, said they would look into it, and that was it."

"What about the boarders living upstairs. Did you know them?"

"I occasionally saw them."

"What were they like?"

"The fella who dressed like a girl," Minnie chimed in. "Surely you remember him."

Oh dear, she's slurring her words. I looked at Minnie and wondered how much she'd had to drink.

"I try to stay out of other people's business."

"He dressed like a woman for cryin' out loud!" Minnie shrieked.

She may not have been drunk, but she was headed in that direction. I gave her a look that I hoped she interpreted as *time to stop talking.*

"So who else lived up there?" I asked.

There was something peculiar about the way Tymon looked at me, and it was making me self-conscious.

"One guy kept to himself all the time. Older man."

"Mike Smith," Minnie blurted.

"I think you told me it was Mark Smith, Minnie."

"Mark, Minnie, Mike. What's the difference?"

She was slumped at an odd angle in her chair, and I was tempted to go over to her and straighten her up...but I didn't want to embarrass her any further.

"Minnie, dear, would you mind if I put a pot of coffee on for us?"

"You hate coffee."

"I thought maybe *you* would like some."

"I don't want any." She looked at Tymon. "Do you want any?"

"I'd love some."

I jumped up. "I'll get it."

I listened to them talk while I attempted to make coffee, something I had actually never done before. My parents had been tea drinkers.

It was hard to concentrate on what they were talking about when my mind was preoccupied with thoughts about why Tymon was denying Anna had a baby. I may not have had solid proof she had a baby at the time of her death, but I knew she did. If that wasn't true, I was—.

Minnie was talking about her late husband, Clarence, but she kept calling him Larence. When I heard her tell Tymon she missed sleeping with him, I quickly finished up my task and rejoined them.

"So, Tymon, you were telling us about the boarders. Mark Smith, the one who died here—what was he like?"

"Like I said, he kept to himself. And his name may not have been Mark Smith."

"Why do you say that?"

"Anna had a feeling, that's all."

"That's interesting. Did she say why she thought that?"

"No, I don't think so."

"And the third one?"

I held my breath, praying Minnie didn't blurt out "Mousey."

"You mean Pussy?"

Good grief.

"Mousey, Minnie! It's Mousey!" Oh, Lord—what he must have thought of us.

"Maybe I should go," Tymon said.

"Please don't, Tymon. I would really like to hear—"

The whistle of the tea kettle interrupted me.

"Please stay. I'll be right back."

"Poor thing doesn't know what the hell she's doing," Minnie mumbled.

When I poured two cups of coffee from the tea kettle that looked like dirty river water, I knew I had done something wrong. I honestly believed the coffee would dissolve in the water. I scooped out as much of the grounds as I could with a spoon and served it to them.

Minnie took one look in her cup and said, "What the hell is this?"

Tymon looked into his and placed it on the coffee table.

"May I speak with you in the kitchen for a moment, Minnie?" I asked her.

She gave me a look as if to say "Who me?" then got up and followed me.

"What are you trying to do to us with that crap?" she asked.

"Minnie, listen to me. You've had too much to drink. I've never made—"

She walked over to the stove and picked up the tea kettle. "You made it in this?"

"Would you please lower your voice?" I asked her in a low whisper. "Now, listen to me. This is very important, and—"

"Go back in there, Betty Crocker. Tell him the real coffee is coming...along with homemade peach cobbler." She pushed me aside. "Go!"

I gave Tymon a weak smile and sat back down on the sofa.

"If Minnie is referring to Henry Sikes, I actually ran into him not long ago at Jake's."

"Jake's?"

Minnie could be heard from the kitchen singing a dreadful rendition of "Home on the Range."

Tymon hesitated before he continued, looking like he would rather have been anywhere but there. "Jake's is a bar in my neighborhood. He recognized me, and we exchanged a few words. Had on expensive clothes, a big gold watch, slicked-back hair. At some point he must have come into some money or something. He never dressed like that when he lived here."

"And the fourth boarder?"

Tymon didn't answer right away.

"I shouldn't be telling you all this stuff. I..."

"Listen, I don't think you know how much I appreciate this information. You see, I never knew my aunt, and the fact that something so tragic happened to her...well, I want to know as much about her as I can. I have no family left, just memories, and I don't even have any memories of her, so whatever you—"

"Some of this is so personal. Maybe she—"

"But she's gone now, Tymon," Minnie chimed in from the kitchen and then resumed singing. "Where the deer and the antelope play."

"I'm sorry," I whispered to him.

"Don't worry. I understand," he whispered back.

Tymon focused on me for a long moment and sighed. His voice was low and soft. "The man who had the room above her, well, they were pretty close."

"What was his name?"

"She called him Al."

"You don't know his last name?"

"No."

"What did he look like?"

"Oh, he was a handsome man. Tall, dark wavy hair, wore nice clothes, drove a nice car."

"Was he living here the whole time you worked for her?"

"No, I'd say he moved in maybe a year after she bought the place."

"And was he still here when she died?"

"Yes, but he was gone right after."

"You don't think he did it, do you?"

"Caused her death? Oh, that thought crossed my mind even though based on what Anna told me about him, I couldn't imagine him having anything to do with it."

"What did she tell you?"

"Nothing specific." He hesitated a few seconds. "Maybe it was just the way she talked about him. I got the impression she cared very much for him."

"I wonder if the police talked to the boarders."

"That I don't know. But I do know they didn't talk to Henry Sikes, because he told me as much."

"I don't suppose my aunt ever mentioned anyone else in her life—relatives, friends...enemies?"

"No. Well, she had a girlfriend who lived nearby. Don't remember her name though."

"Is there anything else you can tell me about her? Anything that would help me figure out what happened to her?"

He had a faraway look in his eyes. "I liked Anna. She was always good to me. Oh, you probably already know this, but she was raised by her aunt and uncle in Mexico."

"Oh, yes, I had heard that, but I never knew what happened to her parents."

"She never talked about them. At least not to me."

"Tymon, do you know exactly how she died?"

His face turned ashen, and he spoke just above a whisper. "They never said in the paper how she died, but there was blood..." He didn't finish his thought. His whole body shifted downward, like the life had been sucked right out of it.

"Blood?"

"I was asked by the bank to get the house ready for sale, and I found some traces of blood." He paused. "Do you think we should check on Minnie?"

We walked to the kitchen only to find Minnie seated at the table... face down in a plate of peach cobbler.

"Do you want me to help with her?"

"No, I'll manage."

"Then I'll be going."

I knew I couldn't keep him there any longer. "Let me walk you to the door."

Tymon opened the door, turned to me, and reached for my hand, which he held for a rather long moment.

"It was a pleasure meeting you," I told him. "And I can't thank you enough for the light you have shed on Anna."

"The pleasure was mine."

I watched him walk away, not knowing what to think of the man.

* * *

The next morning I met with Veronica Van Zandt, but my mind was somewhere else. Tymon was hiding something, of that I was sure, and I would have bet anything it had to do with Anna's baby.

Mrs. Van Zandt handed me the phone bills I'd requested. She had hired me to prove or disprove that her husband Victor was being unfaithful. I called the case the Three Vs. During our initial meeting, when I had asked her if there had been any changes in her husband's personal behavior, she had rattled off all the classic signs of a cheating husband: paid less attention to her and more attention to himself, joined a men's club, wanted her to cook more healthy meals, had less sex, and often worked late. She also told me about some non-textbook behavior that I found interesting. He had been a martini drinker for as long as she'd known him and had recently changed to red wine. And he had come home from a business trip the week before with an unusually neatly packed suitcase.

She told me she'd gone through his wallet while he was taking a bath that morning and was surprised to find a Diners Club card. I wasn't surprised—cheating husbands often spent money on their mistresses using a secret charge card.

After she left, the first thing I did was look for suspicious phone numbers on their phone bills, and it didn't take me long to find one that had been called periodically at very early hours of the morning. My wonderful contact at Illinois Bell gave me the name and address associated with the number—Susan Averill. Mrs. Van Zandt had told me her husband had been going to his men's club on Tuesday and Thursday evenings. Today was Tuesday, so I knew what I would be doing after dinner. My guess was that when I tailed Mr. Van Zandt this evening, we wouldn't end up at any men's club.

After lunch, I delivered several subpoenas, all of which were record subpoenas that could be quickly served to the named companies. At City Hall, I completed a handful of public records checks, one of which was for a troubling case: my twenty-year-old client, Nora Edgar, had found out she was adopted at birth after a hospital worker found her in a storage room. She wanted to find out who her birth mother was. I called it my Storage Room case.

I kept looking at the Green Teen file folder and feeling guilty about not being able to do more. The girl's mother Louise and her sister Flora were at that moment in Detroit looking for Erma, and I was surprised not to have heard from them by now. A previous visit a couple of weeks earlier had proved unproductive for them. But after I was able to locate Erma's father, who was in a small-town jail outside of Detroit, Louise and Flora had insisted on paying him a visit. I had tried to discourage them from meeting with him given his criminal history, but they were determined.

Before I left for the day, I stuck my head in Elmer's door to tell him I was leaving for the day and casually mentioned I was thinking about giving up being a process server because of the potential danger involved.

"Why would you do that? It's good solid work for in between cases. You'd be foolish to give that up."

"But there have been incidents—"

"So bring Danny along on all of them just to be safe."

I told him I'd give it some more thought but that if I did continue, I was going to raise my prices. After I gave Danny his cut, it hardly seemed worth the effort with what I currently charged.

Elmer's sudden interest in what I was doing puzzled me—he never had been before.

* * *

In the office the next morning, I spent an hour writing my Three Vs report for Mrs. Van Zandt. Based on my surveillance, Mr. Van Zandt was either not very bright or wanted to get caught. Why else would he have gone into a popular local bar, sat in the window with a voluptuous blonde, escorted her under bright streetlights to his car, and driven with her to a little run-down motel on the outskirts of town? He couldn't have made it any easier for me if he had tried.

Naomi told me Elmer had her busy doing something personal for him and she hadn't had much time to work on the Mexican caper. That was disappointing, but I had no legitimate complaint, as he was still paying the bulk of her salary.

Louise called me from a Detroit hotel room to tell me she and Flora had connected with Erma's father.

"Apparently, Erma located my jailbird ex-husband, probably under a rock somewhere, and he didn't even bother to contact me. Said he didn't have my number."

"When was this?" I asked her.

"A week ago, before he got arrested for public indecency. Erma told him she didn't like my rules, and that's why she left. Wanted to know if she could come live with him."

"What did he tell her?"

"Hell, no!"

"Nice."

"Oh, he's a real gem, but I'm just happy he said no."

"So what happened then?"

"He said he gave her forty dollars, enough for a bus ticket home and then some."

"At least he did that."

"Mm-hm."

"It's probably a little too long after the fact, but you could go to the bus terminal, show her picture to the agents, and ask if they remember seeing her."

"We were thinking that too."

"Call me with any news, okay?"

We ended the call, and after spending a long afternoon at City Hall, I grabbed a quick sandwich for dinner. Only one lead had panned out at City Hall, but it was the one I had hoped for. My Storage Room client had given me the wrong hospital name. It wasn't Presbyterian Hospital, it was St. Luke's. A clerk in the records department had told me people got those two hospitals mixed up all the time, since they later merged into one—Presbyterian/St. Luke's Hospital. My plan was to pay them a visit the next day in the hope that they kept old records.

THIRTEEN

He Pulled Into Where?

Two days after my encounter with Tymon, Minnie called me. I had tried to talk to her the following day, but she was so hung over she hadn't wanted to talk.

"Got a minute?"

"How are you feeling?"

"Fine. How do you think I'm feeling?"

"I was just—"

"Do you want to hear what I have to say or not?"

"Of course I do."

"Tymon called me this morning asking me the same dumb question. Anyway, we got to talking more about the mystery man, Al, and he finally said he suspected he was Anna's lover."

"Really."

"And he said that Anna confided to him right before she died that she was certain this guy had a wife."

"No kidding."

"I'm having lunch with him tomorrow, at Jake's. I'll do some more snooping."

I wanted to tell her to please not drink, but knowing her likely response to that, I didn't.

"Minnie?"

"Yes."

"Be careful?"

"Gracie?"

"Yes."

"You worry too much."

* * *

I imagined telling a stranger a little about myself.

Hello. My name is Grace Lindroth, but maybe not. It could be Celina Vargas. The woman I think was my mother fled from Mexico when it became too dangerous for her to live with her uncle, who it appears was involved in some dicey business dealings. She ended up in Chicago, where she bought a boardinghouse and then had an affair with one of the boarders, whose last name I don't know and who was married to another woman at the time. I was born, or at least I think I was, and seven months later, she was murdered. Who raised me? Well, it appears it may have been the people who killed my mother.

I'd seen soap operas with less drama.

I kept replaying in my head what Tymon had said. That Anna had questioned whether Mark Smith had been the boarder's real name lent support to the fact that I couldn't find anything on the man—no birth certificate, death certificate, voter registration, Social Security number, business license, census data...nothing. But Minnie had been able to give me the date he died, so all I had to do was tie him to one of the names on the list of men who died in Cook County on that day. I hoped it was a short list.

I couldn't be too surprised that Anna's house had been picked clean immediately after she died. Tymon's understanding was that the medical examiner initially considered her death to be by natural causes until he examined her body in his laboratory and declared it a homicide, so the police wouldn't have treated her apartment as a crime scene at first, so who knows who came and went?

But who would have taken all the furniture, including everything in the baby's room—my room? Had the same person who stole everything stolen me as well?

As much as I would have liked to, I couldn't discount the idea that it was possible my parents had had something to do with her death and my kidnapping. The evidence was there, so as preposterous as that seemed to me, I couldn't rule it out.

One of the most valuable pieces of information Tymon had divulged was that Henry Sikes—the busybody—was still around. I was willing to bet he was a jackpot of information. Unfortunately, I was unable to find residential information on him. My hope was that Minnie would be more successful.

What Minnie had said to me one day about being part of my life and feeling useful again resonated with me. On the way to City Hall to look at death records, I tried to think of something nice I could do for her. Something she would never expect, and something she would truly appreciate.

I had to wait in line at the County Clerk's Office, and when it was my turn, I asked to speak with Flora. When she came out, I told her what I was searching for, and instead of having to jump through the normal hoops, she led me directly into the archives room and showed me where the indices were for the death certificates. She cleared off a desk where I could work.

It didn't take me long to compile a list of Cook County men who died on June 6, 1943. Mark Smith was not among the seventy-three names.

It seemed to me that seventy-three was an awfully big number even for a major city like Chicago, so I asked Flora about it. She disappeared for a few minutes, and when she returned, she explained that soldiers from Cook County who had died in the war were included on the list. There was no way around it—I would need to see the actual death certificate for each man in order to exclude him.

Flora assigned a junior clerk to pull the records for me, ten at a time. It was an arduous task for him but not for me. I was looking for a particular address, for the place of death, something I could determine in seconds.

Two hours into the project, I found it. Marcus O'Gowan had died at the boardinghouse address on June 6, 1943. Cause of death: heart attack. So Anna's hunch had been right—he hadn't given her his real name. But why?

It was disappointing that many of the fields on the death certificate that could have contained helpful information were left blank. What was even more disheartening was that it said he was born in Dublin, Ireland, and was not a U.S. citizen, which limited any other information I would be able to dig up on him. His middle initial was T; his birthday was July 20, 1909; and his cremated remains were buried in Cook County Cemetery. I had to accept the fact that was probably all I would ever know about him.

I drove by my old house on the way home and, being in a sentimental mood, parked a few houses down from it. It seemed so much longer than four and a half years since I'd lived here.

I stared at the front door, a door we had seldom used. A rolled-up newspaper lay on the walk leading to it. When I was young, that had been my job—bringing in the mail and newspapers.

Beyond that door was the living room. We'd seldom used that either. Thinking back, I realized the three of us had usually been in separate rooms, doing our own things.

I watched an approaching car slow down in front of the house. Elmer's turquoise Buick was unmistakable. I wasn't too surprised to see him since he had said he lived in the neighborhood. Not wanting to run into him, I quickly slumped down in my seat.

The next thing I knew, he was pulling into my old driveway!

∽ FOURTEEN ∾

The Ninety-Pound Wuss

I remained slouched down behind my steering wheel, peering over the dashboard, as Elmer's car disappeared behind the row of thick evergreens that lined the side of the driveway.

I wracked my brain trying to remember that conversation in December when I told him about the neighbor boy who'd dropped by the office to see him. I was pretty sure he'd said he lived in the next block, but he'd acted real funny during that conversation, like he hadn't wanted to talk about it. Why would he have lied about where he lived? That is, if he did live there.

A car door slammed. Elmer emerged from behind the evergreens, walked to the front of the house, picked up the newspaper, and returned to the back. I waited another minute, but nothing happened. Not wanting to risk him recognizing my car, I headed for home.

* * *

Well before work the next morning, I drove by my old house again. Elmer's car was in the same spot in the driveway. Either he lived there, or he was close to someone who did.

Later, at the office, Naomi came over to tell me that the name Ignacio Ramirez was so common in Mexico, and Anna's uncle's involvement with Pemex had been so long ago, that she hadn't been able to come up with anything. She appeared as though she was about to say something else but then stopped herself and walked out of the room. She'd been acting a little strange lately—fidgety or something. I couldn't quite put my finger on it. Fearful it might have something to do with the work I was giving to her, I made a mental note to talk to her about it after Elmer left for the day.

Disappointed with Naomi's findings, I went to work on the Storage Room case. Finding birth parents was usually difficult. If an adoption went through an agency, the agency kept tight control of the records. Same thing if it went through an attorney. And if the adoption was illegal, it was even harder to unearth any information about it.

There was another case on my desk that I had recently acquired—I called it my Midnighter case. Flora Walsh from the County Clerk's office had retained me, but a dozen or so of her neighbors were sharing in the cost. For the past three months, she and her neighbors had had a variety of things stolen in the middle of the night from their patios, garages, sheds, and yards. Nothing expensive. In fact, that was one of the puzzling aspects of the case—I was told the burglar had sometimes taken trivial things and ignored valuable items placed right next to them. Stolen items included clothing, food, small tools, toys, bedding, and books.

Flora explained that the police had little interest in these penny-ante thefts, so she and her neighbors had taken it upon themselves to catch the thief on their own. After each neighbor had taken a turn standing watch through the night to no avail, they'd hired me.

I had a little breathing room in the afternoon, and so I went into the back room and combed through all the Attic Finds evidence to see if any bells went off given the new information I had.

I couldn't stop staring at the photo of Anna holding me in the rocking chair. She was looking down at me so lovingly. All you could see was her profile, but even so, you could tell she was smiling. I had never paid that much attention to the picture hanging on the wall behind us, and when I studied it more closely, it looked familiar, but I couldn't place where I'd seen it before. It was a landscape—mountains in the background, a stream on the left, some animals grazing on the right. I couldn't tell what kind of animals, could have been deer. Maybe it was just a print of some famous painting—available in any department store.

I hadn't noticed before either that Anna was wearing a necklace in the photo—a small pendant dangling from a thin chain. Could have been heart-shaped, hard to tell. I thought how nice it would have been to have something so personal of hers, something I could keep near me all the time, something by which to remember her.

A knock on the door interrupted my melancholy. Naomi asked me if she could talk to me after Elmer left for the day. Looked like we were on the same wavelength. Two minutes later, there was another knock on the door. It was Naomi again. Minnie was on hold.

I tried to absorb everything Minnie was telling me, but she was talking so fast, all I got were bits and pieces—something about talking to Henry, who said the police had got it all wrong and his cousin could get in trouble. Finally, I asked her if I could come over later to hear it in person, and she agreed.

The afternoon moved at a snail's pace because I was so anxious to hear what both Naomi and Minnie had to tell me. And then it occurred to me that I had planned to go to Presbyterian/St. Luke's Hospital to look for birth information on Nora Edwards. That would likely take longer than Naomi would be willing to stay, and even if she was willing to stay late, I wanted to get to Minnie's as soon as possible. Nora would just have to wait until tomorrow. I felt a little guilty about delaying a case involving finding someone else's birth parent in favor of my own self-interest, but I figured one more day wouldn't make any difference.

When Elmer finally left, I went out to the reception area to talk with Naomi.

"I hope this doesn't come back to hurt me in the end, but I feel I have to tell you something."

"What is it?"

"Elmer has been paying Danny to keep an eye on you and feed back to him what you're doing."

"What? What makes you think that?"

"I have eyes and ears."

"I'm not surprised to hear he pays Danny for helping him—the same as I do—but why do you think it's to watch me?"

"I've heard Danny tell him where you are, where you're going to be, what cases you're working on."

I had told Danny when I hired him that what I worked on was confidential and not to be discussed with anyone but me. I thanked her for that tidbit of information and returned to my office to tidy up.

Naomi poked her head in my door.

"Good night, Miss Lindroth. I hope I didn't stick my nose where it doesn't belong. If I did, I apologize."

"Don't worry about it. I appreciate the information."

"If what I said gets back to Mr. Berghorn, I'm sure he'll fire me."

"You have nothing to worry about with me."

I wasn't sure what I thought about what Naomi had told me. First of all, she had made the assumption that the money Elmer gave to Danny was compensation for watching me when it could have been for something else. Why would Elmer care where I was and what I was doing anyway? Just to be safe, I decided not to use Danny anymore. I would just have to be more selective about the process-server jobs I accepted.

I finished up and headed out to Minnie's. Upon opening her door, she greeted me with a toothy smile and ushered me into the living room. She poured us each a glass of Scotch.

"So, Detective Lawless, what have you got for me?"

"Don't you get saucy with me."

Saucy? "I was complimenting you!"

"Never you mind."

I laughed to myself—that had been an expression my mother had often used.

"Anyway, like I started to tell you on the phone, Tymon and I met for lunch at Jake's, and all I did was schmooze him because I didn't want him to catch on to the real reason I wanted to be with him. So we talked about stupid stuff while we ate. I told him more about my Clarence, and he told me about how he had cared for his mother until she died. Stuff like that. So afterward, he went his way and I went mine, but as soon as he was out of sight, I went back into Jake's, sat myself down at the bar, and ordered a beer."

Now I couldn't picture Minnie hoisting her squatty little body up onto a barstool and throwing back a few cold ones, but she had surprised me in other ways, so...

"At the risk of interrupting your story," I said, "how do you feel about Tymon? Is he someone you could end up seeing?"

"Of course not. Why do you ask?"

"Because if he is, I don't want you to feel obligated to keep—"

"Look, toots, give me credit for knowing what I'm doing. I've been around the block a few times remember."

"I didn't mean to—"

"Anyway, when I get to know the barkeep a little, I ask him if he happens to know Henry Sikes, and he says, 'Sure, he's part of the landscape around here.' Then he kinda snickers, and I ask him what's so funny, and he says to me in a low voice that Henry had disappeared once years ago and came back a different man. They all wondered who Henry had robbed 'cuz he went from living in a boarding house to buying a house of his own, and all of a sudden he had a nice new car, fancy duds, and a different woman on his arm all the time. All this and the guy had never worked an honest day in his life."

"Henry left the boardinghouse right after Mark Smith—aka Marcus O'Gowan—died, right?"

"Who?"

"I forgot I didn't tell you. You know Mark Smith? Well, his real name was Marcus O'Gowan."

Minnie's hands flew to her hips. "You've got to keep me better informed, Gracie."

She got up from her chair and left the room. I couldn't determine if she was mad at me or was just being flippant...in her own semi-humorous way. I tried to think of what else I hadn't told her. When she didn't return in a couple of minutes, I called her name.

"Be right there," she shouted back.

When she returned, she had an envelope in her hand. She handed it to me.

"You want me to read this?" I asked her.

"Why else would I be handing it to you?"

I removed the letter from inside.

April 25, 1950

To whom it may concern:

I look for my deartháir, Marcus T. O'Gowan, and I think he living in one yours seomra leapa. His family worried and we need find him.

If he live with you, please tell his mother is very sick and like to see him before she die. She love him and miss him.

Here is address. Please write.

Le teann measa,

Darina O'Brady
20 Dawson Street
Dublin

"Well, that fits in with what I found out about him, that he's from Ireland and, in fact, not even a U.S. citizen. So it appears his family was trying to locate him. His mother was sick and—"

"If you believe everything in that letter."

"Why do you say that?"

"Can I go back to my story?"

I nodded.

"You know, this stuff is better than *As the World Turns*. Maybe I should become a real PI. Anyway, I ask him where Henry lives, and he tells me a few blocks from here on Mozart. So I finish my little chat with barkeep and head over to Mozart."

I held my breath—it was only a matter of time before she relayed something she did that was going to get her—or me—into trouble.

She laughed. "You look like you're bracing yourself for a mortar attack or something. Relax, sweetie. I know what I'm doing."

"It's not that—"

"Anyway, so I pay old Henry a visit."

"How did you know which house?"

"I didn't, but Mozart's only two blocks long."

"What did you do, knock on each door until you found him?"

"I started doing that, but it was taking too long, so I just peeked inside mailboxes until I found his name." I felt my jaw drop, and Minnie frowned. "Why are you looking at me like that?"

"Minnie, it's a federal offense to tamper with someone's mailbox."

"I didn't tamper. I just looked inside."

"You shouldn't have even touched it." I didn't know if it was actually illegal to look inside, but I had been taught never to even go near a mailbox to be on the safe side.

She pursed her lips for several seconds before she said, "Look, if you don't want my help, just say so. Here I was going out of my way to—"

"I'm sorry, Minnie. I just don't want you to get yourself in trouble."

"Fine then. End of story."

"What do you mean 'end of story'? What happened next?"

"No. I'm not going to tell you now."

Yet another side to her personality—that of an obstinate child.

"Minnie, *please* tell me what happened."

"Will you let me tell it without your interrupting?"

"I promise."

"Okay, then. So I knock on his door and he answers it. Well, the look on his face is outright terror, and he proceeds to close the door on me."

"So he obviously recognized you. Sorry. Didn't mean to interrupt."

More pursed lips. "Obviously. So I put my foot in the door." She beamed. "You're not the only one who knows that trick. Now, mind you, I'm only five-foot-one, but he's shorter than I am and about fifty pounds lighter, so he's no match for me."

In more ways than one.

"Never was...none of 'em were. Anyway, he's screaming at me in that whiney little voice of his that he doesn't want to talk to me, and I tell him in a nice calm voice that I know all about what he did, and we needed to talk. Otherwise, I was going to the police."

"Minnie! You were taking a bit of a leap, weren't you?"

She stared at me for a long moment, her double chin firmly pressed between the folds. "Do you want me to continue or not?"

I slowly exhaled the breath I had been holding for the past several seconds. "Please do."

"Well, all of a sudden, he quiets down, and I feel the pressure on my foot lessening. He peeks through the crack and asks, 'What do you know?' And I tell him I know enough to get him in a lot of trouble, but I'm a reasonable person and we can talk."

She paused, giving me the opportunity to comment, but I didn't.

"He opens the door all the way, and I go in. Then he offers me a drink, which I take." She got up to refresh our glasses but kept talking. "So I pretend I know how he came into the money, and we play cat-and-mouse for a while. But the more we talk, the more nervous he gets. And the more nervous he gets, the more he drinks. And the more he drinks, the more he talks.

"I'll cut to the chase. I think he stole from Mark, or Marcus, whatever his name is, and then flew the coop. If you dig deep enough, I bet you'll find O'Gowan had a stash of money...or something...and Henry, the little twerp, knew it. And as soon as O'Gowan died, he stole it and ran. But here's the thing. He implicated his cousin in whatever it was he did—said it was *his* plan, *his* doing."

"Who's his cousin?"

"I don't know. He wouldn't tell me that, but if I could get a little closer to what really happened, I bet I could get him to rat out his cousin."

Rat him out? She had been watching more than *As the World Turns.*

I held up the letter still in my hand. "Did you ever respond to this letter?"

"No. I ignored it. I didn't make the connection between Mark Smith and Marcus O'Gowan, so I thought the letter was just a mistake."

"Was there any indication O'Gowan had money, that you saw?"

"None. Of course, I rarely saw the man. When he did leave his room, it was always at night."

"Tymon must have seen his room when he had to repair things, right? I wonder what else he could tell us about him."

"I would think so. Maybe I could work on him some more."

"You have another date with him?"

"It's *not* a date. He said he'd call me." She paused a moment. "He does remind me a little of this old boyfriend I had once though..." Her voice trailed off.

"And?"

"And nothing. That's private."

"You said on the phone something about the police had it all wrong."

"This is where I got a little bold."

No, Minnie, you've already crossed that line.

"I asked him what he knew about Anna's death."

"And?"

"He turned a shade paler, if that's even possible, and said he knew nothing. I knew he was lying, and I told him so."

"Minnie, did it ever occur to you that he may have had a gun or something? Maybe he even killed O'Gowan. Or maybe he killed Anna, and here you are pressuring him and making him nervous and—"

"That ninety-pound wuss?"

"You never know."

"Well, he didn't, so let me go on, or do you want to—"

"No, please continue."

"Anyway, I reminded him that he made it his business to know everyone else's business, so I knew he knew what happened to Anna. And *that*'s when I laid it on him."

Oh, dear.

"I told him I had reason to believe he had something to do with her death, and I was going to go to the police with it."

"You really said that to him."

"I did. I know how to read people. If I didn't, I wouldn't have given *you* the right time of day."

I shut up.

"So we talk back and forth, and all he's willing to say was the police thought it was a robbery gone bad and left it at that, but they had it all wrong, he told me." She paused to take a sip of her drink. "Then he told me he didn't think they even knew she had a baby."

"I knew it!"

"I asked him if he told the police that there was a baby involved."

"And?"

"He said, 'Hell no. None of my business.' We all know what a crock of shit that was. His nose was in *everyone's* business."

"Unbelievable."

"So that's it."

"That's how you left it with him?"

"And I suppose you would have done better?"

"No, not at all. I was just—"

"The way I left it with him was that I would have to think about our little chat and what I was going to do next. Then he gets all serious on me and tries to be my friend, suggests we have dinner sometime soon...says maybe we can help each other out."

"What did you say to that?"

Minnie peered at me over her glasses. "Are you kidding me?"

"Sorry."

FIFTEEN

An Ethical Dilemma

"Grace?"

"Yes."

"Flora."

"Yes, Flora. What can I do for you?"

"Last night, our midnight robber stole Mrs. Huxhold's prize American gensing, and she is hopping mad."

"Her what?"

"American gensing. Apparently, it's a rare plant that takes eight years to mature and produce flowers, and she had been nursing this one along for all that time. And, mind you, she had a small fence around it to keep out rabbits and stuff...and it was just about to flower when—"

"It turned up missing."

"Yep. And she wants whoever stole it charged, tried, and—if possible—hung."

"That might be a little harsh for a stolen plant."

"Tell that to Mrs. Huxhold."

"What does it look like?"

"Hold on a second. I'll read it to you." Flora cleared her throat. "It has the most Arcadian shade of green leaves you'll ever see, each intransigent leaf perfectly shaped, and it had just starting to exhibit a lone limpid but exquisite umbel."

"Let me guess—her words?"

"They're not mine. I don't even know what half of them mean."

"Please tell Mrs. Huxhold I plan to stake out the neighborhood myself, and we'll try to get to the bottom of it. Anything else reported missing lately?"

"I'm embarrassed to tell you this, but I may as well. Last night, my husband and I...well, we got a little amorous in the backyard. He sorta flung my panties, and they landed in the kids' sandbox. I forgot about them until early this morning, so I snuck out there before the sun even came up, and they weren't there anymore.

I asked George if he had brought them in, and he said he hadn't, so I'm thinking someone must have stolen them."

"Your panties."

"I'm afraid so."

"Describe them please."

"Pink with white polka dots."

What I had to put up with in this job.

After Flora's call, I had no sooner started to organize the sudden backlog of work that had accumulated during the previous week when a woman walked in the front door. She asked Naomi if she could make an appointment with someone at NSU Investigative Services. I could see Naomi from my vantage point and watched her open one of those black-and-white composition books, pretending it was my appointment calendar, and told her that there didn't appear to be an opening for several days but if she wanted to take a seat, she would see if one of the investigators could possibly squeeze her in. I loved her style.

Naomi confirmed with me that it was okay to bring her in.

She was tiny, maybe five feet tall and a hundred pounds, if that. My age or a little younger, conservatively dressed in a navy pinstriped pants suit.

Before I could even introduce myself, she took a seat and started talking.

"My name is Fern Herschberger," she said in a soft voice. "I'm trying to locate my birth mother, Anna Vargas."

The woman continued to talk, but for several minutes at least I was barely conscious of what she was saying. My brain seemed to be fixated on the steady tapping sound coming from Naomi's typewriter. Unable to speak myself, I tried to raise my hand to signal her to stop, but I couldn't even move my arm.

Finally, she stopped telling her story and asked me, "Are you all right?"

A wave of something fluttered down my body, releasing me from an apparent hypnotic state.

"Yes, of course. Will you excuse me for just a minute or two?"

She gave me a concerned look and nodded.

I rose from my chair and hoped my legs would carry me.

As soon as I got to the bathroom, I locked both doors and sat on the toilet-seat lid. We had never covered anything like this in law-enforcement school.

The water I splashed on my face rejuvenated my better senses while I tried to digest what this woman had just said. Did she realize who I was? I had to know that for starters. Otherwise, I'd be working completely blind.

Elmer wasn't in, so I unlocked the bathroom door on his side and slipped into his office, trying hard to keep from choking on the stale after-effect of his cigarettes. I used his phone to call Naomi.

"Naomi, listen to me carefully. I need you to find out who referred that woman to me. Does she even know my name?"

"Yes, Mr. Billingsly. I'll take care of that right away. What is your location?"

"I'm in Elmer's office right now, but I'm going into the bathroom in case he comes back. Let yourself into the bathroom through his door when you come in, and please make up something about why I needed to excuse myself for a few minutes."

"Yes, sir. Goodbye."

I could hear Naomi talking to Miss Herschberger, but I couldn't make out what they were saying. I snuck back into the bathroom and waited.

A few minutes later, Naomi came in.

"She said she found your company name in the phone book, and she doesn't live far from here. She's embarrassed she doesn't even know your name."

"Do you believe her? Does she sound sincere?"

"I think so, and I'm pretty good at being right on first impressions."

"What did you tell her about my absence?"

"I said you had a taco salad for lunch, and it wasn't agreeing with you."

"Good work. And for this client, Naomi, I am Lily Lambert. Please remember that." I just hoped *I'd* remember that—I had never used a fake name with an actual client before.

She gave me a puzzled look but said, "Got it."

Naomi left, and I took a couple more minutes to compose myself before returning to my office and new client.

I started talking even before sitting down. "I am so sorry, Miss Herschberger, for rushing out of here like that." I reached out to shake her hand. "I'm Lily Lambert," I said, hoping she was far enough away from my PI license hanging on the wall to be able to read it.

"It's nice to meet you, Miss Lambert. And your receptionist explained. It's happened to all of us at one time or another, believe me."

I took that opportunity to explain my fees, which she accepted without any questions.

"Now, you were saying."

"Yes, I was saying I'd like to locate my birth mother. You see, two wonderful people adopted me when I was an infant, but I didn't find out I was adopted until a few years after they died, almost five years ago."

"You don't mind if I take notes, do you?"

"Not at all."

I asked her why she wanted to find her birth mother.

"I have a boyfriend, and we plan to get married...and have children someday.

And I know someone my age who was adopted and passed down a terrible condition to her baby without knowing, and...well, I wanted to be sure before..."

I knew she wasn't being forthright, but I thought it best to keep the discussion moving. I asked her to tell me all the facts she had—not her assumptions, not conjecture, just the facts.

She didn't respond right away, and when she did, her voice was even softer than before.

"I don't think I have any facts."

Most people don't fully understand the definition of a fact, so I explained.

"For example, what is your birth date, Miss Herschberger?" Was that fair—to start out with that question? How do I separate my objectives from hers?

"January 4, 1942."

Holy...six months before I was born.

"So you may know for a fact that you were born on January 4, 1942, because that's what it says on your birth certificate, or you may think that's your birth date because you were told that your whole life, which wouldn't necessarily make it a fact."

"I have a birth certificate, so I guess I do have at least one fact." She let out a nervous laugh. "I probably have more, but I don't know what's important."

"Who is listed as your parents?"

"My parents' names are on it, but I don't believe they're my biological parents."

I spent the next hour asking her questions, only some of which she was able to answer.

Her story stunned me.

Her parents had died six months from each other—her mother first from cancer. After her father died in a boating accident, she had found adoption papers in a safe deposit box that indicated her birth mother was Rosa Lindroth—my mother! Well, not my real mother...I don't think. But she discovered strange errors on the adoption papers which she thought may have been forged to make it look like a legal adoption when it wasn't. I didn't tell her this, but some of the documents she mentioned should have never left the court and/or the agency.

There were other things that hadn't made sense to her, and she later found clues that led her to Anna's boardinghouse. Over time, Fern located Anna's friend, Esmeralda "Essie" Noe, the same friend Minnie had found for me. She went on to say that in order to get close to Essie, she'd joined Essie's church and became involved in the same activities.

After going to this church for several months, Fern learned from Essie that she had volunteered with her best friend Rosa at the Our Lady of the Angels School after their tragic fire. I remembered that tragedy—it happened in 1958 when I was a senior in high school. That put Essie and Rosa together after Anna's death.

I concluded the meeting by telling her I had enough information to get started on her case and would be back in touch.

At first, I thought it too bizarre that Essie had known both my mother and Anna, but then I thought that was just one more piece of evidence tying all this—whatever *this* was—together in my case. And learning Essie had known my mother, I wondered if I had actually met Essie at some point.

I had an obvious ethical dilemma. How could I charge this woman for investigating a case that would benefit my own interests? And giving her a bogus name complicated matters. That had been a rash decision on my part. In hindsight, I was not sure I should have done that.

The first thing I did was start a background check on Fern Herschberger, which, thanks to the many contacts I'd made, I was able to do over the phone.

I learned that she lived in Portage Park, taught fifth grade at T. Roosevelt Elementary School in Cicero, and had a bachelor's degree from the University of Illinois. She had a valid driver's license, no judgments or liens against her, and no criminal record. Nothing conflicted with what she had told me.

I had been taught in school that a private investigator should never handle his own case. Now I understood why—something happened to the reasoning part of the brain when it was your own case. I walked out to Naomi's desk to clear my head. I hadn't seen Elmer yet, and I asked Naomi about him just to pass the time.

"He *said* he'll be in court all day," she told me, rolling her eyes. "Has me working on his personal stuff."

I glanced down at her desk at what seemed to be a bank statement. It appeared he had her balancing his checkbook. *None of my business.*

"Okay. Well, I'll be in all day, I think."

"Everything okay?" she asked.

"Yes. Everything is okay. Thanks for covering for me back there."

"Um, Nora Edgar called and said she's found another agency to help her and won't be needing your services."

Shit. I had let the Storage Room case slip through the cracks in deference to my own case.

I went back to my office and waited until Naomi ran across the street to buy a sandwich for lunch. Something had prompted me to fish around her desk for Elmer's bank statement. It was from North Community Bank and had been mailed to Waddershins Trust, 5405 W. Ferdinand Street, Chicago, Illinois.

Seeing first-hand that Elmer was associated with Waddershins Trust, the trust that had purchased my parents' house after they died, made me wince. Seeing proof that Elmer was living in my old house on Ferdinand made me sick.

⤳ SIXTEEN ⤳

Doing the Right Thing

Three nights later, at ten o'clock, armed with a flashlight, camera, and a can of Mountain Dew, I climbed the twenty-five-foot chain-link ladder to Flora's sons' backyard tree fort and settled into the five-by-five-foot wooden box that smelled a little like a wet dog. It was my first stakeout for the Midnighter case. I scrunched my legs up under me—there wasn't much else I could do with them—and watched the neighborhood.

It was early April. The cool evening air felt more like a winter leftover than a promise of what spring was about to deliver. Minutes stretched into hours, and I passed the time pondering what to do about Fern. There seemed to be three options. I could continue using the fake name and work on the case like I would any other. I could tell her I had a conflict of interest and couldn't work on her case at all. Or I could come clean and work *with* her.

When one-thirty A.M. rolled around and the only movement I had seen was a large stumpy-tailed cat slinking across the next door neighbor's backyard, I decided to call it a night.

The next day, I decided to make contact with Essie on my own before making a decision about Fern. If Essie could provide more information, it would make the decision easier.

I knew Essie worked, so I waited until after dinner to call her.

"Esmeralda Noe?"

"Yes."

"My name is Grace Lindroth, and—"

She hung up on me.

* * *

I stewed for days, going from surprised to insulted to confused and then to angry.

Essie wouldn't have reacted that way after hearing my name if she hadn't had something she wanted to keep from me.

I had such mixed emotions about Elmer and his connection with my parents' house. The trusting side of me wanted to believe there was a reasonable explanation for his having purchased it and then having lied about living there. For example, it was possible that he had innocently taken advantage of a good deal by buying it and now was embarrassed for me to know because he realized the reason I was not in that house was due to a personal tragedy. But the suspicious side of me didn't buy that story.

And I continued to anguish over Fern. If we worked together, we would have a better chance of resolving the issues than if we worked separately, and joining forces would end my deception of her. What was the worst that could happen? I didn't know the answer to that—a bad position to be in. One thing I did know for sure was that I either had to come clean with her right then or forget coming clean at all. I decided to sleep on it one more night.

The next day, I got ready for work, and as soon as I walked in the office door, Naomi told me Minnie was on the phone.

"Are you sitting down?" she asked me.

"Yes. What is it?"

"That cousin Henry Sikes talked about?"

"Yes."

"It's Elmer Berghorn."

* * *

What I would have given to be able to talk to someone about my situation—someone my age, someone who knew me well, someone to whom I could tell anything and all I would get back was support, someone who made it easier for me to be me. Attempts to rekindle that kind of relationship with Beth proved to be a lost cause—she was too wrapped up in her marriage and pregnancy. Not that I thought there was anything wrong with that. On the contrary, I was very happy for her. I just wasn't very happy for myself just then.

Thanks to the Midnighter case, I hadn't slept well in days, and that had taken a toll on me. I had sat in that damn tree fort every other night for a week and seen nothing. On the nights I hadn't been there, there were reports of stolen items. It was very peculiar, like someone was tipping off the burglar that I was there watching.

Earlier in the day, Naomi had noticed I wasn't myself and had asked me several times how she could help. The problem with giving her work was that most of what I could give to her required me to do some upfront work first, and I wasn't always up to it. That was a problem—I had lost two clients in two days because I hadn't gotten back to them in a timely manner. I felt like things were starting to fall apart.

Fern had left a message with Naomi for me to call her. I had to make a decision one way or another on what to do with her. It wasn't fair to keep stringing her along.

I went out and asked Naomi to call Fern back to see if she could come in to my office at seven o'clock that evening.

* * *

The afternoon and early evening dragged on. Each time I looked at the clock, it was only a few minutes later than the last time I'd looked. Before Naomi left for the day at five-thirty, she brought in a sandwich.

"You can't have your meeting on an empty stomach," she said.

I was lucky to have her.

An hour before Fern arrived, I tried to eat the sandwich, but when the first bite stuck in my throat and wouldn't go down, I put it aside. Damn nerves. I sipped on a cup of hot tea while I waited for her.

When Fern arrived, without saying anything I brought her to my back room where I had spread out on the table all the photographs from my parents' attic.

"Before we start, Miss Herschberger, could you take a look at these photographs and tell me if anyone looks familiar to you?"

Fern took her time studying the photos and then picked up the one of a newborn baby swaddled in a checkered blanket.

"I know lots of babies look alike, but this one looks like me in some of my baby pictures. In fact, I have a picture of me right after I was born wrapped in the same kind of blanket." She glanced up at me. "Same hospital maybe?"

"Let's sit down, Fern. I have so much to tell you."

SEVENTEEN

One of Us Is Wrong

It took me close to two hours to tell Fern everything I knew. When I got to the part about Anna's death, she stared past me for several seconds with a lifeless expression.

"I didn't know that," she muttered.

"Fern, by any chance did you envision a joyful reunion with her if she turned out to be your birth mother?"

"It never crossed my mind that she could be dead. A joyful reunion? No, I guess..."

"Let me explain something to you. Less than fifty percent of these types of reunions result in something positive. Most people wish they had never made the effort in the first place."

She shot me a sharp look. "Is that supposed to make me feel better?"

"No. Just more realistic."

She didn't say anything else, so I continued, but she didn't appear to be listening.

A few minutes later, she said, "I'm not sure if I want to go on."

"Listening to my story?"

"Searching for the truth."

"What's making it less important than it was the day you walked into my office?"

"That she's dead. What's the point if she's dead?"

"That's up to you, but for me, it wouldn't matter if she was dead or alive."

"What do you mean?"

"The first morning I woke up after realizing my parents may not have been my birth parents, it was like waking up with amnesia, like I was living without a past. For me, I won't be whole until I understand my past, and then my goal is to transcend the past, whatever that may be, and develop a meaningful future."

"But you *have* a past with wonderful parents, you told me. Just like I did."

"I know, but it's not complete, and that's a roadblock for me."

Fern nodded in agreement...barely. "I think I understand that. Maybe I need time to think about it...and get over Anna's death. Please continue."

When I finished telling her the rest of what I knew, I leaned back in my chair and asked her what she thought.

Without saying a word, she got up and walked toward the door.

"Fern?"

She opened the door and, after a brief pause, went through it.

I was tempted to run after her, but instead I put myself in her place, her frame of mind, and knew it wouldn't have been the right thing to do. She needed time—at least I hoped that was all it was. If not, I was afraid I had screwed up—big time. Up until I'd told her Anna was dead, I'd thought I had done the right thing by being completely honest with her. Now I wasn't so sure.

I waited thirty minutes until I was confident she wasn't coming back before I went up to my apartment, poured myself a generous glass of wine, and curled up on the sofa. Each minute that ticked by strengthened the possibility that I might have seen the last of Fern Herschberger, and that was upsetting.

The wine calmed my nerves some. I closed my eyes and rested my head on the back of the sofa, letting the savory red liquid glide down my throat. I had decided sipping wine was better than ironing—maybe not healthier but certainly more enjoyable.

The knock on my door startled me, causing a thin stream of wine to slosh onto the sofa. Glass still in hand, I answered the door.

Fern focused on the wine. "Do you have any more of that?" she asked.

We laughed in harmony—long enough to dispel the awkwardness of the moment. I didn't remember telling her that I lived upstairs, but I must have, and I was glad for that, even though I was embarrassed to have anyone see the place.

"You asked me what I thought," she began after tasting the wine. It was humiliating having to serve a guest Mad Dog, but it was all I had. "I don't know what to think, and maybe that's why I left—because I needed to process those thoughts."

"And?"

"The more I thought about what you said, the part about living without a past, the more I thought that may really be the root of my problems as well. Let me clarify something for you. During our first meeting, you asked me the reason I wanted to find my birth mother. Well, what I told you was a lie—the same lie I keep telling my boyfriend, the same lie I keep telling myself really."

"That you want a family medical history before having children?"

"Yes. But in my heart I know the real reason isn't that at all. I'm angry. What kind of person abandons a newborn child? I wanted to confront her and have her explain to me why—why she gave me away. And so when you told me she was dead, I felt like I had nowhere to vent that anger. Keeping it bottled up inside has been painful—physically and emotionally. But you know something? I think sharing it with you has helped."

"You've stirred it up, and that's the first step to releasing it. Now you need to find the truth to push it all the way out."

"It all makes sense. Where did you learn all this?"

"I had to take a few psychology classes in my law enforcement program. At least some of what I learned has paid off. Getting back to Anna—and don't forget we have no proof she was your mother, so whoever your mother was—I've read enough case studies on this to know there are some very legitimate reasons for mothers to choose adoption rather than raise the child on their own."

"Like what?"

"Like they may not have the financial means to provide a safe and healthy place to live. Like they may not have the emotional stability it takes to raise a child. Like she may have been too young to be a good mother. Like—"

"They sound like excuses to me. I'd find a way to make more money. I'd get counseling. I'd ask for help. I'd do whatever it took before I ever abandoned a child."

"You may be stronger than some women."

Fern was silent.

"I hope I haven't overstepped any boundaries," I told her.

She let out a heavy sigh. "No. You're just doing your job."

"I'm trying to be your friend, Fern, not your hired PI."

"Okay, Lily."

"Touché. And one thing we haven't talked about is that it looks like we were born six months apart, and we both think Anna is our mother. At least one of us has to be wrong."

"It appears that way. Unless you were premature."

"Or we don't know our real birthdays."

"Or one of us is lying."

"Will you ever forgive me for that?"

"You know what?" she said. "I am so glad I picked your company out of the phone book that day."

"Me too. But tell me, out of all the PIs listed, what made you pick *me*, if you don't mind my asking."

She stared at me without responding.

"Fern?"

"I'm not sure I should say."

"You don't have to tell me, but considering—"

"I called a bunch of them. You were the cheapest."

I was slow to laugh, and when I did, it came from deep inside my belly.

"By a long shot."

Now we were both laughing so hard, we were swiping away tears.

"In one case, by half," she roared.

"Okay, you can stop now."

It took us a while to compose ourselves, and when we did, we talked for another hour. We weren't able to come up with any new revelations by combining what we knew, but we did agree that Essie Noe was most likely the one who could get us closer to the truth, and it was obvious I wasn't the one who was going to get anything from her.

We parted ways with Fern agreeing to try to get better connected with Essie— just how, she wasn't sure.

I poured myself another half-glass of wine and plopped down on the sofa. I was spent—physically, mentally, and emotionally—but it felt good. I had done the right thing.

I took a last sip of Mad Dog, drew a nice hot bubble bath, and soaked long enough to get prune skin. As I put on my coziest pajamas, I thought about the soothing effect that crawling between the freshly laundered and ironed sheets would have on me.

It was the middle of April, the first mild day of the year. I tried to open the apartment's lone window to let in some fresh air only to find it was stuck. Twenty minutes of struggling later, I managed to get it to open a few inches. The cool, crisp air that wafted in was refreshing.

I crawled into bed and hoped it wouldn't take me long to fall asleep. I didn't want to think about my conversation with Fern, Elmer Berghorn, or my renewed enthusiasm about solving my case until the morning when I had a clear head and was fully rested. Right then, I wanted only quiet, dreamy thoughts.

The acidic smell emanating from what I surmised was the rooftop vents of the dry cleaner two buildings away interrupted my journey to slumberland. What— they ran a night shift? If the odor from whatever cleaning solvent they used was that strong all the way at my place, what was it like for the workers?

I pulled the sheet over my mouth and nose in an attempt to filter the air I breathed and tried to fall asleep.

It hadn't occurred to me that there would be so much traffic outside my apartment at that time of day, and the incessant honking of car horns told me nighttime drivers were no more patient than those behind the wheel during the day.

The dreamy thoughts I longed for must have been hiding somewhere. I changed positions and waited for them to appear.

I hadn't realized there were so many types of sirens—some low-pitched, some high-pitched, some long ones, some short ones, whoop-whoop ones, some off in the distance, and others speeding by right in front of this building.

I closed the window. So much for fresh air.

EIGHTEEN

The Cavalry

I was glad for the weekend—I had spent the latter half of the week working twelve-hour days in order to fit in Attic Finds work, and I had nothing to show for it. I needed the weekend, away from work, to clear my head.

I spent a little time cleaning my apartment and then headed for Six Corners to buy a new pair of shoes—and not from a thrift store. I went to Sears and bought myself a pair of brand-new never-been-worn black Mary Janes.

After running several errands, I picked up some dinner for later and drove home.

Luck was with me—there was a parking space near my apartment door. I juggled the assortment of bags I had amassed until I could comfortably manage them without dropping anything and headed upstairs. At the top of the stairs, I was surprised to find several large boxes blocking my door.

I put everything down, shoved the boxes out of the way, and put the key in the lock. The key didn't work.

What the...?

The boxes weren't sealed, so I peered inside one of them. "That's my toaster," I said aloud. Another one contained my clothes.

I ran downstairs and tried my office-door key. It didn't work either.

I flew back upstairs and frantically searched the other boxes and found my case files. I tore through every box looking for items from the back room, but nothing associated with Attic Finds was there.

Only one person could have been behind this: Elmer Berghorn.

I plopped myself down on the top step, kicking out of my way an array of clothes I had flung out of one of the boxes. I had nowhere to go. And worse yet, the only evidence I had pointing to my real identity was gone.

I looked at all my worldly possessions strewn about me in the filthy hallway. After a good cry, I quit feeling sorry for myself and then beat myself up some for behaving like a helpless little girl. I inhaled a deep breath, marched down the stairs, and headed for the nearest phone booth.

"Minnie?"

"I was just thinking about you. How are you?"

"Not good. I've been evicted from my apartment *and* my office and—"

"What? Well, you get yourself right over here, ya hear? With all your things."

"They won't all fit in my car. I'll have to make several trips."

"Stay right there. I'll have my cavalry come get you."

Her cavalry?

While I waited for Minnie, I put everything back in the boxes and thought of ways to get even with Elmer. What gave him the right to kick me out anyway? He knew the law, and he knew I knew the law.

One hour and several spiteful plots to destroy Elmer later, I wondered if there really was a cavalry coming to rescue me. My stomach was growling. I retrieved the takeout chicken from one of the grocery bags and tried not to think about the ice cream and TV dinners that were gradually defrosting. The chicken was cold and shriveled and bore the flavor of the cardboard box it had been sitting in. I hated that man.

The heavy rap on the street-level door to my apartment startled me. I rushed down the stairs and asked who was there.

"The cavalry, ma'am."

Okay, so that made me smile.

I opened the door to find Minnie, Tymon, and two men—two young, strong men—standing there.

"We're here! Where's your stuff?"

After I showed them what I had, Tymon left to bring his truck around front. When he returned, he told Minnie and me to step to the side and let his young helpers do all the heavy lifting, which they completed in a matter of minutes.

Minnie rode with me to her house.

"Thank you for coming to my rescue," I told her.

"I'm just getting even, you know."

"Even? For what?"

"Coming to mine. And before you ask me what I mean—and I know you're about to—tell me what in the hell is going on?"

I told her all I knew, which wasn't much.

"I don't like the timing—right on the heels of you hooking up with Fern," she said.

"What's that got to do with anything?"

"You're the detective, you tell me."

"You think there could be a connection between Elmer and Fern?"

"So what are you going to do about the missing stuff? You're going to confront him about it, aren't you?"

"I'm not sure what confronting him would do, Minnie. He's not going to hand over the missing items just because I ask for them. I'll probably consult with an attorney to see if I have any recourse."

"An attorney?! That crumb bum throws you out for no reason and you want to go by the law to get back what's legally yours? That man needs a taste of his own medicine."

"No, I'm go—"

"Don't do anything just yet," she said as I pulled into her driveway. Tymon pulled in behind us. "C'mon, let's see what we can salvage from your groceries."

"Minnie, whatever it is you—"

She didn't let me finish—she was out of the car and heading toward Tymon's truck. When I caught up to her, she put her arm around my waist. "Don't argue with me, Gracie. You'll lose every time."

* * *

I woke up and for a brief moment didn't recognize my surroundings. Flowered drapes, stone fireplace, birds chirping outside, the smell of coffee drifting into the room.

Then it quickly came back to me.

Despite Minnie's narrow somewhat lumpy sofa, I felt as though I'd had several hours of quality sleep—stress and exhaustion will do that to you. I'm not sure when I fell asleep, but I think it may have been when Minnie and I were in the middle of a conversation because I don't remember saying goodnight or anything.

Minnie emerged in her robe and slippers carrying two cups.

"I put lots of cream and sugar in yours. Try it. You might like it."

I took a sip of the coffee, and it wasn't bad.

"How did you sleep, Gracie?"

"Okay. And you?"

"Thanks to worrying about you, I tossed and turned all night."

"Please don't worry about me. I'm not going to let the likes of Elmer Berghorn get me down, not for long anyway."

"We're going to get your things back."

"My guess is that they're long gone by now."

"We'll see."

We finished our coffee, and Minnie told me to use the bathroom as long as I needed it to get ready. She had work to do.

In her robe and slippers?

It didn't take long for me to get ready for the day. When I came out, Minnie was standing in her bedroom doorway with her hands on her hips.

"What's the matter?"

"Nothing. What did you say was the address of your parents' house? It's on Ferdinand, right?"

She was up to something.

"Why do you ask?"

"No reason. Just curious."

"If you tell me—"

"What is it?" she asked me.

My eyes were drawn to the picture hanging on her bedroom wall—the one with mountains in the background, a stream on the left, and deer grazing on the right.

"That's the same painting."

"You're changing the subject."

"That's the same painting as the one in the photograph of the woman and baby in the rocking chair. It's the same painting. Where did you get it?"

"I don't remember. It's so old, I...it may have been left here. I don't remember."

"I wish I had that photograph. It could have been taken in this room."

"Don't you worry about your photographs. Now, what was that address?"

I gave her the address.

Minnie and I spent the morning cleaning Marcus O'Gowan's old room and the upstairs bathroom, washing linens, and moving a few pieces of furniture upstairs so I had a comfortable place to stay...temporarily. Minnie acted like an old mother hen when it came to my well-being. And to be honest, I kind of liked it.

Except for the fostering I received from Mrs. Miller, I hadn't been mothered since my own mother had died, and even though it was up for grabs whether she was my real mother, the memories still had an effect on me. My mother had vacillated between two types of mothering: overprotective and indifferent. There were times she fussed over me, made decisions for me, and controlled my every move. And there were other times I didn't even know where she was in the house. What made it difficult was that I didn't know which mother to expect on any given day.

The rollaway bed in my new temporary quarters didn't seem too bad—at least a little wider than Minnie's sofa—and by the time she was through decorating it with bright white sheets, a flowered bedspread, and a few throw pillows, it looked pretty inviting.

We were just about ready to stop for lunch when I remembered to ask Minnie about the attic. She pointed to the ceiling above a three-drawer dresser in the small alcove of the bedroom.

"I don't see anything."

"Look closely."

I stared at the ceiling until I saw a fine rectangular line camouflaged by the linen-like texture of the plaster.

"So how do you get access to it?"

"I have no idea."

"You've never been up there?"

Minnie shook her head.

"Do you have a ladder?"

"There's one in the basement."

"Can we get it?"

I followed Minnie to the basement, and we struggled to carry the six-foot stepladder up two flights of stairs. Hindsight told me it would have been easier to carry it myself—half the time we were pulling it in opposite directions.

I wasn't that steady on a ladder, I soon found out. Minnie was holding it at the bottom, but my legs were shaking, making it unstable. Once at the top, I pushed the trapdoor up and slid it over. I was immediately overcome by a sickeningly musty smell mixed with a urine-like odor.

I gave myself a few seconds to steady myself before I stood on the top step.

"It says 'DANGER – DO NOT STAND ON TOP STEP,'" she said to me.

Too late, I was.

"There's stuff up here. I'm going to look around, if that's okay."

"Be my guest," she said. "You wouldn't get me to go up this ladder," she mumbled.

"It's pitch-black up here."

"Hold on. I'll get the lantern."

"No, wait! Let me get all the way up here first."

I didn't have that much upper-body strength, but somehow I managed to elevate myself up and over onto the attic floor. I peered down through the opening at Minnie.

"Okay. You can go now."

A few minutes later, Minnie returned with the lantern and looked up at me.

"I'm not coming up there to give you this."

"Well, I'm not coming down and then up again. Once was scary enough. In fact, I don't even know how I'm going to *get* down."

She flipped the switch on the lantern and shined it toward me. "How's that?"

I rolled my eyes at her. "Look, all you have to do is climb halfway up. If I lie down on the floor and reach down and you reach up, we can do this."

Minnie took the long cord attached to the lantern, hung it around her neck, and proceeded up the ladder.

"Why do you have it around your neck?"

"You think I'm going to climb this thing holding on with only one hand?"

"Well, what are you going to do once you're halfway up? You're going to have to take it off your neck somehow."

She stopped her ascent and looked up. From there, she resembled one of those troll dolls—small and squatty with large eyes and hair standing straight up—and it was all I could do to keep from laughing.

"I have an idea," she said. She climbed down from the first step, made a hasty sign of the cross, and disappeared. She came back in ten minutes with a roll of tape and a mop.

"What on earth are you going to do with that?"

"Just watch me. Where there's a will, there's a way my Clarence used to always say."

Minnie arduously wrapped the tape around the lantern, affixing it to the end of the mop handle. Then she raised it up to me as far as she could, using the slant of the steps of the ladder to guide it up to me. I lay down on the attic floor and tried to reach it, but Minnie was just a hair over five feet tall and had short arms, so the lantern was still a few inches out of my reach.

"If you go up on the first step, Minnie, I could reach it."

I heard several Hail Marys and a series of grunts before the lantern was in my hand.

"Got it!"

I stood in the middle of the room and held the lantern up to get a lay of the land. One object immediately jumped out at me—a large decorative trunk, about three feet tall and four feet long, a combination of leather, wood, and brass. My heart pounded. Finding an old trunk in an attic—how exciting was that?

∽ NINETEEN ∽
Treasures or Trash?

My excitement had to be placed on hold—the trunk was locked. As I walked back toward the trapdoor, I almost tripped over a metal box. I picked it up and examined it. It weighed about five pounds or so, and it too was locked.

I looked down at Minnie who was still standing at the foot of the ladder.

"You know what we could use?"

"A Scotch?"

"Besides that."

"What?"

"A rope."

"And where do you think I'm going to get a rope?"

"You don't have one?"

Her look served as her response, which was clear.

"Do you have clothesline?"

"Of course."

"Can you bring me some?"

She turned to leave.

"And Minnie?"

"Yes, masser."

She could be funny.

"Something to cut it."

It was just as well I didn't understand what she muttered.

While Minnie was on her mission, I walked the perimeter of the room to make sure there were floorboards everywhere and not any openings between joists where I could fall through. It was a good thing I did this because there were a couple of places where the floorboards were loose.

"So, Miss Einstein, how am I going to get this rope and knife up to you?" Minnie shouted from below.

I couldn't see her throwing the rope up to me—it weighed too much—and certainly not the knife, so I was going to have to come down to get them.

"Too bad there's not a man around," I told her. "They come in handy for stuff like this."

A ringing phone interrupted our conversation, and Minnie disappeared downstairs. She returned a few minutes later.

"Those stairs are going to be the death of me. Tymon is on his way over."

"I better come down then."

"Why? Maybe he can help."

"Do you really want him to see what's up here? What if it's something...well, that you don't want anyone else to see?"

"I didn't think of that."

"Why is he coming over? Just for a visit?"

"No. He has something for you."

"For me? Like what?"

"We'll show you later. Right now, we have to figure this out."

"Do you think he's left already?"

"I don't know. Why?"

"I'd ask him if he has a better ladder."

"This is the last time I'm going to..."

I didn't hear the end of her sentence, but I didn't have to.

I continued to scan the room. It was a nice attic, as far as attics went. I could walk to within just a few feet from the edges without ducking my head. It would have been better with an overhead light though, or at least a window.

Stacks of old *National Geographic* magazines sat in one corner next to an old-fashioned baby stroller, an empty file cabinet, and a pile of tarps. Two boxes sitting in the corner looked interesting. The first one contained women's clothes that appeared to be from the Roaring Twenties. The second box contained scads of old photographs.

I continued my walk around the perimeter and found nothing more.

In the middle of the room was a huge pillar, and leaning up against it were several framed paintings. I couldn't tell whether they were original paintings or prints, but the frames were nice.

I heard Minnie calling me and walked over to the trapdoor.

"How are you doing?" she asked.

"Good. There are a few interesting things up here. Were you able to catch Tymon?"

"Yes. He's bringing a better ladder. I left the back door open for him. I'm *not* climbing those stairs again."

I told her what I had found.

"Let's not mention the trunk to him," she said. "I don't want anyone else to know what's in it before us."

"But that's what we probably need the most help with. It's huge."

"Will it even fit through the opening?" she asked.

"It got up there, didn't it?"

"Good point. Well, let's deal with it later."

I told her about the paintings.

"What am I going to do with a bunch of old paintings?"

"They could be valuable. You never know."

"I doubt——. Here comes Tymon."

"Hello, Tymon," I shouted down to him.

He looked up at me. "Please tell me you didn't get up there using this rickety stepladder."

"'Fraid so."

He moved the stepladder out of the way and raised one of those outdoor extension ladders through the opening in the ceiling. Then he put something that looked like a strip of rubber on the floor in front of it so it wouldn't slip.

My father used to say you can do anything with the proper tools. On one of our rare family outings, my parents took me to Kiddieland when I was seven or eight, and I got stuck in the roller coaster car on the Little Dipper. At the end of the ride, the metal lap bar that holds you in wouldn't unlock. The park staff tried to get me out, but twenty minutes later, I was still stuck in the car. After my father had seen enough, he told my mother he was running home and would be back as soon as he could. He returned with just one tool, and I was freed within seconds. My father and Tymon must have gone to the same school.

Tymon climbed the ladder and stuck his head up into the attic.

"What's that foul smell up here, Tymon?"

"It smells musty. Is that what you mean?"

"Like urine."

"Could be the fiberglass insulation. It can get that way, especially when a room has been closed off for a long time."

"Just about knocked me over when I first opened the trapdoor."

"You're not thinking of bringing that old trunk down, are you?" he asked.

I didn't know how he could even see the trunk with the pillar in the way.

He must have read my mind. "I've been up here before," he said. "Looks the same as it did twenty years ago." He glanced over to a far corner. "Had to fix a roof leak once. Can still see my patchwork."

"Let's get some of this stuff down and worry about the trunk later," I said.

For the next hour, Tymon and I got the items Minnie and I decided were of interest down to the second floor, with Tymon doing most of the work.

Thanks to Tymon's ladder, it was much easier coming down than it had been going up.

"Tymon, can you wait downstairs a few minutes?" Minnie asked him. "We'll be right down. Grab yourself a cold drink if you like."

She handed the metal box to me. "Find a hiding place for this downstairs, will you? Wait 'til I leave, and I'll distract Tymon in the kitchen while you find a place for it."

Minnie grabbed the mop, the rope, and the knife and disappeared out the bedroom door. I waited a couple of minutes, tucked the metal box under my arm, and went downstairs. I shoved it under Minnie's bed before joining them in the kitchen.

"We have something for you," Minnie said.

I couldn't imagine what the two of them would have for me.

Tymon disappeared and returned with a large cardboard box that he set on the kitchen table. I peered inside to find some of the things I had kept in the back room of my office.

"Where did you get this?"

Neither of them responded.

"From my old office?"

Tymon shook his head.

"Where then?"

"Doesn't matter. He found it. Is that everything?" Minnie asked.

I rummaged through the box, and the only things I believed were missing were the bank statements and business cards.

"Where did you found these things if not in my old office?"

"Some things are better left unknown," Minnie said. "That way you can never be implicated."

Implicated meant only one thing.

Tymon announced that if we didn't need him for anything else, he was going to go home. "If you want help with the trunk later, let me know. I'll leave the ladder here just in case."

Minnie walked him to the back door, while I tried to get my mind around what they had just presented to me. The only thing I could think of was that Tymon or someone had broken into Elmer's house or his office and stolen the items for me, and while I was extremely grateful to have my belongings back, I didn't know how I felt about the manner in which they had been secured.

Minnie returned to the kitchen and asked me if I would bring her the metal box.

When I did, she placed it on the table, examined the lock, and then disappeared. She returned a minute later with a bobby pin.

"Are you kidding me?"

"Don't underestimate me."

Minnie fiddled with the lock but couldn't open it. She shook it. "Something's in there. Can't tell what though."

She disappeared again and then returned with a crochet hook. When that didn't work, she retrieved a second crochet hook and worked both of them inside the lock at the same time.

"Have you done this before?" I asked her.

Minnie just smiled and kept jiggling the hooks in the lock until it opened.

She looked at me with a wide grin.

"You're good."

"Tell me something I don't know." She stared at the box. "I'm afraid to open it."

"Why? Afraid something is going to jump out at you?"

She lifted the hinged lid. I couldn't see what was inside, but the look on her face told me it was a surprise to her.

"What is it?"

Minnie took out a piece of paper and handed it to me.

"Bank of Ireland—Irish currency of some sort."

She nodded and turned the box around so I could see inside.

It was filled with bills. I flipped through them.

"They all say one hundred pounds."

We stared at each other for a long moment.

"O'Gowan's?" I asked.

"I told you I thought he must have had a stash."

"Makes sense since that *was* his room down below, so he was the only one with access to the attic."

"Do you think it's still good?" she asked.

"What do you mean? Does Irish money have an expiration date?" The date on the top one was 1942. I flipped through the top twenty notes or so. "1930s and '40s. Want to count it?" I asked her.

"Yeah...over a glass of Scotch."

Minnie poured, and I started counting, creating stacks of ten hundred-pound notes. In the end, we had thirty-seven piles with two left over.

"So how much is that worth?" she asked.

"I have no idea—37,200 pounds. They could tell you at a currency exchange though."

"If it's like a peso, it won't be worth much."

"Good point. Are you hungry?" I asked.

"Famished."

"Do you like Chinese?"

"Love it."

"My treat."

I ran out to pick up dinner, and by the time we finished eating, it was almost eight o'clock. Afterward, too tired to do much of anything else, we said goodnight to each other.

∽ TWENTY ∾

The Key

The next morning, I awoke to the savory smell of bacon wafting up the stairs to the second floor, compelling me to hurry through my morning routine. I joined Minnie in the kitchen and asked her if there was anything I could do to help.

"You can help by letting me take care of you." She turned to face me. "You don't have to be so damned independent, you know."

I tried to stifle a smile. I had become self-reliant because I knew first-hand that people you depend on could be gone tomorrow.

"Yes, m'am," I said to appease her.

She turned back around toward the stove. "Don't get smart with me, young lady. And you need to smile more—it looks good on you."

While Minnie finished cooking, I thought about how different her life would have been right now if she hadn't lost her husband and daughter.

She served me a heaping plate of bacon, eggs, and hash-brown potatoes.

"What—no toast?"

She stared at me for a long moment before smiling a half-smirk. "That better be your sense of humor, Gracie."

I liked teasing her. "So what do you want to do today?" I asked her. "Do you want to tackle the trunk, go through the stuff we brought down from the attic, see how much money you've just inherited? What's next?"

"The money can wait, but one thing I would like for you to find out, if you don't mind, is what right do I have to it? Is there someone you can ask?"

"I don't know who I'd ask off-hand, but I can probably find someone. It's your house though. The money was there when you bought it, so I would think it's yours."

"Well, in the meantime, I want to help you find out everything *you're* after so you can figure out whatever it is you're trying to figure out and move on. *That's* what I want to do next. So you tell me what that is."

"I don't think anything in the attic is going to help me with that, unless there's something in the trunk."

"Let's do that then."

"Let's, as in let *us*?"

"Whatever I can do from down below, I'll do, because you won't catch me climbing up that ladder. But before we go there, I've been meaning to ask you, why do you really think Elmer booted you out?"

"If Tymon found my belongings in Elmer's possession, which I assume he did, I'd say his reason was tied to them somehow. I just don't know how. Elmer's a user—once he gets whatever it is he's after, he's done with you, and that's what I think happened."

"How did you come to meet him?"

"I answered an ad to sublet the office."

"In the paper?"

"No. It was posted on the bulletin board in the small branch library where I used to go all the time. Why? What are you getting at?"

"Looks like that's how he lured you in."

"Which investigative school did you say you went to?"

"I'm just using a little common sense."

"That could be, but I still don't know what he would want with me. Maybe it's tied to him buying my parents' house."

"Remember, he's Henry's cousin. There's that tie-in."

"I know. Well, one thing is for sure—he's hiding something."

While we cleared the table and did the dishes, I told her everything I knew about Elmer.

"Henry's the common factor," she said after drying the last glass. "And I can handle him," she added, rolling up her sleeves like she was getting ready to take him on—physically.

I looked at her in disbelief.

"What? You don't think I can handle that little twerp?"

Nope. I had no doubts.

* * *

Minnie and I had agreed to leave breaking open the trunk for another day. It was supposed to reach eighty degrees, which meant the attic would be a hundred. My room was already unbearably hot, and it wasn't even noon yet.

I decided to try a new approach on the Midnighter case—sitting in that tree fort was obviously not working. An hour after sunset, I drove to the neighborhood where the thefts had taken place, parked the car at the end of the street, slouched down in the seat, and waited.

Forty-five minutes into my watch, I saw movement halfway down the block—three young boys playing kickball. When one of them got hit in the head with the ball and started crying, the game ended and the boys disappeared.

An hour passed without any activity except for the stumpy-tailed cat crossing the street three times, the last time carrying something in its mouth, probably a bird or mouse or something. My mother used to talk about a cat she once had that would catch a variety of critters at night and leave them on her front porch for her to find in the morning.

By midnight, I couldn't keep my eyes open any longer and called it a night. On the drive home, I thought about the necklace Anna was wearing in the photo of her and me in the rocking chair and had an idea. When I got home, I pulled the photo from the evidence box and examined it more carefully.

I retrieved my mother's jewelry box—one of the few personal things I had of hers—and combed through it. I didn't find the necklace, but I did notice that the felt lining at the bottom was loose, so I dumped out the contents onto the bed and picked at the lining until it was halfway up. Underneath was a small envelope. Inside it was a key.

Tymon's ladder was still in the room, on its side tucked behind the dresser so it would be out of the way. It took me a while, but I managed to right the ladder, poke the trapdoor out of the way with the top of it, and then lean it inside the opening. Excited at the possibility that the key might fit the trunk, I started to scramble up the ladder.

Halfway up, the ladder started to slip at the bottom, and there was nothing I could do but fall with it to the floor.

* * *

When I came to, Minnie was saying repeatedly, "You're all right Gracie. You're going to be all right."

All I could see were Minnie's feet—I was lying face down on the floor, my head pounding.

"The ambulance is on the way."

"What happened?" I tried to get up, but Minnie held me down.

"They said to keep you stable, for you not to move. You could have internal injuries."

"What happened?" I asked again.

"You fell off the ladder."

I closed my eyes until I recalled what I had been doing last.

"Where's the key?"

"What key, dear?"

"I had a key."

She patted my head like you would do to a faithful dog and said, "Why don't you just close your eyes and relax until they get here."

"Find the key. I must have dropped it."

"Okay, dear. Whatever you say."

* * *

I spent two days in the hospital—two days too long, if you asked me. I had a concussion, a fractured kneecap, and eight badly sprained fingers. Apparently, I had forgotten to put that rubber thing in front of the feet of the ladder so it wouldn't slip, a minor detail that had cost me dearly.

Minnie was in her glory taking care of me, even though she complained about going up and down the stairs at least a hundred times a day. I didn't need much— just food really—but you couldn't tell Minnie anything. She had a mind of her own.

They told me my knee had a stable fracture, which meant the broken ends of the bones were aligned right, and as long as they stayed that way, it could heal on its own. Unfortunately, the only way they would remain that way was if I stayed off of that leg. At least the concussion had healed, and my fingers would eventually be good as new.

I had been given a set of crutches, which Minnie hid from me. I was not happy about that, but she was my caregiver and, well, my only friend at that point. Someone had removed the two ladders from my room. No surprise there. So that I could get to the bathroom without putting weight on my knee, Minnie rolled into my bedroom a desk chair on wheels.

I told Minnie that I remembered finding a key in my mother's jewelry box and was going to see if it fit the trunk in the attic when the accident happened, but she said she had combed the room and found no key. I wondered if maybe the bump on my head had done something to my memory.

It was the afternoon of my third day out of the hospital, and I heard Minnie coming up the stairs. I could tell what time of day it was by her footfalls on the wooden steps—quick and snappy in the morning, starting to slow down toward the middle of the day, and lethargic and heavy toward evening.

"I brought you some lemonade, dear," she said. "How does that sound?"

"It would sound better in your kitchen."

"You're not supposed to walk on that leg."

"I could use the crutches if I knew where they were."

"Crutches down those stairs? Are you crazy? You must have hit your head harder than we thought."

I glanced over at the area of the floor directly under the attic trapdoor and noticed the glint of something shiny that had caught a ray of sunlight streaming in through the window.

"What's that?" I asked.

"What? Where?"

"Right there, next to that darker floorboard, halfway to the wall."

Minnie walked over to where I was pointing.

"I don't see anything." She took a step toward the window. "This floorboard is loose. I wonder if that happened when you fell."

"Gee, I hope I didn't damage anything when I just about killed myself trying to figure out what was in *your* trunk in *your* attic."

"Just remember, Missy, whose idea it was to go up there."

"It's in the crack. There's something shiny in the crack," I told her.

"I don't see a thing."

Then I didn't see it either because the sun had gone behind a cloud or something. I had one foot on the floor when Minnie stopped me. "You're not going anywhere."

"I'll use the rolling chair!"

"Stay where you are."

"But the key. I think that's the key!"

"I don't see a—"

"Will you do me a big favor?" I asked her.

"That depends."

"Will you please go get your lantern and shine it on the floor, like the sunlight was doing a minute ago?"

Minnie gave me a look that only she could give, but then proceeded downstairs to fetch the lantern. Her footsteps now sounded like she weighed two hundred pounds.

When Minnie returned, I asked her to sit on my bed while I shined the light. "Now do you see it?"

"Yep." She walked over to the spot. "It's down in the crack though. I can't get it."

"Could you maybe get it out with one of your crochet hooks?"

"You mean the ones downstairs?"

TWENTY-ONE

She Wants to Talk

It took Minnie a good half hour to fish out the key from between the floorboards, and when she did, she stuck it in the pocket of her sweater. Why she didn't give it to me I couldn't understand—there was no way for me to get to the attic without the ladder, which I was sure had been stashed away in a place where I'd never find it, probably alongside my crutches. But I didn't say anything.

Before Minnie left to fix dinner, she said, "By the way, I completely forgot to tell you that your lawyer called when you were in the hospital. I must be getting—"

"My lawyer?" I didn't have a lawyer.

"Yes, he said he wanted to talk to you about the money."

"What money?"

"I just assumed it was the Irish money we found. You said you'd look into it for me."

"I'd look into what for you?"

"My rights to it. We talked about that."

It was all I could do to keep my calm.

"What did you tell him?"

"I said you were in the hospital, and I'd give you the message that he called."

"What else did you tell him?"

"Nothing, why? Why are you so upset?"

"Because I don't have a lawyer, Minnie. Someone was trying to get information from you."

"Oh, dear."

"Yeah, oh, dear."

"I'm sorry. He sounded legit to me."

"Think back. What else did you tell him?"

"Nothing."

"Are you sure?"

She threw up her arms. "I don't know."

My stomach began a slow churn as I watched Minnie shuffle across the room toward the door. Then she turned to me and said, "I may have mentioned I still had it here," before she disappeared.

How could she have been so naive? And who was it who had called? Whoever had called was aware of the money, unless Minnie didn't tell me everything. Like maybe the caller had been vague and cunning enough to get Minnie to tell *him* about the money. *Damn it!* I wished *I* had answered the phone.

An hour passed, long enough for an unsettling mixture of anger and resentment to build up inside me, when Minnie came up with my dinner.

"I hope you realize what you did."

"I said I was sorry."

"If someone is bold enough to impersonate a lawyer in order to get information from you about the money, they're certainly bold enough to come after it!"

"So I'll burn it."

"You don't get it. They'll still think it's here and come after it. And then, when they don't find it, who knows what they'll do?" I never should have let her get involved.

She plopped the tray of food on the bed—hard enough to cause most of the peas to bounce up off the plate and scatter everywhere—and abruptly turned away from me.

"I'm going to the grocery store for a few things. Maybe you need to think about things while I'm gone."

I let her go without saying anything more, even though I hadn't gotten everything off my chest. I didn't know what she meant by "think about things," but I didn't care. There were more important issues at hand than trying to figure her out.

I pushed the tray aside and grabbed a pad of paper and pen to start a list of precautions we could take in case whoever had called Minnie paid us a visit. My swollen fingers made it difficult to write, adding to my frustration. After twenty minutes, I had a few things listed in handwriting I hoped I could decipher later, when the phone rang from downstairs.

I sat through ten rings. I could have managed the stairs on crutches if I'd had them. Ten more rings. Someone was determined.

I rolled out to the hallway and into the back bedroom. Scooting down the stairs on my butt was the only way I could think of to get downstairs without damaging my bad knee. If I had been a kid, it would have been fun, but I wasn't, and it wasn't.

Once downstairs, the phone was just several hops away. I was completely out of breath when I answered it.

"Hello."

"What are you doing right now?"

It was Fern.

"I'm talking to you. What are you doing?"

"You've got to come here right away. Essie wants to talk."

"Come where?"

"We're at that little diner on State and North Avenue. Do you know the one?"

"Yes, but I can't come! I fractured my knee and I'm homebound."

"You've got to come, and I've got to go before she changes her mind."

She hung up.

My purse and car keys were upstairs. It took me a while to scooch up each stair backwards on my butt, and when I did, I grabbed my purse and slid back down them in a fraction of the time.

I was almost out the back door when I discovered my car keys weren't in my purse.

"Damn her!" I whacked the wall with the side of my fist, causing a decorative plate that hung on it to come crashing to the floor. Pieces of porcelain scattered everywhere.

I closed my eyes for a moment, perched on one leg, and wondered what else could possibly go wrong. Who could I call? Tymon. I had his phone number, but it was upstairs. No time for that. I dialed "0" and waited for an operator.

"I need the number for Tymon Kossak."

"What city, please?"

"Chicago."

"Spell the last name, please."

I was so frazzled I couldn't think of how it was spelled. "I'm not sure, I—"

"I can't look up a name if I don't have the spelling."

"Can you try K-o-s-s-a-c-k?"

I waited through several seconds of silence.

"I have no listing by that name, ma'am."

"Can you try K-o-s-a-c-k?"

"No listing by that name either."

"Can you try—"

"Ma'am, can you please call back when you have the correct spelling?"

Click.

What was wrong with her? Couldn't she tell how desperate I was?

I didn't know who else to call.

The ringing of the phone startled me to where I almost lost my balance.

"Hello?"

"It's Fern," she said with a tone of despair.

"What's wrong?"

"She left."

"Did she say anything before she left?"

"Grace, all I have is one dime in change for the phone, so I can't talk long. You can't get out?"

I explained my situation. "Can you come here?" I asked her.

I gave Fern the address. She was about twenty minutes away. I wasn't sure who I wanted to see come through the door first—Fern or Minnie. Either way, Minnie was not going to be happy when she found me downstairs and her fancy plate on the floor in a million pieces, but at that point, I didn't care.

I allowed my anger to subside while I waited for Fern—anger at myself for being so careless with that stupid ladder and at Minnie for everything she had done to make my life more miserable than it already was. To think I had just blown the only chance of Essie ever talking to me. I fought to keep back the tears.

When Fern arrived, we settled in at the kitchen table.

"What happened?" she asked after seeing the mess on the floor.

"Plate fell off the wall. Don't ask."

"I won't." She looked around the kitchen. "So this is the house."

"This is it. I'd show you around, but I'm just a little incapacitated."

"I see that."

"So what happened?" I asked.

"So I was working at this ice cream social this afternoon with Essie. It ended at five-thirty, and she was in a pretty friendly mood, so I asked her if she had any plans for dinner, maybe we could grab a quick bite somewhere. And she said okay. So we go to that little diner...I can never remember the name of it...and we're eating sandwiches and talking about church stuff when she gets this weird look on her face, like she's going to cry or something. I ask her what's wrong, and she asks me if I ever had to keep a big secret to myself, one that slowly ate away at me."

"Really?"

"Really. So I said, no I hadn't, but I could imagine that would be a hard thing to do. And she said, 'Well, I have, and I don't know what to do.' So I asked her if she wanted to talk about it, and she said maybe she should, but not with me...with our minister."

"Damn."

"I know. I had to think fast because we were done eating by that time, so I tell her that talking to Reverend Orman would be a good thing, but if she ever wanted to talk friend-to-friend to let me know because I can be a pretty good listener. Then she blurted out something like, 'I know something that could change a girl's life.'"

"Change whose life? Did she say?"

"Not then, but she went on to tell me about this friend she had over twenty years ago who has a daughter who doesn't know about her."

"The girl doesn't know about her mother, or the girl doesn't know about her?"

"I don't remember her exact words, but she led me to believe she knows things about her friend—this girl's mother—that the girl doesn't know, and what she knows could change that girl's life."

We stared at each other for several seconds.

"Anyway, so I'm thinking she's talking about me, but then she says, 'And she called me the other day.'"

"Who called her, the daughter or the mother?"

"The daughter. But I hadn't called her."

"Well, I did."

"Okay, so now that fits. Well, I didn't know that at the time and wasn't sure what to think, so I told her that was interesting because I had a friend with a similar story. And she said, 'Is her name Grace, by any chance?'"

"Oh, my—"

"So I tell her a little about you and, trying not to push her or anything, encourage her to talk to you. And after thinking about it, she asks me if I could call you to see if you could meet us there. So that's when I called you. But when I got back to the table, she was gone."

"Damn."

Just then Minnie burst into the kitchen juggling two bags of groceries. The sound of the broken plate crunching under her feet echoed throughout the room.

"What's going on in here? What are you doing out of your room? What's all this mess?" She looked at Fern. "And who the hell are you?"

"It's a long story, Minnie. Can I tell you later?" I didn't give her time to respond. "Minnie, this is Fern. Fern this is Minnie."

Minnie's face softened. "Okay. You two continue. Don't mind me." She proceeded to put away the groceries.

Fern and I wrapped up our conversation, and she left.

I tried to forget how mad I was at Minnie and filled her in on Fern's call.

"How did my plate get broken?"

"It was my fault. I'll pay for it."

"You can't."

"Sure, I can. Why not?"

"Because it was priceless."

* * *

I had learned in law enforcement school that oftentimes things get muddled right before they get resolved. I hoped that was the case, because nothing was clear to me, including my relationship with Minnie. When I had offered to help her clean up the broken plate, she told me I had caused enough trouble for one day, so I retreated to my room where I stayed for an hour trying to maintain some semblance of composure.

When I heard Minnie clomping up the stairs even more loudly than usual, I didn't know what to expect. She entered my room and stood in the doorway with my car keys in one hand and crutches in the other.

"I'm sorry I hid these from you."

"And I'm sorry I lost my temper earlier today."

"And I'm sorry I messed up that phone call."

"I'm sorry I broke your plate."

"I'm sorry I told you it was priceless."

"It wasn't?"

"I bought it at Woolworth's."

* * *

I called Naomi around noon, hoping Elmer was out to lunch, to ask her if we could meet somewhere after she got off work. In the meantime, Minnie and I agreed to comb through the stuff from the attic.

We spread the contents of one box out on the dining room table and started with a pack of baseball cards. Neither of us had any interest in baseball. Babe Ruth's was the only name I recognized.

We found several theater ticket stubs from 1921, 1922, and 1923, most of them from musicals at the Chicago Theater. A small unframed oil painting was signed P. Cézanne. I knew nothing about art and neither did Minnie. I told her that if she wanted, I could look up the artist at the library to determine if he was listed anywhere.

We pored over hundreds of photographs. The ones that had writing on the back most often referred to two people, apparently a married couple, named Bonnie and Walter. Several of them appeared to have been taken inside Minnie's house. Others had been taken on what may have been road trips. A few of them included other people, but Bonnie and Walter were in almost all of them. Some had been dated, and based on these dates and their clothing, I deduced that Bonnie and Walter had been young adults between 1910 and 1920—the generation before my mother's. I decided for now that they had nothing to do with me.

The phone interrupted the rhythm we had going. Minnie went to answer it.

The dining room was in the opposite corner of the house from the kitchen, but I could still hear Minnie's side of the conversation. She was giving someone a hard time about cancelling plans to meet her. She ended the conversation with, "Don't wait too long to be in touch. I have things I need to talk to the authorities about." Based on her last comment, I figured it must have been Henry.

She was in over her head, but given our recent squabble, I wasn't sure if I should say anything to her. She was so good-hearted, but my gut told me she was destined for trouble.

She came back to our project and picked up where she had left off.

"Minnie, I think you may be putting—"

Her hands flew straight to her hips. "You don't think I can handle myself, do you?"

"It's not that. It's...what if Henry feels trapped and does something stupid? What if he had something to do with that phony phone call? I don't want—"

"Please don't do this to me, Gracie." She paused for a moment. "I haven't felt this alive since...since I had my family." Her last few words were shaky, like she was fighting back tears.

"I don't want you to get hurt, that's all. It's not worth it."

"I know what I'm doing."

"I know you do." No, you really don't.

"What are you doing later today?" she asked.

"With any luck, convincing Naomi to get firmly into my camp."

"Be careful."

"What do you mean?"

"I don't want you to get hurt, that's all."

"Minnie..."

"I hid the money."

"What?"

"The Irish money. I hid it."

"Where?"

"I'm not telling you."

"Maybe I should know where it is, just in case."

"In case of what?"

"Just in case I need to know where it is."

She turned her back on me and muttered, "It's my money. As long as I know where it is..."

* * *

Naomi was five minutes late. I hoped she hadn't changed her mind. I was sitting on a bench in a nearby park that was small and set back from the street. A dozen or so other benches were scattered along a winding sidewalk, but I was the only one there. I started to feel uncomfortable when I realized that if someone bothered me in any way, I wouldn't be able to escape very fast on crutches.

Ten more minutes passed before I saw her come around the corner. She was decked out in a tight black skirt and pink sweater, looking a lot like the late Marilyn Monroe. Had I worn an outfit like that, I'd have looked like a joke, but somehow she managed to pull it off.

"I am so sorry, Miss Lindroth," she said after joining me on the bench. "I didn't think Mr. Berghorn would ever leave."

"That's okay, and please call me Grace."

She looked at my crutches. "What happened?"

I explained my unfortunate incident.

"Can I tell you something before we get started?" she asked.

"Of course."

"I think what Mr. Berghorn did to you was atrocious, and I almost quit over it. The only reason I didn't is because of Candy."

"Candy?"

"My daughter, Candace." Naomi smiled wide, opened her purse, and pulled out a photo.

I hadn't realized she had a child. "She's a beautiful girl."

"Yes, she is. She turns four on Friday. Anyway, Mr. Berghorn is bad news, and as soon as I find something else, I'm out of there."

"What makes you think he's a bad person?"

"Besides what he did to you?"

"Yes."

"For one thing, he has very few clients, and most of those are foreigners who don't understand much English. When I offered to be a translator in the meetings with his Mexican clientele, he flat out refused, said they didn't need my help. He pads their bills with bogus time and expenses…and I have to type them up knowing exactly what he's doing. And then there's that fishy trust he has, Waddershins. Whenever he wants to hide what he's doing, he does it from behind that trust."

She hesitated a moment. "Look, I shouldn't be telling you all this, but it made me so mad when he made me pack up your things—"

"He made *you* do that?"

"Yes."

"Naomi, did you pack up what was in my back room?"

"No, he told me not to touch that."

"Why did he say he was throwing me out?"

"He said you were warned enough about paying the rent."

"That's not true, by the way. I was never late on the rent."

"I didn't think so."

I had enough trust in what Naomi was telling me that I shared with her some of what I was going through, and before I had finished she offered to help in any way she could. I asked her if she could find out how Elmer had come to buy my old house on Ferdinand Street and what his relationship was with his cousin, Henry Sikes, and then I petitioned her to keep her eyes and ears open for anything else. I jotted down the names of all of the players involved in my personal drama before she left.

Naomi was halfway to the street when she turned around and came back to the bench.

"I don't know if this means anything or not. And at one time, I would have considered this private information…but did you know Elmer's wife died when she was just in her twenties?"

"I didn't even know he was married."

"They weren't married very long."

"No kidding."

"And he has a son who's not well, but I don't have any details."

"I kind of wish you hadn't told me that. Now I feel sorry for him."

"I did at first too. But nothing justifies the rotten things he does."

"Yeah, I know."

I hobbled back to my car and thought about the weather on my way home. About all the troops being sent to South Vietnam. About Julie Andrews winning Best Actress for her role in *My Fair Lady.* I thought about anything that would keep my mind off of Elmer Berghorn.

I arrived home to find a note from Minnie saying she was at the currency exchange to see what the Irish notes were worth. At least she couldn't get into any trouble doing that—I didn't think.

I put a pot on the stove for tea, and while I was waiting for the water to boil, the phone rang. It was Louise Fincutter.

"I'm in Detroit again but have reason to believe Erma is back home. I called my house, and no one answered, but that doesn't mean she isn't there. Could you go over there for me?"

"Sure. I can go there and see what's going on. Could we also ask your neighbors?"

"You'll see when you get there, there are no neighbors. If you don't see anything obvious, feel free to go inside. The key is under the middle gnome on the back porch. And if that key is missing, I *know* she's been there."

"I'm on it, Louise."

I left a note for Minnie and set off for Louise's house. En route, I tried to think of a way to get back into Minnie's attic, which reminded me that Minnie hadn't given me the key back. It was clear I wouldn't be able to climb a ladder given my bum knee, and Minnie had been clear she wasn't going up there. Of course, I realized that the key might not be the key to the trunk at all, but I was hopeful nonetheless.

Louise lived on a short dead-end street near Burnham Park. There were only three homes on this street. Hers was the middle one. The other two had For Sale signs out front. Their lawns had turned into fields of weeds, the homes obviously vacant. This, of course, made it difficult for me to conduct surveillance without being conspicuous—why else would I be on this street unless it had to do with Louise?

Forgetting surveillance, I parked the car in Louise's driveway, walked up to the front door, and knocked. A few minutes later, I walked around to the back and knocked on that door. When no one answered, I peeked under the middle gnome that was sitting off to the side. No key.

"What are you doing here?" a voice said, startling me to the point of almost losing my balance—crutches and all.

The girl had a tough look about her—too much makeup, tight clothes, dead eyes. I recognized her from the photographs Louise had given me.

"I'm Grace Lindroth, a friend of your mother's."

"How do you know my mother? I've never seen you here before."

"I'm a new friend. I've seen photos of you. Can we talk?"

"About what?"

"For starters, your mother and aunt are very worried about you."

"I'll bet they are."

"They're in Detroit right now looking for you, and it's not their first trip."

"Can I use your car?"

"What?"

"I said, can I use your car? I need to go somewhere."

She wasn't going to make this easy.

"No, you may not use my car. Do I look like some kind of chump to you?"

"What happened to your leg?"

"I fell off a ladder."

"My mom's a nurse. Is that how you met her?"

"Could we go inside and talk? Standing on this gravel isn't very comfortable for me."

"Only if you take me somewhere afterward."

"We'll see."

Erma and I talked for over an hour. Underneath that rough exterior was a not-so-rough girl whom I rather liked. In the end, she called the hotel where her mother and aunt were staying, apologized for her bad behavior, and asked them when they would be home. Afterward, I drove her to Montgomery Ward where she bought a new outfit with the leftover money she had gotten from her father, an outfit of which I was certain her mother would approve.

* * *

Minnie was waiting for me at the kitchen table.

"So, what did you find out?" I asked her.

Her eyes were wide. She shook her head.

I sat down in the chair opposite her. "What's the matter? Say something."

"You're not going to believe this."

"What? Tell me."

She pulled a 100-pound note from her purse. "See this?" she asked.

"Yes."

"This little sheet of paper is worth $321.28."

"What!?"

"You heard me."

"But you've got 372 of those little sheets of paper."

"The whole way home on the bus, I tried to figure out how much that was, but I kept losing track. I was never good at math."

"I can't do it either without an adding machine, but even if you had just 300 of them and each one was only worth $300, that's $90,000!"

She looked like she might faint.

"Are you all right?"

"Pour me a Scotch. Make it a big one. Pour yourself one too." She seemed to have forgotten I was on crutches.

"Where's the money?" I asked her as I prepared our drinks.

"It's well hidden."

"It needs to be in a more secure place—like a bank."

"But it doesn't even rightfully belong to me."

"Let's think about that. Assume it did belong to O'Gowan. If the man had a will, it would have gone to his heirs. Maybe. He wasn't a U.S. citizen, so I don't know whose law applies. It would go according to Irish law, I guess."

We stared at each other for a long moment.

"It gets a bit complicated, doesn't it?" she said.

"We'll figure it out."

"Gracie?"

"Yes."

"Do you believe in the hereafter?"

What brought that up? "I never thought about it very much. Why?"

"I don't know. I was just thinking about my Muriel. Is she still six years old up in heaven, or is she the age she would have been if she was still here?"

I shook my head. I had enough trouble trying to figure out things that were in the here and now.

✐ TWENTY-TWO ✐

Minnie

I awoke from a fitful sleep, unsure if the reason was the $90,000 hidden somewhere in the house or something else or everything else. It was barely five o'clock, and knowing the chances of my getting back to sleep were slim, I got up and dressed.

I would have liked to have gone downstairs, put a pot of water on the stove, and had myself a cup or two of tea and a piece of toast, but the stairs terminated in Minnie's bedroom, and I didn't want to wake her. She usually got up around eight or so, but I couldn't sit up in my room with nothing to do for more than two hours.

I grabbed my keys and crutches and headed toward the back foyer and out the back door. The outside stairs were steep, but I took my time and made it to the bottom without incident. I retrieved the newspaper from the front walk, let myself in the back door, and settled down in the kitchen with the paper and a cup of Earl Grey.

By eight o'clock, I had finished the paper, drunk three cups of tea, and had nothing to do but wait for Minnie to wake up.

After another half-hour passed, she still wasn't up. She had never slept much past eight since I'd been there. I decided to give her another half hour.

At nine o'clock, I decided I was now worried. I tiptoed as best I could to her bedroom. It was a large room—her bed was fifteen feet or so from the door—and all I could see was a lump under the covers. Feeling somewhat like a cat burglar, I crept toward her. She was on her back with her arms crossed over her mid-section, sound asleep.

I left her alone and decided to wait another half-hour. If she wasn't up by then, I would wake her.

At nine-thirty, I purposely started making lots of noise in the kitchen in an effort to rouse her. I clanked some pots and pans around and waited for her to come through the kitchen door chastising me for making such a racket. I could just imagine her yelling, "What on earth are you trying to do? Wake the dead?" I laughed out loud and decided enough was enough—I was going to go in and wake her.

She seemed so content lying there—like she didn't have a care in the world—almost smiling. I hated to disturb her but figured that if I didn't, she'd probably yell at me for that too.

I touched her arm lightly. "Minnie," I whispered. "Minnie, get up. It's almost ten."

She didn't move.

I gently shook her upper arm.

She still didn't move.

Something was wrong.

I shook her arm vigorously.

There was no response.

"Minnie!" I shouted. "Wake up!"

I clomped as fast as I could to the phone and dialed 0.

"Please. I need an ambulance...right away!" I gave the operator the address. "Hurry, please!"

After propping the front door open with Minnie's umbrella stand, I scrambled back to the bedroom, leaned over her, and listened for breathing. There was none. I checked her wrist. She had no pulse. Her face was stone cold. I tried to lift one of her arms, but it didn't move, like something had it locked into place. I let my crutches fall to the floor and collapsed on the bed beside her.

"No, Minnie, no!"

I sat with her for I didn't know how long, crying, until three uniformed men walked into the room. I picked up my crutches and got out of their way.

They surrounded her bed, so I couldn't see what they were doing. In less than a minute, one of them turned toward me and shook his head.

"I'm sorry, Miss. She's been gone a while."

My good knee became weak, and I feared it wouldn't support me. The attendant who had just spoken came to my rescue and guided me to Minnie's overstuffed chair—her favorite chair. Elbows on my thighs, face in my hands, I sobbed uncontrollably.

"I'll call the medical examiner," one of them said.

A full minute passed before I could look up, and when I did I realized a policeman had joined us.

"Are you okay?" the policeman asked.

I didn't respond.

"Her death appears to be due to natural causes. Do you have any reason to believe otherwise?" he asked.

"No."

Wait. Maybe.

"I don't know for sure," I told him. "Can they check that out?"

"I can recommend an autopsy."

"Just in case, I think they should."

"The medical examiner is on his way," said one of the attendants.

They placed a sheet over her body. I closed my eyes, still in disbelief.

The policeman asked me dozens of questions about Minnie and then explained what steps would be taken next. I nodded but retained nothing of what he'd told me.

He handed me a piece of paper with the number for the medical examiner and information about their procedures.

"Can you stick around to transport the body to Central?" the policeman asked one of the paramedics.

"I'll have to check with dispatch," he responded and left.

Shortly thereafter, the medical examiner arrived and officially pronounced her dead. I left the room when they proceeded to put her in a body bag.

"Is there anyone we can call for you, Miss?" the policeman asked.

"No. She's all I had," I told him through choked-back tears.

Everyone eventually left. Sitting there at the kitchen table, alone with my mournful thoughts, I contemplated how unfair it had been of me to be so hard on her when she had bungled that phone call. It hadn't been her fault. If it hadn't been for me, that call would never have happened.

I had one more cry before crawling back in bed, clothes and all.

* * *

Wilhelmina Ryleigh Lawless died on May 25, 1965—the day Muhammad Ali knocked out Sonny Liston two minutes into the first round for the World Heavyweight Championship title. I knew she would have been pleased that I went to the trouble of digging up that fact. She had loved boxing.

The medical examiner said she died from a massive heart attack and had signs of prolonged heart disease. She had never mentioned anything like that to me. I wondered if she even knew that herself. That she was thinking about her daughter in heaven the night before made me wonder if she'd had a premonition that she would be joining her soon. Knowing they'd been reunited helped me get through the pain of losing her.

Less than an hour after they removed her body, Minnie's phone rang.

"Okay, lady, you win. If I tell you what you want to know, will you get off my back?"

It took me several seconds to catch on to what the caller was saying. Whoever it was obviously thought I was Minnie. I went along with it.

"Mm-hm," I said to him.

"It was Elmer who masterminded the plot to rough up the Irish guy and steal the sweepstakes money. Then the old bloke died before we could carry it out. I ended up with pocket change compared to what that guy won. And Elmer got zip." He paused. "You still there?"

"Mm-hm." It could only be Henry Sikes.

"Who is this?" he asked.

"Minnie."

"And loverboy across the hall from me, he had something to do with it. That's all I know. Now leave me the hell alone."

* * *

The events of the days following Minnie's death were a blur. She had died without a will—or so it seemed—and she had no living relatives. The police had told me that in cases like this, probate court assigned an administrator to handle distribution of the estate. When I contacted the clerk of the Circuit Court, I was told anyone could file a request to be an administrator, so I filed one.

In the meantime, I arranged for her burial. I found no paperwork among her things to indicate where her husband and daughter had been buried or if she had a plot of her own somewhere, so I bought one for her in Mount Olive Cemetery. Tymon offered to pay for half of it. He actually paid for all of it because I had to borrow my half from him.

I picked out a pale blue dress from her closet—she had liked blue. In the pocket I put the photograph of her with her family that was on her nightstand. I thought she might like it with her in her eternal resting place, since it appeared that was the last thing she saw before she went to bed each night.

Tymon and I were the only people present for the brief service in the cemetery's outdoor chapel. It didn't surprise us that no one else was present even though I had put a notice in both the *Tribune* and local *Northwest Side Press*—Minnie had managed to alienate her neighbors and just about everyone else with whom she had come into contact with her gruff demeanor. Unfortunately, they never knew what a kind heart was beneath it all.

The pastor offered a generic eulogy that he probably gave at all funerals for the dearly departed he didn't personally know and then ended it with a Helen Keller quote. "That we once enjoyed and deeply loved we can never lose, for all that we love deeply becomes part of us." That was exactly how I felt about Minnie. She had come into my life when I needed her most, and I knew she would stay in my heart for as long as I lived. Our short relationship had transcended friendship—she had treated me more like family.

Afterward, Tymon came back to the house, I thought mostly to comfort me but also figured maybe he needed comforting as well. We talked about Minnie, her quirky personality, and her changeable moods. He told me that they had been starting to become good friends.

Then, out of the blue, Tymon said something that came as a complete surprise to me.

"I was in love with her."

"Minnie?"

He rolled his eyes. "No, not Minnie. Anna."

Nothing at that point had led me to believe he had been that close to her.

"And did she have feelings for you as well?"

His sigh spoke volumes.

I wondered what he would've thought if he'd known I believed Anna was my real mother. Would he still be sharing this with me? I didn't think I wanted to hear any more, and maybe I should have stopped him—unless he was about to confess something. Like what he knew about Anna's baby.

"Did she know how you felt about her?"

"I never told her. I figured she just thought of me as a handyman, someone to call on when she needed something fixed. Besides, she had something going on with the upstairs boarder, so that was that."

"What was it about her that made you fall in love with her?"

"I don't know. Maybe it was just the way she made me feel when we were together—she accepted me for who I was, appreciated who I was. Maybe it was her laugh...or the way she smelled. Or the way she made my stomach flutter with nervous excitement whenever I was about to see her.

"Sometimes she would bring me a cup of coffee in the middle of what I was doing for her, or a glass of iced tea if I was working up a sweat. And sometimes she would join me, and we'd talk about...I don't know." Tymon's vacant expression reflected his melancholy. "We'd talk about different things—what was going on in the world, the weather. It didn't matter to me what the subject was. Maybe she was like that with everyone, but for me, it was special. She was special."

It didn't seem like the right time to bring up the baby, so I didn't.

TWENTY-THREE

Emotional Overload

S itting there in Minnie's living room the day following her memorial service, I pictured her occupying the other end of the sofa that first time she invited me in to see the place. I clearly remembered that day, examining every inch of the room for clues, even taking notes. I was looking at things in the room a lot differently now.

"We're alone now, you and me," I said to the room.

In going through her things, I found several boxes of rocks—small, smooth rocks of varying shapes and colors—hundreds of them. I pulled a large one from the bottom of one of the boxes and found these words written on it in black marker:

I love you Mommy

I rummaged around and found other rocks with writing on them, mostly words of endearment, obviously written by a young child. Maybe by Minnie's daughter?

As I sat on her bed sorting through the rocks, I noticed the position of the framed photo of Minnie's late husband and daughter on the end table next to me. I had thought before that it had been placed at an odd angle. But now I realized there was a good reason for its position—when Minnie sat in her favorite chair, it was directly facing her.

Bookshelves flanked the fireplace, and at the end of a short row of books was a photograph I hadn't noticed before. I took it down for a better look. Even though it was a black-and-white, I could tell the gardens on either side of the cobblestone path were brilliant with color. Then I glanced at the tapestry hanging over Minnie's favorite chair. It contained the same image. When I took the tapestry down from its hanger, I saw a note pinned to its back.

GRAMERCY GARDENS
MARCH 18, 1960

I was very familiar with Gramercy Gardens—it had been developed when I was a junior in high school, and my French class had volunteered a month of Saturdays to help with the plantings. In fact, we had been the ones who named it. The word *gramercy* has a French origin and means great thanks. The garden had been dedicated to Chicago servicemen and women who'd lost their lives in World War II.

I examined the tapestry more closely and wondered if Minnie had made it herself. March 18, 1960. A chill darted down my back. That was the day my parents had died.

* * *

Minnie had been gone four days when Brenda, my contact at the Clerk of the Circuit Court's office, called me to tell me one other person had filed a request to become administrator of Minnie's estate and that she would get back to me when a decision was made as to who would be appointed. I asked her the other person's name.

"You know I can't tell you that, Grace."

I explained the situation.

"I really can't tell you that," she whispered, "but if you were to come by here and happen to see any documents on my desk that revealed his name when I had my back turned, I would never even know."

"I'll be there in an hour," I told her.

* * *

I wasn't sure why I wasted my time driving to City Hall. I knew before I got there whose name I would see on Brenda's desk.

When I arrived, there was a short line. Two people let me go in front of them—at least the crutches had one benefit. When I reached the front of the line, Brenda turned her back to me. I gazed over the counter at the top of her desk where Berghorn's name had been boldly written on a piece of paper. Brenda turned toward me and mouthed that she would meet me outside in twenty minutes when she was on her break.

It took me fifteen minutes to reach our meeting place. I stood outside and watched the steady flow of people rush past—employees on their way to work, salesmen on their way to what they hoped was a lucrative sales call, lawyers on their way to court. When Brenda arrived a few minutes later, I first explained the crutches and then my concern about Berghorn being administrator.

"I have to be really careful what I say and to whom, Grace. You know how political everything is here."

"I know."

Brenda didn't say anything for a long few seconds.

"I know the judge who's going to handle this. Do you want me to see what I can do?"

"What do you mean?"

"Maybe he can be influenced."

I looked around to make sure no one was within earshot. "As in offering him a bribe?"

"Are you aware of the three I's that everyone involved in our judicial system is expected to withhold?"

"No."

"Impartiality, independence, and integrity. Well, let's just say some of our magistrates may come up a little short in one or more of the three I's."

"No kidding."

"Don't look so surprised. This is Chicago—not all areas of the judicial system are that judicious."

"I could never be a part of that."

"I was just trying to help."

"And besides, I have no money."

"Believe me, this would be such small potatoes compared to what goes on here, no money would be involved. It would just be a little favor."

"Okay, I'm in."

"I gotta go. I'll call you when I know something."

"I owe you, Brenda."

"Lunch sometime?"

"You got it."

* * *

Minnie had been gone less than a week, and I hated the emotional roller coaster I was on. What if I had wakened her earlier that day? Maybe she'd still be alive.

The burden of handling Minnie's affairs compounded the situation. She hadn't left behind a huge estate by any means, yet there seemed to be an endless stream of things I had to deal with in one way or another.

I was grateful that Minnie had kept all her important papers in one place—her underwear drawer. It pained me to be in her dresser drawers, invading her privacy like that. Her smell was in those drawers. By combing through her things, I had learned that the house was mortgage-free, and she had been receiving pension and social security benefits ever since her husband and daughter had died. I had also found the key to a safe deposit box at North Community Bank.

I missed her terribly and didn't realize until I had explored her private possessions how much I had needed a Minnie in my life.

* * *

Brenda came through for me. The week following Minnie's death, she called to tell me I would be getting a letter any day advising me of my appointment to be administrator of Minnie's estate. That was the good news. The bad news was that the court had received a check in the amount of $1,000 to serve as earnest money for purchasing Minnie's house.

"Who submitted it?"

"Waddershins Trust. Does that mean anything to you?"

"It sure does. It's Elmer Berghorn. So how does this work, Brenda? Can he buy it without my approval?"

"In the letter you receive, there will be a date and time for a meeting with someone from probate court who will go over your role as administrator. Nothing can be done before that."

So now Elmer was after Minnie's house. What was with that man?

* * *

The probate court was in a section of City Hall I'd never been in before. I hobbled up and down three staircases before I found Mr. Averill's office. He waved me in.

Norman Averill was middle-aged, wore his hair a little long, and sported a Madras tie. Not exactly the image I would have expected for someone in his position. The top of his desk had nothing on it except for one file folder, a pad of paper, a pen, and a framed photo of Andy Warhol. I hoped for the best.

He began by telling me about my duties and responsibilities, which for the most part included contacting any professionals with whom Minnie had had a relationship, paying outstanding bills, identifying and distributing all her assets, and filing tax returns.

"Are you sure she has no heirs?" he asked me.

"She told me that when she lost her daughter and husband, she was left with no family."

"Are you positive she had no will?"

"She kept all her important papers in one place. I found no will."

"Did she have a lawyer she used for anything?"

"She never mentioned one."

"I ask because maybe she had a will but just didn't keep a copy of it, but her lawyer would have a copy. Since one of your obligations is to contact professional relationships, be on the lookout for a lawyer. The county will get her estate if she has no heirs and no will, and I shouldn't be saying this as a government employee, but I'd hate to see that happen."

"I appreciate that."

He ruffled through the papers in Minnie's file and then peered at me over the top of his glasses.

"There's someone interested in buying her house."

"Oh?"

"It's a Canadian trust named Waddershins. Does that name mean anything to you?"

I must have given him a blank stare a little too long.

"Miss Lindroth?"

"I'm sorry. Yes, it does. I used to work with the man who owns that trust, and he is also the man who bought my parents' home immediately after they died."

"There are people who do that. They watch the obituaries and scoop up real estate at cheap prices. It may not be ethical, but it's perfectly legal."

"As administrator, would I have to sell it to him?"

"You are required by law to advise us of any offers, and if your friend died without a will and without heirs, the county will make that decision."

"What if there are two people who want to buy it?"

"It would likely go to the highest bidder."

"I see."

He gave me the paperwork I would need to prove I had power of attorney over Minnie's estate, and we agreed to meet in two weeks after I had the opportunity to talk to Minnie's professional contacts.

I thought about Berghorn on the walk to my car. Regardless of his motives, I'd be damned if I stood by and let him buy the house.

A moral dilemma floated in and out of my brain on the drive home—what to do with the Irish money. Whose was it anyway? Minnie clearly had said she didn't consider it hers, so in my mind, the state shouldn't get it because it wasn't part of her estate.

I'd be lying if I said the thought had never entered my mind that no one would be the wiser if I just kept the money for myself. I could live comfortably on it for a long time. But a strong sense of integrity that had been instilled in me by my mother kept me from thinking about that seriously. And besides that, I knew the guilt would do me in.

Henry Sikes had told me on the phone when he thought I was Minnie that O'Gowan had won big money in a sweepstakes. That told me it belonged to his heirs—like the woman who had written to Minnie claiming to be his sister. Maybe that's why she had been trying to find him—the money.

How hard should I look for his heirs? All I had was a fifteen-year-old address for his supposed sister. How much time and money was I expected to spend before feeling I had done all I could? How far did I have to go—travel to Ireland and knock on every door?

One thing was for sure, and that was I had to find where Minnie had hidden the bills and get them into a safe-deposit box, like she should have done right from the start.

When I arrived home, Tymon was waiting for me on the patio.

"I was thinking about eating out tonight. Want to join me?"

I hadn't planned anything for dinner. "Sure."

He drove us to Milano's, a little neighborhood Italian restaurant not far from Minnie's. As soon as we sat down and ordered a glass of wine, he rested his elbows on the table and said, "I hope you aren't going to be mad at me for this, or worse yet, mad at Minnie."

I studied his eyes—it was something serious.

"Minnie told me Anna wasn't really your aunt."

I wondered just how long he had known this, how long he had been playing along. Minnie had first met him four months ago in February. He knew the whole time and didn't say anything? My opinion of him dropped a few notches. Of course, Minnie had played a role in this too.

"When did she tell you this?"

"When you were in the hospital."

The end of April. So he'd known for a little over a month.

"Why didn't you tell me this before?"

"She asked me not to, and I respected that."

"What else did she tell you?"

"I know that you're trying to get to the bottom of who your real mother is, and that you think it was Anna. When Minnie died, I knew I had to tell you what she had told me. I waited a week thinking that was a respectable length of time."

"So there *was* a baby."

"Yes. There was a baby."

"A girl."

"Yes, but no one knew about her."

"Henry did."

"That doesn't surprise me. Henry was a busy body. No one else knew."

"But you did."

"She couldn't hide it from me. I was in her home often."

"She was hiding it?"

He nodded.

"Why?"

"I don't know for sure. She asked me not to tell anyone about her, and I didn't...
not until the police after she died."

"And what was their reaction?"

"They said they had talked to everyone—the boarders, neighbors, even where
she banked—and no one mentioned a baby. I tried to tell them Anna was a private
person. I insisted she had a daughter who was now missing."

"And..."

"They dismissed me. Probably thought I was some kind of crazy person."

"I don't understand why she would keep that such a secret or *how* she even was
able to keep it a secret. The baby must have cried."

"I'm afraid I may have helped her hide the child when she asked me insulate the
walls and ceiling of the baby's room."

"Insulate them?"

"So her cries couldn't be heard."

"That's crazy."

"I didn't ask questions."

"She never went out with her? Didn't sit out on the patio? Go for walks?"

Tymon shook his head. "Not that I ever saw."

"I don't get it."

"I think she was either too ashamed to have had a child out of wedlock, or the
father had something to do with it."

"Something to do with what?"

"Hiding the child."

"Why do you say that?"

He hesitated. "Because I think the upstairs boarder Al may have been the
child's father, and Al was married."

I gave that a moment to sink in. I was then more uncertain about Tymon than
ever and didn't know whether to believe anything he was telling me.

"You're upset," he said.

"No, I'm not upset."

"Yes you are. You're wondering whether or not you can trust me." He paused a
moment while he stared into my eyes. "And I'm wondering if you're the daughter
of the only woman I ever loved."

Now I was upset.

"And what exactly would that mean?" I asked.

"Nothing really. It just means—"

"You wouldn't have said that if it didn't mean something."

Tymon squirmed in his chair. "Just that I can finally put a finger on what it was about you that has intrigued me so."

Good God—what was he saying?

"No, *intrigued* isn't the right word," he stammered. "Attracted. No, that's not it either. I'm not very good with words, but do you know what I mean?"

"No. I don't know what you mean."

He didn't say anything—instead he stared down at the table, perhaps searching for the right word, perhaps trying to think of a way out of this.

"From the very first time I met you, I felt some kind of connection. *That's* the word I was looking for. Does that make any sense?"

"Not really."

"I have a picture of her in my wallet. Would you like to see it?"

I nodded.

He fished out his wallet and handed a faded photo to me.

"I told her I was trying out my new camera on different things and asked her if I could shoot her. Pretty sneaky, wasn't it?"

I couldn't take my eyes off the photo. She had some kind of turban on her head—the kind you might wrap around your hair after a shampoo—and was looking directly at the camera. That was the first time I had seen the whole of her face, unencumbered by her hair, a hat, or anything else. Except for being thinner than my adopted mother, she looked so much like her, it was frightening.

"Gracie?"

I carried with me a few of the photos from my parents' attic. I fetched the one of a man holding a baby and handed it to Tymon.

"Could this be Al?"

He studied the photo for several seconds. "Could be. That was a long time ago, and you can't see much of his face here."

I looked again at the photo of Anna he had handed to me. She and my mother had such similar physical characteristics, they could have been sisters. I closed my eyes and tried to retreat to a place in my brain where things made sense. *Could* they have been sisters? If so, would that explain some things?

"Grace?"

"I'm sorry. I can't get over how much she looks like my mother, the mother who raised me. It's uncanny."

He didn't respond.

I handed the photo back to him.

"Did she ever mention having a sister?" I asked.

"Not to me."

We finished our dinners in silence.

I tried to carry on a conversation with Tymon on the drive home, but it was evident he didn't want to talk. The investigator in me tried to come up with a possible reason for that, and then it occurred to me that maybe Tymon hadn't told me everything about his and Anna's relationship. It occurred to me that maybe it had gotten romantic at one point. It occurred to me that he could be lying about the upstairs boarder in order to cover up the truth. It occurred to me that *he* could be my real father.

◦ TWENTY-FOUR ◦

The Will

That night after dinner with Tymon, even though I was overly tired, my eyes wouldn't close. No matter how hard I tried to turn my brain off from thinking about Tymon, Minnie, Fern, and Elmer—I couldn't. I started wishing I could go back to thinking Rosa and Adam Lindroth had been my real parents, like they had always wanted me to think, and forget about everything else.

Had Tymon and Anna had a romantic relationship? A one-night stand? What did I really know about this man? And what was his motive for sticking around Minnie and now me? Was he merely trying to be a good friend, or was he out to get something or to be something—like a father. I didn't know which of these two scenarios scared me the most.

I must have finally fallen asleep because I woke up early to the clock radio playing Bob Dylan's newest song.

> *How does it feel*
> *To be on your own*
> *With no direction home*
> *Like a rolling stone*

How did it feel? Lousy.

My mission for the day was to find the key Minnie had retrieved from the floorboards. It was painful to go into her bedroom. The only thing I had done in that room since she'd died was change the bed linens. I sat in her favorite chair and thought back to the time she had found the key. I'd watched her fish it out, but I couldn't remember what she had done with the key afterward.

I knew she hadn't given it to me. I tried to remember if she had been wearing an apron that day. She was always sticking things in her apron pocket and then forgetting about them. I went to the hook by the back door where she had hung her aprons. Their pockets revealed a few things but not the key.

Back in her bedroom, I checked the pockets of her dresses and sweaters that hung in her closet and eventually found the key in the pocket of her coral sweater, the one I had told her looked so nice on her.

I wiped the tears away and put the key in the change compartment of my wallet where I knew I could find it again.

I decided to spend the better part of the day on the phone contacting everyone in Minnie's address book in order to identify her professional relationships for legal purposes and personal ones to inform them of her passing. There were hundreds of entries. I had started to contact them prior to her funeral, but when all I found were outdated and out-of-service numbers, I gave up on it until I had more time.

After two hours had passed, I was only up to the letter G. That woman must have put every number she had ever dialed in her address book, no matter how trivial. Many of the people who answered the phone didn't even know who Minnie Lawless was. One entry turned out to be the school crossing guard who said he knew exactly who she was—she had often yelled at him for a variety of reasons, none of them justified.

I had stopped for lunch when Naomi called.

"I've been trying to reach you for hours, and all I've gotten is a busy signal."

I told her what I had been doing all morning.

"I have to talk fast. He's in the bathroom. He's back in touch with his cousin Henry, and from what I overheard, it's been a long time since they've talked. Mr. Berghorn wasn't happy with whatever it was that Henry was saying, and I heard your name mentioned..." The tone of her voice suddenly became businesslike. "And what time do you close? Yes, I see. Thank you. Bye."

I supposed Elmer must have finished his potty break.

I waited for Naomi to call back, and when she didn't I continued with my calls.

Later that afternoon, I finished calling every number in Minnie's book. Sadly, my efforts revealed no current personal relationships. Five listings—two banks, an attorney, and two doctors—appeared to have been current professional relationships for her and required an in-person visit so I could prove I had the right to gain access to her personal information.

The house was exceptionally quiet. I would have given anything to hear the familiar sounds of Minnie rattling around the kitchen, fussing with her houseplants, or even making a sarcastic remark about something I had done or said or hadn't done or hadn't said.

I made a sandwich for dinner and was so exhausted that I fell asleep in the middle of *The Virginian* and didn't wake up until the evening news. I figured I'd sleep well that night.

* * *

A few days later, I drove downtown for an appointment with presumably the most important person in Minnie's address book, Raymond Webb, her attorney. He had said very little to me on the phone, which of course I understood. I was confident he'd tell me anything I wanted to know about his dealings with her once I showed him my power-of-attorney document. His office was near the library, and my plan was to go there afterward to see what I could find out about the Irish Sweepstakes, the only sweepstakes I was aware of in Ireland and thus the only lead I had in determining the rightful owner of the stash of Irish bills, which Minnie had hidden so well.

I entered Webb's office on the fourteenth floor of one of Chicago's historical buildings in the Loop. Mr. Webb was a nice-looking man—dark, wavy hair with a little grey at the temples, nice blue eyes, and a friendly smile. His office seemed to reflect his importance, with its rows of matching reference books in the bookcases, collage of certificates and diplomas hanging on the wall, and substantial furniture upholstered in dark burgundy leather. After we introduced ourselves and I satisfied his curiosity about why I was on crutches, he requested my ID and then asked me a series of questions, including how Minnie and I had met and where I had grown up, gone to school, and worked.

When he seemed satisfied with my answers, he explained that he had to verify who I was before discussing anything to do with Minnie, power of attorney or not. I understood that.

"Are you aware that I met with Minnie the week before she died?"

"No."

"She wanted me to draft a will for her."

That caught me off guard. Had she known she was going to die? Maybe that was why Muriel had been on her mind.

"We have a problem in that while I have a draft of the will, it is unsigned, which for all intents and purposes, is the same as having no will at all. Now, I can petition the court to have it become a valid will, but of course I don't know what the outcome will be."

"Did she see the draft at least?"

"No, but it was based on information she had given to me, and that will be my argument."

"It would make things a lot easier, wouldn't it?"

"Yes, it would." He paused. "Grace, she wanted to leave you her house."

I realized I was staring at him, which was rude, but I was so shocked I couldn't get any words out. Why would he even tell me this if there was a chance the will wasn't valid?

"You had no idea."

"None."

"So I want to do whatever I can to validate the will for you. And at no charge."

I didn't trust him.

"I appreciate that."

"She told me about you."

"She did?"

"Yes, she did." He paused again. "I suspect there's a lot more to your story than what she shared with me, but I can tell you one thing...she cared about you and probably would have done anything to help you in your quest to find the truth. And between you and me, I think helping you gave her a purpose in her life she hadn't had in a very long time."

I had to choke back a rush of raw emotion.

"She made such a difference in my life."

"I think you made a difference in hers."

"Did she happen to mention to you that I'm pretty sure I was born in that house?"

"Yes, she did."

The mixed signals he was sending were unsettling. One minute he was all lawyer-like and the next he talked about Minnie like they were friends. I was no lawyer, but I thought he had shared way too much information with me, especially since there was no guarantee he could get the will validated. Why hadn't Minnie ever mentioned him? Apparently, she had told him plenty about me. And why was he so willing to go to bat for me?

"So where do we go from here?"

"I'll petition the court to admit the draft as her final will...and we'll wait."

"How long do you think it will take?"

"Hard to tell. On the low end, maybe ten days. Or it could take much longer. I'll know more when it gets filed."

Before leaving his office, I gave him the name of the probate court representative I had met. He told me he was available to help guide me through the probate process if I wanted to retain him.

It was a short walk to the library, and all I could think about was Minnie wanting me to have her house—the kindest, most generous thing anyone had ever done for me in my entire life—and she wasn't there to thank. I was curious as to whether she had intended to tell me this after her will had been finalized.

I headed straight for the international section where I asked a reference librarian if there was any way to find out the names of the Irish Sweepstakes winners up to and including 1942.

"I can't think of a single resource we have with that kind of information, but wait here a minute." She disappeared and then returned with a piece of paper. "Here is contact information for three large Irish organizations, two local and one international out of New York. I think they would be more likely able to help you." She wrote down her name on the same piece of paper. "But I like a challenge, so I'm going to see if I can't find something as well. Just call me if you find what you're looking for, so I don't spin my wheels for nothing."

My last stop for the day was North Community Bank where Minnie had kept a safe deposit box. After showing my power-of-attorney document and talking to a bank clerk about their procedures, I was ushered into a small room and told to wait. A few minutes later, he returned with a metal box. He unlocked one side of the double lock, and I unlocked the other. As I did so, I found myself hoping there wouldn't be much inside, as I felt like I couldn't take on any more revelations that day.

I quickly went through the contents—her birth certificate, her late husband's and daughter's birth and death certificates, her marriage license, her daughter's hospital bracelet, and several silver dollars. Minnie had been born in 1914, married in 1934, and widowed in 1942. She'd been only twenty-eight years old when they died, just five years older than I was.

TWENTY-FIVE

"You're Not Alone"

I was a block from home and couldn't wait to collapse on the living room sofa. Meeting with Minnie's attorney had been emotionally draining—I was sad, tired, and confused. I hoped to feel better after a nap.

When I inserted my key into the lock at the back door, I was surprised to find it was not engaged. I was certain I had secured the door when I'd left that morning, as I always did.

I slowly opened the door and thought if this was a movie, there would be someone in the audience yelling, *"Don't go in there!"* But it wasn't a movie.

I took two steps into the kitchen and stopped. Every drawer and cabinet had been opened and emptied—food, utensils, plates, bowls, pots, pans, and everything else that had once been in the cupboards were scattered all over the floor and on the countertop. I didn't move. I couldn't move.

I listened for noises, but the house was deadly silent.

Fear overrode all my other emotions. I allowed myself several seconds to calm down before I called the police and then waited for them out front.

It was obvious whoever had done this was looking for something specific, and what was particularly disturbing was that they had conveniently done this when I wasn't home. I hadn't told anyone where I was going or how long I would be gone. Was someone watching me?

Two policemen arrived, checked the house for possible intruders, and made sure all the doors and windows were secured before we walked through the house together. They asked me what, if anything, was missing, and I told them it was hard to tell right off but it didn't appear as if anything was missing. I didn't tell them that it was possible the intruder had found the stash of money Minnie had hidden. I was actually hoping the person *had* found it—that meant he wouldn't be back, and I wouldn't have to spend any more time looking for O'Gowan's heirs.

The police asked me the requisite burglary questions and determined that whoever had broken in had gained access through the back door by pushing it in. They dusted the doorknob and around the jamb for fingerprints but found none. They suggested I have a deadbolt lock installed. I asked them if they were going to dust anything else for prints, and they explained that since it was simply a breaking-and-entering case with no real property damage but for the door, the door was all they'd dust. That didn't seem right to me, but I supposed they had better things to do with their time.

They finished writing notes for their report and told me to let them know within twenty-four hours if I determined anything was missing.

I called Tymon and, without going into any detail, asked him if he could repair the door jamb and install a new lock on the back door. He said he'd come right over.

I tried to ignore the ache in my stomach, the roaring headache, and my physical and mental exhaustion while I cleaned up the mess. I started by locating a large trash bag for the broken items. Picking things up off the floor while I was on crutches wasn't easy. Throwing away items of Minnie's that someone had maliciously destroyed was painful.

Tymon arrived an hour later with his tool box, several strips of lumber, a new deadbolt lock, and a heavy-gauge security door chain.

"What on earth happened?"

"Someone broke in while I was out running errands." I filled him in on what I knew and how the police had handled it, leaving out a possible tie-in to the money.

I continued cleaning up the kitchen while Tymon worked his magic on the back door.

"I never did like the way this door was constructed. By the time I'm through with it though, it will be completely burglar-proof. What do you think they were looking for?"

"I'm not sure. It doesn't look like anything is missing, at least as far as I can tell."

"You're not safe here. You know that."

"Can you go with me upstairs? I haven't been up there yet."

"Did you hear me, Gracie?"

"The police went up there, but—"

"You're not telling me everything."

"I've told you everything I know. I don't think it's a big deal. Neither did the police. Will you go upstairs with me?"

He gave me one of those *I'm not through with this subject* looks and followed me to the staircase. I gestured for him to go ahead of me since it took me a while to maneuver myself up the stairs.

In my room, things that had still been in boxes from when I'd moved in were strewn about as was everything from the dresser drawers and closet. Even the mattress from the rollaway bed I slept on had been thrown to the side.

A cigarette butt next to a crumpled-up photograph on the floor caught my eye. I carefully picked the photo up by one corner. It was the one of Anna holding me in the rocking chair. The cigarette butt could have belonged to whoever did this or even one of the policemen, but my suspicion immediately went to Elmer.

"Tymon, can you do me a favor?"

"Anything."

"Try to find a box of Baggies in the kitchen and bring it up here."

Photographs are wonderful for capturing fingerprints. I wasn't sure what would be gained by having the cigarette butt, but it could do no harm collecting that as well.

I walked over to the edge of the room and looked up at the ceiling trapdoor that led to the attic. It was in perfect position. I didn't think whoever had rampaged through the house would have put it back so perfectly if they had gone up there, nor would they have put the ladders back in the basement. I suspected the trunk was safe.

Tymon returned, and as I turned toward him, the tip of my right crutch slid between two of the floorboards. In order to catch my balance, I was forced to throw all my weight onto my left leg, the one with the bad knee. I screeched in pain loud enough to be heard in the next county.

"Gracie! Are you all right?"

"I'm okay. I just landed on my bad knee."

Tymon took my arm and led me over to the bed, where I completely disregarded the missing mattress and sat down too fast and too hard, hurting my tailbone.

"Damn it all!" I snapped.

"What's the matter?"

Suddenly, I felt like I was in a pressure cooker and someone had just opened the relief valve—there was no controlling the flood of tears that came streaming down my face.

"What's the matter? I'll tell you what's the matter!" And then, through sobs and tears, I blurted out the litany of issues both large and small that had been building up inside of me for the past few months, ending with the fact that Minnie's passing had left me sad and alone. I was sure Tymon didn't understand half of what I was saying through all my blubbering. When I was finished, I was so embarrassed about my loss of control, I didn't know how I would ever be able to look that man in the eye again.

He sat down on the bed, put his arm around me, and said in a soft, calm voice, "You're wrong about one thing, Gracie. You're not alone."

TWENTY-SIX

A Loud Knock

Knowing someone had broken into my home—well, the home in which I was staying—and touched all my things was unsettling. I wanted to wash everything that could be washed and throw away everything else. My body was so tense most of the time that I had to keep reminding myself to relax. If Elmer and Henry were responsible for the break-in—and I was sure at least one of them was—they would pay for it one way or another.

I didn't know what I would have done without Tymon. He insisted on sleeping on the sofa that night just in case the intruder returned, and he said he planned to stay around for a little while the next day. Still, I needed to be careful around him. Maybe that wasn't fair of me, but at that point, I didn't trust anyone. And if Tymon had in fact had a romantic relationship with Anna and hadn't told me about it, I couldn't trust him either. For all I knew, he could have had some covert reason for hanging around me or been in cahoots with Elmer or Henry.

In the morning, I hobbled down the stairs to the kitchen, where I found Tymon drinking coffee.

"I hope you don't mind. I helped myself."

"Of course not."

"Can I pour you a cup?"

"No, thanks."

"Feeling better today?"

"Much."

"I want to fix that floorboard so you don't get your crutch caught in it again," he said as he got up from the table.

"Okay."

I started the tea kettle. Five minutes later, Tymon was back in the kitchen with a shoebox.

"What's that?" I asked.

He sat down and slowly shoved the box across the table toward me without saying anything.

I laughed. "Nothing is going to jump out at me, is it?"

He maintained a sober face.

I lifted off the lid. The box was filled with 100-pound Irish notes.

I glanced up at Tymon, and we stared at each other for several seconds.

"Where did you find this?"

"Under the loose floorboard."

"So that's where she hid it."

"Who?"

"Minnie."

He didn't say anything.

"It's a long story."

He stood up. "So you know about this?"

I nodded.

"Well, I don't need to know. I'm going to fix that floorboard now."

I did a quick count of the bills to make sure all were there. Four hundred. Four hundred? I had counted three hundred and seventy-two of them with Minnie. Where had the other twenty-eight come from? I recounted. Exactly four hundred. I counted a third time. Same thing. Could I have miscounted the first time? The damn bills couldn't have multiplied on their own.

Tymon was back.

"All done, Miss Gracie." He sat down with me. "So do you suppose that's what they were after?"

"I don't know. Maybe."

"You're not safe here. They could come back."

"They won't come back. Whatever it was they were looking for—if they were looking for something in particular—they didn't find it."

"You never know. If I were you, I'd put that money in a safe place and stay in a hotel or something until this cools down."

"I can't afford to do that."

He glanced down at the box and then at me. "Are you kidding me?"

"It's not my money, Tymon."

"I'll lend you the money to stay in a hotel. What are you going to do if they come back here and you're here? Hobble away from them? You're defenseless on those crutches." There was certainty in his tone.

"I'll get an attack dog."

"You're taking this much too lightly. Promise me you'll think about what I've said."

"I promise."

"I can stay if you want."

"I don't think that's necessary."

"Lock the door behind me."

"Don't worry about me. I'll be fine."

I looked at all the money, afraid to admit he might be right.

* * *

I started out sleeping in my bed upstairs, but every creak, gust of wind, and car that went by made me jump. After two hours of lying there with my eyes wide open, I got dressed and went downstairs to sleep, but not before lining up pots and pans, tin cans, and anything else I could find in front of the doors so that if anyone did try to get in I would hear it.

The next morning, every muscle in my body ached from sleeping crumpled up in the living room armchair—the most centrally located piece of furniture. Minnie didn't have as much as an aspirin in the medicine cabinet, so I added that to the list of things I needed at the store.

The money made me nervous, but I had to keep it in the house until Monday when the banks were open. It was currently inside a flour sack in the freezer, the only place that hadn't been disturbed during the break-in.

The phone rang, and I didn't have to answer it to know it was Tymon. He'd called to check on me no less than four times since he'd left. I supposed he was genuinely concerned, but even though I thought I could probably trust him, his attentiveness was making me uncomfortable. He said he was going to come over later in the day to drill holes in all the window frames and then secure them somehow with large nails stuck in the holes. As long as he didn't nail all the windows shut, I didn't care what he did.

Savoring the last of Minnie's chamomile tea, I made a list of what I needed to do on Monday. I was running low on cash and hoped I had enough to buy at least some staples. Naomi had been forwarding my mail to me, and the checks I'd received from clients had carried me so far. I checked my wallet. Twenty-eight dollars. With any luck, when I was done I'd have enough left over to put a few dollars' worth of gas in my car. I checked the change compartment. Another dollar seventy-five and the key from my mother's jewelry box that I hoped opened the trunk in the attic.

I stared at the key. That wasn't her key. That was the key to Minnie's safe deposit box. Where had I put my mother's key? Or *was* that my mother's key? Confused, I went to Minnie's dresser drawer where I thought I had left her safe deposit box key, and it was there, right where I had left it. I placed both keys side by side on the dresser. Except for the grooves, they were identical.

While examining them, I managed to turn them over enough times that now I didn't know which was which, but I guessed that didn't matter. What mattered was that the key I had found in my mother's jewelry box now looked like it could be for a safe deposit box and not the trunk.

I went upstairs and dumped the contents of the jewelry box onto the bed. Her watch caught my attention. I had never really looked at it very closely before. It was a Rolex. Expensive. I don't remember ever having seen my mother wear it. I put it back and continued with my original mission.

Initially, I had found the key hiding under the loose felt lining at the bottom of the box. I pulled back the entire lining to reveal a tiny piece of paper with the number 708 written on it. Minnie's box number at North Community Bank was 351. Did all banks use the same kind of key and numbering system?

I racked my brain for the name of the bank that had taken over my parents' house after they died, thinking maybe they had a box at that bank. Now that I thought about it, it would have made sense since I hadn't found any of the documents among their things one might have expected to find after they died, like my parents' birth certificates or their marriage license.

I supposed that even if I had known at which bank the box was located, I wouldn't have been able to access it. For Minnie's box, I had power of attorney, but I didn't have anything like that for my parents. I would call Minnie's attorney on Monday and ask him what I could do about it. If they'd had a safe deposit box, my birth certificate could be in there. I didn't know why I—ace PI that I was—hadn't thought of that before.

* * *

That night, I slept well, probably because Tymon had burglar-proofed all the windows. But for him to be completely satisfied, I feared I may have still needed a ten-foot barbed-wire fence surrounding the house.

The next morning, I thought about leaving the house, and the idea made me nervous. Or maybe it was the idea of coming back to it that scared me. Or both. But I had errands to do, and I had to face that fear sometime—I refused to be a prisoner in my own home.

When it was time to go, I triple-checked all the windows and double-locked the back door. Somehow I managed to get to the car on my crutches while carrying a shoulder bag across my chest, keys in one hand and in the other a metal nail file that Tymon made me promise I would carry with me whenever I left the house. "The neck and eyes are the best places to jab someone if you really want to hurt them," he had explained. "That's if you can't knee him in the groin." I was also wearing a whistle around my neck in case I was attacked and needed to get someone's attention. It was almost not worth going out.

As I drove to the bank, for some reason I was reminded of a conversation Minnie and I had had over a few Scotches one evening when she asked me where I saw myself in five years. I told her I didn't know, wouldn't know until I knew who I was. She'd quoted one of her late husband's favorite authors, Napoleon Hill. "A goal is a dream with a deadline," she had said. I liked that quote. Then she advised me to not be like her and wallow my way through life without dreams and goals. I vowed never to lose sight of that wisdom.

I neared Six Corners and parked the car in an open lot—another one of Tymon's suggestions—and armed with the power-of-attorney letter, I entered Minnie's bank and asked for her safe deposit box. The clerk brought it into a small room assigned to me and unlocked his half while I unlocked the other. As soon as he left, I opened the box and realized there wasn't enough room in it for the thick stash of money I had. I rang for the clerk and asked if I could rent a larger box. When he came back with the new box and paperwork to sign, I noticed the new key was a different style than the one for the smaller box. I asked him about it.

"We probably have six different style keys here," he said. "Most banks do."

I showed him my other key. "So this other key I have could belong to any number of banks?"

He examined the edge of the key.

"They all have serial numbers. Do you want me see if this is one of ours?"

"Sure." I had never noticed a number stamped on the edge—more of my first-rate investigative skills hard at work.

He came back in a few minutes with a thick ledger.

"It was ours."

"Was?"

"It went to the city's unclaimed property office on...let's see...June 1."

"Of this year?"

"Yes."

"You're kidding."

"No ma'am. When someone fails to pay the rent, we try our best to locate the owner or, in cases where the owner died, their heirs. And if we can't locate anyone, we're obligated to keep it five years, and that was up on June 1."

Ten days ago. What timing!

After the clerk left, I put everything in the new box and—taking a chance that he was available to see me for a few minutes—drove to Minnie's attorney's office. There I learned that Mr. Webb was in court, so I left him a message about my parents' safe deposit box.

My next stop was the District 16 police station, where I picked up a copy of the police report on the break-in and dropped off the crumpled photo and cigarette butt I had found after the ransacking. I asked the policeman behind the counter if I gave him the name of who I thought did it, could they see if their fingerprints matched those on the photo. I already knew the answer to this question but wanted to hear it from him.

"Not without probable cause, lady. What would you like us to do with the cigarette butt?"

"I thought it could be evidence. If you have a suspect and he smokes that brand..."

"Whatever you say."

My next stop was the Ace Hardware store, where I picked up ten rubber doorstops. After buying a few essentials at the grocery store, I had enough cash left for three gallons of gas.

The first thing I did when I got home was place three rubber doorstops under each of the outside doors. I wasn't sure how secure that was, but it beat the pile of pots and pans I had been using. Then I made some lunch and thought about where I should be focusing my time—seeking revenge on Elmer, working on Attic Finds, or getting a life. It was a tough call. I was grateful when the phone interrupted my thoughts.

It was Fern. She told me Essie hadn't come to church on Sunday, and when she'd asked one of the elders about her, he'd said she moved away and didn't leave a forwarding address. Fern had then called the Cicero Baird & Warner office where Essie worked and was told she no longer worked there.

I would have kicked myself if I could have.

"Moved away? Just like that?" I asked her.

"That's what I was told. I asked around, and no one seems to know anything."

"Great. So where does that leave us?"

"You're the private eye. Can't you do something to find her?"

"I could. But then what? It appears she doesn't want to tell either one of us what she knows."

"I've been thinking about that. What could she possibly know that is so remarkable that it would change someone else's life and make her so afraid to say anything that she ups and moves away? I don't know anything that would fit that scenario."

"It must have something to do with Anna's death, don't you think?"

"So let's say she knows who killed her. And let's say when Essie said it would change a girl's life, she was referring to you. Would that change your life?" she asked me.

"Depends on who it was, I suppose. I don't know. Maybe if we put our heads together we could come up with something. Want to come over?"

We planned to get together Friday after work. She'd bring the pizza—I'd supply the beer.

While I waited for Tymon to arrive to fix a leaky pipe under the kitchen sink, I called each of the Irish organizations the reference librarian had provided to ask them for a list of Irish Sweepstakes winners. None was able to do it straight away, but all three agreed to see what they could find.

A loud knock on the back door startled me. I figured it was Tymon.

I opened the door with a big smile only to find myself standing face-to-face with Elmer Berghorn.

∽ TWENTY-SEVEN ∾
Desperation

Without saying a word, Elmer shoved me out of the way and closed the door. I stumbled several steps back and teetered for a few long seconds before dropping one of my crutches, which he kicked to the side. To regain my balance, I grabbed onto the corner of the large island in the middle of the room.

"What do you think you're doing?" I asked.

Five feet in front of me, Elmer stood with his fists clenched, his eyes narrow slits. In the eight months I had worked in the same office with him, I'd never seen his face look anything like that—so distorted and perverse. The scant light that trickled in from the small window onto his face caused him to appear more apparitional than human.

"Where is it?" he asked in a hoarse whisper.

"Where is what?" I asked inching back away from him.

"You know what I'm talking about."

"No, I don't."

What does he have in his hand?

"I know you found it."

He edged closer, and I took a long step back, struggling to balance on one crutch, the thumping of my heart against my rib cage only adding to my unsteadiness.

"You better leave before I call the police."

He took another step toward me, and I took another step backward. My back was now up against the refrigerator. I scanned the island for something I could use to hit him or throw at him if I needed to, but there was nothing within my reach. I considered confessing to having the Irish money and offering to take him to the bank for it. I didn't know how far I should go and also didn't know how far he *would* go.

He glanced over at the phone on the other side of the kitchen and arched a sly brow. "No, you won't."

"You need to leave." I was barely able to get the words out.

"Not until you hand it over, and if you want to find out how serious I am, continue to play dumb."

He started to take another step closer, and when I raised my remaining crutch up toward his head in an effort to stop him, he snatched it out of my hand with a vicious yank and threw it across the room. The formidable sound of it slamming against the wall caused me to jump. I considered running but was afraid my knee wouldn't hold up to that. The rush of blood that surged through my veins made me feel faint.

"If you don't hand it over, Gracie," he said, spitting out my name like it was poison, "you'll need someone a lot better than your boy Tymon for protection."

That he called me Gracie was unnerving—only Tymon, Minnie, and my mother had ever called me that.

"Look, Elmer, I don't have anything you—"

"And if you even think of calling the police, try this on for size, golden girl. I don't suppose you know that my dear cousin Henry is dead. Poor soul. I found him crumpled up in a heap on his cement patio." He relaxed his posture, almost like he was enjoying a little chitchat with a friend. "And wouldn't you know it, just the other day he was telling me about how your little Miss Minnie made some threats against him. Now the police think he fell off his second-floor deck after having a bit too much to drink—which, knowing that boozer, was a likely story. But if I told them *you* were the one who made those threats, I think that would open up a nice little investigation ...making your life a living hell."

"What makes you think they'd believe you?"

"The grieving relative? The one who found his poor broken body that evening?"

"You'll never get away with it."

He took another step closer, his face so tense it looked like it might shatter. I glanced to the right, but there was nothing to hold on to, so I sidestepped back to the island, putting more distance between us.

"Too bad Mommy and Daddy aren't around to help you," he said sarcastically.

My body stiffened at the remark, the anger rising up in my throat like bile.

"You leave them out of this."

He took another step closer, forcing me back one more step along the base of the island.

"Oh, I know all about your parents, darlin'," he said with lips curled in icy contempt. "I know about their connection to this house and, best of all, what's hidden here."

I continued stepping backward until I reached a corner.

"You're bluffing."

For every forward step he had taken, I had moved two steps back, but eventually I had nowhere to go. I was halfway around the island—ten feet from the back door in one direction and ten feet from the entrance to the hallway in the other. Given his position directly across the island from me, he could have easily caught me before I reached either escape route, even if I had been able to run.

He laughed. "Bluffing, you think? Think again."

"You won't get away with this." I couldn't remember if I had already said that.

"What, telling the police you threatened Henry? Oh, I'll get away with it all right. Because my friend Naomi will back me up on it."

I was pulled back to a psychology class exercise I had gone through in school. I forced myself to relax—first my facial muscles and then my neck and on down my body—until I was able to collect myself and speak to him calmly. I kept my voice low and steady, taking on as much of a sympathetic tone as I could muster.

"Elmer, I know why you're doing this. You're a desperate man, and I completely understand your motive." My heart was beating so vigorously that I couldn't hear my own words, but I kept talking anyway, hoping that what I was saying made sense and had the right impact.

"What the hell are you talking about?"

"I know about your son and your wife's death."

A wave of red took mere seconds to ripple up his neck.

"You don't understand shit!" he said, almost choking on his rage.

"But I do. How *is* your son?"

"Stop talking about him!"

"Is he doing better?"

"Shut up!" he bellowed.

Then his demeanor shifted. His eyes rolled skyward, and his body haphazardly swayed from side to side. He cried out, "It wasn't her fault!"

Both of his hands were now palms down on the counter, his arms stiff as metal rods. The veins on the top of his right hand stood out from the tight grip he had on what appeared to be a ring of keys.

"It was *my* fault for forcing myself on you, Hazel! I'm so sorry," he said through a prolonged wail. His gaze was still directed up, and I didn't think he knew at that instant where he was or who else was in the room. "If it wasn't for me, you'd still be here."

Then his voice transitioned from quivery and loud to soft and contrite as though something had broken the spell of his rage. "I tried to get him the help he needs, but I never could afford it. And he deserved that help." He whimpered as if surrendering to his failure as a father. "He still does."

The atmosphere in the room turned eerily calm, sending shivers down my back.

Elmer turned to me, and as abruptly as his remorsefulness had come on, it disappeared.

"And you're the one keeping my son from his treatment! So let's just do this the easy way, you annoying little twit, or you'll—"

"Or she'll what?" Tymon barked as he boldly walked into the kitchen, a foot-and-a-half-long pipe wrench dangling from his hand.

Elmer turned toward Tymon, and the two of them sized each other up like two male lions competing for the same territory. Elmer didn't take his eyes off Tymon. Tymon didn't move from his wide stance just inside the back door. They both stood erect and silent.

Without warning, Elmer bolted toward the hallway and disappeared. Tymon ran after him.

"No!" I shouted after Tymon. "Let him go."

I heard the bang of the front door against Minnie's copper umbrella stand and then the shriek made by the screen door Minnie had often said needed a little WD-40.

I wanted to sit down but was too afraid to move.

Tymon came back into the kitchen, gathered my crutches, and helped me to a chair.

"Did he hurt you?"

"No."

"How did he get in?"

I didn't respond.

"Do you know him?"

"Yes."

"Who is he?"

"That was Elmer Berghorn."

"The guy who locked you out of your office and apartment?"

"Mm-hm."

"How did he get in here?"

"I feel pretty stupid about this, but I thought it was you, and I opened the door without looking to see who it was."

"Gracie."

"I know. I know."

"What did he want?"

"I think he had something to do with breaking in here. I think he knows about the Irish money, and I think he thinks I have it or know where it is, and he wants it."

"That's a lot of thinking."

"I know, but that's what I think."

"And what if I hadn't come in when I did?"

"I don't know what he would have done."

"Gracie, you can't—"

"I know. It was stupid of me to open the door without knowing who it was, and I won't make that mistake again."

His unrelenting stare prompted me to keep talking.

"It's okay now. He's gone and—"

"It's not okay now," he said. "I saw the look on his face. I'm going to call the police."

"No, don't."

"But he was a threat to you. You can't let him get away with that."

"He's more of a threat to himself than me."

"It's your call, but I don't understand why you don't want to report this."

I wasn't sure I fully understood that myself.

"He won't be back," I told him. The look on Elmer's face when he had poured out his soul to his late wife had convinced me of that. I'd seen the gut-wrenching pain in his eyes when he assumed responsibility for his wife's death—something I suspected he had never contemplated before.

"You can't stay here, Gracie."

"I'll be fine."

"You said that after the break-in. You were wrong then too."

He wasn't going to let it go.

"Look, I have extra bedrooms. Come stay with me."

"And how long do I stay away?" My stomach was so upset, I was afraid I might be sick. "Tymon, I'm not leaving this house. It's all I have right now."

He shook his head. "Then let me move in with you. I can take one of the rooms upstairs, and you can move down to Minnie's room."

Move in with me?

"Nothing more is going to happen."

"You're being naive. He's not going away as long as he thinks you've got something he wants. You may leave out your back door one day, and he'll be holed up in the bushes or something or behind the garage when you're getting into your car. You're not safe here, and I'm not going to let you stay here alone."

Not going to let me? Who did he think he was?

"Tell me you'll stay with a friend then. Anything but staying here alone."

"I'm not leaving."

Tymon got up and walked toward the door. "I'll be back in thirty minutes with a few of my things. Lock this door behind me." He paused. "Thirty minutes."

Now what? I didn't want him moving in with me. I didn't even know if I should trust him. After all, I had trusted Elmer.

I locked the door and plunked myself back down at the kitchen table. Of course I trusted Tymon. But I still didn't want him to move in with me. If Tymon knew about Elmer's threat to tell police I had something to do with Henry's death, he'd be making plane reservations for me to go to some other country right now.

Had Minnie been here, she would have said, "It's after noon. Pour yourself a Scotch, Gracie." God, I missed her.

Elmer's behavior had frightened me—it had been like seeing two, maybe three, entirely different people inhabiting the same body. I had never witnessed anyone become that emotional, that pitiful, and that desperate.

"Desperate people do desperate things," my mother's voice whispered in my ear. Observing him behave like I just had made me think that desperation might have been Elmer's driving force.

If I allowed Tymon to move in, which room would he take? The only one with quick access to the downstairs was the one above Minnie's bedroom, which would be right above where I'd be sleeping. I was supposed to feel comfortable with that?

He'd said it hadn't been her fault. Did his wife think she had caused her son to be ill?

He'd be back soon. What was I going to do?

Elmer knew about my parents, or had he said he knew about this house?

I'd need separate space from him.

He had mentioned Tymon. Should I tell Tymon this?

I'd put a lock on my bedroom door.

He called Naomi his friend. Were they in cahoots?

The phone was ringing, but I didn't want to answer it. I needed to figure this out. Shoot—it could be him.

"Hello."

It was Naomi, and she was talking so fast I had to strain to understand her.

"He just stormed in here saying, 'Tell Danny to meet me at the house.' Then he grabbed something from his desk drawer and ran out. I thought you should know. Gotta go. My other line is ringing."

I heard a car door slam and scrambled for my crutches. When I peered out the window, I expected to see Tymon's car in the driveway. Instead, there were two cars, and I didn't recognize either one.

TWENTY-EIGHT

Roommates

My heart pounded so hard my chest hurt. I was frozen in the spot where I stood, too afraid to look out the window again. There was a knock at the back door. I waited. Another knock.

"Gracie!"

It was Tymon's voice. But who was with him?

"Open up. It's me."

"And who else?" I asked through the door.

"Let me in, and I'll explain."

"No."

"Gracie, it's me. I'm alone. Let me in."

I crept to the back door and peeked through the curtains. Just Tymon was standing there. I unlocked the door but not the security chain.

I glanced past him. Only one car remained in the driveway. "Whose car is that?"

"A friend of mine's. He's going to leave it here for a few days so it looks like there are more people in the house."

"Another car just left. Who was that?"

"That was Jack. Carl, the owner of the car sitting in your driveway, needed a ride back to his house. Gracie, everything is okay."

"Where's your car?"

"On the street."

I stared into his eyes, which were full of compassion. Feeling a little stupid, I unlatched the security chain to let him in.

He chuckled. "I'm glad you're being more cautious about who you let in, but really..."

"Get in here. I have to tell you something."

I told Tymon about Naomi's phone call.

He didn't say anything for several seconds.

"Sit down, Gracie."

His gaze was so intense, I had to look away.

"How do you feel about having a few boarders until things get resolved?" he asked.

"What?"

"I'm pretty sure I can get three of my poker buddies to stay in the other upstairs rooms for a while. That means four more cars going in and out of your driveway—lots of activity—and four able-bodied men around in case there's trouble."

An hour earlier, I hadn't wanted one person staying with me. Now he was suggesting four. My head told me this was absurd and not to agree to it. But my stomach was saying something entirely different.

"Can I use your phone?" he asked.

"Of course."

One by one, Tymon called Jack, Otto, and Carl to ask them if they would help him out by staying in the rooms for a few nights. I did not attempt to stop him. When he was done, he turned to me and said, "I have loyal poker buddies."

"I can see that."

"Before we go upstairs and see what needs to be done for their arrival, I have to ask you what you want to do about Berghorn."

"What do you mean?"

"Did he do anything to you that could result in him getting arrested?"

"Sort of. He made one idle threat—"

"What kind of threat?"

"Not one that made me fear for my safety or anything..."

"What threat did he make?"

I didn't answer right away—as much as I despised Elmer, for some reason I felt the need to protect the vulnerable side of him that had spilled his heart out on the kitchen countertop.

"Grace."

"Yes."

"Tell me what he said that threatened you."

"It wasn't anything really. I may have—"

"Tell me."

I repeated what Elmer had said about telling the police I'd had an argument with Henry right before his death.

"That's extortion, isn't it? You would know better than I."

"Maybe."

"And you don't want to press charges against him?"

I thought about that for a moment and then shook my head.

"Why did you tell me to let him go the other day?"

"Because there's another man inside of him that needs rediscovery right now."

"I don't understand you."

"I'm pretty sure he's done things far worse than this. I'd rather they get him on something bigger, down the road."

"You're sure?"

"Mm-hm."

"If you change your mind, you'll let me know?"

"I will."

We spent the next half hour listing what each of us had to do before the guys arrived. I hoped they had simple needs, because I didn't have much to offer them. We moved all my things from O'Gowan's old room on the second floor to Minnie's bedroom on the first, and the furniture in that room to the room above Minnie's bedroom, where Tymon was going to sleep. Each of the other rooms had a bed, a small dresser, a lamp, and a chair. I put clean sheets on the beds, dusted off the dressers, and put all the extra towels and linens I could find in the upstairs bathroom.

It was eight o'clock, and I was tired and hungry. I checked in on Tymon who was under the kitchen sink fixing the leak with the heavy-duty wrench that he had brandished like a weapon earlier.

"I called Otto, and he's bringing a pizza with him for us. I hope you like it loaded," he said.

"I'm so hungry, I could eat anything."

As he slipped out from under the sink, he said, "I'm done with my list. How about you?"

"Done."

"Gracie?"

"What?"

"I know you're uncomfortable with all this."

"I'm okay with it."

"No, you're not, but as smart as I think you are, you have no sense for when you're in a dangerous situation, and *somebody's* got to look after you."

"Tymon?"

"What?"

"Thanks."

TWENTY-NINE

The Connecting Puzzle Pieces

If someone had told me a few days earlier that I'd be living with four men, three of whom I had never met before, I would have called that person crazy. But during the first night of their stay, I slept better than I had slept since Minnie had died three and a half weeks earlier.

First thing the next morning, I quickly got dressed and grabbed some juice and a bagel for breakfast before my roommates began to stir. Tymon's cohorts were younger than he was—somewhere in their forties. They were all bachelors, I was told—I wasn't sure if any of them had ever married. Jack was an electrician, Otto a toolmaker, and Carl a chef. Based on the way they interacted with each other—the way they bantered, slapped each other on the back, and joked around—I could tell they'd known each other for a while. Their camaraderie was enviable.

I spent the day arranging my things in Minnie's bedroom, careful not to disturb her things too much or change the way she had the room organized. It was hard to be in her room—where she had slept, kept her personal things, and died. The dirty laundry in the hamper, her toothbrush in the bathroom, the half-read book on her nightstand were all painful reminders. I couldn't imagine throwing any of her things out like they were trash.

I finished in Minnie's bedroom a few minutes before Fern arrived with a pizza—I'd almost forgotten she was coming over. I didn't have the heart to tell her I was sick of pizza, having had it twice in the last twenty-four hours. At least the one she brought wasn't "loaded," like the one that was still lying in a heap at the bottom of my stomach. We agreed to talk before we ate.

The first thing I did was explain the activity in the backyard, where Tymon and the gang were rebuilding Carl's transmission.

"They look harmless enough. How long are they going to be here?"

"As long as Tymon thinks I'm not safe here alone, I guess."

"You don't sound too happy about it."

"I'm sleeping better, and that's a good thing, but... Anyway, let's talk about Essie. I've been doing a lot of thinking about her. When you last met with her, she was on the brink of telling you something important and then changed her mind."

"Right."

"What if we could do or say something to make her change it back?"

"Like what?"

"If *I* knew something that would change a person's life, I would be more compelled to tell them if I knew they were going down the wrong path by not knowing. Does that make any sense?"

"I'm with you," Fern said. "So let's say, for example, that Anna is really your mother, and your mother Rosa kidnapped you after Anna died."

"What made you say that? Because bizarre as that sounds, I think that could be possible."

"I don't know. Anyway, so let's think about what path you could be taking that would cause her to spill her guts. It has to be something with big consequences."

"I agree."

We sat in silence for several minutes.

"So what's the worst thing that could happen to someone—that they die!"

"That's a little extreme, don't you think?" I said.

"We have to get her attention."

"I know, but—"

"I've got it!"

"Tell me."

We spent the next hour hatching an outrageous story about how I was despondent over not knowing who my parents were and had threatened to kill myself if I couldn't get to the bottom of it. Who could ignore that?

Afterward, over a sausage-and-black-olive pizza and a couple of beers, we sat in the living room and talked about all sorts of things unrelated to our stories. It felt good to be with her...like a friend.

Fern left, and the more I thought about our plan to deceive Essie, the more it pulled me back to my first encounter with Minnie—when I'd told lie after lie in order to get information from her—and the less I liked it.

* * *

It took me a while to get back into PI mode as I prepared to search for Essie Noe, and when I did, I realized just how much I didn't like doing that kind of work. Being away from it helped me to fully appreciate that fact.

I wanted to see if anyone was living in the house Essie used to rent, and if so, what they were doing with her mail. When I told Tymon my plan to surveil the house, he insisted on coming with me. To avoid an argument, I agreed. So far, his manning the house with his poker buddies had created few problems and relieved me of most of my anxiety, so I couldn't very well question his judgment on this.

On the way to Essie's old neighborhood, Tymon told me a couple of stories about Anna. I could tell by the inflection in his voice that he still carried a torch for her after all these years. I asked him why he had never married.

"Before or after Anna?"

"Both."

"I was forty when we met, and I had just lost my mother. Up until then, I was taking care of her. My mother had polio and was restricted in most everything she did. There wasn't any time for girlfriends. I had to work to support us."

"And your father?"

"He died shortly after I was born. Pneumonia."

"I'm sorry to hear that. Must have been tough back then."

"It was, but we managed."

We parked a few houses from Essie's old house, which was in one of Cicero's many blue-collar neighborhoods, and patiently waited for something to happen.

"And after Anna?" I asked, continuing with our conversation.

"After Anna died, I spent the next several years kicking myself for not pursuing her, not being there to save her. She'd be alive today if—"

"You can't think that way, Tymon. You're—" At that moment, I saw a woman slip out the side door. "Look!" I said, pointing to her. We waited in silence as she walked to the mailbox and sorted through the mail. She put some of mail back into the box, flipped up the red flag, and then turned and walked back into the house.

"Bingo. That tells me the post office doesn't have a forwarding address for her."

"How do you know that?"

"If they did, they wouldn't be delivering mail to her here."

"You're good."

"Not really. Anyway, so I can't use my post office ruse."

"What's that?"

"I can't tell you. It's not...well, let's just leave it at that."

"What now?"

I started the car and headed for home. "Essie sold houses for a living, and I know they don't get their commissions until the house closes, so there's a good chance she has earned commissions she hasn't collected yet, which means she still has ties to Baird & Warner."

"You *are* good."

"Not really."

"So now what?"

"I don't know. I wish I knew someone who was connected in the real estate field."

* * *

A week after the boys moved in, I told Tymon over breakfast that I believed the coast was clear and they could go home now.

"How do you know the coast isn't clear because of us being here?"

I didn't have an answer for that.

"But you guys must be anxious to go back to your homes, your normal routines."

"Do you hear any of us complaining?"

"No, but—"

"We're here for the long haul, if needed, and if you keep feeding us Sunday dinner, you may never get rid of us."

You would have thought the pot roast dinner I had made for them over the weekend was the first decent meal they had eaten in months. Well, not Carl, the chef, but the others. I had resolved to make that a weekly tradition for as long as they were there. It was the least I could do.

Later that morning, a woman from the Irish American Heritage Center called me to say she had some information. Tymon offered to drive me there. I didn't argue.

It was a short drive to the Center, and once we got there Tymon asked if I wanted him to wait in the car. He knew more about what I was doing than anyone else at that point, so I figured what was the difference. I told him to come in with me.

We were greeted at the entrance by a docent who showed us to the management office. The office manager who had called me earlier motioned for us to come in and sit down.

"I was able to find a list of sweepstakes winners for three of the years you requested," she said. She slid a piece of paper toward me. First, second, and third prizes had been awarded four times per year. I quickly ran down the list with my finger. Halfway down was the name Marcus O'Gowan. He had won it in May 1941.

"Thanks. I found the name I was looking for," I explained. I started to slide the list back to her when I noticed his name listed again—this time in November of the same year. I asked her if that could be a mistake.

"No. Until recently, he was the only single person to win first prize twice. Imagine that."

"That must have been some amount."

"And I wish I could give you the amount, but they keep that confidential."

I thanked her, and we left.

"So how does that help you?" Tymon asked me on the way to the car.

"First of all, it explains the second box of money—the one you found."

"There's more?"

"Minnie and I found a slightly smaller amount in the attic."

"Where is that then?"

"I don't know. She hid it. I thought you'd found it until I counted it and it contained more bills than the first one."

"Holy—"

"I'm now sure the money was O'Gowan's, and my guess is that he moved here to get away from people who were after it—relatives maybe, friends, who knows. He changed his name, found the room in Anna's boardinghouse, and lived there like a hermit."

"A rich hermit."

"A very rich hermit."

* * *

I awoke at three-thirty A.M. and couldn't get back to sleep, so I got up and curled up in Minnie's favorite chair with a novel. After reading for a bit, it occurred to me how I could get Elmer off the trail of the O'Gowan money once and for all.

Feeling quite pleased with myself for hatching such a clever plan, I dressed, made myself a pot of tea, fetched the paper, and stirred up a batch of blueberry muffins. It didn't take long for the fragrance of the muffins to start wafting through the house, reminding me of Minnie, who always had something baking in the oven.

From my vantage point at the kitchen table, I saw Jack leave for work. Otto soon followed. I'd seen Carl leave mid-morning a few times. Tymon never left unless it was with me.

I had to admit, there were still times that I was uncertain about Tymon. I wanted to believe he was this very nice person who had been in love with Anna, felt a connection with me, and expected nothing in return. But I didn't know any of this for sure.

I worried that I trusted him more than I should. Here he was, living upstairs with open access to my living space. He had installed a lock on the door at the top of the stairs that connected our bedrooms, and we kept it locked. But it was a double-sided lock, so if either of us wanted to gain access to the other's space, we could. He had assured me he kept the door to the hallway on the other side of his room locked at all times, so at least the other three didn't have access to the first floor.

Tymon knew almost everything about me—my past, my present, my dilemmas, and my vulnerabilities. I supposed if he was going to pull anything on me, he would have done it by now.

I went back and forth about his intentions—most of the time leaning toward positive. Still, it nagged at me.

My thoughts drifted to Essie Noe as I sipped my tea. I wished I knew if she had moved far away or just far enough to drop out of sight for a while. I considered going to the library and perusing the most recent Sunday *Tribune* real estate sections to see which houses she had listed. But Tymon would want to accompany me, and I hesitated asking him to watch me scour through newspapers for hours.

I heard Tymon's signature knock at the back door. He could have let himself in via the staircase in my bedroom or by using his back-door key, but he didn't. In that respect, he behaved more like a neighbor than a roommate, and for that I was grateful.

I let him in and told him to help himself to a muffin or two. Like every other morning, he had made a pot of coffee up in his room and brought down a cup of it in a large Snoopy coffee mug.

"So what's on your agenda today?" he asked.

I told him about what I thought I might be able to find by poring over old newspapers.

"Let's go. When do they open?"

"Are you sure you want to sit with me while I do this? It could take hours."

"I am capable of reading, you know. If we split it up, it will take half the time."

"Are you sure?"

"I wouldn't have offered if I wasn't."

"They open at ten."

Tymon told me he wanted to check under my hood for something or other that he said sounded off the other day. While he did that, I called Naomi to ask her if she'd help me turn the tables on a certain someone she had previously referred to as a "no-good low-down rat-fink skuzzball." She said she was in and could stop by over the weekend if it was okay to bring her daughter. We agreed to meet on Saturday morning.

Tymon told me I had a couple of belts that needed replacing, so we planned to take his car to the library and then stop by the neighborhood mechanic's place to get the belts. He asked me on the way what I thought would happen when I found out once and for all who my parents were.

"I'm hoping it will give me enough peace of mind to allow me to move on with my life. I don't have anything if I don't have my identity."

"This is really important to you, isn't it?"

"I feel stuck not knowing, if that makes any sense. It's like doing a jigsaw puzzle—there are puzzle pieces you can put together and you see parts of the picture, but until you find the pieces that connect them, there's no whole picture."

"But what if you never find those connecting pieces, Gracie? What then?"

I didn't have an answer for that.

Once we arrived at the library, we went to the reference section where they had the past issues of the *Tribune*. We made ourselves comfortable at a table in the corner of the room and got to work.

There was no one near us, so we talked while we flipped through the newspapers. At one point, I asked Tymon if he had ever worked in any capacity other than home maintenance.

"No. Devoted my whole life to it. Started out helping my mother around the house, then as a teenager helping neighbors. After high school, I had to work to help support my mother and me, and that was all I knew."

"It sounds like it worked out pretty well for you though."

"I can't complain. I live a simple life, but I'm comfortable."

"When did you retire?"

"The minute I became eligible for Social Security last year. I still do some things." He smiled. "For special people."

Two hours and eighteen months of Sunday *Tribunes* later, I had six leads.

⌒୭ THIRTY ୭⌒
It Was Elmer

It was Saturday, and I was sitting on the patio with a cup of tea waiting for Naomi and her daughter to arrive. The previous day, the doctor had said I could finally ditch the crutches. After I'd been on them for seven and a half weeks, I was considering creating a nice bonfire out back in which to burn them. As I waited for Naomi, I considered the calluses on my hands and the irritated skin under my arms, wondering how soon my body would get back to normal.

Tymon was the only other one home. The "boys" had gone off to a White Sox game.

Naomi and little Candace arrived right on time. Naomi's weekend outfit was just as provocative as her work attire—tight-fitting Capri pants, a polka-dot v-neck top, and patent-leather slingbacks. Candace had hair so blonde it was almost white. Her bright blue eyes and wide smile matched her mother's.

I had bought a few things to keep Candace amused while Naomi and I talked. I figured you couldn't go wrong with a coloring book, crayons, and bubbles for a four-year-old.

Naomi introduced me as Miss Lindroth.

"Hi, Candace. How old are you?"

She held up four fingers and eyed the bubbles.

"Do you like to blow bubbles?"

She nodded.

I unscrewed the lid on the bottle of bubbles and handed it to her, and she ran off to play.

The first thing Naomi said was that she couldn't wait to get out of Elmer's office.

"He's as shady as they come, and he expects me to just go along with it. I don't know if he's breaking the law or not, but I'm sure much of what he does wouldn't pass the code of ethics I know lawyers have."

"Do you have any leads on another job?"

"A couple. But nothing close yet."

I took the next twenty minutes or so to explain my plan to divert Elmer's attention away from the money...and me.

"Count me in. I'll gladly help you with this. In fact, it will be my pleasure!"

We chatted for a while longer, long enough for Candace to color a picture for my refrigerator, and then they left for a birthday party.

I felt good but knew I'd feel even better on Monday when Naomi placed what I'd hoped would be a live hand grenade at Elmer's feet.

* * *

After a painstaking hunt for phone numbers, I called the first name on my list of Essie Noe leads. I was hoping the sellers still had a relationship with her and knew how to reach her. Essie had listed this man's house for sale the same month she'd disappeared.

That call didn't pan out—the man told me he'd changed his mind after listing his house with her and had taken it off the market.

My second and third calls were to people whose homes had been listed by Essie in February, four months before she disappeared. No luck there—both had been sold and closed upon before she disappeared.

Call number four was to a disconnected phone number.

Call number five rang fifteen times with no answer.

A woman who confirmed her house was still for sale answered the last number on my list. I told her I might be interested in buying it and asked her who at Baird & Warner her realtor was. She told me Esmeralda Noe.

"No kidding," I told her. "I happen to know her, but she recently moved out of the area. Is she still handling your sale?"

"Yes, as far as I know. I haven't heard otherwise."

"I think she may have moved out of state."

"I wouldn't know anything about that."

"Has her number changed? I still have her old number."

"I just call the Baird & Warner office when I need to reach her. Would you like that number?"

"No, thanks. I have it. I'll give them a call. It was nice talking to you."

It was a long shot, but I called the Baird & Warner office.

"Hello, may I speak with Esmeralda Noe, please?"

"She's not here, but I can put you through to someone else who can help you."

"I was hoping to talk to Esmeralda. Will she be in later today?"

"I don't expect her in. Are you sure someone else can't help you?"

"Actually, this is personal, but this is the only number I have for her." I forced my voice to crack. "A very dear friend of ours passed away, and I wanted to tell her about it. Would you happen to have another number for her?"

"I really can't give that out, Miss. But I can take your name and number and give her the message."

"I'm afraid that won't do any good. I live in Benton Harbor and am on my way to take a train in for the funeral. She would have no way to reach me."

"I'm not allowed to give out personal information. I'm sorry."

She was sticking to their policy no matter what.

"I understand. Thanks anyway."

Looked like I still had the ability to make stuff up on a moment's notice—wasn't that grand?

I tried the unanswered phone number again. Still no answer.

I no sooner hung up the phone, and it rang. It was Naomi.

"I thought you'd never get off the phone," she whispered. "Can't talk long. It worked, and is he mad! Pacing his office, pounding on his desk, swearing up a storm. Gotta go."

It paid to know people in the right places. I opened up the Chicago *Daily News* to page twenty-three:

> The owner of NSU Investigative Services must have made one
> family in Dublin, Ireland more than a "wee" bit happy when
> she informed them she had located the missing $250,000 worth
> of Irish notes that their dearly departed relative had won in two
> separate Irish Sweepstakes drawings. The money has since been
> returned to its rightful owners.

Of course, just two copies of that bogus page had been printed—one for Naomi to give to Berghorn when he overheard her talking about it on the phone, and one for me so I could gloat about it every once in a while.

* * *

No one knew that it was my twenty-third birthday. I'd thought about telling people but then decided against it. Birthdays should be happy occasions, and except for my satisfaction over duping Elmer, I wasn't feeling particularly happy then.

On a long shot, I retrieved my box of family photos hoping I would discover something of value, something I had overlooked or that hadn't made sense before but would now.

I examined a photo of a crowd of people in front of Wrigley Field—more specifically, in front of the blue and white HOME OF CHICAGO CUBS sign. It occurred to me that if someone had been taking a picture of the sign, it would have been centered in the photograph. Instead, the crowd of people was front and center. I stuck the photo in my pocket.

After wasting an hour looking at photos I had examined a hundred times before, I hopped on the bus to meet Fern for lunch, hoping I could draw out from her more information about Essie, things that could lead to her whereabouts—hobbies, favorite foods, friends, relatives. Sometimes the smallest tidbit of information could turn into a viable clue.

That day, I was traveling without Tymon, who had agreed that since Elmer thought the money was gone, it was safe enough for me to be out and about by myself. I suspected his need to protect me would end soon, but admittedly I had mixed feelings about that. I had gotten used to having someone looking out for my well-being—a male version of Minnie.

As soon as I got off the bus, the smoky aroma coming from Eddy's Rib Joint hit me, reminding me of those special occasions when my father would bring home full rib dinners for us. I walked a half-block down the crowded sidewalk past a bank, two dress shops, a hair salon, and a drugstore until I reached the restaurant.

I spotted Fern seated in a booth next to the windows overlooking the sidewalk. We greeted each other with a quick hug.

As soon as we ordered, I showed her the Wrigley Field photograph.

"Look closely at the people in front of the building. Do you recognize anyone?"

Fern examined the photo and slowly shook her head. "No."

"What about the woman in front who is gazing directly at the camera. Does she look familiar to you?"

"Not really."

"Could it be Essie?"

She continued to stare at the photo. "Could be, but it's hard to tell." Several seconds passed. "It could be." She turned the photo over and read the back. "1941."

"How old would you say Essie is now?"

"I'd say somewhere in her fifties."

"So let's say she's fifty-five. That would make her thirty-one in that photo."

"The woman in the photo could be that age. What if it is her? What does that tell you?"

"Not much except that maybe she liked baseball, enough to have her picture taken in front of the stadium."

"That photo was taken the year before we were born."

"I know. I was thinking about that."

"Any leads on finding her?" she asked.

I told her about my calls to Essie's clients.

"Needle in a haystack," she said.

"Something like that. Do you know what kind of car she drives?"

"She doesn't. Takes public transportation everywhere."

I got excited. "Really? Why didn't you tell me that before?"

"I didn't think it was important."

"It's important. Knowing that, and being fairly sure she still has ties to Baird & Warner to finish up any sales she started before she left, I'd guess she must still be in the area, close enough that she can take public transportation."

"That must be why you're the PI. So now what?"

"I'm going to call for information in every suburb to see if they have a new listing for her."

"What about right here in Chicago?"

"I've got that covered. I called for a Chicago listing on her every day for two weeks after she disappeared. They would have had one by then if she was here, so I stopped."

"Unless she doesn't have a phone. Or is staying with someone."

"She has to have a phone—she's a real estate agent. But she could be staying with someone. She never mentioned being close to anyone?"

"No. She was pretty quiet about herself. I had a hard time getting anything out of her. She talked about a niece, but I don't think she ever mentioned her name."

I told her about tricking Elmer into thinking the Irish money had been given to O'Gowan's relatives.

"Nice one! So are all your boyfriends gone then?"

"Very funny. No, not yet. Tymon is being extra cautious."

"So what else is new?"

"I know."

We finished our lunch, said goodbye, and headed for different bus stops.

When I arrived home, I found Tymon on the patio drinking a cup of coffee.

"Did you have a nice lunch?" he asked.

"Yes, and I was only mugged twice."

"I won't rest until that hoodlum is completely out of the picture. You know that."

"Out of the picture? What do you want...him dead?"

"I'd settle for incapacitated. Sit for a minute, I have something to tell you."

His expression was serious.

"What's wrong?"

"I went over to Jake's while you were at lunch and ran into Henry Sikes."

"I thought he was dead!"

"Looks like that's what Elmer wanted you to think."

Now I felt stupid for not having checked that out.

"So what did he have to say?"

"A lot. Henry develops a very loose tongue when someone buys him drinks." He leaned in toward me, his arms resting on his thighs, his hands clasped together. "Gracie, Elmer Berghorn was responsible for your parents' deaths."

THIRTY-ONE

Revoked

My body went numb. I wanted to ask Tymon to repeat what he had just told me but was unable to speak.

"Breathe, Gracie."

I hadn't realized I wasn't breathing.

"That's hard to believe, Tymon. But you said Henry was drinking, so how can we..."

"Henry wasn't crazy drunk when he told me that. And my experience with people and alcohol is that it doesn't create thoughts, it just brings them out."

The notion that someone—someone I knew, for Pete's sake—had done something that resulted in my parents' deaths was incomprehensible.

"What did he do?"

"Now bear with me. It's a bit of a long story. We know Henry left the boardinghouse the same day O'Gowan died—Minnie told us that. And we know from the bartender at Jake's and others that Henry started flashing money around about that same time, so I figure he broke into O'Gowan's room at some point after his death, stole whatever cash he could find, and fled."

"What a creep."

"This next part, I think, will surprise you. Apparently, right after O'Gowan died, Berghorn was arrested and went to prison."

"Prison! For what?"

"Henry said embezzlement and a bunch of other stuff."

"Holy..."

"I know. Meanwhile, from prison, Elmer is hounding Henry to locate Al, the boarder who had the room over Anna's bedroom."

"Why?"

"Al left the boardinghouse right after Anna was killed—the next day, in fact. And Henry had told Elmer at some point that he had seen Al and O'Gowan talking with each other on more than one occasion. And since O'Gowan was such a recluse, Elmer thought it odd that he would be talking to Al. He thought maybe Al had found out about O'Gowan's money and had somehow gotten his hands on it after O'Gowan died."

"Whose mind works like that?"

"Berghorn's, apparently. Anyway, as Henry put it, 'He wasn't the boss of me, and he was in prison, so he couldn't see what I was doin' or not doin'.' So without putting much effort into it, Henry kept an eye out for Al, and...what do you know? One day, he sees him coming out of your house on Ferdinand Street."

"My house?"

"Your house."

"So Al knew my parents."

"It looks that way."

"So what year was this?"

"He didn't say, but I got the impression it wasn't long after O'Gowan's death."

"He died in June 1943. I was just a year old."

"Okay. So to appease Elmer, Henry said he just made something up about keeping a watchful eye on Al and every once in a while seeing his car at the Ferdinand address. And he does this periodically throughout Elmer's prison sentence."

"So then Elmer gets out of prison—"

"How long was he in prison?"

"I don't think Henry said. Anyway, he gets out and sets up this law practice—"

"How did he do that with a criminal record?"

"I don't know, but we both know he did. Well, he couldn't make enough to properly take care of his son, and he couldn't stop thinking about O'Gowan's winnings even after all that time."

"Okay, so stop there for a minute. You're saying Elmer was obsessed over O'Gowan's money so he could provide for his son?"

"According to Henry."

"Naomi told me his son was ill. Did Henry give you the impression that Elmer's son had a long-term illness?"

"No, he didn't say that."

"Did he say that's why Elmer went to prison? The embezzlement and other stuff, did he take those risks for his son?"

"You ask good questions. I don't know."

The thought of Elmer doing it all for his son was no justification for it, but it sure made me think about him as a man. What that meant to me was that his bad behavior wasn't an indication of his character. It was an indication of his situation—a situation so dire that it blinded him to ethical concerns.

"I'm sorry. Please continue."

"Would you like to take a break?"

"No, I'm good."

"So Elmer tells Henry to show him the house on Ferdinand where Al keeps going, and he gets it into his head that whoever lives there may have a connection to the money."

"That seems so far-fetched."

"I thought so too. So he digs into your parents' business and finds out they have this nice home with a very small mortgage, a new car, and some other things all on your father's wages at the Soo Line Railroad. He becomes convinced your father somehow benefited from O'Gowan's fortune."

"So he kills them?"

"Hold on. I'll get to that."

"It's hard to hold on when—"

"I know. I know. So Elmer wants to search the house, but of course he can't do it when there are people living there, so he gets this harebrained idea to force them out long enough for him to snoop around. It was winter, according to Henry, and really cold."

I was unable to hold back the tears—it was like being confronted with their deaths all over again.

"March 18," I said through my blubbering. "Extremely cold...sub-zero."

"So his plan was to cut off their gas line so they would have no heat, forcing them out of their house until the gas company could find the problem and fix it."

"But why did he have to kill them?" I cried.

"According to Henry, he didn't intend to. He just wanted to force them out long enough for him to search the house."

"But that's crazy!"

"I know that, and you know that, but my impression from Henry was that Elmer was a desperate man. Desperate men don't think logically."

"Go on."

"Whatever he did caused carbon monoxide to back up into the basement, where apparently they were at the time. And they were overcome by it."

I struggled to speak. "Had he picked another time, I would have been in the house too."

"I know, sweetie."

"So did the rotten...did he get what he was looking for?"

"He didn't get O'Gowan's money, of course we know that, but according to Henry, he fraudulently got access to one or more of their bank accounts and then further took advantage of their deaths by buying the house."

I shook my head in disbelief.

"How could he do that and still sleep at night?"

"Desperation is like an addictive drug—it controls your brain, your thinking. Nothing else matters."

I closed my eyes and tried to make sense of it all.

"Are you okay?" he asked.

I nodded with my eyes still closed.

"So let me try to recap here," I finally said. "Henry finds out O'Gowan has a stash of money and tells his cousin Elmer about it. Elmer concocts a plan to rob O'Gowan, but before he can implement the plan, O'Gowan dies unexpectedly. Henry steals whatever he can from O'Gowan's room and flees. They both know O'Gowan won a lot more than that in the sweepstakes, but Elmer can't do much about it because he's been hauled off to prison.

"Then Elmer gets out of prison and—thanks to Henry—thinks there's some connection between Anna's boardinghouse lover Al and my father, which by some convoluted logic makes him think there's a connection between O'Gowan's money and my father. So he can search our house, Elmer tries to force my parents out of it by cutting off the heat in freezing weather but bungles that and kills them. And like that wasn't bad enough, he then takes advantage of this heinous act and buys our house—probably at a low price—and steals from my parents' bank accounts."

"That's pretty much how I understand it...at least according to Henry, and I found him to be quite believable."

"Right. He's not smart enough to make this kind of stuff up. You know that's probably why I was rushed out of that house afterward—because Berghorn was pushing to buy it. And I know from Naomi that he has connections with North Community Bank where my parents had a mortgage. He probably paid someone off to get me out of there as quickly as possible."

"There are no words to—"

"Wait a minute!"

"What?"

"I don't have it anymore because Berghorn stole it from me, but I found a statement from North Community Bank among my parents' things. The name on the account had been torn off, but I'll bet that was the account Berghorn stole from. If that was a current statement, there was close to $8,000 in that account. And there were two other bank accounts, one in San Diego and one in Mexico."

"How much was in those?"

"I don't remember now. That lousy..."

"So then Berghorn found you—"

"Thinking either I had O'Gowan's money or I could lead him to it."

Tymon didn't respond.

I couldn't stop shaking my head. This kind of thing didn't happen to ordinary people.

"Elmer killed my parents." My emotions completely took over again, and before I could do anything about it, I was crying uncontrollably. Tymon rushed over to me, placed his strong hands on my forearms, and lifted me up from the chair.

"Let's go inside, Gracie."

Once inside, I got hold of myself, and my grief quickly changed to anger.

"That son-of-a-bitch can't get away with this!" I pounded the side of my fist on the kitchen counter, causing Tymon to jump and me to wince in pain.

Tymon led me to one of the kitchen chairs, put a pot of water on the stove for tea, and then joined me.

"What kind of person does that?" I asked.

"One desperate for money?"

I got up and grabbed a piece of paper and pencil from the kitchen drawer.

"What are you doing?"

"Wait here a minute." I went upstairs to retrieve the envelopes that contained all my important papers and notes related to Anna and my parents.

"I'm creating a timeline. I need to understand this better," I told him when I returned.

When I was finished, I read him the following:

Nov 10, 1939	Anna buys the boardinghouse
Jan 4, 1942	Fern is born
Jun 28, 1942	I am born
Jan 23, 1943	Anna is murdered
Jan 24, 1943	Al leaves the boardinghouse
May 29, 1943	Minnie buys the boardinghouse
June 6, 1943	O'Gowan dies
June 6, 1943	Henry leaves the boardinghouse
	Berghorn goes to prison
	Berghorn gets out of prison
Mar 18, 1960	~~My parents die~~ Elmer kills my parents!
Aug 10, 1964	I start working out of Elmer's office

I glanced up at Tymon, who was intently staring at me.

"I wonder how much time Berghorn had after O'Gowan died and before he went to prison," I said. "Why didn't he break into the boardinghouse to look for the money?"

"Sorry. I forgot that part. Berghorn had told Henry to break into the boardinghouse and look for the money, but I'm not sure if it was before or after he went to prison. Anyway, Henry was content with what he had already stolen and gotten away with, so he lied to Elmer and told him that he broke in, searched every inch of the place, and didn't find anything."

I didn't respond.

"You've got that look on your face. What are you thinking?" he asked.

"I don't know yet. But one way or another, Elmer Berghorn is going to pay. And Tymon?

"Yes."

"Today is my birthday."

* * *

At three A.M., as I lay in bed wide awake, all I could think about was how Elmer had reeled me in like a fish getting me to sublet from him and then held me captive until he had no more use for me. And I'd been oblivious to every bit of it. *Well, Mr. Berghorn, you will pay for everything you've done...if it's the last thing I ever do.*

If it hadn't been for Berghorn, my parents would have still been alive.

I would've had no reason to think they were anything *but* my parents.

I would've had a job as an interior decorator that I loved.

I wouldn't have been sitting on almost $250,000 that wasn't mine.

I would've had a normal life for a twenty-three-year-old.

Now I was agitated and, knowing I'd never fall back asleep, I got up and dressed and headed for the kitchen.

The second I opened my bedroom door, the tantalizing smell of something chocolate wafted in. Tymon had his back to me and was taking something off the window sill when I entered the kitchen. When he turned around and saw me, he almost dropped the pan.

"What are you doing here?" he asked.

"I live here...remember?"

"Now you've spoiled the surprise."

"What surprise?" I asked.

"Just promise me you'll act surprised after dinner this evening."

"You baked me a birthday cake?"

"What are you doing up so early? I still have to frost this thing."

"Want some help?"

"Well, if you're not going to leave, then yes, you may as well help me."

I stared at him while he iced the cake, something I'd never seen a man do before. I don't think my father had ever set foot in our kitchen. Tymon wasn't half bad at it.

"You don't seem to be helping," he said.

"You don't seem to need it. So where did you get cake ingredients? I know it wasn't from this kitchen."

"There's a little all-night grocer in Edgewater."

"You'd better stop doing nice things for me, or I won't let you leave."

He laughed. "I dropped off my rent check the other day, and the landlady told me she thought maybe I'd skipped out on her."

"I can imag—"

"What's wrong?" he asked.

"I just remembered something." I jumped out of my chair. "I'll be right back."

I returned with the receipt in my hand.

"This." I waved it in the air.

"What's that?"

"It's a receipt for a basement build-out in our house that I found after my parents died. Do you know what that is?"

He took the receipt from me.

"Doesn't say much more than that," he said. "*Material and labor $278.15. May 5, 1943.*"

"That was a few months after Anna was killed. She died on January 23."

Tymon's eyebrows arched. "Basement build-out. The only thing I can think of is—"

"It's a room."

"What?"

"A room. Like the one downstairs." I felt the adrenaline pumping through my veins. "I'll bet they had a room built in their basement like the one downstairs."

"Wouldn't you have seen it growing up?"

"If it looks anything like this one, I never would have even known it was there. And besides, the only things down there were the furnace, hot-water heater, and washing machine. I never went down there."

"Maybe the safe is in there," he said.

"I wonder if Berghorn realizes there's a room down there."

"You don't even know if there *is* a room down there. All you have is a receipt."

"I'll bet you any amount of money, there's a hidden room down there...unless he's had it torn out."

"So now what?"

"Now what?"

"What about the room? What can you do about it?"

"Oh, I don't know. Probably just let it eat me up inside until I know if it exists or not."

Tymon put the finishing touches on the cake and placed it in the pantry.

"Show me your surprised look," he said upon his return.

"Don't worry, I won't disappoint. Who's going to be here?"

"Never mind. At least something will be a surprise."

"Tymon, do you think Berghorn had anything to do with Anna's death?"

"No, I don't."

"You answered that quickly. What makes you so sure?"

"The way Henry was talking so openly yesterday, he would have said something. And besides, what motive for killing her would he have had?"

"I suppose you're right. But Henry knows something about who killed Anna. At least, Minnie thought so."

"I'm not so sure. He was spilling everything to me. I think if he knew something, he would have said something."

"Maybe he doesn't even know what he knows."

"I'll connect with him again if you think it will help, but not this soon—"

"Oh, I wasn't suggesting that."

"When the time is right, I'll continue my chat with him. Gracie?"

"Yes."

"May I take you to dinner tonight—a late birthday celebration?"

"Thank you. I would like that."

"Pick you up at six then?"

"See you then."

I went out the front door to retrieve the paper, and when I returned I decided to go to City Hall and do a background check on Berghorn. I didn't know why it hadn't occurred to me before to do that.

* * *

I hadn't been to City Hall in a while, and I hoped my regular contacts remembered me. Research would take twice as long if I had to follow their usual protocol.

My first stop was the County Clerk's Office, where I found Flora on duty. After some small talk, I handed her a piece of paper with Berghorn's name on it and asked to see his birth certificate, marriage license, and documents for any judgments or liens against him. She asked me to come back in an hour.

Next I went to the County Archives department to see if he had ever served in the military. He had not, which was odd given he must have been somewhere in his twenties during World War II. Ha! Even they didn't want him. It also surprised me to find there was no record of him having an Illinois driver's license. Either he was driving without one or he had an out-of-state license.

When I returned to the County Clerk's office, Flora handed me copies of Berghorn's birth certificate and marriage license and told me she'd found no judgments or liens. I thanked her and headed toward Business Affairs to try to find his license to practice law. I had no contacts there and had to take a number and wait my turn.

While waiting, I examined the birth certificate.

Elmer Edward Berghorn, Jr.
Born December 1, 1916
Garfield Park Hospital
Mother: Agnes Joanne Berghorn
Father: Elmer Edward Berghorn, Sr.
Father's Occupation: Self-employed

Nothing very interesting.

He had married a woman named Hazel Osgood on February 14, 1942. Valentine's Day—how sweet.

When my number was called, I was escorted to a room of ten or so microfilm readers and shown where to find business licenses. They were filed by year, so I had some guesswork to do. Four years for a bachelor's degree and three more years of law school would have made him twenty-five, putting graduation in 1941, so that explained why he hadn't served in the war—he was probably in law school.

Two hours later, after scrolling through miles of microfilm, I finally found it—a State of Illinois license to practice law issued by the Superior Court on June 14, 1940.

Next stop, Clerk of the Circuit Court, where I asked for Elmer's criminal record and was told to come back in an hour.

Thinking that I should have asked Flora for the death certificate for Berghorn's wife when I was there, I walked back to the County Clerk's office and requested it. I went back a half an hour later and read what was on the sheet of paper Flora handed me.

Elmer's wife had died on December 25, 1942—Christmas Day...by suicide. I read farther down the page and gasped.

Next of Kin: Elmer Edward Berghorn, husband, 22
                Warren, son, 6 mos

She had taken her own life when their son was only six months old. I looked back at their marriage license. February 14, 1942. If my math was right, Hazel had been five months' pregnant when they married. During Elmer's emotional rant, he had said that something wasn't Hazel's fault, that it was his fault for forcing himself on her and that but for him she would still be here. His fault that she'd had the baby or his fault that she'd committed suicide? Or was it something else?

I walked back to the Clerk of the Circuit Court to see if they'd found Berghorn's criminal record. The man behind the counter escorted me to a back room where I was asked to wait for a few minutes. That surprised me. As a regular citizen, all I had was a right to know of the existence of specific court documents—I couldn't actually view them like law enforcement could.

The clerk returned with a small stack of papers.

"If you want copies, you'll have to come back. The duplicator is down."

"Okay."

This man did not know what he was doing. If for some reason he thought I was law enforcement, he should have asked for my ID. Dilemma time. It was a felony to impersonate a law enforcement officer. But I hadn't technically impersonated one. It wasn't my fault the guy was stupid.

This was something I had vowed never to do—intentionally break the law or even overstep boundaries.

I stared at the document on top before deciding what to do. A copy of Berghorn's law license with the word REVOKED stamped across it in red stared back at me.

I combed through the rest of the documents.

⁀ᴐ THIRTY-TWO ℗⁀

Happy Birthday to Me

So Berghorn was practicing law without a license. Now *that* was interesting. I wasn't sure yet what I was going to do with this information, especially since I hadn't gotten it on the up-and-up and there was more I needed to unearth in order to have the whole picture. As much as I wanted him to get what he deserved, I made a promise to myself that I would be patient and thorough and take no hasty actions.

Tymon's familiar knock interrupted my thoughts. I peeked out the side window to make sure it was him and opened the door.

"Ready?" he asked.

It was a twenty-minute drive to the Italian Village, one of Chicago's oldest restaurants and one of my favorites. I told him on the way that Berghorn had been convicted on eleven counts of tax evasion, embezzlement, money laundering, and bribery.

"How long was he in prison?" he asked.

"I still have to dig up that information."

I told him about Elmer's wife's suicide and the baby she left behind.

We reached the restaurant and parked, and I took his arm as we crossed the street. He gave my arm a little squeeze.

"So what now, Gracie?" he asked.

"I don't know. He's practicing law without a license by preying on people who don't speak English. How low is that?"

"Pretty low."

"That needs to stop."

We were seated right away and continued with our conversation.

"So he could go to prison for that as well?" he asked.

"I would think so. And for causing my parents' deaths…and for breaking into my home. Well, not my home, but…"

"But it should be." Tymon leaned in and lowered his voice. "I shouldn't be telling you this, but I'm going to anyway. Minnie wanted you to have that house after she died. She said she was going to will it to you."

"Tymon, I could kiss you."

He looked scared.

"Don't worry. I won't. Here's the deal." I told him about Minnie's draft will. "I think there might be more of a chance of the court legitimizing her will given your statement. I'll call her attorney tomorrow."

"You deserve to have it. After all, it's where you were born."

"I guess I don't have proof of that yet, but in my heart, I know it's true."

He lifted his water glass up to mine. "Happy birthday, Gracie."

Dinner with Tymon was enjoyable. After getting the subject of Berghorn behind us, we talked about Anna, my parents, our childhoods, his mother—all things family.

As we talked, I was reminded of something I had heard years ago: Family is not an important thing, it's everything. I had never thought much about that quote before meeting Minnie—her family had meant everything to her. And the same was true of Tymon to some extent—I could see it in his face when he talked about his mother. I had to add Elmer to that list—most of all Elmer.

When we got home, Tymon's three poker buddies were sitting on the patio drinking beer. They serenaded me with the worst rendition of "Happy Birthday" I had ever heard. It was delightful.

The next day I called Minnie's attorney—now also my attorney—to tell him that Minnie had told Tymon about wanting me to inherit the house. He said if Tymon came in to make a statement, he would amend it to the petition.

"I have some other news for you," he told me. "I have a court date for you to claim your parents' safe deposit box. September 10."

"September 10? Why so far out?"

"That's a pretty normal backlog for circuit court."

"Okay. I'll try to be patient."

Two and a half months off. I figured a lot could happen in two and a half months.

* * *

Before I could decide what to do about my newfound knowledge of Berghorn's shady business practices, I had to make sure I had all the information required to do it right. I had read too many case studies in which someone had gotten off scot-free due to sloppy or insufficient investigative work, and that was not going to be me.

I was aware of four state prisons in Illinois: Joliet, Stateville, Pontiac, and Menard. The first three were relatively close to each other and not that far from Chicago. Menard was much farther, in the southern part of the state. I called the closest three and was told the same thing: prison records were open to the public but only if you came in person. Stateville and Joliet prisons were near each other, both about an hour's drive from Chicago. Pontiac was an hour farther south. And Menard was at least another five hours beyond that. I asked Tymon if he would like to join me on a trip to Joliet, Stateville, and Pontiac prisons, hoping I would find what I was seeking in one of them and not have to travel all the way to Menard. He said yes and offered to drive.

Stateville Prison in Crest Hill was first on our list. I had heard a lot about this maximum security prison—a fifteen-building compound situated on several hundred acres.

On the drive, Tymon told me about a time when he thought he had seen Anna a year after she died.

"Almost got myself arrested. I was doing some extensive remodeling work in a house on Kinzie Street because one of the kids had left the bathtub water running and flooded the place. What a mess."

"What section of Kinzie, do you remember?" Our house on Ferdinand was just a block north of Kinzie, but Kinzie was a long street that ran from one side of the city to the other.

"All I remember is there were a mess of railroad tracks across the street. Why do you ask?"

"Just curious."

"Anyway, I was going there every day for weeks when one morning I saw this woman pushing a baby carriage. I could have sworn it was Anna. There was traffic, so I couldn't stop to look at her more closely. I drove around the block, but by the time I reached the spot where I had seen her, she had disappeared."

"That must have been upsetting."

"You got that right. In my head, I knew it couldn't have been her, but my heart wasn't listening to my brain at the time, and I kept driving around that area looking for her like a crazy person. The next thing I know, a police car is behind me with its flashing lights on. Apparently, someone had called them to say there was a suspicious man in a truck combing the neighborhood."

"Oh, dear. So how did you explain to the police what you were doing?"

"I told him the truth—that I thought I saw someone I knew and was just trying to find her. He told me if I didn't leave the neighborhood, I'd be arrested for prowling."

"I wonder if it was the woman with the baby carriage who called the police."

"I don't know, but every day after that, I looked for her on my way to and from that house on Kinzie."

"You never saw her again?"

"No. I never saw her again."

Driving up to the prison was intimidating—if the thirty-foot concrete wall surrounding it didn't remind you of the type of people who were confined within, the numerous guard towers looming over the wall did.

At the main entrance, we showed our IDs and explained the nature of our business. We signed in and then were escorted to the administration building. A guard took us to a small windowless room with a table and four chairs. We sat in silence until an older matronly woman came in and asked us to write down the name of the person who was of interest to us and for what years.

I wrote down ELMER EDWARD BERGHORN, 1944 TO 1958.

The woman glared at me like I had just asked her for a piece of the moon.

"It's not like we're the FBI with those fancy computers, you know."

"I'm sorry if it's an inconvenience, but I am told they *are* public records, so..."

She left in a huff.

"What? Did I give her too many years to look up?" I whispered.

"Probably. I wonder if they still do malaria experiments on the inmates here," Tymon whispered back.

"They really did that? I thought those were just rumors."

"No, I think it's true. The inmates would volunteer in hopes of a shortened sentence."

I got the chills. "It's creepy in here."

Miss Sourpuss finally returned forty-five minutes later and handed me back the piece of paper. "No one here by that name for any of those years. I'll show you out."

"Would it be possible to see inside one of the round inmate houses? Peek through a window or something?" I asked.

She gave me a blank stare.

"It's just that I've heard they're pretty unique, and we've come such a long way..."

"This isn't a tourist attraction. We don't give guided tours."

"I thought maybe just a—"

"Follow me," she mumbled.

We walked down a short hallway to a waiting room. On the walls were photographs of the interior of some of the buildings that housed the inmates.

"This is as close as you're gonna get. They're called roundhouses, by the way."

Hundreds of cells, four stories high, lined the walls inside each of the roundhouses. In the center of the floor was a three-story watchtower where someone inside had a clear view inside all the cells. It was impressive.

"Seen enough?" she asked.

"Yes, thank you."

She directed us from behind until we got back to the guardhouse, where we picked up our IDs and signed out.

"Nice place to visit, but I wouldn't want to live there," Tymon said with a smirk.

Joliet Correctional Center was a much older prison and not at all like Stateville— no concrete wall surrounding it and just one building on a much smaller piece of property. An armed guard greeted us inside the main door. We went through the same drill and were ushered into a waiting room.

After waiting a full hour, the young man came back with the piece of paper I had given him with Berghorn's name and possible years as an inmate. On it he had written JULY 5, 1943 TO FEBRUARY 2, 1958.

We were led back to the reception area where we picked up our IDs, signed out, and exited the building.

I skipped down the walk leading to the parking lot. I could hear Tymon behind me laughing.

Elmer Edward Berghorn had spent fourteen-plus years in prison for tax evasion, embezzlement, money laundering, and bribery. Looked to me like the Joliet Correctional Center deserved a failing grade in rehabilitation.

∽ THIRTY-THREE ∾

The No. 54 Bus

The first thing I did when I got home from our prison road trip was add some dates to my timeline to make sure everything fit.

Nov 10, 1939	Anna buys the boardinghouse
Jun 14, 1940	Berghorn gets his law license
Jan 4, 1942	Fern is born
Feb 14, 1942	Berghorn marries Hazel Osgood
June, 1942	Berghorn's son Warren is born
Jun 28, 1942	I am born
Jan 23, 1943	Anna is murdered
Jan 24, 1943	Al leaves the boardinghouse
May 29, 1943	Minnie buys the boardinghouse
May/Jun, 1943	Henry and Elmer plot to rob O'Gowan
Jun 6, 1943	O'Gowan dies
June 6, 1943	Henry leaves the boardinghouse
Jul 5, 1943	Berghorn goes to prison
Feb 2, 1958	Berghorn gets out of prison
Mar 18, 1960	~~My parents die~~ Elmer kills my parents!
Aug 10, 1964	I start working out of Elmer's office

One possible scenario I envisioned was that Berghorn had been desperate for money after his son was born with a condition that was expensive to treat, so he embezzled money and didn't pay his taxes. If he went to prison in July of 1943, that meant the Feds had probably been close to nailing him in the preceding months, and Berghorn knew it. That must have been when he got desperate enough to plan to rob O'Gowan.

I struggled with the ambivalence I felt toward Elmer—his doing bad things for a good reason. I couldn't condone any of his wrongdoings, but I understood why he did them. Not only did I understand why, but I admired him for it. Somewhere along the line, he must have lost sight of the consequences of his actions.

I felt a moral obligation to turn him in for practicing law without a license, and I had all the information I needed to report him to the State's Attorney's office. But with most of his clients having been illegal immigrants with little to no rights, the consequences of his actions would likely have been greatly diminished. And I kept thinking about his son, who was better off with Elmer home to care for him than behind bars. My finger was on the trigger, but I was reluctant to squeeze it.

There were obstacles to consider with respect to getting him on other things. It would have been nice if Elmer's fingerprints had been all over that photo he'd crumpled up and left behind when he broke into Minnie's house. And as for my parents, so much time had passed, and the only strong evidence against him would be testimony from Henry—and how likely was he to make a statement against his own cousin?

I wasn't sure what to do, and it wasn't something I felt comfortable discussing with anyone else. My mind kept drifting to a place where I didn't want it to go— doing something underhanded to make sure Elmer paid for what he'd done. Had I been certain of not getting caught, I might have given in to that temptation.

* * *

When Tymon came down to steal some coffee, I told him I was going to stake out the Baird & Warner real estate office for a couple of hours a day until I spotted Essie. It had been over three weeks since Essie had disappeared, and I was afraid if I let any more time pass, I'd never find her. He didn't like the idea.

"I thought you said she doesn't work there anymore."

"Apparently, she doesn't work at that location, but she could still work for them, and she still has old clients."

"That's a long shot don't you think?"

"Maybe."

"And you'll be a sitting duck."

"For who?"

"Berghorn."

"I think he's lost interest in me. As far as he knows, O'Gowan's money is long gone."

"And what if he's after more than just the money?"

"Like what?"

"Wasn't it you who decided there may be a secret room in the basement of your old house? And then when he busted in here that day and demanded you give him something, he didn't say what, did he?"

"It was the money."

"Maybe it wasn't the money. Maybe it was the combination to the safe he found in that room in the basement."

"Which I have."

"You have what?"

"The combination to the safe."

"Then that settles it. You're not going."

"And I see that neither are you." I wanted to take back those words.

"I've been here this long..."

"What about the other guys?" They'd been there for three weeks. "I think it's okay if we relieve them from their duty, don't you?"

"C'mon. The poker games are great."

He made me smile.

"Tell you what. I'll do the daily stakeouts with you. We'll bring sandwiches and eat lunch in the car every day while we watch the place."

"A daily picnic."

"Something like that. How will you know it's her by the way? You've never even seen her, have you?"

"No, but Fern has, and she's described her for me. And she doesn't drive, so that's another factor for narrowing it down."

"Start tomorrow? Pick you up at eleven?"

"Okay."

When Tymon left, for some reason I was close to tears.

As I sat there, I began to realize that maybe I did know why. I was twenty-three years old. I had no permanent place to live. No job. No real identity. There was an ex-con out there who might think I had something he wanted, and I had close to $125,000 in a safe deposit box and another $125,000 hidden somewhere in the house that was clearly not mine.

I had myself a good cry before tackling the laundry that had been piling up for three weeks and then looked forward to all that ironing.

* * *

Tymon and I were on our first stakeout together. We parked in a bank parking lot across from the Baird & Warner office in full view of their front door and the two nearest bus stops. Other than that, the landscape that held us captive was completely uninteresting.

I had packed a sandwich and bag of chips for each of us.

"What does she look like?" he asked.

"According to Fern, she's quite plain—medium brown hair, wears modest clothes, sensible shoes, no makeup. But you must have seen her back in the day if she and Anna were friends."

"People change. Look at me. I used to have a full head of dark, wavy hair."

"A real Valentino then?"

"I could turn a head or two back then. Anyway…you have a receipt for this safe, and it's dated when?"

"It was in either late 1939 or early 1940."

"And the date on the basement build-out receipt?"

"A few months after Anna was killed. May, I think. May of 1943."

"And when did Minnie buy the place?"

"Close to Memorial Day, 1943. What are you thinking?"

"I told you before there could have been a safe in Anna's hidden room in the basement, and the timing would have been right that Anna bought it right after she bought the house. Your parents had the room in their basement built shortly after Anna died, and they could have moved the safe in there."

"That makes my parents look like criminals."

"On second thought, a floor safe couldn't be easily maneuvered up and down a ladder. Those things are heavy."

"How heavy?"

"I'm thinking since it was called a floor safe on the receipt, it's got to be bigger than one you would set on a shelf or something. So it's going to weigh at least a couple hundred pounds."

"Could they have hoisted it up and down with a rope?"

"I suppose if they had the right equipment, but we're talking a big deal here. That wouldn't be something you could do without someone noticing."

"Someone like Henry?"

"Someone like Henry." He glanced at his watch. "It's one-thirty, Gracie."

"Okay. Let's call it a day."

* * *

Tymon and I were back in the Wells Fargo Bank parking lot at midday for the fifth day in a row, and there had been no sign of Essie. If the bank had had better security, they would have questioned what we were doing there every day by now.

On the positive side, the stakeouts had given us the chance to talk about every subject imaginable, and the more I got to know Tymon, the more I liked him. It had taken me a while, but now I was convinced he was just an all-around good guy, and it seemed such a shame he had been alone all his life.

On the drive back home, Tymon surprised me with his question.

"Do you trust me, Gracie?"

"Well, we're living in the same house. You know more about me than anyone else on this earth. You have access to every room in the house. Yes, I think I can say I trust you."

"Enough to tell me where you keep the combination to the safe without really telling me?"

What was he up to? We weren't sure if there even was a safe, let alone where it was.

"Why?"

"Why what?"

"Why would I do that?"

"Because I asked you to."

* * *

Early the next Saturday morning, not without hesitation, I put the combination to the safe in the cookie jar. When Tymon came down for his usual morning coffee, I told him to help himself to a cookie. He thanked me and left.

I was glad it was the weekend and that I had a break from our midday stakeouts. They took a big bite out of the day—three hours counting driving time. Still, I wanted to continue for another week, and Tymon hadn't shown any reluctance, so that was going to be my plan.

The phone rang. I couldn't imagine who would be calling so early—it was barely seven o'clock.

"Hello?"

It was Fern. She'd had an Essie sighting.

"I was coming into church after stupidly agreeing to manage a Saturday daycare room full of two- and three-year-olds when I saw her stepping onto a 54 bus."

"Did you call after her?"

"She was too far away."

"Are you sure it was her?"

"I know it was her. I recognized the dress she was wearing."

"How long ago was this?"

"Not more than ten minutes ago. I came in here hoping to run into someone who could give me some information, like why she was here, but—wouldn't you know it—no one is around right now."

"You think she was in the church?"

"There are only two reasons you'd be at that bus stop on a Saturday: to come to this church or to come to the off-track betting parlor next door, and I'm quite sure she wasn't betting on horses."

"Fern, I gotta go. I have a hunch."

"Okay."

"What color dress was she wearing?"

"Beige with a wide black belt and black epaulets."

"See ya!"

I jumped in my car before Tymon could catch me and headed for the Baird & Warner office, thinking she might go there next. I parked in our usual surveillance spot in the bank parking lot and waited. No sign of Essie.

After fifteen minutes of tapping my fingernails on the dashboard, I drove to Essie's church and waited for a 54 bus to come by. When it did, I followed it so that I was familiar with the route. When the northbound bus turned east on Montrose, I figured that must have been the end of the line and it was going to turn around. According to the odometer, it had been four miles between the church where Essie had boarded the bus and the end of the line—four miles and thirteen stops.

I decided that little adventure had been a complete waste of my time. With that long of a route and that many stops, she could have gone anywhere. The only interesting thing was the route ended at Montrose Avenue, which was 4400 north. Minnie's house was on Belle Plaine Avenue, which was 4100 north. Ha! She could have walked to my place from there.

Shit!

I drove as fast as traffic allowed, which was not fast enough. Why did all the slowpokes have to pick right now to be on the road? The giant maroon Buick in front of me was going slow enough to be in a funeral procession. Must have been an old man driving it. They get that way.

When I finally got home and drove down the driveway, I saw Tymon standing on the patio.

"She was here, wasn't she?" I asked him after I jumped out of my car.

He nodded.

"How much did I miss her by?"

He glanced down at his watch. "Half hour."

"Damn it!"

I ran back to my car.

"Where are you going?"

"To see if I can catch her before she gets on the bus."

"Wait!"

I ignored his plea and barreled out of the driveway, almost sideswiping a parked car. It was five blocks to Cicero Avenue where she would get back on the bus, if that was even the bus she would take to wherever she was going. I kept my eyes peeled for her beige and black dress, but I didn't see her anywhere. A ride around the neighborhood proved to be fruitless.

Tymon was still on the patio when I returned.

"Sit down," he said pointing to one of the patio chairs. "I'll tell you what happened."

I plopped down next to him. "Lay it on me."

"I was sitting right here when she walked up the drive, and as soon as she got within twenty feet or so, she must have recognized me, and she turned right around and ran off. I called out her name not knowing for sure it was even her. I yelled, 'Please come back! It's okay!' But she was halfway down the block by the time I got to the sidewalk. I would have gone after her, but—"

"No, you did the right thing. You'd have scared her even more if you'd gone after her."

"I'm so sorry, Gracie. I feel just awful that I—"

"Don't feel bad. It wasn't your fault. If I hadn't rushed off like I did, I would have been here when she came and that wouldn't have happened. I'm surprised she recognized you after all this time."

"I am too, especially since during the three or so years I worked here, I saw her only occasionally. Why do you think she bolted like that?"

"I'm thinking she was expecting to see me here, and when she saw you, of all people, she probably couldn't rationalize fast enough why you would be here, and she panicked."

"I'm sorry."

"You'll never guess where I just was."

"Where?"

"Fern called to tell me she just saw Essie get on a 54 bus outside of the church where Essie used to go. I thought knowing that bus route could be helpful in finding out where she is staying, so I jumped in my car to where she got on the bus and followed it."

"And the reason she was on that bus was to come here."

I hoped I didn't look as foolish as I felt right then.

THIRTY-FOUR

The Floor Safe

I called Fern to tell her about the No. 54 bus escapade.

"It would be funny if it wasn't so unfortunate. I wonder if she's been scared off for good," she said.

"God, I hope not. I could just kick myself. Now, even if I find out where she lives, I can't approach her, at least not so soon after this happened. And the more time goes by, the less likely it is I'll be able to find her. I really know how to screw things up!"

"Aw, don't be so hard on yourself. You know, I've been thinking about this. When she and I had dinner that day, and she told me she had this secret that she was thinking of talking to Reverend Orman about, maybe that's what she was doing before she got on that 54 bus. And maybe it was he who recommended she speak directly with you."

"Makes sense, and I hope you're right, because if you are, she may be back."

"What's next?" she asked.

"I don't know. Essie is the only one I know with the answers."

"No, she's not. If I'm right, Reverend Orman has them too."

"He's not going to tell anyone, least of all me."

"Maybe he would if he felt pressured to do so."

"What are you suggesting, that we beat it out of him?"

"No. Maybe just rough him up a little."

"You're sick, Fern."

"I've been called worse."

* * *

Raymond Webb called me to say he had a hearing date for the validation of Minnie's draft will—August 2. Three weeks away. He felt good about it, especially given

Tymon's statement.

When I got off the phone, I started setting the table for dinner—Tymon was bringing Chinese food. It had surprised me earlier when he'd said he had a few errands to run and would be back in a couple of hours. He hadn't left me alone for that long since moving in, which I had to admit didn't bother me anymore.

Tymon's familiar rap on the back door made me smile. There were certain things I'd miss when he was gone.

He had a wide grin on his face.

"What's going on?" I asked.

"Nothing," he said unconvincingly, as he entered the kitchen with a large bag.

I finished setting the table while he unloaded the food, which we didn't bother taking out of the white cardboard containers.

"There is no safe," he said before either one of us took a bite.

"What?"

"There is a room in Berghorn's basement, very similar to the one here, but it's empty."

"I know you don't want me to know how you know this, but can you at least tell me that everything went okay...without incident."

"He'll never know anyone was there. Someone had already hacked through the cement wall to get in though."

"Someone?"

"Not us. Someone before us."

"Well, I hope it was Berghorn. And when he finished hacking down the wall, I hope he looked up to find the trapdoor that he could have used to get in. Serve him right. Anyway, the room was empty?"

"Completely."

"But who knows what Berghorn could have removed from it."

"Right. I'm sure your parents didn't build it for nothing."

"I'm getting tired of all these dead ends."

"Gracie?"

"Hmm?"

"At some point, are you going to let go so you can get on with your life?"

"And give up?"

"Letting go doesn't have to mean giving up."

"I suppose."

"And I realize everyone's different, but sometimes maybe it's better not to search too hard for it."

"Why?"

"You could get hurt in the process, or worse yet, find something that makes the situation even more troublesome."

"I guess it's a matter of whether or not it's worth the risk," I added.

"Exactly."

"Tymon?"

"Yes."

"It's worth the risk for me."

* * *

A floor safe couldn't just disappear, I thought, as I lay wide awake several hours before daybreak. Like Tymon had said, since the receipt described it as a floor safe, it had to have been heavy and bulky. He said he remembered seeing something covered with a tarp in Anna's hidden basement room that could have been a safe—the size of a small dresser. A floor safe would obviously—.

"You idiot!" I said aloud.

It was three A.M., but I didn't care. I threw on a robe, ran up the stairs to Tymon's room, and pounded on the door.

The door swung open, and there stood Tymon, wearing nothing but his boxer shorts, his hair a tousled mess.

"What's wrong?"

"It doesn't sit *on* the floor. It sits *in* the floor."

"Huh?"

"It's a floor safe! A safe that's built into the floor...flush with the floor so you could throw a rug over it or a piece of furniture, and no one would ever know it's there."

He looked dazed.

"Okay," he said unenthusiastically.

"I'm sorry I woke you. I got excited. We can continue this conversation in the morning."

"Well, I'm up now," he said. "Let me get dressed. You make the coffee."

He wasn't as excited as I was, but that was okay. I charged down the stairs, threw on some clothes, and went to the kitchen. While I made a pot of coffee, which Minnie had eventually taught me how to do correctly, I fantasized about finding the safe and uncovering all sorts of missing pieces to the incomplete puzzle that was my life. This could be a red-letter day.

Tymon used the inside staircase to enter my space. I supposed he figured that since I had rousted him out of bed he had the right to do that. And he did.

"I'm really sorry, Tymon. Please don't be mad at me."

"I don't think I could ever get mad at you, Gracie, not for real. Just give me a cup of coffee."

We sat down at the kitchen table.

"So what's this about the floor safe?"

"The floor safe Anna bought isn't one that sits *on* the floor. It's one that gets implanted *into* the floor. That would make a lot more sense than a big clumsy one that would be next to impossible to get down a ladder into that basement room, doesn't it?"

"Have to agree with you there. So let me guess. We're going to search every inch of floor for the safe."

I flashed him a wide smile.

"That's what I thought. But what makes you think it's still here?"

"Because it was hidden, and whoever cleaned out this place after Anna died didn't know it was there. Could be."

"We'll soon find out, won't we?"

"Do you want me to make you some breakfast before we start?"

"That would be wonderful."

When Tymon finished his breakfast, we started in the living room, moving each piece of furniture, peeling back the area rug, and looking underneath it for suspicious cracks in the hardwood floor. We found nothing in the living room, foyer, or dining room.

Minnie's bedroom also had hardwood floors, and like the living room, there was a large area rug covering ninety percent of it. The trapdoor to the basement room was under the bed. A thin leather strap affixed to it served as the means to open it. And several feet from it was a thin outline, about a foot square, about the right size for a floor safe.

I looked at Tymon.

"I'll get something to pry it open," he said.

He returned in a few minutes and slipped a putty knife into one of the cracks. The suspense caused me to stop breathing until he lifted the thin ply of wood out of its cradle and placed it to the side. Underneath was a sheet of tar paper. Tymon lifted up the tar paper to reveal a combination lock, situated in the middle of what appeared to be the top of a metal box.

I raced to my dresser drawer and pulled out the scrap of paper that had the combination written on it.

L4, R29, L60.

I dialed the numbers, and when I heard a click, I let out a high-pitched yelp. I pulled up on the recessed handle and carefully lifted open the lid to the box. The suspense was invigorating but at the same time seemed to settle my nerves.

∽ THIRTY-FIVE ∾

Open Floodgates!

The safe was empty.

"If Anna had actually used this safe, why was it empty? No one would have even known it was here."

Tymon shook his head.

"I wonder if Al knew about it."

"Maybe. I wish we knew who he was. You don't remember anything more about him other than what you've already told me?"

"No."

"When Henry called here and believed I was Minnie and started to spill his guts, he said something about the loverboy across the hall having something to do with Anna's murder."

"Didn't seem like that kind of person."

"People snap sometimes."

"I suppose."

"And Henry's nose was in everybody's business."

"I know, but—"

"And we know he left right after she died. Why was that?"

"I still don't think he had anything to do with it."

"You look tired."

"I am. After we put this room back together, I think I'll take a short nap."

It was approaching five A.M., but it seemed much later. Tymon went back upstairs. I settled myself in the living room to think.

* * *

The phone woke me up. I must have dozed off in the living room chair—not surprising since I had gotten up at three in the morning. I glanced at the mantle clock—half past nine.

It was Naomi.

"Are you going to be home later?" she asked. "I'd like to stop over after work, if that's okay."

"Sure. I'm—"

"No, I'm sorry you must have the wrong number. Goodbye."

She hung up. Berghorn must have stepped out of his office.

I knew Naomi well enough to know she wasn't coming over to chitchat. Something was going on.

I had nothing better to do, so I figured I'd spend some time at City Hall to see what I could find out about Bonnie and Walter Thomas, the names written on the backs of the photographs we had found in Minnie's attic. As soon as Tymon came down, I told him where I was going.

I drove to the County Assessor's office where they kept a paper trail of real estate ownerships. I didn't have good contacts there, so I had to wait in line. An hour later, I had confirmation that Bonnie and Walter Thomas were the first owners of the house and that it had been built in 1910. Nothing earth-shattering, but at least that put the Thomas name to rest.

* * *

I could tell Naomi was upset.

"Let's sit in the living room," I suggested. "Can I get you something to drink? Wine, something stronger?"

"No. If I have a drink, I'll get just that more agitated."

"Ice water?"

"Thanks. It's so god-awful hot today."

She wasted no time or words as soon as I returned with her beverage.

"Elmer Berghorn is scum. No he's lower than scum. Do you know what he's doing right now?"

I shook my head.

"Two people, two illegal immigrants without driver's licenses, strangers to each other, get into a car accident, and one is seriously injured. Each comes separately to Mr. Berghorn for advice, and he accepts both cases! Now I know a little bit about conflict of interest, and I know he can't do that."

"Right. There are rules of conduct that prohibit that."

"And he's got me doing the billing. These guys are probably so scared, they keep paying his bills. And they don't have that kind of money. I know they don't. He's shameless!"

"I'll tell you what's even more despicable, Naomi. He doesn't even have a license to practice law."

"What?!"

"I found out recently it was revoked twenty years ago."

"Well, that explains a few things. I've got to get out of there. What a horrible man."

"Do you think you could stick it out just a little longer to give me time to have him caught by the right people?"

"How long would that take?"

"Not long, I hope. And, Naomi, when it's over, if you need anything to tide you over in between jobs, I can help you with that."

"Just tell me what I have to do."

Learning Berghorn's latest escapade incited me to trigger the opening of the floodgates that would hopefully sweep him into a jail cell where he belonged.

THIRTY-SIX

The Trunk

I had sufficient evidence against Berghorn to file a complaint with the Illinois State Bar Association—one compelling enough in my mind to solidly implicate him. The big question was whether the people with the power to put him away agreed with that premise.

I was careful not to implicate Naomi in the gathering of evidence or present any information that could be construed as illegally seized or else I'd be incriminating myself. It was a delicate balancing act. When I finished entering the information on the appropriate complaint form, I drove to the ISBS's regional office near City Hall and, ignoring my stomach spasms, hand-delivered it.

I didn't feel good doing this. The investigation would likely result in Elmer being fined, made to reimburse people for his fees and any damages, and possibly incarcerated. The fact that he had many illegal immigrants for clients—people with so few rights—was even more troubling. What would happen to them? And it pained me that the bar association's investigation would have nothing to do with his causing my parents' deaths.

I hoped I had done the right thing.

The next morning, Tymon agreed to join me in the attic to see if we could get the trunk open without breaking it. If we couldn't, then I'd have to wait to see if I legally inherited the house, in which case I figured the trunk would be my property and I could break into it if I wanted.

It was the middle of July, and each day the local weathermen stated how many days in a row we'd had record heat. The heat would have had less effect on everyone if they hadn't kept reminding us of it. I was grateful that Tymon had installed a fan in one of the front windows—the air it pulled through the house made it somewhat bearable. Other people were more creative—Naomi had shared with me that she put her underwear in the freezer to keep cool.

Tymon was still living with me, though his buddies had moved out. The other guys came over just often enough to give the appearance of constant activity. This arrangement suited me fine.

With all that had been going on in my life since Minnie had died, I hadn't given much thought to her neighbors, and none had approached me either. Now with a succession of men coming and going all the time, I suspected there was a lot of tongue-wagging going on behind my back. Oh, well.

Tymon arrived carrying his long extension ladder and a rubber strip, the same rubber strip I should have used to avoid that nasty fall back in April. We both smiled, and we both knew why.

"Here, let me carry that," I told him. "Where would I buy one of these, by the way?"

"I'll give you one for Christmas," he said with a straight face.

Tymon was tall enough to stand on a chair and open the trapdoor to the ceiling. He pushed it to the side and situated the ladder and rubber strip, and we climbed up. It had to be 100 degrees in that attic.

He shined light on the trunk with his flashlight.

"I believe they call this a steamer trunk," he explained.

"What's a steamer trunk?"

"Any trunk with a flat top. They were called that back when people used them for luggage on steam-powered ships and trains. The flat tops made them stackable."

"How do you know so much about everything, Tymon?"

"I've been around the block a few times, Gracie. I see and hear things."

He aimed the light on the lock. Underneath it were the initials ISR.

"I didn't notice that before," I said.

He shined the light on the top of the trunk.

"I'll bet you didn't notice this before either," he said, pointing to a key sitting atop the trunk.

"You've got to be kidding me!" I picked up the key, put it in the lock, and turned it. The clasp popped open.

We looked at each other in disbelief, and when we'd stopped laughing, Tymon tried to nudge the trunk with his foot.

"There's something heavy in there."

"I'm afraid to lift the lid."

"Want me to open it?" he asked.

"Yeah, you do it. I'm going to get ready to run."

He grinned. "Why? Whatever is in there is dead by now."

"Cut that out. This is creepy enough."

He lifted the lid and exposed a tray sitting on top. Inside the tray were three light-colored bags tied off with thick string.

Tymon lifted one of the bags out of the tray. It jingled.

"This weighs a ton."

"Open it."

He took a Swiss Army knife out of his pocket and cut the string. When he did, coins came spilling out. Tymon shined the flashlight on one of them. At its center was an image of a woman with outstretched arms and wings. On the left was engraved 50 PESOS. On the right, 37.5 GR ORO PURO. And on the bottom, "1821" and "1947."

"Why the two dates?" I asked.

"I'm not sure. Maybe 1821 is some important date in Mexican history?"

"Could be."

"It says it's 37.5 grams of pure gold," he said. He poked the other two bags, which made the same jingly sound. "Three bags of them."

I had two letters to Anna from Nacho, who I presumed was her uncle in Mexico. Naomi had told me Nacho was a nickname for Ignacio, which would fit the first initial of the monogram on the trunk. And the Mexican coins made sense in terms of where he had lived.

"How much is 37.5 grams of gold worth, do you think?" I asked.

"An ounce is worth thirty-some dollars."

"How many grams are in an ounce?"

"I have no idea, but let's say each coin is an ounce."

"And would you say there are at least 250 coins in each bag?" I asked.

"Probably."

I did the rough math in my head. "That's at least $7,500 a bag."

"Times three bags."

"Let's see what's underneath."

His brow dripping with perspiration, Tymon lifted the heavy bags out of the tray.

Inside the trunk were numerous smallish items wrapped in brown cloth. I picked one up and tore off the cloth to find a layer of foam padding. Someone had gone to a lot of trouble to protect whatever was inside. I removed the padding and revealed a jade figurine—a beautifully carved salamander.

"As much as I want to see what all is in there, I can't take much more of this heat," he said.

"Feel up to carrying them downstairs?"

We dragged the trunk over to the hatch door. Tymon went halfway down the ladder, and one by one I handed him the items. When we were done, the floor of the room that used to be O'Gowan's was a sea of brown lumps.

"Before we unwrap these, let me get us some drinks."

Tymon and I spent the next few hours unwrapping a variety of unusual-looking figurines, clay masks, and jewelry—many of them quite beautiful and all appearing to be Mexican. And then we counted the coins, all 1,123 of them.

"Are you thinking what I'm thinking?" I asked him.

"I have no idea what you're thinking." He handed me an envelope.

"What's this?"

"It was in one of the coin bags."

The sealed envelope had Anna's name written on it.

"I can't open this."

"Why not?"

"It's not mine."

"The owner can't open it."

"I don't feel right opening it."

"You could wait to see if you inherit the house, and then it would be legally yours. But I would say it's yours anyway. She was your mother."

"I don't know that for sure."

He smiled. "*I* do."

THIRTY-SEVEN

Anna's Letters

Tymon and I placed the items from the trunk into three large garbage bags and stashed them in the basement until I could figure out what to do with them. I put the letter to Anna in my nightstand drawer.

The cache of what appeared to be valuable art was a reminder of the photographs I'd taken of the paintings we'd found in the attic earlier. I'd never had the film developed, so I put that on my mental list of errands for the afternoon.

I puttered around the house until the sudden rain shower let up and then headed for Six Corners where I dropped off the film and stopped at the bank to withdraw money from my savings account.

Something compelled me to drive by Berghorn's office on my way home. I pulled into a parking space across the street and stared at the front door. The more I thought about how nice he'd been in the beginning—how he'd helped me buy a car and move into the apartment upstairs and arranged for Danny to accompany me to places that were too dangerous for me to go alone—the more contempt I had for the man.

Naomi had told me that my half of the office remained vacant. I wasn't surprised—everyone else was probably too smart to be taken in by him. I wondered if he periodically had a good laugh over what he had pulled on me.

I was just about ready to pull out of the parking space when I heard the gradual increasing sound of a siren. I waited for it to pass, but it didn't. Instead, a couple of unmarked police cars with blue lights flashing from their dashboards pulled up in front of Berghorn's office. Two men in dark suits jumped out of the first car and rushed in through the front door. The two remaining men stood outside of their car and appeared to be having a casual conversation.

I put my car in park and turned off the ignition, not believing my good fortune to be able to witness first-hand what I hoped was Berghorn's arrest.

Five minutes later, Berghorn emerged with his hands behind his back, escorted by the two men. The perspiration glistening on his muscle-tight face was visible from clear across the street. I didn't want him to see me, so I started to slouch down in my seat. Too late—he looked directly at me. He mouthed something I couldn't discern, but I didn't have to—the evil look he gave me spoke for itself.

The police car with Berghorn in it left. I waited another fifteen minutes until the other two officers emerged from his office, each one carrying a box of what I presumed was evidence. As soon as they pulled out, I walked across the street and through the front door to Naomi's desk.

"Naomi?" I called out.

Naomi came around the corner smiling.

"You knew it was going to come down this afternoon?" she asked.

"No! That's the beauty of it. I just decided to drive by and, as luck would have it, I saw the whole thing. I haven't heard one word from the Bar Association."

"Well, I have. I had to go downtown and answer a bunch of questions, not once, but twice." Her face lit up. "You should have seen the look on his face when those agents came storming in here. First, surprise. And then, complete horror. It was all I could do to keep a straight face."

"What did they say to him?"

She picked up a scrap of paper from her desk and, straining to deepen her voice, pretended to read from it. "You're under arrest for practicing law without a license, insurance fraud, forgery, mail fraud, and driving on an expired driver's license."

She switched up her voice to sound pathetic. "But Officer, there must be some mistake."

Then she went back to the deep voice. "There's no mistake, Berghorner."

In her own voice, she said, "Now that was funny, the way he mispronounced his name."

Back to the deep voice: "There's no mistake, Berghorner. You're coming with us."

"So what happens now?" I asked.

"I was instructed to stay here and wait for a federal investigator."

"Federal?"

"That's what he said."

"I better leave then. Will you be all right?"

"Yeah."

"Call me if you want to come over afterward. I'll be home."

"I will."

She gestured toward her desk drawer and then left the area.

I opened the drawer and removed a two-page list of Berghorn's clients, tucked it inside my blouse, and left.

On the drive home, it hit me that things couldn't have worked out any better: he'd be going back to prison where he belonged, and I wasn't feeling the least bit guilty for having had something to do with it. I turned up the volume on "I Can't Get No Satisfaction" by the Rolling Stones. Not me. I had just gotten plenty of satisfaction.

After I got home, I drafted a script I would use to call Berghorn's clients, telling them that Berghorn was not a real lawyer and giving them the names and phone numbers for two legitimate ones. Naomi had agreed to be with me when I actually called them in case they needed an interpreter.

It had been a tiring day, but I had to make another attempt at solving the Midnighter case—it had been almost five months since Flora had engaged my services. The thefts had continued, and I had no leads. Most recently, a Zippy the Chimp hand puppet had been taken from the backyard of a family who now had a very distraught three-year-old on their hands. Knowing I would be out very late, I took a two-hour nap first and then drove to that neighborhood.

I hadn't been parked for longer than ten minutes when some movement in the front yard two houses down caught my eye. I sat in silence in the darkness and observed someone or something sauntering across the street. I turned on my headlights to find the same stumpy-tailed cat I had seen on previous stakeouts. When it sensed the light, it dropped something and ran.

I got out of my car and walked to the place where the cat had dropped the item. It was a fully cooked turkey leg.

Since it was too late to knock on Flora's door and tell her what I had observed, I drove home to catch a few hours of sleep before work the next day.

* * *

I called Flora first thing in the morning.

"I think I know who has been stealing things around the neighborhood," I told her.

"Who?"

"He's a large fellow, short brown hair, big green eyes, and a stump for a tail."

"Huh?"

"It's a cat, Flora."

"A cat?"

"That's what I think. Do you know a cat like that in your neighborhood?"

"No. But in the next block there's a cat lady—that's what we call her because nobody knows her name. We don't know how many cats she has, but we suspect it's quite a few." She gave me a description of the cat lady's house and approximate address so I could investigate further.

That afternoon, I drove to the cat lady's house to see if any of her cats fit the description of the turkey-leg bandit. Seeing nothing telltale in her yard, I knocked on her door.

The foul smell that wafted from within when the door opened overwhelmed me. An older woman, unkempt, with missing teeth and stubbled chin whiskers, asked me what I wanted. I explained the reason for my visit, and after I convinced her I wasn't with Animal Control nor interested in removing any cats from her premises, she admitted that she had a cat that fit the description of the bandit.

"He's been getting out lately, but I have no idea where he goes."

I told her about all the missing items from the neighborhood.

"Could be him. I don't know."

"Would it be possible to have a look around? See if any of the missing items are here?"

"Be my guest."

The house was in the same unkempt condition as the woman...maybe worse. Cats were everywhere—one on top of the refrigerator, several around the woman's feet, two going at it in the dining room, and a mom with kittens on a dining room chair. I glanced around as we walked through the house but didn't see any of the missing items.

"His name is Stumpy," she said as she led me toward the back of the house. "Never did know what happened to his tail. I saw him coming out of the shed out back the other morning. We can look in there if you want."

The shed she had referred to was missing a door and half the roof. We walked inside to a large stash of items piled in the corner—toys, clothing, linens, balloons, and right on top a pair of pink polka-dot panties.

"He's our thief, all right. Would you have a couple of bags I could put all this stuff in?"

While she was getting the bags, I pushed some of the items around with my foot only to find three dead mice at the bottom of the pile. I was grateful when the woman returned with a pair of gloves along with the bags.

"Can you try to keep Stumpy inside from now on?"

"I'll try."

* * *

The next day I arrived at circuit court early for the hearing of Minnie's will and waited for Raymond. When he arrived, he explained what to expect in the proceeding. He didn't think I would have to say anything—he'd do all the talking.

We were soon ushered into the courtroom where we waited for the judge.

I was more nervous than I ought to have been. I felt guilty inheriting the house, until I reminded myself that Berghorn had put down a thousand dollars in earnest money in an effort to buy it after she died. I felt I would have done anything to see that *that* didn't happen. I mused at what would happen to the thousand dollars—I doubted they would send it to him in prison.

The entire hearing lasted all of fifteen minutes. In the end, the judge admitted Minnie's draft will as her final will, which meant I was the beneficiary of her house and its contents.

After Raymond and I left the courtroom, I asked him something I had been curious about for some time—why he had told me about Minnie wanting me to have the house before her will had even been validated.

"Because one way or another, I was going to make sure you got that house."

"Why?"

"Grace, I watched that woman slowly transform from a young, vibrant wife and mother when she was married to Clarence to a miserable old coot after she lost her family. I tried to help her along the way, give her advice about how to get back on track. My wife did too. But she never took any of it. Then you came along, and I started to see the old Minnie reappear. You were going to inherit her house if it was the last thing I ever did for anyone."

"Sounds like you knew her personally."

"I didn't see any reason to tell you this before, but she was my sister-in-law. Clarence was my brother."

"I had no idea. I'm so sorry for your losses—a brother, a niece, and now Minnie. When did you learn of Minnie's death?"

"When you called me."

"I'm so sorry. Had I known about you, I would have—"

"You didn't know."

"But your last name is Webb."

He smiled. "I changed it after I passed the bar."

"Why?"

"Would you go to an attorney named Raymond Lawless?"

I had to laugh. "I guess not. Thanks for sharing that story about Minnie. It means a lot."

I thanked him for all his work, and he told me what he had to do next to get the deed transferred to me. I asked him if there were any exceptions to what was legally mine with respect to the contents of the house.

"Can you give me an example?" he asked.

"Like what if I found something in the house that I suspected belonged to someone else but I didn't know who?"

"Generally speaking, when you buy—or, in your case, inherit—a house, you inherit everything in it, even if it's hidden. But that doesn't mean someone else couldn't also have a claim to it, and then a court would have to decide who has the better claim."

"I see."

"Grace, I have to tell you about a rather odd stipulation in the will. I'm not sure if this is going to make any sense to you or not, but here goes." He pulled out a copy of the will and read an excerpt. "If Miss Lindroth decides to plant any bushes on the property, they can only be winterberry bushes, nothing else."

Now *that* made me laugh.

"You may have this copy," he said.

We parted ways, but before I headed for home, I skimmed over the will. Minnie had had a substantial amount of Chicago & North Western Railroad stock, which she left to a foundation that took care of families of railroad employees who had lost their lives on duty.

She had been a kind soul.

* * *

The next morning, I waited for Tymon to come down for coffee so I could tell him the news.

"So what is making you smile so big this early in the morning, Gracie?" he asked.

"You're standing in *my* kitchen, I'll have you know."

He reached out to shake my hand.

"Congratulations. You deserve this house."

"Thank you. I feel at home here."

"Have you given any thought to what you're going to do with it?"

"Do with it? I'm going to live here."

"I mean the upstairs. It's an odd layout even if you were to rent out the rooms."

I gave that a moment's thought. The income would be good, but living with boarders? I didn't relish the thought, especially given the peculiar make-up of the last body of boarders residing there.

"I'm not sure if I would do that."

"Maybe you'd want to convert it back to its original state then—a single-family home."

"Maybe. I haven't thought about it, to be truthful."

Tymon paused before saying, "I suppose I should be going now that Berghorn is out of the picture." His melancholy expression reminded me of a quote I'd heard: *Don't cry because it's over. Smile because it happened.* I knew I would miss him.

"I'm sure you want to get back home and into your normal routine again."

He didn't respond, didn't even seem to react.

"Can you stay a while...I mean, while I open that letter to Anna?" I asked.

"Sure."

I left to retrieve the letter from my bedroom, and when I returned, Tymon was gone. I waited a few minutes, and when he didn't return, I was at a loss as to what had just happened. This couldn't be the way he was leaving—without saying goodbye.

I felt just awful. Should I go after him, or allow him to do this his own way? But I didn't want our relationship to end like that. Then I realized that I didn't want it to end at all.

I heard a familiar knock at the back door and heaved a sigh of relief.

"It's open, Tymon."

He came in—it was obvious he'd been crying.

"What's wrong?"

He sat down at the kitchen table across from me.

"I'm sorry. You said 'letter to Anna,' and I lost it."

He held up a white envelope.

"I wrote this to her in July of 1942." He turned it around to let me see it was still sealed. "I never gave it to her."

He pushed it across the table toward me.

"You want me to read it?"

"I want you to have it. You were the reason I wrote it."

I stared into his eyes for an explanation but received none.

"I'm not following you."

"I told you I loved her."

I nodded.

"After you were born, I wanted more than anything to take care of the both of you. I fantasized about it every night when I went to bed, and I woke up every morning wondering if this would be the day I would get up enough nerve to give her the letter. Until it was too late.

"When it became clear to me that the police weren't going to try to find you, I looked for you on my own. Every time I walked by a mother pushing a stroller, I'd peek inside, wondering if maybe it was you. Later, I walked by schools during recess wondering if one of the little girls was you, hoping that was the case because that meant you were okay. I even contacted the FBI at one point. They said they would open an investigation, but I don't think they ever did. They said I wasn't giving them very much to go on. I bugged them until they finally said they would keep the case open, but for now there wasn't any more they could do."

He sat slumped in the chair, looking defeated as if this had all just happened.

"You asked me one time why I hadn't pursued a relationship with anyone after Anna was gone. Because I couldn't. She was the only woman I could think about."

He looked away from me for a moment, and when his eyes reunited with mine, I knew he was about to say something heartfelt.

"Gracie, the minute you walked into this house, I knew it was you. Minnie didn't have to tell me later that Anna wasn't your aunt. I could have told her that."

Tears too powerful to blink away filled my eyes.

"You must have really loved her."

"I adored her. I want you to read my letter to her...not now though. Read it when I'm not around."

When he wasn't around. After he left my kitchen...or this world?

He gulped and blew out a stream of air through open lips.

"I'm okay now. Let's read the trunk letter."

Now it was my turn to gulp. I opened the letter and read it aloud.

March 3, 1940

Dear Anna,

I am sorry if you have been trying to reach me. I have been on the run. Margarita is in a safe place. Things don't look very good for me though, and I'm afraid when they catch up to me, it will be my demise.

I have accumulated substantial wealth during these past few years, and what I invested in coins and artwork I want to share with you, my dear niece. These items can be sold in the U.S. for enough money to take care of you for a long time. Life is short—enjoy yourself.

This will likely be the last time you hear from me.

Te amo y te extraño.
Nacho

The letter deepened the emotional state I was already in.

"That pretty much confirms my suspicion that Anna's uncle made a lot of money working in the Mexican oil industry, probably illegally or at least underhandedly. So he put his wife in a safe place and sent Anna to the U.S. Who knows what happened to him."

"And he tried to salvage at least some of what he had acquired by sending it to Anna."

"Looks like it. The letter is dated 1940, the year after Anna bought this house."

"I wonder if she even opened the trunk. The contents looked untouched."

"And the letter was still sealed."

"I wonder why," I asked him.

We sat in silence for a long moment shaking our heads.

"I'd say you're a pretty rich girl."

"If he got it illegally, I don't think I want anything to do with it."

"Gracie?"

"Yes."

"You remind me so much of her."

* * *

Before I went to bed that night, I put the still-sealed envelope from Tymon on the nightstand intending to read it in the morning when I was more rested.

Two hours passed while I lay in bed, eyes wide open. I turned on the lamp beside me and opened the envelope.

Dear Anna,

If you are reading this letter, it means I must have finally mustered the courage to give it to you.

You've touched my life in ways you'll never know, and I would give anything for the opportunity to try to do the same for you. I love you, Anna. I think I have from the very beginning. My mother used to say, 'When it's real, you'll know.' Well, I know.

You deserve to be with someone who is there unconditionally for you, to protect you, support you, someone to laugh with you when it's funny, and hold you when it's not. Someone to help raise your beautiful daughter, play with her, watch her grow up. I want to be that person.

You'll have to forgive me for unburdening the feelings I have for you in a letter rather than face-to-face. Finding the right words to express what I feel in my heart doesn't come easily for me, and if I were to attempt to tell you in person, I'm afraid it would come out all wrong or maybe not at all.

I don't know how you're going to react to this letter, but regardless of your feelings for me, I promise you I'll always be there for you and Celina, and that's a promise I intend to keep.

Love,
Tymon

It wasn't easy reading someone else's love letter. It was even harder knowing the writer could be my father.

⤳ THIRTY-EIGHT ⤳

Bad Timing

I sat in my living room fantasizing about what my life might have been like if Anna, my father, and I had still been a family. If this had been their home, I might have been there with my husband and infant daughter visiting. Or I might have just come home from college where I was working on my master's degree. Or I might have been in town visiting for a few days, away from my home in New York or Los Angeles or…Timbuktu.

Each time I studied this room, I saw it in a different light, or maybe I was just in a different place in my life and saw most things differently.

The court date to determine if I could take possession of my parents' safe deposit box was five weeks away. I barely had enough cash—cash that I could truly call my own—to get by on until then.

If the box didn't reveal the truths I was after, I made a promise to myself to forget the identity crisis and move on—no matter what. That promise was one that was very hard to swallow.

Before picking up the photos of the paintings in Minnie's attic, I ran by the Illinois District Court office to see if I could find out Berghorn's hearing date. When they told me none had been set yet, I was disappointed but not surprised. These things took time. Unfortunately, until I knew this man's fate, I couldn't relax.

I picked up the photos and browsed through them in my car. I then drove to the library and started researching the artists. Three names stood out: Diego Rivera, Frida Kahlo, and Angel Zarraga. If the paintings were authentic, they could be worth something.

My next visit was to an art appraiser recommended to me by the Art Institute of Chicago. The appraiser examined each photograph without expression.

"They're quite impressive. Are you interested in selling them?"

"For now, I'm just interested in what they're worth."

"I'd like to see them in person."

"They're pretty bulky, and I wouldn't want to damage them in handling."

"Could I come to them?"

"Is that the only way you could appraise them?"

"Yes."

"I can arrange that. Do you appraise other Mexican artwork—figurines, jewelry, masks?"

"Yes."

We arranged for him to come to my house the following week.

"I hope you have these insured," he said before I left.

When I got home, I called Raymond Webb to ask him if he could recommend an insurance provider for the artwork. I spent the rest of the day unwrapping the artifacts that had come out of the trunk and photographing them for the insurer. I threw in the small Cézanne painting that Minnie and I had found in the box of photographs that belonged to the couple who owned the house before Anna.

* * *

I asked Tymon if he would come down when the appraiser arrived. Not that I believed I needed a witness or anything, but as I had learned the hard way, you can never be too sure about people. I had transformed the dining room into an art gallery for the occasion. In total, there were twelve paintings, twenty-seven figurines, ten pieces of jewelry, and six clay masks.

Gordon Decker from D&E Appraisers arrived at two o'clock. With him was Benita Cruz, whom he introduced as an expert in Mexican art. Tymon joined us moments later. Benita, whose role was to authenticate the artwork, separated herself from the rest of us.

"While Benita is confirming the artwork's authenticity, I am going to make notes on each piece and examine its condition," Gordon explained. "Then I'll go back to my studio and find out what similar pieces have sold for to determine a fair market value for you. Is that what you expected from me?" he asked me.

"Yes."

"Good."

Tymon and I sat at one end of the room and watched them work. I didn't have to see the final appraisal to know these were valuable pieces—I could tell by the way they handled the pieces and looks on their faces. Gordon finished first and joined us.

"What does Benita look for exactly?" I asked.

"She's very familiar with these artists and can tell a fake. She's mainly looking for certain brushstrokes and color tones."

When Benita finished with the paintings, she proceeded to the figurines.

"With the rest of the pieces, unless it is signed, she'll just authenticate that it is Mexican and, if she can, will determine from which civilization it came—Mayan, Toltec, Colonial. She's good at all of that. I'm not."

I excused myself while I fetched a tray of lemonade and glasses from the kitchen. It looked as though they were going to be there a while.

Gordon, Tymon, and I discussed current events, sports, and the weather while Benita continued her work. She finished at five-fifteen.

We bade Gordon and Benita good-bye, and Tymon helped me rewrap everything and put it all back in the basement. According to Gordon, it would take two to three weeks to complete the appraisal.

Later, as Tymon and I sat at the kitchen table eating Chinese food, I told him about my plans for a small dinner party the following week to celebrate my new house. I had invited Fern and Naomi. The three of them had never met.

"Are you sure you want me there?" he asked.

"Of course, I want you there. Why do you ask?"

"Oh, I don't know. You three girls..."

"It won't be a hen party, if that's what you're afraid of. I promise."

"What can I bring then?"

"Courage."

"Gracie."

"Sorry. Couldn't pass that one up."

* * *

My dinner guests would be arriving in an hour, and I still had a lot to do. A pork roast was in the oven that pretty much took care of itself, but I still had to prepare the green beans, potatoes, and salad fixings. The peach cobbler I had baked in the morning was sitting on the kitchen window ledge. It had been one of Minnie's favorites.

I was on the way to my bedroom to change clothes when the doorbell rang. Couldn't imagine who it could have been—it was too early for guests.

"May I help you?" I asked the woman standing on my porch—middle-aged, average height and weight, wearing a pale blue dress.

"Grace Lindroth?"

"Yes."

"I'm Essie Noe."

Whatever I had been thinking the moment before instantly disappeared from my consciousness. After an awkward moment of silence, I was finally able to speak.

"Essie. Please come in."

I opened the door to let her into the foyer. At once, she glanced into the dining room where the table had been set for four.

"I've come at a bad time." She turned toward the door and reached for the doorknob.

"No, not at all. Please don't leave."

"But you're having company. I'll come back."

"It's just a casual dinner. You could even join us and—"

"No, I'll come back some other time," she said. Before I knew it, she was out the door.

I wanted to shout, *Please don't go! I need you!* But I didn't.

"May I call you?" I asked instead.

She kept on walking, and when she reached the sidewalk she turned left, quickened her step, and disappeared down the block.

My heart felt like it had dropped as far down in my chest as it could go, and I had a hard time walking into my bedroom. So close! I dropped down on the bed and started feeling sorry for myself.

The doorbell again rang. I raced to the door.

It was Fern.

"Well, don't look so disappointed," she said. "You were expecting someone else? The Queen of England maybe?"

"Very funny. Come on in."

"I came a little early to see if I could help you with anything. What's up with the face?"

"I'm running a bit behind. Make yourself comfortable while I change. If Tymon or Naomi comes, would you let them in? But check through the window first to make sure it's them," I said halfway to the bedroom. "I'll explain later."

I tried to calm myself down while I slipped into a new dress I had purchased for the occasion. For the next few hours, I had to forget Essie had ever come here. I could do that. Sure, I could do that.

I heard Tymon's familiar knock at the back door as I was putting on a little lipstick. Fern was going to have to introduce herself.

As I passed through the kitchen to check on dinner, Naomi pulled into the driveway. I let her in the back door.

Tymon had on a suit and tie. Bless his heart. It was mid-August, and he had dressed up for my dinner party. I hoped he had enough sense to take off his jacket before he roasted in it.

I put on my best hostess face and brought a tray of drinks into the living room.

My guests were talking about the new television series, *I Spy*.

"You do realize it's not that exciting in real life," I chimed in. "Most of the time, PIs are sitting around waiting for something to happen or doing something very mundane—not chasing spies and gorgeous women."

"If they showed that, nobody would watch it," Fern said.

I laughed. "I'm just trying to set the record straight, that's all."

We spent the next half hour talking about television, celebrities in the news, and Beatlemania, a subject on which Tymon had little to contribute. At seven o'clock, I herded them into the dining room.

Dinner conversation centered on the house and what I was going to do to it to make it my own. Naomi, who knew my whole story by then, asked how it felt after all those years to be living in the same house in which I had been born.

"Well, I'm still not one hundred percent sure I was born here, but it feels good," I told them. "Like I belong here. Like I'm home." I tried not to get emotional.

"Do you ever feel her presence," Naomi asked. "You know—your mother's?"

"Don't tell me you believe in ghosts." Tymon said to her.

"Yes, I believe in ghosts. You don't?"

"There's no such thing. Whenever something happens they can't explain, they call it a ghost."

"Grace?"

"I have to admit, I feel something in this house, something in the atmosphere, but I'm not sure it's her ghost or anything."

"Safe response, Grace," Fern said.

"I try."

"What about aliens, Naomi?" Tymon asked. "Do you believe in them too?"

"Now you're just teasing me."

"Okay, you guys, why don't you continue this conversation in the living room."

After I cleared the table, I brought in a tray filled with plates of cobbler and beverages. I was about to take my first bite when Fern got up from the sofa and handed me a gift-wrapped package.

"This is from all three of us."

All three of them? They had just met on this night.

"You guys shouldn't have bought me anything. I didn't expect *that*."

"Well, we wanted to," Fern said through laughter.

"What's so funny?"

"It wasn't easy for us to connect. I'm surprised we were able to pull it off without you knowing...you being a PI and all."

"That just goes to show you how bad I am at that. I didn't suspect a thing."

I unwrapped the box and lifted out a beautiful crystal bowl.

"This is gorgeous, but you really shouldn't have."

"We thought you might be a crystal kind of gal."

We spent the next hour talking, laughing, interacting like old friends, and when they left, I felt so good about things, I almost forgot I had missed talking to Essie three hours earlier.

Tymon offered to help with the dishes, but I declined his offer. I hated crying in front of people.

THIRTY-NINE

The Photo

"Gracie, if you don't mind me saying, you look a little lost these days." Tymon and I were sitting at the kitchen table. The hearing that would determine the fate of my parents' safe deposit box—and potentially my fate as well—was still two weeks away.

"I suppose I do feel a little lost. There's so much I could be doing, should be doing. Instead, I do nothing, and it's driving me crazy. At least when I was doing PI work, I was helping others, contributing something."

I chose not to admit to him that after balancing my checkbook the previous day I had realized I'd made a math error in my favor and was down to forty-seven dollars and twelve cents. My savings account didn't look much better.

"Have you heard from Essie?" I had told Tymon and Fern about Essie's visit the previous week.

"No, not a word."

"What about the Irish money? Have you decided what to do with it?"

"According to my lawyer, it's rightfully mine, but I'm not at all comfortable cashing it in." Even if I *was* a month away from going back to a steady diet of ramen noodles.

"It would be interesting to know if the inheritance laws in Ireland are similar to ours."

"Yes, it would."

Later that afternoon, I called the Irish American Heritage Center to ask how I could find out about a will executed in Ireland for someone who had died in this country. The woman on the phone told me it was different in Ireland in that there was no central registry of wills. She believed the best source would be the solicitor who had prepared it. She asked if I knew what county the man had been from. I told her I wasn't sure, but it could have been Dublin.

"Dublin, the city, is the capital of Ireland, so there are many solicitors there.

Wouldn't be easy to find. And you say he died how long ago?"

"Twenty years."

"So there's a chance the solicitor is gone as well. It might be easier to locate friends or family. I can give you names of a few organizations that help people in the U.S. find relatives in Ireland, if you like."

"Not now, but I may call you back for that."

I retrieved the letter Minnie had received from O'Gowan's supposed sister. It was dated April 25, 1950—almost fifteen years earlier. It had been signed by Darina O'Brady, who had provided an address underneath her signature. Who knew if she was even still alive, never mind still residing at that address?

I called the Irish American Heritage Center back.

"I'm sorry to keep bothering you with this, but do you know where I can find a current phone book for Dublin?"

"*That* I can help you with. I get one every year."

"Can you tell me if it lists a Darina O'Brady at 20 Dawson Street?"

"Hold on a minute, and I'll check." She came back to the phone a couple of minutes later. "Sorry. There's no one in Dublin listed under that name."

* * *

"Ready?" Raymond asked me.

I hadn't believed this day would ever come.

"Yep."

"Relax, Grace. This is going to go fine."

He wasn't the one who would be affected by the judge's decision.

A clerk let us into the courtroom, where we waited for the hearing to start.

I wondered if judges realized the significance of their decisions. And how did I know if this judge was going to be fair and impartial? The nameplate on the judicial bench read LESLIE KRAMER. What if he was some old codger who didn't want his children to inherit a dime of his, and he put me in the same light? And who judged the judges? What made them qualified to make life-changing decisions?

I sat there desperately clinging to what little was left of my optimism.

Judge Kramer walked into the courtroom, and I was instantly heartened—she was tall, young, and smiling.

She asked Raymond a bunch of questions to which I assumed she already had the answers. Formalities, I supposed. Her last words were, "Possession granted for both boxes."

Both boxes?

As soon as she uttered those words, I felt liberated—relieved of the angst that had weighed me down for so long, an angst that was soon replaced with one of a different nature. But two boxes?

Raymond and I left the courtroom and waited for someone to bring the boxes to us.

"Did you know there were two boxes?" I asked him.

"Yes, I knew. But I didn't want to tell you beforehand. You've been fretting enough about just one box."

I smiled. "You do understand why, don't you?"

He returned the smile. "Yes, Grace, I do."

The clerk arrived and handed me two metal boxes. I thanked him. Raymond escorted me out to my car. He had other business at City Hall, so we parted ways. He went to the Clerk of the Circuit Court to file a routine claim. I went to my car to discover who I was.

I had parked in a garage two blocks away, on the top floor, facing a wall. I cracked both windows to ensure ample airflow—if I discovered something life-changing, I didn't want anything hampering my ability to breathe.

One box was decidedly lighter than the other one. I opened that one first. In it was a lone envelope, unsealed. I breathed deeply and read the letter.

January 5, 1942

Dear Baby Girl,

I address this letter to you, but if I'm going to be completely honest, I am writing it for my benefit as well. I did not give you a name. I did not want that attachment, that additional guilt. I am unable to care for you. I am barely able to care for myself these days.

I know you are going to a good home, a loving home with two people who will take very good care of you. I know that for a fact. I checked them out myself.

Your real father is Adam Lindroth. He left me in July of last year. I didn't know it at the time, but I was three months pregnant with you. I don't know where he is, and I do not believe he is ever coming back.

When I saw your face for those few brief moments after you

were born, I thought my heart was going to break. When the
nurse came in and asked me if I was ready to "give you up,"
I cringed. I wasn't giving you up. I was giving you the life I
wanted you to have, the one you deserved. I did this out of love
for you and nothing else. I hope you understand this in time.

All the love I have left to give I will to you.

Your mother,
Rosa

The letter had been written the same year I was born. My mother—the person
I *called* my mother—had given birth to a daughter almost six months before I was
born. But why would she have given up a baby for adoption and then adopted me
soon afterward? It didn't make sense.

I reread the letter. It wasn't clear if she had written it one day, one month, or one
year after she had given birth.

Then it occurred to me that maybe the baby was me. That maybe my birthday
wasn't really June 28. Maybe it was January 5. She could have written the letter
right after I was born and then changed her mind when my father came back. But
why would she have kept the letter? It was hard to imagine my mother having had
to deal with something like this—she wasn't that strong of a person.

Rosa's emotions seemed raw in the letter, which made me think she had written
it shortly after she had given birth. January 5. Wait...Fern's birthday was January 4.
January 4, 1942.

Rosa could have been Fern's real mother. That had been Fern's first inclination,
after all. Everything seemed to fit—the birth date, the loving adoptive family.

I secretly wanted Rosa to be Fern's real mother, not mine. I felt a strong kindred
bond to Anna that would be difficult to abandon.

The baby she was referring to had to be one of us.

The thoughts in my head were scrambled and indiscernible. I needed to be
home when I opened the second box.

* * *

When I got home, there was a note on the counter from Tymon saying he was there
if I needed him. At that moment, I realized I felt closer to that man than I had to my
own father. My plan was to call him after going through the second safe deposit
box...as soon as my emotions allowed it.

I nestled into the large upholstered chair in my bedroom—Minnie's favorite chair—my feet up on the matching ottoman, the second safe deposit box on my lap, and a cup of chamomile tea next to me for additional support.

As soon as I realized that the document on top was Anna's will, I looked away from it. What were my parents doing with Anna's will?

I took a sip of tea and tried to relax while the hot liquid glided down my throat. I hadn't expected this to be so hard.

After taking a deep breath, I began reading.

WILL of Anna Thalia Vargas

I, Anna Thalia Vargas, a resident of Chicago, Illinois, hereby make this WILL and revoke all prior Wills and Codicils.

1. PERSONAL INFORMATION

   a. I was born on August 1, 1904, in San Diego, California.
   b. I am not married, and I have never been married.
   c. I have one living child, Celina Thalia Vargas, born June 28, 1942.

2. BENEFICIARIES

   a. To Esmeralda Noe, I bequeath my Rolex rose gold watch and the sum of $250 to care for my cat, Tobias, in the event he survives me.
   b. To Tymon Kossak, I bequeath my 1938 Buick.
   c. To my precious daughter, Celina, I bequeath all my remaining real property, bank accounts, and stocks.

3. PERSONAL REPRESENTATIVE

   I appoint Martin Torres of Higgins, Fletcher & McKenzie as Executor of my WILL, and if he is unable to serve, then I name Walter Higgins of Higgins, Fletcher & McKenzie as alternate Executor.

   I, Anna Thalia Vargas, hereby sign this WILL at Chicago, Illinois, on this August 1, 1942.

Anna Thalia Vargas
Anna Thalia Vargas

WITNESS: I hereby state, under penalties of perjury, that on
this first day of August, 1942, at Chicago, Illinois, I observed
Anna Thalia Vargas who proved her identity to me, declare the
above document to be her WILL. She signed the document in
my presence. She appeared to be an adult, of sound mind and
memory, acting of her own free will, and not under any force or
duress. I am now signing my name on the WILL in her presence.

Margaret Everest
Margaret Everest
1405 West Plymouth Avenue
Chicago, Illinois

I leaned all the way back in the chair. Seeing in writing my birth date linked to
a child with my unusual middle name convinced me I was Celina Thalia Vargas.
And if that was true, then Anna Thalia Vargas was my mother. I let that sink in for
a moment and savored the joy that welled up from deep within. But the feeling was
short-lived as I was reminded that this further implicated my parents in having had
something to do with Anna's death. I leaned all the way up against the back of the
chair and closed my eyes for a long moment. Running through my head were the
same horrible thoughts about my parents that I had tried to suppress for the last
five years.

The will was dated August 1, 1942, a month after I was born, six months before
Anna had died. She had left her watch to Essie and money to care for her cat. And
she had wanted Tymon to have her car. That was so sweet.

Two people had left me the same house some twenty years apart. No wonder it
felt like home.

I stared out the window—at nothing really—trying to absorb the simple reality
of it all.

When the room came back into focus, I picked up the next item, which was
an outdoor photo of my parents and me when I was a baby. I stared at my mother,
whose hair appeared quite dark. As far back as I could remember, my mother,
Rosa, had had light brownish-red hair. I turned it over. Nothing had been written
on the back.

The telltale white letters on a black background told me the next item was a
birth certificate. I carefully unfolded it.

Celina Thalia Vargas. Born June 28, 1942
8 lbs, 12 oz
Chicago, Illinois
Cook County
Nine-month term

I basked in the glory of this defining moment, trying to hold on to the feeling of sweet certainty that rolled over me, because I knew the sensation would soon evaporate, never to be recaptured.

I continued reading. There was a check mark beside the box labeled "Illegitimate." I stared at it blindly, unaware I was crying until a tear made a direct hit on the word.

The box for the father's name had been left blank. Anna's address was listed as the boardinghouse address, now my address.

I slowly let go of that place I hadn't understood for so long, and I mentally prepared myself for going down a path that Anna had started to pave for me. I fantasized about developing new hopes and dreams and becoming my new self. Emerging into the person that I was destined to be felt...I couldn't explain the feeling really. New...different...exhilarating.

Eventually, I was calm enough to proceed, but instead of reaching for the next piece of paper, I fished out a piece of silver jewelry from the bottom of the box. The necklace was unmistakably the same one that was in the photo of the woman sitting in the rocking chair holding me, the woman I then knew for sure was Anna. I put it on, closed my eyes, and held the pendant in my hand for several seconds.

The next item was Rosa's birth certificate. The only information on it that I didn't already know was her birthplace—Kansas City, Missouri.

The last two documents were death certificates for Anna's parents. Arsenio Vargas had been born in Monterrey, Mexico, in 1876. Maryanne Thalia Palmer Vargas had been born in San Diego, California, in 1880. On both certificates, the place of death was listed as San Diego, and the date April 13, 1910. Their cause of death was listed as accidental, which could have meant just about anything. They died when Anna was just six years old. So my grandmother had had the middle name Thalia too. And it appeared my grandfather had been Mexican. Interesting.

At the bottom of the box was the most beautiful christening dress I had ever seen. It was obviously handmade, crocheted I believed, at least thirty inches long, way longer than an infant, ivory in color. The stitches reminded me of hundreds of seashells all sewn together with pale pink satin ribbon running through them. Tiny pink-and-white flowers randomly speckled the gown.

I folded the dress the same way I had found it and put everything back in the box.

I was disappointed Anna's death certificate wasn't in there, as I'd hoped it would shed more light on things. City Hall didn't have it on file either, but given City Hall's recordkeeping and Chicago politics, this wasn't too surprising.

I kept staring at the photograph of my parents and me and wondered why it had been put in there and not with our other family photos. My father was so handsome in it, with a head of wavy hair most women would envy. I didn't remember him being that handsome, but then I supposed kids didn't ever think of their parents in that way when they were growing up with them.

It was an interesting photo—snow on the ground, us standing in front of a light-colored house. Ours had been a light color—yellow—but there wasn't enough of the house showing in the photo to tell for sure if it was ours. After studying it further, I decided I didn't think it was our house because there was a winterberry bush peeking out above the snow, and my mother had never been able to get a winterberry bush to grow in the summer, let alone make it through a winter.

And then an alarm went off in my brain.

I ran outside to the front corner of the house where there was a large winterberry bush, the one that I had used to coerce Minnie into giving me the time of day nine months earlier.

I held out the photo in front of me at arm's length and compared a cracked board midway up the first floor of the house to the same cracked board in the photo.

This photo of my parents and me had been taken in front of Anna's house.

"Looks like you've got things figured out."

Her voice startled me. I turned around to face Essie.

"Not really, but I think I'm about to. Let's go inside, my friend."

FORTY

A Rhetorical Question

My heart was thumping up against my rib cage as I led Essie into my house. This could be it. I felt like running around to every window and door to make sure they were locked and she had no escape route, but I didn't. Instead, I poured each of us a glass of lemonade as we settled in the living room to talk.

Essie's eyes explored the room, but the expression on her face told me there was some exploration going on in her heart as well.

"Good memories?" I asked her.

"Wonderful memories." She teared up and then laughed. "I told myself I wasn't going to do this. So much for that." She pulled out a handkerchief and dabbed her eyes. "Anna and I had many a talk in this room. And laughs. And tears. It's funny—she used to sit right where you're sitting, and I would sit right here. Every time, like they were assigned seats. And sometimes we would pick up where we had left off the time before, as if only minutes had elapsed instead of days."

"Sounds like an enviable friendship the two of you had."

"It was."

I gave her a moment to surrender her memories to the present.

"So, where do I start?"

It was a rhetorical question, so I didn't respond.

"I met Anna shortly after she bought this place. I used to live a block from here, over on Warner. I was out walking my dog one day when he suddenly became excited and broke away from me. He bolted across the street to this house and disappeared into the backyard.

"I called him several times from the front walk, and when he didn't come, I walked down the driveway to the backyard. Well, Junior had chased a cat up a tree and was guarding what he now considered to be his territory. Anna came out the back door to see what all the commotion was about. I fetched my dog. We talked, and the next thing I know, we're friends."

"For how long?"

"Until she died. But let's not jump ahead, if that's okay."

I nodded in agreement.

"We had been friends for less than a year when—"

I waited several seconds for her to continue. She seemed to be staring at my neck, perhaps lost in a thought. If she was now having a change of heart about telling me everything, I'd scream.

"You have her necklace on," she said.

"You recognize it after all this time?"

"I gave it to her."

Now it was my turn to well up. "Well, that makes it even more special." I was suddenly reminded of Anna's will. "Wait here a minute," I told her. "If you move, I'll—"

She laughed. "I won't move. I promise."

I retrieved the Rolex watch and handed it to her.

"This was her good watch," she said.

"She wanted you to have it."

"How do you know that?"

"It was in her will."

"She had a will?"

"I found it in my parents' safe deposit box, which the court awarded to me just yesterday."

She smiled. "Looks like my timing was finally right."

"Do you know what happened to her cat?" I wasn't sure why that was of interest to me after all these years, but I asked it anyway.

"Tobias? The black cat?"

"According to her will, she had set aside $250 for you to take care of her cat in the event it outlived her."

"Tobias died before Anna." She paused. "I used to call him Toby, and she would always correct me. Toby apparently is a dog name, not a cat name, at least according to her." She handed the watch back to me. "I can't accept this. You keep it."

"She wanted you to have it. *I* want you to have it."

She caressed it for a few seconds. "I always admired this watch. I used to tell her that when she wasn't looking I was going to steal it from her."

"Well, now you don't have to. And I'm sorry I interrupted what you were saying about when you first became friends. Please continue."

"I started to say that it was less than a year after we met, I think, when she met Al... Obviously you know about the boarders who used to live here."

"Yes, I do."

"So Al moves into one of the rooms. It was January 1...I don't know why I remember that date, but I do. Anyway, at first Anna wasn't going to take in another boarder. In fact, after she had lived here a short while, she didn't like the idea of having boarders at all. But there were three of them here when she bought the place, and she didn't have the heart to kick them out. Anyway, Al must have been pretty convincing back then because she let him have the only vacant room, which was the one above her bedroom."

"The one with the internal staircase."

"Yes, and that made Anna nervous, even though there was a door at the top of the stairs that locked from her side."

"But she let him move in anyway."

"Anna had a hard time saying 'no' to people in need. So he moves in, and it wasn't long before they became friends. And shortly after that... more than just friends."

"A romantic relationship?"

"Yes. And it was only after she fell in love with him that...well, he told her he was married."

"That must have come as quite a blow to her."

"She definitely didn't see it coming. She was devastated. We talked about it a lot. Talked about it. Cried about it. He told her his marriage was over and it would just be a matter of time until they would divorce. And she accepted that. But then things got *really* dicey when Anna discovered she was pregnant...with you."

I could feel the emotion welling up in my entire body.

"I'm sorry. I was sure you knew. I should have broken it to—"

"No, I knew. You just validated it. Sorry. I don't know why that struck me so. Please go on."

"Are you sure? We could take a break."

"No, I'm fine. Go on."

"So now she's pregnant, and Al is still married, and he hasn't talked about getting a divorce since that first time, so Anna's not sure where she stands with him."

"So what was his reaction to her pregnancy?"

"He was happy about it. Said he and his wife had tried to have children for years but weren't successful."

"I'm beginning to not like this man."

"I understand your feelings, believe me, I do."

"So you knew him pretty well."

"Only through Anna. I never spent more than five minutes at a time with Al, just long enough to exchange pleasantries before and after Anna and I did whatever it was we were going to do together." She paused. "One thing I should clarify is that Anna never said a harsh word against him. She said he was everything she could ask for in a man. He was attentive. He bought her things. He was sensitive to her needs."

"Apparently not all her needs," I chimed in.

"No, but other than that—and, for sure, it was a big *that*—he was great, according to her."

"You would think once Anna became pregnant, he would do the right thing."

"I think he liked their arrangement just fine. I don't think he had any intentions of divorcing his wife."

"And Anna went along with it."

"Anna was in love—what more can I say."

"Then I'm born."

"Then you're born, and their life goes on."

The phone rang, and I ran into the kitchen to answer it. It was Tymon saying he was aware Essie was there and asking if I needed anything. Tymon didn't miss much. I told him I'd call him later.

I brought the pitcher of lemonade to the living room on my way back and refreshed our drinks.

"You realize Tymon is the reason I didn't stay here to wait for you to come home that day."

"We figured that. But why?"

"Can you imagine my surprise when I saw him? Here, it took me I can't tell you how long to get up enough nerve to talk to you, and then I see Anna's old handyman at your house. I think I was in shock."

"When you're finished, remind me to tell you how we met."

"All right. So they have this rather peculiar living arrangement until you were about six or seven months old." She hesitated. "Before I go on, how much of what I've said so far did you already know?"

"I suspected pretty much all of it. I just had no proof."

"This is where it's going to get messy. I highly suspect you don't know this part."

I may have appeared calm on the outside, but inside my body there was a firestorm going on.

"I hadn't talked to Anna for several days when she called me...hysterical. She asked me if I could come over, but not to her house. She gave me an address in the Austin neighborhood. I dropped everything and drove there.

"When I arrived, Anna met me at the door, and she looked like hell. Excuse my French, but I don't know how else to put it. It looked like she had aged ten years since the last time I'd seen her. I could tell she'd been crying. Her hair was a mess. Her clothes were scruffy, and she had a black eye. My first thought was Al had beaten her up. Anyway, we went into the living room, and she told me the most horrific story I had ever heard or even read in a novel.

"Three days earlier, when Al was at work, his wife had paid Anna a visit. Anna had let her in the house and the conversation started out okay, but the more they talked the more bizarre the woman's behavior became. And when the baby—when *you*—began to cry, the woman went berserk and got physical with her."

"How do you mean, physical?"

"Like his wife got up and started pounding on her. Anna was sitting in a chair when this happened, but she managed to get out from underneath her and ran into the baby's—um, your—room, grabbed you and headed for the back door. But the wife ran after her. Anna said she tried to escape out the back door, but it was locked, and while she was fumbling with the lock, the wife came at her with a butcher knife that she'd picked up from the counter. Anna ran back to your bedroom, put you in your crib, closed the door, and turned around to face her. The two women scuffled and before long ended up back in the living room. The woman kept trying to stab Anna, and then...somehow... Anna got the knife away from her and stabbed her right in her chest."

I was so confused.

"You mean the other way around, don't you?" As soon as I said it, I knew it was a dumb question—how could Anna be telling Essie this story if she had been the one who had been killed?

Essie stared at me for several seconds and then looked like she was going to cry. "Essie?"

"Listen to me carefully." Her voice was shaky, and I wondered if she was going to be able to get the words out. "Anna killed Al's wife." She paused, but not long enough for me to get it. "Grace, the man who moved into the room above Anna's was your father."

"I know. You told me that."

"Your father...Adam Lindroth."

FORTY-ONE

Regarding Anna

I couldn't say how long it took Essie to tell me that the man who had raised me, the man I had thought was my father for the first seventeen years of my life, the man I had then doubted was my real father for the past five years—Adam Lindroth—was, in fact, my real father. Time must have shut down for me in the stunned silence that followed her telling me this.

"Do you need time for that to sink in?" she asked.

I nodded.

"I'll be right back. I need to use the restroom."

My brain must not have been working properly because all kinds of ridiculous scenarios were running through it. I felt the sweat building up on my forehead and dripping through my cleavage. I wished Tymon was there. I needed someone to hold me and make me feel safe. He could have done that.

Essie returned. "Are you okay?" she asked.

"I'm so confused."

"I know you are. But hold on tight, Grace, the story's not over."

I closed my eyes for a brief moment and tried to control my breathing, which was coming in short gasps.

"Okay. Go on."

"Adam's wife...was Rosa Lindroth."

"I, of all people know that, Essie."

"It was his wife who died that day—Rosa Lindroth."

"Essie, my mother died with my father when I was seventeen. In their house. Carbon monoxide poisoning. I was there."

"*Anna* died when you were seventeen, hon."

I stared at her for several seconds. I didn't believe her. She had the whole thing confused.

"No, she was murdered when I was just a baby. I have the newspaper articles."

"The woman you called mother all those years—that was Anna."

The tears began to gush—there was no stopping them. I felt like I was floating in time, somewhere between what she had just said and what it actually meant.

"What are you saying?" I cried out through wails.

She didn't wait for me to gain composure. "After she stabbed Rosa, Anna called Adam at work, and he told her not to do anything until he got there. She wanted to call the police and tell them what happened—that she had killed Rosa in self-defense. But Adam had other plans. He sent Anna and you to his home in Austin while he straightened up the room, cleaned up the blood, and put some of Anna's clothes on Rosa before he staged her body on the sofa."

"To make it look like what?"

"I'm not sure what he was trying to make it look like because he put Anna's purse near her, with her driver's license and everything else still in it except money, so maybe he wanted it to look like she was robbed. I don't know."

"Did Anna know what he was doing?"

"At the time, I don't think so. But eventually he told her because she told me about it."

"It's hard to believe the man I knew as my father could have done all that."

"I'm sure it is. Anyway, then he got busy moving Anna's things to his house. Not everything of course. He left enough behind to make it look like she had lived there. But not your things. He removed all your things."

"So it didn't look as though a baby had lived there." That matched what Tymon had told me.

"Exactly. Then after Adam hauled away Anna's things, he called the police and told them he was worried about his landlady and asked if they could check on her. He waited for them, identified the dead woman as his landlady, Anna Vargas, and left."

"So he intended for the police to think the dead person was Anna from the get-go."

"It looks that way."

"And she went along with it?" My disbelief suddenly morphed into anger. "And then Adam went back to his house like nothing happened and played house with Anna, and all those years I was growing up, she played the role of Rosa. Do you know how much time I have invested in trying to find out who my real mother is, how much of myself I have put into this, just to find out—. All this time I longed to have a life with my mother, my real mother, and I could have...but I didn't...because she... I shed tears over that woman's grave, for God's sake!"

I stopped my rant.

"I'm sorry. You're the last person I should be yelling at."

"I understand. Believe me, I do. Look, Anna didn't want anything to do with it at first. Trust me. It took a lot of convincing on Adam's part and a lot of soul-searching on her part before she went along with it, and she carried that guilt her whole life."

"Even so, I don't think anyone could have convinced me to do that."

"Adam was an expert manipulator. He knew just how much charm and praise he had to give in order for her to give in. And he had a knack for creating a false sense of fear and doubt in her, not to mention the guilt he laid on her. Eventually, she became blind to his faults and surrendered to his will completely. I think the guilt of it all did her in."

"How he was able to transform her into someone she really wasn't was so unfair. I just figured she was always very passive, easily influenced by others."

"Far from it, I'm afraid."

"So, afterward, you and Anna stayed friends?"

"Well, yes and no. Adam was clear he didn't want her to tell anyone about what happened, including me, so we had to hide our friendship from him. It was rare we could meet in person. Most of our conversations took place over the phone when he wasn't around."

"You could have gone to the police."

"I could have, but Anna begged me not to. She convinced me no good would come out of that. So I promised her I wouldn't."

"What about her other friends?"

"She didn't have any other friends that I was ever aware of."

"Why? Because he wouldn't allow it?"

"That may have been part of it. Then afterward..."

"Afterward what?"

"It wasn't the same. She wasn't the same person afterward."

We both laughed—in the very same instant getting the irony and humor of what she had just said—a much-needed break for me, maybe for her as well.

"So you think you were her only friend *before* all this happened?"

"I think so."

"She had lived there a few years. She hadn't made friends?"

"I don't know for sure, but I think she was embarrassed about her lifestyle, how she could support herself without working, and then later the affair with Adam and a child without being married."

"What I don't understand is how the police didn't know there was a baby in the house when Anna died. The nursery was there. And Tymon tried to tell them, but from what he told me, they thought he was crazy. Surely others knew—neighbors, the local grocer, people where she banked. They must have seen her pregnant."

"Anna didn't show much until toward the end, and then I would run errands for her. And those first few months after you were born, I would sit for you whenever she needed to go out. It doesn't surprise me that no one knew about you."

"So what were her plans for later—when I wanted to go out and play, when I was old enough to go to school?"

"I don't think she thought that far ahead."

"What about Rosa? Didn't she have friends? Or relatives. And what about their neighbors? They would know Anna wasn't her."

"My only guess is that Adam had been as controlling with Rosa as he was with Anna. And as far as neighbors, look at your old house—tall evergreens on both sides and in the back. Park across the street. It was very private."

"That it was. Even when I was small, I remember feeling so isolated playing in the backyard, fenced in by all the trees. Many times I tried to escape to the front of the house where it was more open. I wanted to see other people, but out front was off limits for me. To this day I'm uncomfortable being surrounded by too many trees."

That memory pulled me back to my childhood and my mother's peculiar behaviors. She had spent a lot of time by herself, off in her own world, and didn't always seem that interested in me or what I was doing. Had Adam been that demeaning?

"I can understand how what she went through would change her," I said. "Look what she had hidden her whole life. And something tells me he wasn't much of a comfort to her. I think I understand now why she was the way she was."

"How do you mean?"

"Distant most of the time with me but not with my father. She was more in tune with him than with me. She looked for and then followed his lead, almost to the point of being subservient. I remember one time my best friend Beth's mother told Beth how proud she was of her for something she had done. When I heard those words of praise, I thought how much I would have loved to hear my mother say something like that to me, even just once."

"But she *was* proud of you. I know she was."

"Well, she never said it to me."

"She was a changed person. I don't know what else to say."

"You left off when Anna assumed Rosa's identity."

"Part of Adam's plan was to—"

"And what about Anna's, or I should say Rosa's, death certificate? I couldn't find one."

"Adam saw to it that it would never resurface."

"Did the police ever suspect Adam had something to do with it?"

"I don't know, but Anna later told me he had given them a phony name."

Thoughts were running through my brain faster than I could process them.

"Looks like Adam thought of everything," I said. "Except the attic. Why did he leave all *that* behind?"

"You mean the paintings and things from her uncle?"

"Yes."

"Much to Adam's protest, Anna wanted nothing to do with any of that. She loved her uncle, but she was sure he had acquired those things...underhandedly, shall we say."

"That's why she left the key to the trunk out in plain sight."

Essie chuckled. "That's exactly why, but she never told Adam that. She told him she had sent it all back. So you know what all was in the trunk?"

"I've had it appraised."

"Worth a lot?"

"A substantial amount." I stopped for a moment and smiled. "It's funny. I was never sure what I was going to do with it, but I told Tymon that if it had been gotten illegally, I didn't want anything to do with it. Looks like I may have inherited at least one of her traits."

"Grace?"

"Hmm?"

"You've inherited more than just one of her traits." She paused. "You really have."

More tears. I liked her.

"So now they have all of Anna's things. Then what?"

"They settle into Adam's house—the house you grew up in."

"The one he and Rosa had lived in? That must have been difficult for Anna—living in that house."

"Oh, she didn't like it, but she had no choice, because Adam wasn't about to leave that house."

"Why?"

"Adam had a younger sister who disappeared when she was just in her teens, and they had been close. The police had considered her a runaway. Anyway, he never gave up hope that one day she would return, and when she did, he wanted her to be able to find him. How much do you know about Adam's parents?"

"Nothing. They died before I was born."

Essie raised her eyebrows.

"What? That was a lie too?"

"Well, I'm not sure. He never knew his father."

"I didn't know that."

"And his mother went to prison when Adam was ten or twelve."

"What?"

"The way Anna told me the story, Adam and his sister lived with their mother and uncle, and one day when his uncle was off somewhere, Adam fell off a woodpile or something and broke his leg. His mother didn't drive, but his uncle's car was sitting in the driveway, and she decided to drive Adam to the hospital."

"And she had never driven a car before."

"Right. And on the way, she lost control of it and hit an old man and his grandson who had been walking down the road."

"Oh, my. What happened?"

"They died, and Adam's mother went to jail for manslaughter."

"Manslaughter? But it sounds like it was an accident."

"She was driving without a license, on the wrong side of the road, and she was speeding."

"Gross negligence. So what happened to him...my father?"

"The uncle raised him and his sister, until his sister disappeared, that is."

"In the same house I grew up in? On Ferdinand Street?"

"Yes."

"And what about her, Adam's mother?"

"She died in prison, but I don't know when or how."

"I'm in shock. I never heard any of this!"

"Probably not something your father was too proud of."

"Did Adam visit his mother in jail?"

"Every Sunday. There was a fair amount of guilt there—if Adam hadn't been playing on that woodpile, she wouldn't have been in prison."

"Then at some point, Adam married Rosa. How long were they married?"

"I want to say eight or nine years. I'm not sure."

"And then Adam leaves Rosa, takes a room in Anna's boardinghouse, and has an affair with Anna."

"Yes."

I was finally getting it, but it was all so wrong. Rosa had deserved better. So had Anna. And even Essie. Adam was another story.

"You know where Rosa is buried, right?" I asked.

"Yes, I know."

"So Adam and Anna just let the city handle things...like she was just some poor indigent soul?"

"I know. That was horrible, but if they wanted to avoid the consequences for Anna, they had no other choice."

"That's appalling."

"There's something I want you to know, Grace. I wanted to get to know you as you were growing up, but it was impossible with your father in the picture. I worked, sometimes seven days a week, but being in real estate I did occasionally manage to visit you and Anna during the day when your father was working. But that stopped as soon as you were old enough to talk."

"You thought I would say something to him?"

"Yes. I tried other ways though. I would actually go to your school whenever I could when I thought you might be outside for recess, and I'd watch for you. I wanted to come over to you, hug you, tell you I was your godmother and would always be there for you, but I couldn't. Anna made me promise I wouldn't. She didn't want to create problems between them."

"You're my godmother?"

"Adam never even knew about the christening."

"I have the christening dress."

Essie closed her eyes, squeezing out a lone tear. "I made that dress for you."

"You did?"

"I patterned it after the wallpaper in your bedroom."

"The pink-and-white flowers?"

Essie laughed. "Took forever to sew on those darn flowers."

"It's a gorgeous dress."

"Thank you. Anyway, as the years went by, Anna and I stayed friends, but like I said, unbeknownst to Adam."

"Tell me about Anna before she met Adam."

"When I met her, she was fun to be with and a real looker. Took pride in the way she dressed, did her hair. She had this one outfit that I swear turned every man's head she passed. The blouse had short butterfly sleeves and a crossover neckline that showed just a tease of cleavage. The skirt flared out at the bottom and swished around her perfect legs when she walked. Both were made of this robin's egg blue silky fabric that seemed to flow behind her like water. And the most amazing thing about it was that she had no idea how attractive she was, how many heads she turned. She was that unpretentious.

"She loved her independence, reveled in it. And she had a great sense of humor—I didn't know half the time whether she was being serious or pulling my leg. Always upbeat, even when things didn't go as well as planned.

"Then he came into her life, and she eventually became... I don't know...tired and, well, each year she put on a little more weight, didn't dress like she did before. But she said she was happy, so..."

"That first part didn't seem at all like my mother, that's for sure. Just the opposite. I'm curious about her hair color. What was her natural color?"

"Dark brown, almost black. Looked beautiful with those green eyes of hers. But she changed it right after...the incident."

"To brown with some red in it."

"Like Rosa's."

"That explains some of the photos I found. This whole thing is so sad. Whoever said 'Love is blind' knew what they were talking about."

"I think Shakespeare gets credit for that." She paused. "Anna told me he was a good father to you."

"He was. I mean, I have no complaints as far as that goes. I never wanted for anything. He treated me okay."

"I snuck into your eighth-grade graduation, by the way."

"No kidding."

"And I was going to contact you after your parents died, but I just couldn't do it." She bit her lip and shook her head. "I'm so sorry I didn't. I should have."

"Don't be sorry. I managed."

"That was the worst time of my life, so I think I know how hard it was for you," she said through a swallowed sob. "I should have been there for you. And all because of that damn room."

"What room?"

"The one in the basement."

"What about it?"

"Do you know about it?"

"I know about it now. Not back then."

"Both rooms?"

"Mm-hm."

"She had the one built in this house to hide things her uncle sent her. There was a time that room was packed with stuff. She knew it wasn't right, but he was her uncle, her only father figure, and he was good to her, so she went along with it."

"The room was empty when I found it."

"She would hold things for him until he sent her instructions as to what to do with them. What you found in the attic was the last shipment he had sent to her. He wanted her to have it."

"And the room in the basement of our house?"

"That was Adam's doing. He wanted a secure room available in case Anna's uncle sent more things. Anna hated that room, and they frequently argued about it."

"So her uncle knew she had moved?"

"I guess so."

"Did he ever send more things to her?"

"Not to my knowledge."

"So that room was always empty?"

"Not entirely. Anna kept a journal. She said she started keeping one as a teenager in Mexico. At one time, she had hundreds of them, but after she moved in with Adam, she destroyed all of them except the current one—that one she kept in the rafters inside that secret room. I'd completely forgotten about that until just now."

That explained how Berghorn knew all that personal stuff about Anna and me. He had probably torn that room apart looking for the money and had found the journal. It made me sick to think he'd read her personal thoughts.

"Essie, when my father lived here as a boarder, you said Anna called him Al."

"She found out his real name after they moved in together."

"What about his last name? What did he use?"

"I'm a little confused about that myself. I'm almost positive Anna told me his name was Al Lindstrom or something close to that. Then, when she found out his real name was Adam, she told me he had told her Al was a childhood nickname— his initials being AL. But she later denied telling me his last name was Lindstrom. She said she knew all along it was Lindroth. I think he lied to her about both his first and last name, and she was trying to cover up for him."

"I would have been out of there."

"Frankly, I'm not surprised she covered for him."

"Why?"

"First of all, she loved him. At least, that's what she told me. And he protected her."

"And if she crossed him, he had one heck of a secret to hold over her head, didn't he?"

"Of course he did, but don't forget he was an accessory to her crime."

"Right. I remember my father saying more than once that he wished he could retire early and move far away."

"That was his plan."

"Really."

"In some ways, I felt sorry for him."

"How so?" I asked.

"I think what happened to him as a child determined the man he became."

"Maybe."

"I also think what happened to his mother influenced him in the way he handled the situation with Rosa. Even though his mother had killed someone by accident, she still had to go to jail. Knowing what it was like for her there, he didn't want Anna, the woman he loved, to have to go through that."

"This is all so complicated."

"I know. Grace, are you aware of the floor safe in this house?"

"Yes. It's empty. Did she have that installed as well?"

"Oddly, that was here when she bought the house. She replaced it because the previous owners didn't leave behind a key. She used to keep money in it. Dirty money from her uncle that she would send on to someone else after a period of time."

"Essie, tell me how Fern fits into all of this."

"Fern?"

"Fern Herschberger."

"You tell me. I didn't know she did."

"I only met her six months ago." I told her about Fern walking into my office that day and the items she had found among her parents' things after their deaths that led her to believe either Rosa or Anna had been her real mother.

"Did she know who you were when she came to your office?"

"She said she didn't."

"Did she know who I was?"

"Yes."

"So her friendship with me wasn't coincidental—it was just a sham."

"Please don't be mad at her. She was desperate to find out about herself...just like I was. It's probably hard to understand unless you've been there."

"I can assure you Anna was not her mother."

"I'm sorry I upset you."

"That's okay." Her voice was so soft I barely heard her. "I shouldn't be casting any aspersions on her. I was the one who did wrong."

"How do you mean?"

"We should have been having this discussion long ago."

"You were just being loyal to your best friend."

"I guess."

"Do you know Elmer Berghorn?"

"Never heard of him."

"He caused my parents' deaths."

"What?"

"He's in prison now, but not for that." I filled Essie in on my ordeal with Berghorn and the story about O'Gowan's sweepstakes winnings.

"That's unbelievable. How long is Berghorn in for?"

"Seventeen years."

"I hope he rots in there. So that recluse boarder was wealthy?" she asked. I gathered she was referring to O'Gowan.

"Quite."

"Well, I don't think Anna knew anything about that. At least, she never said anything to me, and we pretty much told each other everything."

"Minnie didn't either."

"Minnie?"

I told Essie about Minnie—how we had met and our subsequent relationship.

Essie laughed. "They could make a movie out of all this."

"I know. Want to hear something funny? That day you came here and were surprised to see Tymon, do you know where I was?"

She shook her head.

"Following the 54 bus. Fern saw you get on it that day, and I thought knowing its route might lead me to where you were staying."

"I took that bus to get here."

"I know that now. Why did you leave your house in Cicero, by the way?"

"Because you were getting close and making me nervous, and back then I was still in the mindset that I wasn't going to talk to you."

"What changed your mind?"

"I finally confessed everything to my pastor, Reverend Orman, and he advised me to talk to you."

"Then I say, 'Thank you, Reverend Orman.'"

"I don't know about you, Grace, but I'm exhausted."

"Me too."

"Maybe we should call it a day."

"Can we stay in touch?" I asked.

"I would like that." She glanced around the room. "You know, I walked by here a year or two ago just for old time's sake. Stopped for a minute out front to take a long look at it. The day lilies were in full bloom...so pretty. And then this irate lady comes rushing out the door asking me what the hell I was looking at. I tried to tell her I was just passing by, but she wasn't having it. I never did *that* again."

I laughed. "I'm sure that was Minnie. A raging bull on the outside, but a real sweetheart on the inside. Remind me sometime to tell you about our first meeting."

Essie stared at me for several seconds before tearing up.

"You remind me so much of her," she said.

Under different circumstances I wouldn't be sitting in this lovely screened-in gazebo enjoying the seventy-degree weather with just enough of a breeze to usher the sweet scent of the neighbor's lilac bushes over this way. Tymon designed the gazebo after a barn he saw in Wisconsin. Octagonal in shape, it can easily hold eight people, but more times than not, there are just the five of us in here.

I can see my rock garden from here as well as from my kitchen window. I used Minnie's rock collection to create it. As I was digging into one of the boxes of rocks, I came across the metal lock box containing 372 hundred-pound Irish notes—the first money Minnie and I discovered in this house. She had hidden it well.

The winterberry bush I bought Minnie as a peace offering didn't make it, but I took a picture of it when it was still partially alive. The framed photograph sits on the nightstand next to my bed beside a long, smooth rock that has the words "Best Friends" scrawled on it in black marker.

Regarding Anna, now that I know her whole story, I have a hard time accepting her as my real mother. The Anna who gave birth to me was my real mother. The Anna who raised me was a superficial rendition of the real Anna disguised as someone else, and to be honest, I don't know how I feel about that person now.

As for my name, I've gone back and forth on which one I should use. The woman who gave me life named me Celina, but I've been known my whole life as Grace. For now, I go by Grace. But who knows—someday, I may change my mind about that. And someday I may change my mind about how I feel about the woman who raised me.

If it wasn't for Anna, the five of us wouldn't be together, not like this anyway. The money I received for the Mexican artwork and gold coins she left behind will fund NSU Immigration Services for a very long time. I think she'd be proud of me. I hope she would anyway.

I glance around the open-air room at my cohorts who helped me form this organization and now play an important role in keeping it functioning.

Naomi makes sure we all have what we need to do our jobs and serves as interpreter for my Spanish-speaking clients. She dresses much more conservatively these days, realizing that her former "too hot to handle" persona was her peculiar way of making sure she didn't attract a man she could potentially like, realizing now that not all men are like her abusive father. She recently became an active member of the PTA at her daughter's school and has been talking regularly with one of the single fathers she met there. I hope that works out for her. She's a wonderful person and a good mother.

Tymon, my only permanent boarder, does here what he's done his whole life—he fixes things. And I'm not just talking about physical things. He's also good at fixing misguided souls and broken spirits. I don't know for sure that he's not my real father—he and Anna could have had an affair that she never disclosed to Essie—but that's not important to me. The gifts I have received from him on my journey to find the truth far outweigh the need to know whether he or Adam was my biological father. If he had relations with Anna and someday wants me to know that, he'll tell me.

Fern continues to teach second grade—even won the regional Teacher of the Year award this year—but on weekends, she's in my dining room teaching English to our non-English-speaking clients. When Fern realized she was the baby in the letter Rosa wrote, she cried. And when she told me that she and her boyfriend were going to get married next month and asked me to be her maid of honor, I cried. Then when she thanked me for helping her get on with her life, we both cried. We're best friends now, which is pretty amazing given my mother was responsible for her mother's death.

My dear friend Essie still sells real estate for Baird & Warner and, in her off hours, helps to transition immigrant families who are living in my boardinghouse to permanent homes. I liked Essie from the beginning, but I like her even more now that she's discovered a new person inside herself after being relieved of the burden of keeping Anna's secret for all these years.

I wish I could say Minnie was here, helping out in her own unique way. I wish she had lived long enough for me to understand her. She was gruff and sometimes difficult, yet my guess is what she wanted most in life was to be accepted by others, be part of a family again if she could, and take care of people. I don't understand why she got in the way of herself like she did. I think about her often, and I don't think I'll ever stop missing her.

I realize now that Minnie and I were a lot alike in that we were not living full lives. And even though, in the end, we each changed that for ourselves, there may have been easier ways for us to go about it. But then we wouldn't have met, so I have no regrets.

What do I do for this organization? I make sure that indigent immigrants who desire American citizenship and need legal advice are aware of the services available to them so they do not get taken by the likes of Elmer Berghorn.

And speaking of Elmer, he has agreed to work with prison officials in setting up a free legal counseling service for his fellow inmates who are not U.S. citizens in exchange for my creating a trust fund for his son—from proceeds I earned selling off the Mexican coins and artwork—to make sure the young man gets the medical care he needs. He eventually told me his whole story, and it was touching.

Elmer and Hazel married when she was five months pregnant, something that shamed her and her family. Their son, Warren, was born premature with several health problems, and then a month later was diagnosed with spina bifida, the most severe form of it. Hazel blamed herself for their son's illnesses since she had not sought medical treatment during the early months of her pregnancy when she was so desperately trying to hide it. Apparently, that burden was more than she could bear, and she took her own life.

Warren is currently twenty-five, cannot do anything for himself, has serious gastrointestinal problems, is learning disabled, and has gradually gone from wearing braces on his legs to using crutches to using a wheelchair to now being bedridden. The finest doctors in the world could have helped him at one time, but not now. Sadly, it's too late. All I can do is ensure his basic needs are met and he's as comfortable as possible.

I do not regret being the catalyst for Elmer's incarceration—prison is where he belongs. But that doesn't mean I have no respect for him. You see, I realized something profound from Elmer's actions. I realized that things that happen to you in the past can mold you into someone you're not. I think about that often and how it holds true for so many people in my life, but especially Elmer.

Since opening its doors in January, I'm proud to say NSU Immigration Services has helped forty-seven adult immigrants on their way to becoming productive U.S. citizens—people who want better lives for themselves and their families and are willing to work for it. All twenty-three of their children are enrolled in school and doing well. I know this because my services require them to check in with me periodically. And they're happy to do this—they are proud of their accomplishments, proud of their contributions to the good of this country they now call home. I love what I do, and I'm good at it, if I do say so myself.

All 772 hundred-pound Irish notes are still in a safe deposit box. My boyfriend has Irish roots, and we've talked about going to Ireland someday. I don't know how serious he really is about me, or I am about him, but it sure would be nice to find Marcus O'Gowan's relatives and give them the money he won—relieving me of the burden of having something that doesn't belong to me.

The Attic Finds case is now closed. Even though I wasn't very good at PI work, I guess I did okay with my most important case. I may have taken too long to solve it, floundered at times, botched some things along the way, and broken some rules, but I did discover the truth I was after. Perhaps others wouldn't have gone through what I did to reach this point, but for me, I couldn't face the future without understanding my past.

Discovering the truth about my parents didn't make me a different person like I thought it would—but it did allow me to shed the veil of uncertainty I was wearing so the real me could shine through. I visit their graves on holidays and anniversaries. I visit Rosa Lindroth's grave too—usually with Fern.

I look toward the neighbor's lilac bushes and smile—the stray black cat I see every once in a while sits motionless on his haunches among the bright purple flowers, eyes fixated on me. As soon as I look away, he'll quietly disappear—he's done that before. I pretend he's a descendant of Tobias, the black cat my mother had when she lived here. And that connection warms my heart.

∽ OTHER BOOKS BY FLORENCE OSMUND ∾

The Coach House

This book is not only thought evoking but also a genuine pleasure to read.
—BestChickLit

1945 Chicago. Marie Marchetti flees from her devoted husband when she realizes he is immersed in local corruption, only to discover it's the identity of her real father that unexpectedly changes her life more than her husband ever could.

Daughters (sequel to *The Coach House*)

Civil rights, gender roles, and political postures are carefully, realistically, and sensitively present in this story.
—Pens and Needles

Discovering who her father is leads Marie Marchetti to discover who she really is and where she belongs, driving her to seek peace and truth in her life. But unexpectedly, the most life-altering consequence of her reunion grows out of an encounter with a twelve-year-old girl named Rachael.

Red Clover

Red Clover is a wonderfully written detailed story about a man overcoming his upbringing and becoming his own. The finished product, both the man and his story, are exemplary.
—Ray Paul, Windy City Reviews

The troubled son of a callous father and socialite mother determines his own meaning of success after learning shocking family secrets that cause him to rethink who he is and where he's going. Lee Winekoop's reinvention of himself is surprising; the roadblocks he confronts are unnerving; and the cast of characters he befriends along the way is both heartwarming and amusing.

∽ೖ ೩∾

Books are available on Amazon http://www.amazon.com/author/florenceosmund
Or the author's website http://florenceosmund.com/buy_the_authors_books
Or at book stores who order from distributors Ingram or Baker & Taylor

If you enjoy my books, I would greatly appreciate your taking time to write a short review on Amazon and/or Goodreads.
—Florence Osmund

ABOUT THE AUTHOR

After more than three decades of working in corporate America, Florence Osmund retired to write books. She earned her master's degree from Lake Forest Graduate School of Management and forged an active career in administrative and human resource management. She currently resides in Chicago where she enjoys all the things that great city has to offer and (of course) reading and writing.

If you are a new or aspiring author, Florence invites you to visit her website where she offers considerable writing advice, book promotion and marketing strategies, and many helpful website links.

Contact Information

E-mail: info@florenceosmund.com
Website: www.florenceosmund.com
Facebook: www.facebook.com/florenceosmundbooks
LinkedIn: www.linkedin.com/in/florenceosmund
Twitter: @FlorenceOsmund
Goodreads: www.goodreads.com/user/show/8800692-florence-osmund
Amazon: www.amazon.com/author/florenceosmund

CPSIA information can be obtained
at www.ICGtesting.com
Printed in the USA
LVOW13s0252170517

534791LV00011B/614/P